DEFINITELY BETTER NOW

DEFINITELY BETTER NOW

AVA ROBINSON

MIRA

MIRA™

ISBN-13: 978-0-7783-1059-4

Definitely Better Now

Mira
22 Adelaide St. West, 41st Floor
Toronto, Ontario M5H 4E3, Canada
MIRABooks.com

Printed in U.S.A.

For Erik

ONE

For the past 364 days, I've been taking life one day at a time. Starting tomorrow, my life, my sobriety, will be measured in years.

I looked over my shoulder as I hit the period on my keyboard, making sure for the hundredth time that none of my coworkers at Richter & Thomas Financial Consulting could see what I was doing. I should have been finding the best shade of green for our newest Facebook ad. That was my charge in my critical role as Marketing Assistant #2. To the three colleagues I shared an office with, it was an average Thursday. But to me, it was a very special day. And this very special day required a top secret Word document.

The marketing-and-communications office was a repurposed, windowless conference room tucked away on the twelfth floor of a building in the Flatiron district of Manhattan. We had four desks shoved into the center of the room. Vanessa Zhao, Marketing Assistant #1, sat beside me. Our boss, Jermaine Johnson, sat across from me. And across from Vanessa was Colin Taft, who worked on video and kept his headphones on all day. My desk was the closest to the door, which meant that if anyone had to get up and go to the bathroom, they'd be able to glance at my computer. So writing a top secret speech was a risky choice. But I couldn't help it—there was no other time I'd be able to collect my thoughts.

When I woke up tomorrow morning, I'd be one year sober. And tonight, to celebrate that feat, my AA group was having a party for me, a party where I'd be expected to speak from the heart. The thing was, I was terrible at speaking from the heart. My heart was shy. It didn't like crowds. And while my sponsor, Lola, had told me I didn't need to write anything down, I couldn't help myself. I wanted to say the right thing, and after living with myself for twenty-six years, I knew I'd never be able to say the right thing off-the-cuff. Maybe someday, I'd get there. Maybe that day would even be tomorrow.

I'd been waiting to feel like a fully polished, emotionally stable version of myself for a year now, and tonight, everything would finally click into place. In AA, after a full year of sobriety, the rules change. Your sponsor loosens their grip on the reins. They trust you more, maybe let you go a day or two without calling. It wasn't that I wanted to talk to Lola less, but I was ready to be out of this early sobriety, everything-is-fragile phase. I wanted to move into the no-more-curveballs phase.

As if my thought spirals were contagious, my computer's cursor suddenly transformed into a spinning wheel. It spun itself into a frenzy until both Word and InDesign quit in protest. That's what I got for having two applications open on this ancient PC. But it didn't stop there. After InDesign sputtered out, the whole screen faded to black. I gave my monitor a slight shove. "Not again."

Vanessa took off her headphones and rolled two inches closer to me, leaving less than a foot between us. "You think you lost everything?"

"We'll see. Maybe she's in a good mood." I thought about the words I had typed—whole paragraphs containing my deepest, darkest, dirtiest secrets—and who might read them when they resurfaced. What kind of maniac was I, writing those things at work?

To exist within these walls, I'd created another person. I called her "Work Emma." Work Emma was exceptionally professional and was not open about her sobriety. If she were to one day tell someone, she would do so gracefully: seltzer in hand, hair pinned into a French twist, with just the right amount of red lipstick. It certainly wouldn't be through writing a cringeworthy personal speech and then having that speech pop open as a recovered Word doc.

Vanessa shook her head. "She's never in a good mood."

It was true. My computer was our small office's resident aristocratic, corset-wearing woman; she would faint at the drop of a hat. Any goodwill I tried to point her way only crashed against her like waves off a rocky coast. As sure as I was that the moon would rise in the night sky, I was sure that my computer would randomly shut down and fuck me over.

As I crawled under my desk, Jermaine said, "Just message IT!"

I would, I absolutely would. But Work Emma was a conscientious and thoughtful coworker and knew that if she messaged our IT associate, Darren, without at least unplugging and plugging the computer back in, he wouldn't come down.

I poked my head back up. "Anything?" I asked Vanessa.

She shook her head no. "I'm messaging," she said.

Before I crawled back up, I noticed something tucked between the under-desk filing cabinets. A stack of Post-its must have slipped between my desk and Jermaine's. I grabbed a pencil and used it like a fishing rod. Vanessa said something I couldn't quite make out. Darren was probably on his way. The pencil made contact. I looked at the top Post-it and blinked in surprise.

It wasn't my handwriting. Was it a password? No, it couldn't be; there were spaces. It read—in neat, typewriter-like script—*Life is a journey, not a destination.*

I flipped to the following note: *Today is the first day of the rest of your life.* And usually, any version of Emma that read that would scoff and roll her eyes. Work Emma especially didn't care for clichés. But today wasn't a day like any other. So I didn't scoff. Instead, I did something much more embarrassing and blinked back a tear. Getting this dusty yellow note today felt like fate. Because after tonight, everything would be different. And tomorrow, the note wouldn't be meaningless, cliché, or trite. It would be true.

A knock on our office door jolted me out of my reverie. I sat up quickly, hitting my head on the underside of the desk. "Fuck," I said a touch too loudly.

"Emma!" Jermaine called in a good-natured tone. "I don't think I've ever heard you curse before!" Work Emma was a polite young woman. She'd tossed cursing away with the cocaine.

The first thing I saw as I crawled out from under the desk was not Jermaine or Vanessa lending me a helping hand or even Colin continuing to ignore me. There was a man I'd never seen before opening the office door. I was on my hands and knees, so my perspective might have been altered, but it looked like he was tall. The kind of tall where he didn't stand up straight. A lifetime of comments must have created a slight hunch to his shoulders.

"Did you call IT?" His voice had a bass-like quality that would vibrate the sidewalk if played through booming car speakers. His dark hair was straight except where it curled over his slightly too-large ears, and he had exactly seven moles. I shouldn't have counted—he probably saw my eyes crisscrossing over his face and knew exactly what I was doing—but I couldn't help myself.

"Yes?"

"Are you okay?" Was he calling me out for staring at him? I blinked away the thought. No, he was commenting on the fact that I'd yet to get out of cat-cow position.

"Ben! Back to simple fixes? I thought you were too big of a

deal to get under desks anymore," Jermaine said as he stood. I watched as their hands met and Ben's curled around Jermaine's, enveloping it.

"Everyone else is busy." He shrugged.

It was really time for me to stand up. I brushed the dust off my knees. Ben was tall and, if I was being completely honest with myself, also beautiful. His dark brown eyes caught mine. I darted my gaze to the ceiling.

"You sure you still know what to do?" Jermaine continued with the teasing tone of a jovial father figure. "Ben here got a big promotion a few months back, and while I thought that might be enough to get him to come out to Friday Night Drinks with us—"

"Yeah, well, IT is still IT," Ben said, cutting Jermaine off. A hint of pink colored his cheekbones. His skin showed the beginning of every emotion. But there was no reason for him to blush. I was the one who'd embarrassed myself.

"What's the problem?" he asked me.

"Well, uh, my computer. We call her Mrs. Bennett because she's very Mrs. Bennett–y. Bad nerves, you know?" I said, sticking the Post-its on my desk.

Ben looked at me with a sharply furrowed brow, as if he was unsure of my sanity.

"From *Pride and Prejudice*? She's the mom? Always almost fainting?" I said as though I was asking him, although he clearly knew less about Jane Austen than I did.

He huffed something that was a little too surprised-sounding to be a real laugh. "I don't think I've ever had anyone describe a computer problem using a literary analogy before."

"It's not a helpful diagnostic. It froze and turned off, which it does not infrequently, but now it won't turn back on."

"Hmm, in that case, I might have gone with Billy Pilgrim." Ben's eyes were on me. He hadn't even touched my computer yet.

"I don't know who that is, but I have a feeling you said it just to stump me."

The left side of his lips lifted in a smile. "I might have," he said. "But I also think it works. He's the main character in *Slaughterhouse-Five*. Classic unreliable narrator, always getting unstuck in time."

"Very different vibes. We'll have to trade copies and see which is more fitting." It was a joke, I promise, I meant it as a joke.

But then Ben said, "A book club for diagnosing computer malfunctions. That sounds like a good way to get me to start reading again." What I thought was him blushing earlier had been only a gesture at the act, because now his face was betraying him.

I giggled. It was high-pitched and sounded foreign to my own ears, as if my vocal cords had forgotten that particular vibration. I was lucky I hadn't started playing with my hair.

Vanessa wheeled her chair into my field of vision to raise her eyebrows. It was the reminder I needed. Work Emma didn't publicly flirt with coworkers.

"Well, shall we?" I said, gesturing to the computer.

After a few minutes of Ben kneeling beside me—he absolutely refused to take the chair no matter how much I offered to swap—he got up and declared that it was time I get a new computer. Apparently, having the director of IT come down instead of Darren made a big difference. Where Darren fiddled and fidgeted with wires and ports, Ben told me he'd be back in a few and then picked up the computer and carried it away, and with it the beginnings of my incriminating speech. I was nervous about feeling vulnerable with my AA group, but that was nothing next to the sudden terror I felt about being vulnerable in front of Ben—who was an entirely unknown quantity. At least if he was bringing me a new computer, maybe my old files, including my speech, would never see the light of day.

I was left with an empty desk. Without a computer, there was nothing for me to do. Minutes collected into an hour and then started to pool into a second one. I couldn't miss my party tonight, no matter how long Ben kept me. But I was supposed to go to dinner at Mom's before—she was my date for the evening—and now that I was out a computer, my collected thoughts had spilled all over my mind. I had no idea what I'd say in my speech. My stomach squirmed at the thought. I imagined all eyes on me, watching me stumble over words that should be smooth and effortless.

I poked my head over Jermaine's computer. "Hey, do you think…maybe…it's almost five?" Perfect. Work Emma strikes again.

"Why don't you call Ben?" Jermaine said. "See if he needs you to stay or needs passwords or something." I silently thanked my higher power that I'd simply memorized the password my computer came with, *xYjg67bq*, rather than making up my own and having to reveal anything about myself to Ben. God forbid he learn the name of my childhood turtle, Spinach.

He wasn't hard to find in the company directory: his name sat right where it was supposed to, on the first line of the IT Department. Benjamin Nowak, Director of IT. My stomach gave a slight and nonsensical flip as I dialed his number.

"Hey, sorry it's taking me so long," he answered like we were in the middle of a conversation. "I'll set you up in a few minutes. Then it'll be off both our plates tomorrow." I didn't quite trust his sense of time. He'd said earlier he'd be back in a few minutes, and that turned into two hours. "Unless you have somewhere to be?"

This was the problem with Work Emma: she never had anywhere to be. She certainly wasn't about to announce to Ben, and allow the entire marketing-and-communications office to overhear, that she was going to an AA party held in her honor. There was only one possible way out of this situation: I'd have to lie. "Oh, well, I have a doctor's appointment."

There was a pause on the other end of the line. As if Ben was weighing my lie in his mind. Yes, it was rare to have doctors' appointments after 5:00 p.m., but I was sure they happened occasionally. It wasn't so obvious.

"No worries. Would you mind getting in a bit early tomorrow so we can get you set up?"

I had wanted to take a secret personal day tomorrow. Call out sick and then do something to celebrate myself. Go on a long walk through the city, throw my hands (metaphorically) into the air, and (even more metaphorically) let out a scream of relief. But another excuse didn't come into my mind, and the truth was so far from the tip of my tongue, I couldn't even imagine what it tasted like.

"Eight thirty okay?"

TWO

"Is it dry?" Mom asked as she took a bite of the chicken she'd roasted us for dinner. We were in the same apartment we'd moved into when I was twelve. We'd bounced around for a few years after my parents had gotten divorced, Mom slowly giving up being a professional modern dancer for a job as a dance teacher at LaGuardia High School. Once she got full-time work, we could afford more than a sublet, so we'd moved into this fourth-floor walk-up on the Upper West Side. It was a one-bedroom that we'd divided into two, using bookcases.

"A little, yeah," I said. Then, noticing the expression on her face, I added, "But the flavor's great."

She shook her head. "I knew something was off when the recipe said to cook it for two hours." Mom wasn't a culinary goddess, but she fed me every night of my childhood, and there was a poetic sweetness to her feeding me tonight, on my last night of a different sort of childhood.

My AA group, Hudson Group, called tonight's celebration a "Watch." We threw them for every member who made it to one year sober. It was part birthday party, part graduation, and part AA meeting, all thrown together in the back of an Upper

East Side diner. Although some people in Hudson Group came to their Watch alone, it wasn't uncommon for people to bring a spouse or a few friends. Sobriety wasn't just about us. As the often-uttered phrase went, *Alcoholism is a family disease*, so it only made sense that sobriety should be a family celebration. I was only bringing Mom. I couldn't imagine walking into that diner tonight with anyone else by my side.

As for my dad, I didn't even tell him it was happening. That conversation wouldn't have gone well. I'd learned over this past year that it was better if we avoided the topic of alcohol or alcoholism on our quarterly phone calls. And even if we could suddenly, magically start discussing AA, he hadn't been down to the city from his house in the Catskills in years. He would never come for something like this. Something of mine.

"Should we scrap it and order in?" Mom asked.

"No!" I took another big bite. The meat was as dry as baby powder on my tongue. "Thank you for cooking for me, Mom."

"It's sweet that you still want me to, even though you're all grown up."

"Is twenty-six so grown up?" As the years went on, I was feeling younger and younger. My body was aging, but my soul was Benjamin Button–ing. Sobriety had cast a newness over the way I viewed the world. There were so many firsts open to me again, even after a year: first trip sober, first night out sober, and even first kiss sober.

"I think by any standard or measurement, twenty-six is pretty damn grown up, hon." She took one more bite of the chicken, gritted her teeth, then spit it out. "I can't do this. Stop being polite, and let's order a pizza."

She stood, plate in hand, and walked across the invisible divide that separated the kitchen from what we called "the dining room." I followed her, laughing. The kitchen had always been my favorite part of this apartment. It had a permanent smell of coffee that was just on the wrong side of burnt. Somehow, Mom had made so many cups of pour-over coffee with water straight from a singing kettle that the smell had embedded itself into the drywall. It was the only room with a window that looked out on anything besides a brick wall. In the kitchen, I could spend hours staring outside as the cars and people streamed past on Ninety-Sixth Street.

A phone call to Ray's later, now with pizza grease dripping down her fingers, Mom finally got around to her latest favorite subject: setting me up with her neighbor's nephew. Even though said nephew lived in Washington, DC, worked incredibly long hours, and was certainly not sober, she'd gotten into her head that we'd be perfect together after he came for dinner, saw a photo of me, and apparently said I was pretty.

"So, after tonight, you can finally date, right?" she asked, mouth full of cheese. She was going for a long setup, but it was unnecessary; I could see her conversational tactics from a mile away. She hadn't been the kind of mom who always wanted me to be in a relationship until recently. But a switch had flipped around the time one of her best friends' sons had gotten married. I knew my social media feed would be covered in weddings and babies in a few years, but it seemed as though that was happening now for Mom. Her friends' kids were getting married and having kids of their own, and she was watching it all with envy on Facebook.

"It's all kind of fortuitous because Gates will be in town in a couple weeks—"

"I promise you I won't be interested in Gates," I said. "We have nothing in common."

"You haven't even met him!" Her voice was shrill. She took a breath that seemed to pain her and then continued in an almost pleading tone, "Emma, I get worried about you. You've been alone for so long."

"I've been single, but I haven't been alone. I'm not lonely." That used to be true, but I wasn't sure it had been recently. The nights curled up on my couch had started to feel long, my duvet was less cozy, and the single dinners I made for myself weren't tasting like independence anymore. "And anyway, just because I *can* date, it doesn't mean I feel *ready* to date."

"When will you be ready?"

"I don't know! I don't have a timeline. And it's not just dating that's going to change tonight. I'll also be able to sponsor other women, and be a little more independent from Lola."

But if I was being very, very honest with myself, it wasn't the idea of leading another young, confused girl, whose skin was still off-gassing vodka, through the steps that made my palms sweat. No, Mom was right: the sweat was due to the fact that my year of sponsor-mandated celibacy had ended. As far as AA was concerned, I was a grown woman now. If I wanted to take my closed-off heart and cases of emotional baggage for a spin on the New York City dating scene, no one would stop me. But was I ready to date? Well, that was a different matter entirely.

It wasn't like I still felt the way I did a year ago, when the very thought of going to a restaurant and making polite conversation over glasses of sparkling water seemed unendurable. After all, sitting down to make amends to your mother and confessing that it was you who accidentally gave her crabs ten years ago by using her towel after sleeping with a skateboarder you met in Washington Square Park really gave a person a new perspective on how awkward a conversation could be. It's not an easy thing to admit you let her believe that it was her boyfriend and that you let her break up with said boyfriend, and the whole time she was angrily emptying the drawer she'd given him in her dresser and telling you not to trust men when you got older, you knew it wasn't the well-meaning theater director who was a liar, it was you: her teenage daughter.

Over this past year, I'd told her all that and so much more and watched her eyes change from afraid to disappointed, over and over, and I didn't once look away. So, yes, I was changed. I was better. And after tonight, after my Hudson Group celebration—my Watch—I'd be one year sober and an entirely different person. I just wasn't sure if that person would be ready to open herself up in the way dating required.

"Why do you care, anyway?" I asked Mom. "It's not like you haven't modeled how to live a fulfilling single life." She'd had boyfriends, but nothing really serious since my dad. Although I was aware that when she'd leave the apartment with smoky eyeliner and the rich scent of her sandalwood perfume, she was going on dates, she'd never returned hand in hand with a man. While sometimes I worried about her being lonely, her life seemed full: she had two best single-mom friends, Gloria and Terri, who also lived in the neighborhood. The three of them were always darting from yoga in the park to new plays at Lincoln Center. Their group chat was more dynamic than any I'd ever been a part of.

"Because I care about you, about your happiness." She sounded defensive. I narrowed my eyes at her. "And Gates—"

"Cut the Gates bullshit. You're being weird."

"I am not. Are you excited for your speech?"

"Oh my god, the only topic I want to discuss less!"

She stood and picked up the pizza box, offering it to me, then putting it in the fridge when I shook my head. While her back was turned, she said, "It's just, someday, I might not be as available as I am now. For you to drop by."

"What does that mean?" I followed her to the sink, where she turned on the faucet to start washing our dirty plates.

"I just— I want you to have another person to lean on. It would be good for you."

My phone vibrated on the table. I grabbed at it, grateful for the interruption until I saw who it was.

Lola: I thought you were getting here at 9?

It was now nine fifteen. I thought I'd told her I planned to come at ten. Did she forget, or had I been too scared to tell her I wanted to break with tradition in this way? I couldn't remember. Usually, Watch celebrants got to the diner at nine to start schmoozing, but the whole thing was making me so nervous that I'd decided I really didn't need to be there a whole three hours before I gave my speech.

Emma: Sorry, got a bit waylaid at my mom's. We'll be there by 10!

"Who is that?" Mom asked.

"Lola. I guess I fucked up the time I was supposed to get there."

She rolled her eyes. "Lola has rules for everything, huh? Well, she's wrong in this case. There's no such thing as being late to your own party."

As Mom and I sat on the crosstown bus over to Gracie's Diner, I fidgeted with the one-page speech I'd typed up at home after work. I wouldn't pull it out, but it felt like a safety blanket sitting in my pocket. My thoughts had been collected, and they were right there against the warmth of my thigh. I'd gone to my first Watch the week I met Lola—the same week I'd crawled out of my apartment three days dry and chosen a random AA meeting on the New York Intergroup website. In most AA groups, you chose your own sponsor, someone who you might've heard speak and had a connection to. But sponsorship worked a bit differently in HG. When the woman beside me asked who my sponsor was after that first meeting, and I said I didn't have one, a choreographed dance quickly happened that ended with Lola shaking my hand and telling me she was excited to work with me.

I'd been terrified of going to that first Watch. Socializing? Being out late? Looking new people in the eye without a drink in my hand? Those were things I simply could not do; I'd proven it to be impossible over the last ten years. But the Watch was happening after the Tuesday night meeting that Lola insisted I go to, and before I could think of an excuse, I was following her up Second Avenue and blowing up balloons for a woman I'd never met.

The "birthday girl," Carey, didn't walk in until hours later. By the time she did, I'd heard countless women, all of whom seemed way too cool to be sober, talk about how much they loved her. She grew large in my imagination. Who was this person who'd enchanted Manhattan's reformed Uptown socialites and Bushwick hipsters alike?

Carey lived up to the hype. She was in her twenties like me and had a bleached Mia Farrow pixie cut and a prairie dress covered in blue flowers. She was self-deprecating about her past and glossy-eyed with hope about her future. She said, "It's moments like this that I thank God for making me an alcoholic because if I wasn't, then I wouldn't know the bliss of sobriety." I'd balked, knowing that the bra I was wearing still had dried vomit crusted into the worn lace, but desperate to drink again anyway. But other people nodded along. They even cheered.

My speech wouldn't be like hers—I'd never be able to pull off a pixie cut (my jawline was nowhere near defined enough), nor would I be able to casually sit on a table with my ankles crossed. I could only do my best.

Pulling open the front door of Gracie's, I tried a deep breath, but it came out as a stutter.

"Emma!" Lola said, throwing her arms around me. "Congratulations!"

I murmured my thank-you into her magnolia-scented hair.

We broke apart, and I made my introductions. This was the first time Mom and Lola were meeting. It was awkward having them side by side. It wasn't like they didn't have things in common. They were both confident New York City women who easily called me on my BS. But, since getting sober, my mom and my sponsor had been my only two real confidants. Which meant that they'd both heard me complain about the other ad nauseam—cue the awkwardness.

"It's so good to finally meet you!" Mom said, pulling Lola in for a hug of her own. "Thank you so much for helping Emma this past year! I can't believe what a transformation it's been!" Mom was using the smile she usually paraded past men right before she told them her name was "always Jacqueline, never Jackie" and declined their invitation out. But there was something earnest in her eyes, and I hoped Lola could see through her plastered smile.

Lola seemed taken aback. When I'd described my mother, I often talked about the ways she resisted or disagreed with this process. She hadn't wanted me to drink but also seemed uncomfortable about my calling myself an alcoholic and centering my life around AA. Even though she'd been desperate for my dad to change his life exactly this way when they were together, she'd been mildly alarmed that I, the daughter she thought took after her in every way, couldn't just learn to moderate her drinking. She was happy to say goodbye to the Sunday afternoons when she'd arrive at my Brooklyn apartment to find me still in bed, where I'd been for anywhere between four and thirty-six hours, with vomit in my hair and shards of broken glass from the previous night scattered across the floor. But she also hadn't wanted me to stop going to gallery openings with her even though they carted out free wine.

"Thank you for being such a great support system for her!" Lola returned. "This is one of the reasons I love Watches so much—we finally get to see the whole picture, not just the people who support Emma within the rooms, but also the people who are supporting her outside of them."

This was going better than I'd expected. I should have had more trust in both of them. We were all on the same side, after all.

"I'm sorry...but are there no men here?" Mom asked, looking around curiously.

Lola politely followed Mom's gaze across the room. "Doesn't look like it." She shrugged.

"Will there be?"

I pinched Mom's arm where Lola couldn't see. She took a half step away from me, committing to the line of questioning.

"Some might show up later, or it might end up being just the girls tonight!"

"Hmm."

I realized I'd probably avoided telling her how gender-segregated Hudson Group was. It wasn't as if we were separated by some edict from on high—it was just that we did almost everything within sober "families." My sober family was made up of Lola, her sponsor, and any other sponsees Lola or her sponsor had. It was like a family tree that branched out in a million directions. Since Hudson Group had hundreds of people, we used sober families as a smaller subset. And since there was an AA-wide practice that encouraged sponsoring people of the same gender, my sober family was exclusively women. But now I could tell Mom was reframing my decision to be single the past year in this new context and deciding it had more to do with HG's influence than she'd previously thought.

Before she opened her mouth again, I cut in: "Can we help in any way? I'm so sorry we're later than expected!"

But everything was already set up, and the back area was full of people. I knew all of them by sight, but I would have only been able to name about half of them, maybe 60 percent with a gun to my head. Just like when I went to Carey's Watch a year ago, most people were here because it was considered polite, and they'd get points with their sponsor for showing up. I was worried that because I didn't have any close friends I hung out with outside of meetings—Lola only had one other sponsee, and although she came to meetings, she was rarely around otherwise—my Watch would be noticeably smaller than most. But word had spread through the fruitful grapevine and Hudson Group members had shown up for one of their own.

Looking around, I was confronted with the bodies in the space, milling about, watching me wait for midnight, and I realized how nervous I was. All of these people were going to hear me speak. They were going to listen to my story. Worst of all: Mom would be listening. There'd be nothing she hadn't heard before, but I hoped it wouldn't echo in a new way for her in a room full of people. Although I'd promised myself no one else would remember what I said, I couldn't really say that was true. After all, Carey's words still rang out in my mind all these months later. Some newly sober young woman might hear me speak tonight, and instead of being inspired, like I was with Carey, they could feel revolted. Maybe they'd see the tremors in my hands and wonder where all the miracles sobriety promised were. Clearly, if I was still nervous and stuttering, I wasn't better, and if I wasn't better, why should they try?

I'd qualified at regular AA meetings, but that format made it feel completely different. In those meetings, after I shared my story, other people would raise their hands and speak about how they related. Maybe they'd latch on to my divorced parents and tell a divorce story of their own, or perhaps they'd understand the grief I felt having betrayed people I loved, and they'd talk about relationships they'd lost in their own life. Cross talk wasn't allowed, but it was a conversation. Tonight, on the other hand, was a speech. On the spectrum between cry for help and Oscar acceptance, this one was feeling heavy, golden, and statuesque.

My quiet nervousness became too much for even my own mother, and she started to weave her way around the room, meeting and talking with people. Every few minutes, I'd see her gesture in my direction and point me out to her latest conversation partner. They would sometimes smile and wave and other times furrow their brow in confusion as if they were just now seeing me for the first time.

Finally, Diane, my lone sponsee sister, showed up, ordered a slice of key lime pie, and posted herself next to me at the back of the room. She was a fortysomething stand-up comedian who'd had a few walk-on parts on sitcoms. "You know this is my first Watch?" she said. "I thought I'd have a terrible time, and I wasn't wrong, but you look like you're having a worse one."

"Your first Watch? I must have been to a dozen by now."

"Really? You dig the atmosphere or something?" She gestured at the tables full of abandoned coffee mugs.

I laughed. "No, of course not. But Lola told me to come, so I came."

"Hmm," Diane said, leaning back to study me. "Me, personally? I don't do everything Lola tells me."

"Well, I don't, either." I thought of the example of arriving here tonight a whole hour late, but I didn't think Diane would count that. "But it doesn't really hurt to go to them. And Lola thinks it helps."

"Yeah, but—"

I couldn't let her finish; her questioning of Lola was rubbing an area already chafed by Mom's earlier comments. "I feel like a lot of this stuff is simple. I want to get better. I don't want to drink, and I don't want to be the person I was when I was drinking. If I have to follow some rules I don't fully understand or go to events that are a little awkward and a little boring to do that, then so be it. I trust Lola, and she says this will help."

"I guess that's the part I struggle with," Diane said. "There are parts of who I was when I was drinking that I liked. I want to be as funny as I was. I want to be as spontaneous as I was. I don't want to drink, but I wish I could keep everything else the same, you know?"

"No," I said, the force of my voice surprising us both. "I don't want to have anything to do with who I was before."

"Okay, girlie. I hear you."

We sipped our coffees and let the other partygoers fill the silence between us.

I tore at a loose thread on the hem of my cherry red dress as Lola stood to introduce me. It was '90s vintage that I'd bought off Etsy for the occasion. The breathable cotton was necessary in the heat, but I hadn't had time to wash it, and it smelled unfamiliar in the way things do when they come from a stranger's house.

"Hello, everyone! It's getting close to midnight, so I think we should get going!" Lola started, and after a few specific thank-yous and welcomes, she told the room the story of the tradition of the Watch: "Years ago, when this group was first founded, one of the original members relapsed on the night before their first anniversary of sobriety. They were able to come back to the fold, and the following year, the night before their first anniversary, the group gathered around them, in this very diner, to watch and make sure they made it through the night sober. It became a tradition. The first year of sobriety is one of great change, where we're essentially young children learning to walk again. Most people who relapse do so during the first year, and if you can get through the pain and discomfort of building a new life, you have a better chance of making it in the long haul. Many of our rules only apply to the first year of sobriety..." She paused to allow the room a chuckle. I heard a raucous hoot from a table in the back. "And so, in addition to being a little insurance policy to make sure folks make it across the finish line, the Watch has become a celebration—almost a graduation ceremony.

"So, without further ado, I want to welcome Emma to stand and talk to us about today versus this day last year."

My stomach twisted in anticipation. Today a year ago. My last day of drinking.

I stood. I noticed a fresh coffee stain on the skirt of my dress.

The cherry red now wore a small splash of mud brown. Another way I'd be different from Carey.

As I reached her, Lola gave me a hug, then gestured to me with the tight-lipped smile of pageant mom. Applause.

"Hi," I started. The room was full of expectant eyes sitting wide in friendly faces, but the same fears I'd had earlier pulsed through me. What if no one related to what I was saying? What if I ended up convincing someone *not* to stay sober?

I started again: "Thank you all for coming." Another breath. What had I written down earlier?

I thanked Lola for her guidance and spiritual leadership. I thanked Mom. I thanked the community, whatever that meant. Then there was no one else to thank, and it was time for me to start my story. "I wasn't born into a big family. I didn't have any siblings, and when I was nine, my parents got divorced. My dad moved out of the city, and I didn't see much of him.

"When I was growing up, before the divorce, before I had ever tasted alcohol, it controlled my life. I heard about it every day when my parents fought. The short version is she wanted him to drink less and he wanted to drink more. Before high school, all I knew about drinking was that it was powerful enough to blow up your life. There was nothing casual or relaxed about drinking. I've heard people in meetings talk about alcohol becoming their god, and I think that was true for me even before I'd had a sip. To drink or not to drink was the question that pumped through my mind as a child. And that was sad, and I was lonely, but when I was fourteen, I met Susannah and the question was suddenly answered."

I wasn't sure how much Susannah to include in my speech. When I'd practiced it, I never talked about the scuffed vintage satin heels she wore in ninth grade, or how her laugh was clear and sharp and it seemed like she thought everything I said was funny. Instead, I'd practiced talking about the casual way she spoke about drinking forties on school nights and how easy it was for us to change "school nights" into "lunch breaks" by the time we got to tenth grade.

But I ended up saying it all, talking about how she was my first and only and truest best friend. And how after ninth grade, we never left each other's side. We both stayed in the city for college and forewent dorms in favor of shared apartments at the end of train lines. The long rides, late nights, and twenties scraped together for bags of weed and coke were all ours to share. She was mine, and I was hers. Anything I did, from throwing up on the kitchen floor, because I missed the sink, to blacking out and waking up in the wrong borough in the bed of a man who I didn't remember meeting, was funny because she found it funny. And because if that was my Wednesday night, her Thursday would be just as bad.

Until she met Brian. His man bun was dumb but having to share her was even dumber. Suddenly, she thought all the things I did were messy instead of funny. And I hated Brian more than I hated anyone I had ever met. Including my dad—which was saying a lot.

Another breath.

"And so, because I was jealous, and because my jealousy made me hate Brian, and I didn't know how to get him to leave, I did the one thing that worked best in the past when I wanted men to leave. I tried to sleep with him."

I released a chuckle, and the crowd laughed with me. There was a magic to AA meetings that allowed everything to be laughed at. Even though this wasn't technically a meeting, a spell had been cast when enough alcoholics entered the room. We could laugh at anything—even the most horrible mistakes, mistakes that ended marriages or ended in jail time—because we were all facing whatever happened together. Your worst fear is suddenly funny when someone is holding your hand. That same camaraderie and companionship I'd found with Susannah, I glimpsed it here.

"But Brian did not reciprocate. Instead, he told Susannah what I did, and to my shock, she decided to move out of our apartment and in with him. So I sat around drinking and bitching about her to all our friends until I had no one to drink with or bitch to anymore.

"That was tolerable for a few months, until it seemed like she really wasn't coming home. And without her there to laugh with me, throwing up on myself didn't seem funny anymore. It seemed so, so sad. Thankfully, I found this meeting, and Lola, who guided me through the twelve steps. And now I can stand here in front of you all, proud of who I've become." Had I said enough? Did they believe me? "I'm grateful to be an alcoholic because if I wasn't, then I wouldn't know the peace of sobriety."

There was applause. It was alright. I exhaled. As long as no one realized I stole the last line from Carey's speech, then it was totally alright. I looked up at the clock in the doorway; it was 12:06 a.m. My first year of sobriety was officially over and the rest of my life had begun.

THREE

Today is the first day of the rest of your life. The slogan from the Post-it played on a loop in my mind. The sunrise was arching through my linen curtains and dyeing the stark white walls of my studio apartment a shy lavender.

Choppy recollections of words and phrases I'd said in my speech the night before started to pierce through as I woke up. They rode to the front of my mind on waves of self-doubt. Did anyone feel the way I felt? I wished people had said more than congratulations to me last night—that they'd whispered their own secrets and strengths to me. Maybe then I wouldn't have had to rip off part of Carey's speech. But the Watch wasn't a time to doubt the process. The Watch was a time to celebrate. Even though sobriety didn't feel like pink-cloud peace to me, I'd done the right thing by not mentioning how I didn't feel fully there yet. After all, I didn't really know where *there* was. I wanted to feel grateful for being an alcoholic. I wanted to be so blissed out that everything that had come before felt worth it. But I didn't. I still felt like things would have been easier if I was normal.

It was 7:30 a.m. on Friday morning, which meant that even

the near-constant buzz of Crown Heights was hanging back. The spiraling part of my mind started releasing its hold as soon as my feet hit the sidewalk. I passed coffee shops scattered with a few early risers typing away on their laptops, restaurant workers hosing down strips of concrete dirtied by a busy night, and bodegas selling rolls dripping with gooey eggs and cheese. All of the people I passed had their own full lives. They were tending to bank accounts, families, broken hearts, blistered dreams. My problems were small. I had a vulnerability hangover from the Watch. Life would go on.

I almost made it to Eastern Parkway and its canopy of tall oaks offering cover from the mid-September sun when my phone rang.

Dad.

I clicked Decline without thinking. He'd caught me by surprise is all. We hadn't spoken since I visited Phoenicia a few months ago, and I thought, after the way it went, we'd take a longer break. I wanted us to, at least. I'd call back. Just not today. Not this morning.

My dad was born Robert but had taken the Hindu name Kirtan after a life-altering visit to India with his partner Gaurapriya (formerly Laurel). The last time I saw him, he was celebrating the start of his second Saturn's return and wanted his family and community to gather around him. I, as his only child, counted in that group. Had it been a year earlier, depending on the mood I was in, I would have let the invite sit unanswered or I would have taken the bus up, bringing only shrooms and the romantic notion that a weekend away would help me "detox" from whatever mess I was leaving behind in the city. I'd had no idea what a trip up there fully sober would be like, but the email informed me that Saturn's return was an astrological rebirth, and since I was also in a time of great change and reflection, I was optimistic.

It took about five minutes for him to hand me a glass of white wine. I kept saying, "I'm good right now, but thanks," until he asked what was wrong with me. I told him I wasn't drinking anymore.

"At all?" he asked, stepping closer. I noticed the yellow of his teeth and the fermented smell of his skin. Gaura was on the far side of the room with three of their friends, but I still worried she could hear us.

I had hoped that with his astrological rebirth, our relationship would have a rebirth of sorts, too. As a kid, I'd go up to the Catskills for the summer to visit him. The older I got, the shorter those summers became, as I wanted to spend more and more time in the city with my friends. The weeks I stayed in the Catskills with him were spent mainly alone and tucked into the latest fantasy series until I turned fourteen and started bringing Susannah, and we'd hang out on the porch and smoke weed. My dad mainly stayed out of our way. We'd pass him in the hall and break into fits of giggles, and he'd let us off with a knowing wave. Eventually, I asked him if he wouldn't mind buying us beer, and it only took a few months to wear him down until he started leaving an extra case on the basement stairs every time I visited. We didn't talk about it, but I'm sure a piece of him felt like I was choosing his side in the fight that broke up our family. I answered the question "to drink or not to drink" with a resounding gulp.

"No, Dad, not at all."

"As a temporary fast of sorts?" His eyebrows furrowed.

"It's forever. Well, hopefully forever. I wasn't doing well with drinking." I didn't want to mention AA. It had been a lightning rod in my parents' marriage. The first time I ever heard of AA was in muffled shouts from their bedroom. My dad would say he was an artist, he needed to relax for his creative process. And he only ever drank beer and wine, which barely counted. He thought Mom was crazy, overreacting. When I first started drinking in high school, I thought he was right. What was the big deal? After all, I didn't remember him drunk as much as I remembered the fights about it.

"And your definition of forever includes this weekend's festivities?"

"Yes, it does. I won't drink at the party. I can't do it to myself anymore." I stared at an ant crawling on the countertop between us. It was thick-bodied and dark black against the indigo tile.

"Were you drinking spirits?" he asked.

I nodded. Now that I was looking for them, I found two more ants. I wondered if my dad and Gaura had a house policy about not using poison that would harm animals.

"You know," he started, "my father was an alcoholic."

I, of course, knew this about my grandfather. He'd died in a nursing home when I was twelve, but my last visit with him was etched into my consciousness. He couldn't remember my name, but he kept asking if I could sneak him in some scotch. When Mom was recounting the beats of the divorce to me years after it happened—the two of us curled up on the couch like best friends in a distorted rom-com—she told me that my grandfather's obvious alcoholism was my dad's greatest evidence that he wasn't one. He wasn't falling down. He wasn't hitting people. How could they be in the same category?

"And I've found it's hard liquor that people really have problems with. That's how I've managed to control my drinking all these years. Beer, white wine—it doesn't cause the same problems."

I nodded, even though all I wanted to do was rip the glass of wine out of his hand and bash it against the wall just to show him how out of control a glass of wine could make me. But I knew that fantasy was giving me too much credit; if I really took it out of his hands, I'd bring it to my lips, not the wall. I crushed the ant closest to me under my thumb.

I got to work while the offices were still dark. Each of my steps triggered an automated fluorescent flicker as I walked down the hall. It was going to be a long workday, and that's what I should've been focusing on. Richter & Thomas was considering launching a new marketing campaign to target Gen Z. Convincing eighteen-year-olds on TikTok to invest in their retirement funds wouldn't be easy. But that wasn't my focus at the moment. Instead, I was thinking about Ben. About what it would be like to be alone with him for thirty minutes. It would be the closest thing I'd had to a date in over a year. Which was sad, because meeting an IT guy before 9:00 a.m. to set up my new work computer was obviously not a date. My nerves were in great shape.

Ben arrived at 8:19 a.m., opening the office door with a computer in his arms. "Oh, I thought I'd beat you here," he said, placing the clunky PC gingerly on my desk, next to the monitor that wouldn't need replacing. Had he wanted time with my computer without me here? "Trying to get out of your comfort zone?" he asked.

"What?" I looked up at him. I was sitting in my chair, which was infinitely better than being on my hands and knees, but I was still surprised by how far I had to tilt my head back to make eye contact.

He pointed to the stack of neon Post-its. The one that was now on top read *No one ever grows up standing still in their comfort zone.*

"I didn't write that. I would never write something like that." I might have spoken too sternly, but it felt imperative that he not think I was the kind of woman who doodled silly sayings on yellow Post-it notes. Work Emma could be a lot of things to a lot of people, but I couldn't send her so far afield that I lost control of her completely.

"You're a fan of comfort zones, then? Happy to stay put?" I couldn't quite read the expression on his face.

"I'm not pro or anti. I just think platitudes are stupid," I said.

He still hadn't sat down, even though Vanessa's empty chair was only a foot away. "Most of the time, anyway."

"I guess most of the time we can be friends, then." He smiled, finally sitting. His left incisor was ever-so-slightly folded over his canine. He was being chatty. In a teasing, bordering-on-taciturn way. "My least favorite has got to be 'Everything happens for a reason.'"

I smiled back. "Because there's a lot of bad things happening out there for no reason?"

"So you haven't heard of the lizard people controlling our international institutions?"

I guffawed—not something Work Emma was supposed to do. It wasn't a polite or demure sound. "I have, actually. I also spend too much time on YouTube." My algorithm leaned more toward twentysomething girls living boring lives virtually in *The Sims 4*, but even so, YouTube had tried to show me some pretty out-there conspiracies.

"YouTube can be a dangerous place." He smiled wide again as if pleased with himself for making me laugh.

"I think the worst is 'Live every day like it's your last.'"

He plugged in my new computer as he asked, "Because it's dangerously close to YOLO or…?"

"No, because that saying works for people who are too scared to do anything reckless, not people who are too reckless to be scared."

"And you're the latter?" I felt his eyes roving over my face. Is this how I looked when I was counting his moles?

I nodded. "I think I'd be dead if I thought like that." I couldn't remember the last time I'd said something so honest to someone I worked with. Work Emma didn't do honesty and vulnerability; it's what made her Professional.

Ben blinked at me. And then again. In my manifesto about why I should think before I speak, I could use this as a key footnote. Even when something seemed banal to me, it was probably a statement that was not fit for the corporate workplace. I broke eye contact and said, "Have you ever been to Maine?"

If I'd surprised him by my sudden change in direction, he didn't let on. "No. Is it nice?"

"I haven't been, either. But it's in New England, so I would assume it has salty air, clapboard houses, and high-quality fried seafood. What's not to like?" I was rambling, but it didn't matter. I'd done what I meant to do. Changed the subject. Stopped his weird blinking.

"I'm from Upstate New York, which has embedded a kind of weird rivalry with New England in me. Why does New England get to be romanticized all the time? If city people want to peep leaves, they can get just as good of a look in New York." His fingers moved against the keyboard as he spoke; setting up computers clearly came so easily to him he barely had to think about it.

"Oh, but upstate is so different!" I said, spinning in my chair. This chair had never spun before, I was sure of it. "There are no quaint towns and no dogged Puritan spirit. Leaf peepers aren't just looking for the hills full of cascading red leaves; they want the red leaves contrasted with the bright white steeple of the church where hard-nosed Puritan ministers used to preach about the evils of witches."

"You're speaking with quite a bit of authority, but let me tell you, upstate has both."

I rolled my eyes. "Upstate is full of hippies, and then, if you go farther up, hippies and apple farmers."

"What makes you so sure?"

"My dad lives there." Did Work Emma have a dad? I don't think I'd ever mentioned my dad before at work.

"Oh yeah? Where?"

"Phoenicia, right by Woodstock."

"I don't think that's fair. You're judging the entire state off the mecca of hippy-dom."

"Are hippies and Woodstock somehow related? I had no idea!"

"Did your dad retire there, or…?"

I could've said anything, but the truth slipped out: "He's lived there since I was nine. I mainly grew up down here with my mom."

"A city kid, then?"

I nodded. "How about you?"

"I'm from Troy." He scrunched up his face, trying to assess if that would mean anything to me. He guessed correctly—I'd never heard of Troy, outside of Homer—and continued: "It's a bit north of Albany, which has fewer picturesque churches and more midcentury brutalist office buildings stuffed with corrupt state politicians."

"What's not to romanticize?" I tried to ask with a straight face, but it broke by the second syllable of the sentence. He laughed, too. Was I good at this? Maybe talking to attractive men while sober wasn't so hard. I must've built it up in my mind. "Is Troy nicer than Albany?"

He shrugged. "It's greener, at least."

"Hey, and maybe being from there is what made you so beautiful." I heard the words as they were coming out of my mouth and felt a heavy dose of shame crash over me. It turned out that I was not good at this. I was, in fact, wildly terrible.

"Being from Troy?" He looked confused. The joke was so bad I'd almost confused myself.

"I'm so, so sorry. I was trying to make a Helen of Troy joke. I also now remember Helen wasn't even from Troy, she was kidnapped and taken to Troy, so it doesn't even make sense." I was stammering. I was blushing. The marketing-and-communications office of Richter & Thomas Financial Consulting was my own personal hell on earth. "I'm really sorry."

"So you were saying I have a face that could set one thousand ships to sail?" His voice was sarcastic as he gestured to himself like the very idea was a joke. But it wasn't. There were no long eyelashes or soft lips, and he certainly didn't have Helen's famously blond hair, but there was a beauty similar to that you might find in the midcentury office buildings he said dominated his hometown: his features were pointed. His jaw, nose, and browbone were drawn with the same defined hand I could imagine created an architect's blueprints.

I could have used his sarcasm to deny the whole thing. But instead, I said, "That's what I meant, yeah." I was earning my recklessness back. But it was worth it. I wasn't going to let him walk around thinking his face was something to be laughed at.

His smile fell. "I think that, as a son of Troy, I would actually be Paris, not Helen." He paused. "And I would be promised the most beautiful woman in the world to bring home."

We were making eye contact. My breath was so shallow it was only reaching my collarbones. "I should not have mentioned Homeric poetry."

He shook his head, clearing it. "It's okay," he said. The tips of his ears were red where they stuck out of his hair.

At some point during my awkward stumbling, my monitor had lit up. I gestured to it, eager to move on. "Is this good to go?"

"Yeah, go ahead and enter your password. It's a new computer, but since we save everything to the cloud, it'll have all your old data on it." He pushed the keyboard and mouse toward me.

All my old data? I should have been relieved I didn't have to start my hunt for the perfect green all over again, but the feeling was overshadowed by the sudden terror that my speech was about to pop up. "Will what I was working on yesterday be there?" I had to know before I started typing.

"Oh, the project you were working on when it froze? Maybe. Let's try." He looked at my hands expectantly. I didn't move them. "Do you know your password?"

"Yup. I know it." There was no way around this. No lie I

could tell to avoid typing it in. My fingers traced their familiar path across the keys. I hit Enter.

"Might take a minute to boot up the first time." A minute. A whole minute that I'd have to live with my stomach in my throat. I stared at the spinning blue circle in the center of the screen.

"So, uh, what neighborhood do you live in now?" Ben asked. He was trying to make conversation, but my whole focus was on what was about to happen.

"Crown Heights." I couldn't look at him.

"And do you live with roommates or…?"

"I live alone." The screen flashed. The generic Windows desktop image appeared. No applications were open. "Oh! Here it goes!" I sounded too excited. I could hear it, but I couldn't help it.

"Yeah, give it another second," he said.

"For what—" But just as the words left my mouth, I saw it. InDesign and Word were both opening. It was going to happen. There was no way I could stop it. The Word doc, my speech, popped up and took over the entire screen. Crisp and incriminating. I lunged for the mouse and minimized it as fast as I could. "That was nothing!"

"Okaaay," Ben said, drawing out the word.

"It was a creative writing exercise." I had to say something to explain it. "Not work related, sorry."

"No worries. Do you write?" Even though my computer was clearly functional, Ben was making no moves to leave. Instead, he was settling in. Leaning back. Chatting.

"That was the first time. It was a joke. Something I'm doing with my friends." I couldn't stop the lies. They were bubbling out of me at a rapid pace. Ben was nice, and cute, and funny, but I needed this morning to end. For him to even have glanced at my speech made me feel like I was standing in front of him not just naked, but naked with my skin peeled off. Like he was seeing the blood pour through my muscles and fall to the office floor.

"So," he started, "I was wondering, do you have lunch plans?"

"I bring my lunch." It was true. Every day, I brought a glass Pyrex of rice and beans. It was boring, but it was also cheap. Although I felt living alone was necessary for my sobriety, it was barely affordable and I had to save wherever I could.

Ben stood up and pushed in Vanessa's chair, but before he walked out the door, he said, "Oh, well then, maybe, would you want to grab a drink after work sometime?"

My mind went blank. I should have added up where his questions were heading. But I was so distracted and out of practice, I hadn't seen it coming.

"I'm sorry. I'm busy tonight." I kept my eyes on the floor. I didn't want to see his face change from nervous to disappointed or embarrassed.

"Oh. Of course. No problem. Earlier, it seemed like... Never mind." He walked to the door, reached for the handle, and then asked, "Do you have a boyfriend?"

The question surprised me enough that I looked back at him. "No!" It slipped out, but I should have caught it. A boyfriend would be a good excuse, a sturdy lie. But for some reason, I didn't want Ben to think I had a boyfriend. My mind started spinning. "I just have a lot going on right now. This week. Today. That Word doc you saw..."

The truth was so close, I could feel the syllables on the back of my tongue. I could tell him. I could just say that I was sober. That I was a recovering alcoholic, and he saw my speech celebrating one year sober, and I got embarrassed because no one in the office knows and I have no idea how to tell them, but he seemed so nice, and— "It's actually my friend's boyfriend's funeral. He died in this sudden terrible accident and, you know, so, she's having a funeral. Tonight. And I was helping her with her eulogy. That was the Word doc you saw."

That was not what I meant to say.

FOUR

I got a whole bench to myself on the train ride to the Upper East Side for my Hudson Group Tuesday night meeting. Tuesdays were the big meeting night. Couldn't miss it. Couldn't reschedule it. Everyone in Hudson Group was required to be at Tuesday's meeting. Hudson Group had meetings seven days a week at 7:00 p.m., and each day of the week had a theme. When I'd joined, Lola had put me on Monday, Tuesday, Thursday.

None of the HG meetings were typical for AA. Tuesday night was just speakers, and no one who wasn't predetermined was welcome to share. On nights like tonight, I could relax, listen, and take information in. Mondays were the reverse—I was always on edge.

Monday's meeting was a nightmare—truly. The first time I went, I thought someone had reached into my subconscious and created something out of my worst fears. It was the boggart of events. It wasn't in a church like all the others were. Instead, it was in a public high school auditorium. Most public New York City schools were built during the New Deal in the 1930s, and all of the auditoriums looked the same: narrow wooden stadium-style seating facing a stage with thick red velvet curtains, surrounded by grand ten-foot windows. At some point between the '30s and when I was a kid in the '00s, the windows had been covered in latticed metal bars so no one could jump out. To open a window, you'd have to stick a long pole through the bars just right, latch it on, and heave it up. Teachers who'd been around for a few decades—the ones with weary eyes, voices grown husky from yelling at mischievous students through thick New York accents—were always the best at this. No one who attended the Monday night meeting could ever quite manage it. Before the bars, they might've been nice rooms. And maybe if I hadn't sat through so many tiresome assemblies in my thirteen years in New York City public schools, I wouldn't have thought anything of the atmosphere. But the atmosphere was only where the horror of the Monday night meeting started.

The meeting worked like this: there would be a speaker, and that speaker would speak for ten minutes about one of the twelve steps and the work they'd done on it. They'd go up on the stage and stand in front of the red velvet curtains with nothing more than a mic to block them from the audience's view. You might think, Fine, what's the harm there? But here's where it got bonkers: the speaker would then point to someone, *anyone*, in the audience, and whoever they pointed to would have to go onstage and share for three minutes. Then that person would point at random to the next person, and so on. There was no volunteering or refusing. You were supposed to sit back and go with God's will. But mostly I'd sweat through the entire meeting, my nerves on edge, my stomach dropping with every finger-point into the crowd.

Somehow, blessedly, in the five months I attended, I never got picked. I wore head-to-toe black, shrunk down in my tight wooden chair, and prayed for the full hour. Even though I wasn't too sure about the whole Higher Power thing, I would still beg the Universe not to let me get picked. When I completed my fifth step, I finally asked Lola if I could switch to Saturdays.

She didn't let me feel great about it—there was talk about how Mondays might help me grow, and the group wouldn't let anything truly bad happen to me—but when I kept asking with increasing desperation, she finally let me switch. Saturday was a meditation meeting. It was very peaceful.

On Tuesdays, I always met Lola forty-five minutes early at the Starbucks around the corner on Sixty-Third and Lexington. As usual, it was full of people having hushed conversations with their sponsors. New York City was full of AAs if you listened for them. There might be people on the F train whispering about making amends, people walking down Central Park West talking about making more time for fellowship, or people tucked into the corners of coffee shops all across town murmuring the words of *12 Steps and 12 Traditions* aloud to themselves. I gave muted waves and head nods to a couple of people I knew before sitting down at a small table across from Lola.

"So," Lola said, "we haven't hashed things out since the big day. How are you feeling?" She was wearing a delicate white eyelet dress that I would have sweat through in minutes in the September heat. I hadn't thought about my clothes until that very moment. I was wearing a light blue button-down and a black skirt. It was pretty much what I wore every day to the office.

I couldn't help myself; I stole a quick peek at Lola's engagement ring as I told her I was feeling fine. It was still massive and gleaming, just as it had been when I met her. Lola had been in a relationship when she got sober, which meant she didn't have to be celibate for a year. The logic behind not recommending new relationships was that a recently sober person might replace their addiction to alcohol or drugs with an addiction to sex or love. I wasn't so sure you couldn't become addicted to what you already had—my new daily ice-cream habit could attest to that.

"Should we dig in?" she asked with raised eyebrows.

I nodded, pulled up my Notes app, and opened the long-running file titled "Resentments."

Meeting with your sponsor wasn't like going to therapy or chatting with a friend—at least, not the way Hudson Group did it. Our discussions were all based on our resentments. We made a list every week, and then every week, we said them aloud and let them go. The Big Book taught us that our resentments were what made us sick. Alcoholics had a particular ability to blame the world around them instead of themselves. Bill W., the author of the Big Book, gave the example of how he believed it wasn't his fault he drank; it was his nagging wife, the asshole who fired him, or the president for sending him to war. I might not have been a macho early-twentieth-century stockbroker like Bill was, but I had my own version of his logic. I used to think I deserved to get drunk because I had weird parents and a weird childhood, but in the end, I was the only person who had to deal with the consequences of my actions.

I led with a recurring item on my list: my dad. I still wasn't sure what our relationship was going to be now that I was sober, and I resented him for making me figure that out. "He called me on Friday, actually. I missed it."

"Did you call back?" Lola asked.

"No, I didn't." Lola consistently gave me advice about "being in service" to my dad. She believed that if he saw how successful my life was without drinking, he might follow suit. I shied away from the pressure of that belief. "He left a voicemail, but I didn't listen to it."

"Why don't we listen to it together?"

"Now? Here?" I wiped my palms on the smooth polyester of the work skirt I'd gotten on sale at Target.

She nodded at me, and I took a deep breath. I didn't play it for Lola. I held the phone close to my ear as my dad's familiar voice poured through the speaker: "Em—it's Kirtan. Dad. Give me a call when you can."

"It's nothing," I said to Lola, relieved. "He's just asking me to call him back."

"Why don't you?"

"Now?" I asked for the second time in less than a minute.

"It seems like you've built up this moment, this call, maybe more than you need to. It could be a casual hello. And if it's not, what better time than sitting here with me in fellowship before we gather with our community?"

I could think of several better moments. All of them involved me sitting alone. I shook my head no.

"Give it a try," Lola said.

I didn't know what to do besides what she told me. I hit Call.

The phone rang twice. And then a third time. It occurred to me suddenly that he might not answer at all. That I could get through this moment having gained points with Lola, all while avoiding a conversation with my dad. My pulse slowed. Things could go my way.

"Hello?" His voice was rough. It sounded tired, like maybe I'd woken him. Anxiety pumped through my bloodstream. I didn't want to be talking to him here like this. I wanted us to have a casual relationship that didn't require the support of a sponsor.

"Dad? It's me? You called? On Friday? Sorry it's taken me a while to get back to you."

"Emma. Oh. Where are you?"

"In a Starbucks." I made eye contact with Lola, and she gave me an encouraging smile. "Is everything okay?"

He took a breath. It blew through the speaker of the phone like a gust of wind through leaves, rustling the conversation. "Yeah. 'Course. I was thinking of coming down there. It'd be nice to see you."

"Coming down here?" I asked.

To my knowledge, my dad had only been back to New York City once since he moved away almost two decades ago. Whenever the city was mentioned in his presence, he usually said the incredibly stereotypical *I'm so glad I got out*, *I don't know how you do it* or *You know there's a big world out there, Emma. You don't have to live there just because you were born there.* He prided himself on having lived in and then lost New York—like it was a habit he'd had to kick. The people who still lived here, including my mother and I, were wasting their lives in a self-imposed prison.

His last trip had been about a decade ago, when he came to introduce me to Gaura, as well as to his own new name and identity. *Robert* had been rebirthed as *Kirtan*, and I was having a hard time getting to know his new personality. I was a senior in high school, and they'd asked me to meet them for lunch and a yoga class in an old townhouse on a side street in the depths of Chelsea. I'd been out with Susannah the night before, and I hadn't slept. The soft metallic drip of cocaine was still tinkering its way down my throat, and my eyeliner was unwashed and pilling against my skin like a sweater that had seen better days.

The class wasn't like any I'd ever been to before. We didn't do any downward dogs or crunches disguised as boat poses. Instead, we just sat and breathed. We closed one nostril and then the other, over and over, faster and faster, until my head floated off my body, and all I felt was rage. I was furious about the way my dad and Gaura looked at me during lunch, like I was wrinkled and dirty—in need of a good deep cleaning. And, worse, like it was them who could provide that for me. The audacity shocked me silent. It felt as if he'd spilled a drink, walked away, and then came back in to ask why the rug was ruined. I trembled thinking about each sly look they gave each other when I stumbled over answers about school.

I was lost until Susannah met us for dinner and repeatedly forgot their self-given names. Each time Laurel or Robert slipped past her lips, the pressure that had wound itself around my lungs eased. What did it matter what they thought of me, when I had her? Each time she let her tongue dart between her teeth to sound out the many *l*'s in Gaura's former name, I bit back a laugh. Susannah thought they were dumb, which meant it didn't matter that I couldn't breathe properly, that I was failing chemistry and only applied to CUNY schools, or that I didn't have a connection to my spiritual self.

"Yeah, it's been too long since we've been in the same city, or the same room, as each other," my dad said over the phone, bringing me back to the present.

It'd been less than a year, and we'd certainly gone longer. "I'm just surprised," I said. I stood up, needing to regain an ounce of privacy, and walked over to the corner to stand beside the trash, straws, and room-temperature milk.

"I want to see my kid. That's not such a big deal, is it?" There was a sharpness to his voice, anger smoldering around the edges of his words, but I still couldn't tell if he was drunk.

"No, no. It's a good surprise. I just thought something about the city was painful to your soul." I should have shut up. I wished I could have Susannah by my side again, winking at everything he did and rolling her eyes recounting it later. But she was long gone. I'd have to go into this one alone.

"I don't know what you're talking about, Em. Sure, it's a place where it's hard to feel a connection to the bounty of nature, and I think you know that for my spirit, in particular, I need to be connected to—"

"I'm pretty sure you said it was a steel monument built to honor the worst of humanity's tendencies." My tongue had never learned to form the words *you're drunk* in his presence, but I could argue about this.

"I never said anything of the sort. You're such an exaggerator." I could hear him rolling his eyes. "I think it'd be good to come down soon."

I wanted to force the point, to make him admit those were the exact words he said. They'd engraved themselves into my memory as soon as they were out of his mouth. But he was moving through the conversation so quickly, I couldn't help but be pulled along. "Soon? What does *soon* mean?"

"Do you think you could find me a place to stay close to your apartment?"

"What do you mean by *soon*?" I said, stepping aside for someone who was throwing away a half-eaten egg-white bite. I had no idea what he'd think of my place, my small top-floor studio, my little white-walled oasis, the only place that had ever been only mine. I couldn't imagine him curving his linen-clad shoulders through the doorway.

"Pick a weekend in the next month." My dad ran his own framing business in Kingston. His profit had never been great, but his cost of living was low. If he wanted to, he could close the shop for a weekend.

I wished I could open the calendar on my phone and see a list of important appointments, invites to dinner parties and book launches and museum-exhibit openings I already had to choose between. But I didn't have it in me to lie. "My schedule is wide open."

My nerves hummed after I ended the call. His behavior didn't make sense to me, but it never had before, either.

"That wasn't so bad, huh?" Lola said as I put the phone down on the table between us and took my seat again.

"No. It wasn't. He said he missed me. That's why he called."

"Aw, sweet. See? Building bridges isn't as hard as we make it out to be."

I looked around at the tables nearby, unable to meet her cloying gaze. "Yeah, it's nice. It's also just odd?"

"Not that odd for a dad to miss his daughter, right?" Lola didn't get my family at all. But that wasn't going to change in this conversation. She, as she often did, told me to pray for him. There wasn't much else you could do for an active alcoholic. We said the third step prayer aloud together in hushed tones.

"God, I offer myself to Thee—to build with me and to do with me as Thou wilt. Relieve me of the bondage of self, that I may

better do Thy will. Take away my difficulties, that victory over them may bear witness to those I would help of Thy Power, Thy Love, and Thy Way of life."

I replaced *God* with *Universe* in my mind to make it feel more real. But today, I still felt like I was whispering into the wind—or rather, the artificial breeze created by Starbucks' HVAC system.

"Who's next?" Lola asked.

"Ben," I read from my phone.

I gave her a brief rundown of Ben asking me out on Friday and how I felt surprised and flustered.

"What would be a way out of this predicament?" she asked, but I knew she already had a particular answer in mind.

"Telling him what I was doing with the Word doc. Telling him that I'm sober. But I just— I'm not comfortable telling people at work yet." The more we talked about letting the world know exactly who I was, the more aware I became of the people around us. Did they know what kind of conversation we were having?

"Have you gotten to know anyone at the office? It's going to be hard to feel like you can open up to people if you don't get to know them and let them get to know you."

"Not really. Vanessa, who I sit next to, is nice. We're friendly." Vanessa and I were bordering on more-than-coworkers and edging toward friends. We Slacked throughout the day, making guesses about what could be on Colin's playlists and sending each other eyeroll emojis whenever C-Suite made proclamations about giving back or corporate responsibility. But I wasn't sure how Work Emma could be friends with someone. If I was being brutally honest with myself, I wasn't sure how Real Emma could, either. I hadn't made a real friend since everything imploded with Susannah.

"Would you want to hang out with Vanessa?" Lola asked.

"Maybe. She's asked me to come out for drinks on Friday a few times. I just feel awkward being the only one not drinking—"

"And having people ask you why you don't. Right?"

"I hate it." I hadn't been into a bar in a whole year. I didn't know what it would feel like. But I didn't think it was the alcohol that would scare me. I wasn't looking forward to it, but I knew I could withstand the scent of whiskey and wine without my resolve crumbling. I just didn't know how to act when everyone around me was drinking and I wasn't. I would be the lone rusted gear in an otherwise smooth machine.

"Do you think you could try going for one hour? It's always nice to be friendly with your colleagues." Lola was more social than I was, and so I felt like I should follow her advice. Her Instagram was full of pictures of her at underground bars and elite gallery openings. She could stand next to people who had glasses of wine in their hands but have her own hand empty and a smile on her face. I wanted what she had.

"Go for an hour. People will be relatively calm in the first hour, no matter what. Remember, people aren't thinking about you that much. They're thinking about themselves."

I nodded. It was true.

"You're a year sober now! You don't want to spend your entire life hiding in the rooms. I mean, what would happen if you got invited to a wedding or a birthday party?"

I wasn't likely to get any invitations anytime soon. I thought of Susannah again. Her birthday was in two weeks. I shrugged in response.

"The point of sobriety is to live a full life, and full lives include some people who drink. I don't want you to limit yourself to only our tiny section of the world."

I didn't want that, either. I didn't want an infinite number of weekends with Netflix, library books, and dinners cooked for one. Maybe she was right: small steps into the social world of Richter & Thomas could be just the steps I needed to take.

The crowds appeared as soon as Lola and I turned the corner onto Park Avenue. Hudson Group was not like AA from the movies. There were no circles of folding chairs holding up downcast middle-aged men in church basements. No, Hudson Group told its members to dress up and fill Christ Church on Sixty-First and Park every Tuesday. The church was half a block wide and, according to rumor, built from leftover granite from the Brooklyn Bridge. Even though the meeting took place on the Upper East Side, the *Gossip Girl* neighborhood, people came from all over the city to attend. It would take me an hour on the subway to get home, and I knew people who'd have longer commutes. But it was worth it because HG felt like going to a Ted Talk hosted by Tony Robbins and Brené Brown.

I immediately fell in line, back with Diane, as Lola started chatting with her own sober sisters. "Who do you think will be speaking today?" she asked. "An old man in a suit…or?" It was almost always an old man in a suit.

"Could be a politician's daughter in a fashion-forward blazer," I said.

"There's always that outside chance. Or a young CEO who still thinks he has the whole world ahead of him," Diane added. Hudson Group had created a beautiful and permeating delusion that addiction was nothing to be ashamed of and that no one would judge you for overcoming a mental illness, especially if you caught it before you did anything too noteworthy. Every Tuesday, the speaker would say addiction was the best thing that ever happened to them because it gave way to sobriety. I, on the other hand, felt like there was a layer of dirt under my skin that I couldn't scrub off. I was pretty sure as soon as I told other people I was in recovery, they could see it, too. It was why I hadn't been able to bring myself to tell Ben the truth the other morning.

Guided by volunteer ushers, we all piled snugly into old oak pews. With the crowds tonight, we were lucky not to have to sit in the balcony. Although it wasn't strictly enforced, men generally sat on the left and women on the right.

The chatter died down as I was further squished into the pew. I had been lucky enough to get an aisle spot, but now the deceivingly smooth wood of the banister was digging into my hip. I looked up—the balcony was indeed full. People in their office wear were falling all over each other to get into the church on time. The speakers were taking their places on the chancel. I checked my phone before silencing it. It was 6:58 p.m., and the meeting would start precisely at 7:00 p.m. Not a minute later.

An usher bent down and tapped my shoulder. "Excuse me," she said.

I nodded, trying to be quiet.

"We have one more. Do you think you could squeeze?" the usher asked.

"Oh," I said. I turned to Diane and passed the whisper on. Scraps of space were found between thighs. I was able to move about eighteen inches from the aisle.

"Thanks!" the usher said and then pushed a young man into the seat beside me.

In my entire year coming to Hudson's Tuesday-night meeting, I'd never sat next to a man. He was blond, blonder than me, and small. I nodded at him. He nodded at me. He wasn't particularly handsome. I wouldn't have noticed him if I passed him on the street or sat across from him on the subway, but I had to reckon with the fact that our thighs were touching, denim on polyester, and this was the closest I'd been to a man since I got sober.

I'd committed to not dating or sleeping with anyone in my first year of sobriety, but I knew plenty of people who'd broken that rule. It's not like I would've gotten kicked out of AA if I had. People didn't get kicked out of AA. But I couldn't afford to break the rules. I didn't trust myself to veer even a little bit off course. It was like the saying *One is too many, and a thousand is never enough.* That saying was about drinks, not broken rules, but I was sure it could be applied to both.

The speaker was delivering what seemed like, at least from the crowd's reactions, a lively qualification. But I hadn't heard a single word. My brain, against my best advice, shoved Ben's face into my mind's eye. I tried to push him back out.

People brought friends and loved ones to Tuesday's meeting. It was open, which meant that people who didn't identify as alcoholics could come and listen. I hoped I could walk down these crowded aisles whispering in someone's ear one day. Mom would come if I asked her, but I didn't think it would dispel her feelings about the group I'd joined. I could see her rolling her committed-atheist eyes when we all joined hands in prayer. Since no one could see inside my head, I was allowed to imagine that future person would look like Ben. A lot like Ben. It was just a daydream. His ship had probably sailed. I had to move past him. Get over it. Maybe find a boyfriend online.

I barely noticed when it was time to stand and join hands to close the meeting, but Diane's elbow in my rib cage let me know. I followed the small blond man out of the pew to the edge of the church to join the giant circle forming across pews and under stone archways. I held his hand on my right—his palm was warm but not sweaty—and Diane's on my left. Together the entire circle closed out the meeting with the Serenity Prayer.

"God, grant me the serenity to accept the things I cannot change..."

I couldn't change the past. I couldn't change what happened last week or last year.

"The courage to change the things I can..."

Could I change the future? Could I go out into the world again and really announce myself, blood bare of alcohol?

"And the wisdom to know the difference."

I hoped so. And maybe Lola was right. I could start by telling the truth, the whole truth, to someone at work.

FIVE

The office clock ticked from 4:59 to 5:00 p.m. Had this been any other Friday, I would have been watching my entire team walk out the door and wishing them well. They would have told me I should come along, that there was always room for me, but they'd eventually have given up and laughed their way down the hall. And I would have sat still and waited for the voices to die down so I could slip out alone. But this was not any other Friday—I had finally accepted Vanessa's invitation to join the rest of the office at Friday Night Drinks.

Jermaine stood and stuffed things into his saddlebag. Putting on a big smile, he lifted his hands and declared, "Folks! It's happening much later than we originally thought, but after six long months of waiting, our baby Emma is coming to Friday Night Drinks! First round's on me!"

Colin swiveled in his chair. "You better order the most expensive drink on the menu, Emma. Otherwise, you're wasting this rare and golden opportunity."

"It's called 'the Floozy.' It's vodka and muddled strawberries with a daisy floating on top," Vanessa said, leaning over.

Now was the moment. Better now in my comfort zone than

out there at the big, loud bar where weird memories and spirals of self-loathing might kick in.

They don't care, I recited to myself. *Just say it.*

"I actually don't drink. So it'll be a very cheap seltzer for me, Jermaine!" I could hear myself trying too hard, a false sense of cheerfulness to my tone. My hand involuntarily scratched a sudden itch on my chest.

"Lucky me." Jermaine laughed, then patted me on the back on his way out.

I turned off my computer and slowly packed my bag. Colin walked out next, telling us he'd see us downstairs.

Vanessa gave me a soft smile. "So, is this the big secret that's had you avoiding hanging out with me?"

"Yeah, pretty much," I said.

"Are you comfortable telling me why?"

I couldn't meet her eyes. I thought about how Work Emma would disappear for Vanessa if I told her. To Vanessa, I would no longer be the polite young woman who couldn't curse without surprising people. I would be damaged and defective. I didn't want to lose the narrative that had made me feel so safe and solid. But I had to bite the bullet. "I'm in recovery," I said.

"Recovery?"

I'd forgotten how immersed in AA lingo I was. How it had become my whole world, how the words they'd taught me had become as essential as the ones I first spoke as a child.

"Recovery. As in, I'm recovering from alcoholism." The words were slow and stilted, like I didn't form them often. But I did, I reminded myself. Every time I raised my hand in a meeting and said, *Hi, I'm Emma, and I'm an alcoholic.*

"Oh. I'm so stupid. Of course," she said.

"You're anything but stupid, Vanessa."

"Okay. But am I kind of a dick for asking you to come to Friday Night Drinks so many times?"

"No," I said. "I'm not scared of the bar. Really. I just hate feeling like the odd one out." One of those things was true, at least. I was also a little bit scared of the bar. It had been over a year since I was last in one.

"Can I help with that?" she asked.

She could've. I liked the idea of having someone stay sober with me, unglassed eyes I could turn to for support, but I didn't want to ask that of Vanessa. She loved Friday Night Drinks. Who was I to take that from her? And besides, Over-a-Year-Sober Emma didn't need that kind of support, right? "No, don't worry about it," I said.

"Okay, if you're sure. But, Emma, I'm glad you told me. We've been sitting next to each other for months. I feel like you know everything about me." She laughed. "I'm honestly a little surprised I didn't know something so major about you."

Had I hurt her feelings by keeping my cards close to my chest? That hadn't been my intention. But she was right, she'd been open with me. I knew about her childhood growing up in the suburbs of Detroit, her early figure-skating dreams that had been dashed when she hit puberty and got other priorities, how her parents wanted her to go to med school, and how even though she was living in the city and making a decent salary, she still occasionally felt like she'd disappointed them. I knew I hadn't given her enough in return, but Friend Emma had never exactly been great at her job, and work had been my focus these last few months.

The bar was around the corner from the office, tucked away on a side street and bearing the nondescript name of Bar 28. On the ground floor of a frightfully thin building sandwiched between two modern glass towers, it was a cavern full of exposed brick archways and old oak booths. "There's a downstairs, too," Vanessa said, then added with a wink, "That's where all the good stuff happens." The old me would have assumed that the good stuff was bumps of cocaine passed along on phone screens and unprotected sex in public bathrooms, but was that the kind of thing my coworkers were getting up to on Friday nights? Or was Vanessa joking about the occasional drunken make-out?

She started toward the back and, along the way, said hello to at least five people, only three of whom I could name. There wasn't a single thing about this place that wasn't bar-like. It had that smell of stale beer and dim lights. There was a buzz of conversation mixing with the low din of '90s alt-rock.

My eyes kept flicking back to the wall of half-filled bottles of alcohol. Amber shined past the sepia Knob Creek label. Light flickered off Bombay Sapphire like glacial streams pouring over ancient stones. The mirror made the wall look never-ending; the geese in flight on the Grey Goose bottle repeated into infinity.

But all around me, the pieces of my colleagues' personalities I'd only caught glimpses of in the office pulled my attention. Dan from Reception was holding court telling a story of his days in a Phish cover band, Michelle from Content was sipping a martini and smiling coyly at her phone, and Jermaine was already the center of everything, buying drinks and making promises to get everyone dancing. In a funny way, it felt like the first time I was able to see a bar for what it was to most people, a place to build community and let loose. To me, it had only ever been one of two things: either a place to lose myself entirely, to be out-of-body blackout drunk, the kind of drunk where memories can't be made or revisited, where moments exist and pass away in an instant; or somewhere I feared, where that great haunting euphoria could take over no matter what I did to avoid it. But today, over a year after I'd had my last drink, it was starting to look like a building with brick walls and echoing laughter. I thought maybe Lola was right and it was just a place—the only meaning it had was the meaning I gave it.

Whiskey caught my eye, mimicking a copper waterfall as the bartender poured it into a waiting tumbler. I looked away, but I could feel it twinkling behind me. It didn't have to mean anything.

We stopped at a booth where two young women Vanessa introduced as Izzy and Maria were sitting. They both worked in Customer Relations and had the exact same long bob. Maria had it in black and Izzy in red. Vanessa shrugged off her coat and took out her ponytail, her long dark hair falling to her waist and causing Izzy and Maria to erupt into giggles and applaud at her show. I clapped a beat too late.

"Everyone's usuals?" Vanessa asked.

Izzy and Maria nodded in tandem.

I started to speak, but she cut me off.

"I heard you in the office, Em—the house seltzer is coming right up," she said while grabbing her wallet from her coat pocket.

She walked toward the bar, and my eyes followed her. Maybe Lola was wrong. This wasn't a room filled with whatever meaning I gave it. There was enough alcohol here that I could get drunk from bathing in it. I didn't even have to let it touch my lips. I could just fall into it, let it seep into my bloodstream through my skin.

I pulled my gaze away, only to be greeted by Izzy and Maria looking at their phones. I didn't know what to say. I'd never had a conversation with either of them. Should I compliment their twin haircut? No, obviously you can't compliment two people's haircuts at once. Should I ask how they liked working at Richter & Thomas? No, how boring. Could anyone really say financial consulting was their passion? I doubted it.

"So," Izzy started, placing her phone on the table, "are you not drinking right now?"

I should have asked the stupid work question.

"No, I don't drink," I said. This wasn't like in M&C. I didn't know these people. I didn't trust them. I was overly paranoid. "You guys have great haircuts," I tried.

"Thanks," Maria said, running her fingers through her blowout.

But Izzy continued, "Like you don't drink ever? Or are you on antibiotics right now?"

"No, never," I said. I didn't try to force the conversation another way. I knew from experience it wouldn't work.

"Not even on New Year's or at a wedding?"

"In neither of those scenarios would I drink." I felt like a PSA.

"Have you ever tried it?" she asked.

This was a question I'd been asked before. It surprised me the first time, but I'd gotten used to it since. I chalked it up to my general wholesome appearance: the relative youth, the lack of visible tattoos. Apparently, to some people, it was more believable that I'd never had a drink than that I'd already had an uncountable amount and given it all up. Never trust appearances.

"I have, yeah. And now I don't." This was a simplified version of my life story.

Izzy nodded a slow continuous nod, like she was in the process of putting things together. Silence fell over our booth. I didn't hold anything against Izzy; I would have asked the same questions two years ago.

Vanessa, with the poise of a seasoned waitress, gave us each our favorite drink. My seltzer had a sprig of rosemary and a floating slice of lemon. At my expression, Vanessa said, "I asked them to zhuzh it up a bit."

I gave her a faint smile. I wanted to say more, to pour out profound thanks for this small nod of inclusion, but I feared any attention I gave to the seltzer would start Izzy asking questions again.

Vanessa started talking about how the bartender reminded her of her first high school boyfriend, and then suddenly, everyone was discussing the horrors of trying to give blow jobs with braces. I'd never had braces, so I had no strategy to contribute. Was that another whiskey double the bartender was pouring? I read the label—Widow Jane. They made that in Brooklyn. Susannah and I used to talk about doing a distillery tour, but we never got our shit together enough to go to Red Hook on a Sunday afternoon.

"You know, Emma," Izzy said, pulling my attention back to her, "I used to have a coke problem in college."

Ah. So her slow nods had amounted to something. She'd put it together. Vanessa looked from me to Izzy and then back again. Maybe she thought I'd made my recovery public knowledge. That we had been discussing my alcoholism while she was grabbing our drinks. That her friends had been bonding.

"And since then, I've had this rule. I never have more than four drinks a night," Izzy continued, making meaningful eye contact with me. I congratulated myself for only glancing down at her Negroni once.

"What are you talking about, Iz?" Maria asked. "You're being so weird. Also, you had like seven drinks last Saturday," she laughed.

"No. I didn't," Izzy snapped.

"You know, I've never had a real online dating profile, but I was thinking of setting one up," I said. It was an offering. I couldn't go any closer to the topic of drinking. The bar on the other side of the room felt like a distant drumbeat of an approaching army. I had to take a detour and weave the conversation into a different swamp. I hoped my lack of a dating life was equally interesting. That, I could offer them.

"Really?" Izzy said, her face softening.

"Would you want to set one up, like, tonight?" Maria asked.

"We could help you," Izzy said. "You're so hot it's going to be, like, crazy easy."

I laughed, hoping it sounded natural. "I leave it entirely in your hands."

Vanessa looked at me, a question furrowed into her brow. I could probably beg her to get me out of this, but if it turned the tides of this conversation, I'd do it. I didn't want to keep talking about how weird and damaged I was. Sober Emma could still be fun, and fun girls let their friends set up online dating profiles for them. What was the worst that could happen?

"You better go ahead and give us your phone, and we'll give it back to you when we're done," said Maria.

"You want me to give you full control?" I asked.

"We won't post until you say it's okay!" Maria said.

"Actually, I don't trust you to have any good pics on your phone," Izzy said. "Let's do a little photo shoot first. Do you have any lipstick on you?"

After that, it all happened so quickly. Lipstick on and hair down and mussed up, I was posed in the booth, against the brick wall, and with various combinations of other people.

Apparently, after the photo shoot ended, they didn't need me anymore. Izzy, Maria, and Vanessa sat close together with their heads bent over my phone. They were hard at work creating Dateable Emma, a fictional version of me that would attract legions of good-looking and emotionally available men. I wondered what she'd be like.

I was glad they had something to focus on. Because when Ben walked in with the rest of the IT department, I knew my face would have betrayed me in an instant. It didn't occur to me that he'd be here. I thought Jermaine mentioned that he didn't usually come. While I might be fine with Izzy, Maria, and Vanessa setting up a dating profile that I had no plans to actually use, I was not fine with them knowing about my real-life, real-embarrassing crush on Ben. I knew they'd tell me I should go for it, and then I'd have to tell them that things had already gone weird and sideways. Before I knew it, my whole life story would be on the table next to Izzy's second Negroni. Better not to start down that path.

I went up to the bar. I couldn't help myself. Not to get a drink. I just needed a moment away from all the chatter about the new-and-improved virtual me. And also because Ben was at the bar, with his suit jacket off and his shirtsleeves rolled up to his forearms.

Would he pretend he didn't know me? Would I pretend that our previous interaction wasn't the catalyst for me being here tonight? Would all of the pretending grow around us until it was as firm as the truth? Maybe we wouldn't even have to pretend. Maybe anything that had ever existed had disappeared in the week since I'd seen him last. He was kitty-corner from me, leaning on the dark oak with his back to the bar and talking to his fellow IT-er Darren. Darren's eyes trailed my hands as I tore at an abandoned napkin. Ben's gaze followed his.

I saw the moment he realized it was me standing beside him. His relaxed stance solidified. I almost smiled, but I didn't quite manage it. "Hi," I said. "I didn't know you came to these."

He rotated toward me and the bar and away from Darren. "It's Mike's birthday," he said, gesturing to a tall man looking at his phone in the corner. In an instant, he'd raised his hand to call the bartender over. "What are you drinking?" he asked.

Both he and the bartender awaited my answer. "Oh, just a seltzer, thanks." I wasn't sure who I should be looking at, but I couldn't keep my gaze off Ben.

"You sure? It's my treat."

I nodded, my attention hooked by the scraps of napkin glued to the skin of my fingertips.

"Always good to stay hydrated," he said. Why had I thought there'd been anything between us? I couldn't think of a single thing to say, and apparently, neither could he.

"I don't drink." I hadn't meant to say it. But now it was out there, sitting between us beside the napkin I had torn to shreds. I should have followed it up with the Whole Truth™ but I couldn't—who might overhear me? It was one thing to be honest with Ben and an entirely different thing to admit my powerlessness over alcohol in front of the entire office, especially as they were currently standing at an altar of it.

Ben raised his eyebrows a millimeter, and his gaze got stuck on me. He was puzzling me out. Perhaps things were clicking into place in his mind. I hoped so.

"Two seltzers, then," Ben said to the bartender, who was still waiting for our order.

"And another pilsner!" Darren called as he slid into the space between us. "On his tab!"

Two seltzers. He was just being polite, but the phrase wrapped itself around me, holding off the stench of spilled beer and the glint shining off the wall of liquor. I felt a grin spreading across my face and stifled it. He was just being polite. Or maybe, just maybe, he wasn't only being polite. Maybe he wanted to join me where I was. Vanessa had offered not to drink with me, but Ben hadn't offered. He took the action I needed someone to take. If he was just being polite, he was really good at it.

"Ben was just telling me about his army days," Darren said. His eyes were on the wrong side of glassy. He had clearly nominated himself as some kind of wingman.

"I wasn't," Ben said, staring at the assuredly fascinating woodgrain of the bar top. "We were talking about work."

"Were you in the army?" I couldn't imagine it. When I thought of veterans, I thought of country songs and corn-fed boys, not suit-wearing New Yorkers. But Ben wasn't really either of those things, not entirely. He was an upstate kid who'd veered down here on a winding road rather than a straight one.

"Not really," Ben said. "I mean, yes, I was. But not for long. And I was very young." I wondered if there were photos of him at eighteen in uniform on his parents' wall.

"But he still knows his way around an AR-15, right, man?"

Ben looked at Darren, and it was like the rest of the bar disappeared, but not in a good way. "I highly doubt that Emma cares about how specific guns work. And that's not something I want to brag about, man." The word *man* hung off the end of his sentence like a taunt. He was clearly pissed at Darren.

Did Ben have a Work Ben? Did he feel like Darren had blown up his spot? Was I not the only one at this bar who had versions of themselves they'd rather keep hidden?

The bartender delivered our drinks and Darren picked his up first. "Alright, whatever, bro," he said before walking away.

Ben reached for one of the seltzers, lifted it to me, and said, "It was nice seeing you, Emma." He was going to walk away.

I grabbed his forearm; his skin was hot against my hand. "Wait," I started, but then didn't know how to continue. I wanted to tell him the truth. I didn't know how close I would get to the Whole Truth™, but I hated having this lie sitting between us. Would I hate the feeling of the truth more? I wasn't sure, but I told Lola I'd try to come clean. "About last week…"

"Oh. Right. The funeral." He said the words like he'd already guessed I'd been lying. He put his seltzer back down on the bar. Maybe this wouldn't be so hard, then.

"I got flustered. I wasn't thinking, and I lied. There wasn't a funeral. I wasn't writing a eulogy. I shouldn't have said I was. I'm so sorry."

His gaze was stubbornly attached to the bar as I spoke. He couldn't bring himself to look at me. This was exactly as hard as I'd thought it would be.

"I'm really sorry I made you so uncomfortable," he said after a long a beat of silence.

"No, no!" I reached out to grab his arm again, but then thought better of it. "You didn't make me uncomfortable. Not in that way. I was writing something personal, and I got so embarrassed. It wasn't something I'd want anyone at work to see. I made myself uncomfortable."

"Okay," he said, bringing his gaze up to meet mine. He probably wanted to know what was on that Word doc, and maybe I should have told him. But I'd gotten as close as I could get to the Whole Truth™ tonight.

"So maybe we can be friends? Or maybe, I don't know, the lunch sounded nice?"

"If you're sure," he said.

"I am—" I started. But then I heard Maria's voice calling my name across the bar. "I should go back." I pointed behind me. "But I am. I'm sure about lunch."

He took a sip of his seltzer and nodded. I didn't think he fully believed me. But he didn't have much of a reason to. I wondered what would have happened if I hadn't asked for a seltzer. What if Drunk Emma had been at the bar? Would he have gotten us both a double whiskey? Maybe as it burned down our throats, he wouldn't have minded if I laid a hand on his arm, if I pulled myself around to his side of the bar and tucked myself under his arm. I could've leaned up, smoothing my hand across his chest, and whispered hotly into his ear. Together, we could've found out what kind of stuff happened downstairs.

I shook my head. And reminded myself what that would have looked like in reality—not the fantasy version: I couldn't just have one shot, so I'd have to have too many, I'd vomit or black out and he'd have to put me in a cab home before we could even kiss, I'd be mortified the next day thinking about all the things I'd said and probably didn't mean, and he'd never ask me out again, feeling grateful that he dodged a bullet.

One of the reasons I wanted to get sober, and wanted to *stay* sober, was because I was exhausted from all my interactions being clouded by the fuzzy veil of a couple of drinks. I always felt like what I did when I drank didn't matter, but that was also the problem: I did almost everything drunk, so nothing I did ever mattered—at least not to me. Which meant I was walking around living a purposeless life, easily distracted by the scent of anything new that would blissfully numb me out. Sure, maybe I did fewer things and talked to fewer people now that I was sober. But now all of the words that came out of my mouth at least meant something to me. Maybe Drunk Emma would have convinced Ben to fuck her. But I'd rather be Sober Emma, slowly learning more about him.

I returned to the table, fresh seltzer in hand. Vanessa's eyes met mine.

"We're done!" Maria cried as I squished into the booth across from her.

"Alright, let's see," I said, but I knew I didn't sound excited enough. This moment should have been full of giggles and glee, but I was stuck in the moment that had just passed. Had I said the wrong thing to Ben? Was it stupid to confess? Did it make me seem unstable?

"Before we hand it over, promise you won't get mad," Izzy said.

"Why would I get mad?" I asked, carefully avoiding any promise not to.

"We know we said we'd keep it a draft, but then Vanessa said—" Izzy started.

"Keep me out of it!" Vanessa interrupted, downing the rest of her drink.

"Fine, we all thought, not just V, that it might be good for you to see how much interest you got in a few minutes," Izzy continued.

My heart sank. My phone was going to be full of dicks. Both literally and metaphorically, I was sure it would be a parade of dicks.

"Okay, well, we can always take it down. It's just the click of a button. But when it's in draft, you can't see the guys! And that's the fun part!" Maria said.

I forced a smile. "Well, let's take a look!"

They turned the phone around, and I wouldn't have recognized myself at all.

The profile picture they'd chosen was not one we took during our photo shoot. It was of me over at the bar talking to Ben, except Ben wasn't in the shot. He wasn't awkwardly cropped out, either; it just looked like I was standing at the end of the bar, looking out at my friends. I was blushing, just slightly, and smiling softly. The bar lighting had turned my sometimes ruddy hair into gold waves that spilled everywhere. I looked pretty. I was going to let myself admit it. It was a good picture.

"I snapped that one a second ago," Vanessa said. "I was on my way to the bathroom and saw you there at the bar."

I had a feeling she was telling me this so I would know that the whole world hadn't witnessed my moment at the bar. That it'd only been her. Maybe being Real Emma with Vanessa wasn't a bad idea after all.

"It's a nice picture. Thanks," I said.

I swiped through the rest of the pictures, most of which had been stolen from my photo stream. There was a selfie I'd taken on my fire escape as the sun was setting, me goofing around with Gloria's Australian shepherd, and a bikini picture from years ago.

"Okay," I said, turning the phone back to them. "I'm deleting this one. I'm twenty-one in this. I don't look like that anymore." Susannah had taken the picture five summers and a lifetime ago, when we spent afternoons before our restaurant shifts out on the Rockaways. I hadn't been back since Drunk Emma transformed into Sober Emma.

"Fine," Izzy said.

"Told you," Vanessa added.

I scrolled to the bio portion of my brand-new dating profile, which I was sure would make me cringe.

Emma, 26

Marketing, NYC

Native New Yorker who's lived in every borough but Staten Island. (Yes, I know where the best pizza is. No, it's not Roberta's.)

I walk everywhere, even if it's pouring.

I'd rather dress down than dress up.

I don't drink, but you can.

"This isn't terrible!" I said in a squeak. That was a lie. It made me want to jump off the tallest building I could find. It was too personal. Too real. Too public. "How did you know all this?" There. A somewhat neutral statement.

"I've sat next to you for six months, Emma. You mention how much you hate Roberta's at least once a week," Vanessa said. Maybe I hadn't been quite as closed off with Vanessa as I'd thought.

"Well. It is annoying that they—" I started, but then froze when I saw matches start pouring in. "Oh my god, I can't do this! There are real men out there, looking at me!" I shoved my phone back into Izzy's hands.

"Okay!" she squealed. "But I'm going to swipe all over the place!"

"Wait!" Maria said, grabbing Izzy's fingers.

"Oh my god," they both said in unison.

"What is it?"

"Just the hottest guy in our office," Maria said and turned the phone to me and Vanessa on the other side of the booth.

Mitchell, 32
Finance Executive, NYC
About me: I'm career driven and I like to call the shots. I love Hamptons summers and Vail winters. There's not a challenge I'm afraid of. Don't be surprised if you see me on top of Everest one day.
About you: You're not ready to settle down yet and looking to have some fun.

"Shoot me," I said. "His bio is so gross." There he was, Mitchell Brady: the chief content officer of Richter & Thomas. His first picture was of him with his hand on his chin, apparently staring off into the distance, but with his shining rose-gold Rolex sharply in focus. I don't think we'd ever spoken. He worked in the actual Finance wing, which meant he made probably ten times more money than I did. And judging by how well his suits fit, he wasn't afraid to show that off.

"He already swiped right on you!" Izzy said.

"He must not recognize me," I said. "Probably only looked at my hair and my age."

"Well, I guess he'll find out soon! I swiped right, too!" Izzy laughed.

"You didn't!" I grabbed the phone and deleted the app with shaking hands.

"Whoa, Emma! Way to overreact. You can always unswipe," Izzy said.

"Okay, okay," Vanessa said, easing through the tension between Izzy and me. "Let me tell you all about this total dick that messaged me last week."

And then my brief and uncomfortable moment in the sun was over. Finally. I'd survived a social work thing. I could go tell Lola that I'd done it. I talked to five whole people. I let them get to know me, at least a bit. And I got to know them. I could probably take a break now. There was no reason to make a habit out of this, right?

SIX

Monday was full of emails, captions, and moving text around on images until Jermaine asked if we could chat for a second. He looked nervous. Was he going to fire me?

"It won't take longer than a minute. We can just step into the staircase," he said.

We didn't have our own conference room at M&C, so if we ever needed one, we'd reserve one on another floor. This very rarely happened. Usually, if two of the four of us had to work together, the other two would put on their headphones. So whatever Jermaine needed to talk to me about was too serious to have Colin and Vanessa overhear but not serious enough that it required HR and a conference room.

Jermaine opened the door to our small office. "Ladies first," he said with a forced laugh.

"Thanks." I stepped through.

He gave me a tight smile as we stared at each other, surrounded by the solid concrete.

"Is everything okay?" If Jermaine wanted to talk about a personal problem of his, surely he would have chosen someone else. Anyone else. But maybe he'd found out I was in AA and he wanted to quit drinking? It would be a surprise, but some alcoholics were very good at hiding.

"I'm probably making too big a deal of this. It just never goes well."

"What never goes well?" Was he about to ask me out? No. That was impossible. He was my boss. I reported to him. Also, I distinctly remembered him mentioning a boyfriend.

"It's that time of year again. Well, I guess this will be your first holiday season with Richter & Thomas, so you wouldn't know. But maybe you've heard?"

Holiday season? It was September. Did we not get Christmas off and he was nervous to tell me? "I'm not really a holiday person," I said so he would worry less.

Somehow, that made him look even more stricken. "I didn't know that."

"Yeah. I'm a bit of a grinch." I spent my childhood Christmas Eves eating Chinese food and watching *Casablanca* with Mom, which was fine. But then Christmas Day she'd put me on a bus upstate. Trailways buses on Christmas Day were not typically full of holiday cheer. I remember watching car commercials around the holidays that showed whole families piling into shiny new cars that sailed over snow and sleet as the family sang carols and wore matching scarves. The bus didn't feel like that. It was full of lonely people, and I was one of them.

After I arrived at my dad's house, we'd always decorate a big pine tree he had on his front lawn with Christmas lights, but he'd soon disappear into himself, his words getting slower and softer, and I'd feel so far from home. When I was eighteen and started working restaurant jobs that didn't give me the holidays off, it seemed like a good excuse to stop making the trek up there. It had been eight years since I'd spent a Christmas in the snowy Catskills.

Jermaine's voice brought me back to the present, and the cold concrete staircase: "Well, like most offices, we have a holiday party."

"Okay?"

"Most people don't think about this, but it's a lot of work to plan a big holiday party for a staff of our size."

"Sure. Of course." This was my first real office job, so I had no idea how office parties got planned. I'd studied communications at City College and worked at restaurants throughout and in the years afterward. When I first got sober and really wanted to get out of the restaurant scene, my boss offered to let me do marketing for their restaurant group instead. After that, I was able to get a job at Richter & Thomas. I wasn't fully qualified, but I think they were desperate for someone who knew their way around TikTok.

"And party planning isn't exactly in anyone's job description," Jermaine continued. "So, the way we do it here is we have a Fun Team that plans the party every year."

"That seems reasonable." Jermaine was fun; he was a natural fit for the Fun Team. Maybe he just wanted to tell me he was going to be extra busy leading up to the holidays?

"But we started to have an issue, because, well, to be honest, no one wanted to be on the Fun Team."

My heart sank.

"So we decided that each department would choose a representative to serve for a one-year term."

"It has to be Vanessa, right? She's so social. Do you want me to tell her?" I reached for the door handle.

"No, Emma." Jermaine stopped me, his voice taking on a softer bad-news tone that I'd heard on a thousand episodes of *Grey's Anatomy*. "Vanessa did it last year. I'm sorry. I nominated you."

"When? Is it too late to change it?" This is what I got for being Work Emma, for not telling Jermaine I was sober. Although I wasn't sure being a recovering alcoholic was an immediate get-out-of-jail-free card.

"We all gave our nominees at the monthly department heads meeting this morning."

"Will there be an election? Surely I'll lose."

"No. Sorry, *nomination* is just the word we use. You're on the Fun Team."

"But I'm no fun!"

"You enjoyed yourself on Friday!" Jermaine was trying to make Friday more than it was. I hadn't even really thought about going again. I certainly wasn't in any position to plan the biggest work event of the year. "And I think it will be good to have someone less…outgoing on the team. You'll bring an interesting perspective."

"Jermaine," I started. But he was already opening the door.

"It's going to be fine, Emma, I promise. The Fun Team meets weekly on Wednesdays at one p.m. in the big conference room on twelve. You'll get a calendar invite shortly." He gave me an encouraging shoulder squeeze before he walked away.

This was a step too far. A single Friday Night Drinks was one thing, but months of planning the holiday party? It would be more than I could bear.

On Friday evening, I met Mom at our favorite neighborhood restaurant: Flor De Mayo on Broadway. It was a Peruvian Chinese restaurant that served the best fried pork chops in New York, with a complimentary side of plantains. I rolled my eyes in ecstasy between bites. Being celibate wasn't so bad as long as I had a steady supply of fried food.

Mom, who was always able to savor her meals more than I could, took up the conversation where I'd abandoned it when our plates arrived: "So, what ended up happening at the work thing?"

"Nothing really. Some of the girls made a dating profile for me, but then I deleted it."

"Can you undelete it? I want to see all the cute boys that want to date you!"

The app had felt like an oppressive weight back in the bar, but now it felt like a game. Nothing would come of it. I was safe in the little bubble that burst into existence whenever Mom and I were together.

I pulled the dating app I'd deleted back up. Izzy had lied about my data being gone. It was all still there as soon as I entered my email. I looked at the messages I'd received in that brief moment when my profile was live last week. To my surprise, there were no dick pics. The mythos around dating apps hadn't borne any fruit, yet.

Mom moved over to sit next to me on the bench seat, and we started swiping through the swaths of available men. They were more like paint swatches than humans. I imagined myself at Home Depot trying to find a color for my bright white walls under the fifty-foot ceilings and fluorescent lighting. How could you tell from a three-by-three-inch sample? It was all so performative, and I knew that's how my profile read, too. I couldn't see a way to find the humanity, as if social convention had forced us to pixelate ourselves until all meaning was lost.

Every once in a while, we'd argue about which way my finger should go, right or left. Mom had a taste for artistic, hipster-looking guys with well-groomed mustaches, whereas I couldn't imagine dating an artist, and didn't have to think too hard to understand why. My parents had both moved to New York to be artists and prioritized their own quests for truth and beauty above stability. I wanted to be with someone who would reverse that equation.

A message popped up. I opened it and then dropped my phone, like the entire device was a cockroach that had fallen from the ceiling and landed in my lap.

"Who was that?" Mom said, picking my phone up.

"No one!"

"It says Mitchell? He has nice eyes."

I peeked across her shoulder and read the message from Mitchell Brady, CCO of my company: Fancy seeing you here ;)

All things considered, it was a relatively unoffensive message. It could be interpreted as a joke, as lighthearted communication between cordial colleagues.

"I work with him. Well, not *with* him. I don't see him on a day-to-day basis—"

"Then you already have something in common! You should respond!"

"He's my boss. I mean, not my boss because we don't work in the same department, but he's like *a boss*."

With that in mind, I wrote back. Haha!

I clicked Send and then typed out three possible additional messages.

~~Izzy from work made this profile for me and I think she swiped on you last week!~~

That would be throwing Izzy under the bus, so I deleted it. If Vanessa and I were ever going to move past being Work Friends—and the more I got to know her as Real Emma, the more I wanted us to—I should maybe try to be friends with Izzy and Maria, too. Or, if not friends, then at least friendly.

"Wait, stop typing and deleting so fast. I need to get out my reading glasses!" Mom said as she rummaged through her purse.

"No, just let me do this."

~~I think some girls from work swiped on you last week at Friday Night Drinks. Let's just pretend we didn't see each other.~~

"No, that's not very nice." The reading glasses had been gathered quickly. But I agreed with her; it sounded too "the lady doth protest."

~~I'm new to this, but I heard it was the polite thing to do to swipe right on people you know?~~

"Go back to your side of the table," I told Mom.

"No! It's just starting to get good!" Her reading glasses slid an inch down her nose.

"Please, Mom, go look at your Facebook for ten minutes."

When she was seated and had pulled open her crossword app, Mitchell replied again. You have a nice profile.

Well, that was weird. I wasn't sure how to get out of this conversation. What are you supposed to say to someone you work with, who works in a different department but who definitely has more power than you, who you've accidentally matched with on a dating app? I didn't remember this being in the company handbook. Although, to be fair, I also hadn't read it.

Emma: Thanks.

Mitchell: Tbh, I'm surprised to see you on here. You give off serious not-single vibes.

Emma: So you've seen the poster-sized framed portrait of my boyfriend on my desk, then?

Mitchell: Whoa, open relationship?

I let a whole minute pass. Mom raised her eyebrows, asking me if I was done. I shook my head. I'd wanted to diffuse whatever sexual tension came part and parcel with matching on a dating app. But I didn't want him to start going around the office telling everyone I was in a nonexistent open relationship.

Emma: No, it was a joke.

Mitchell: Sweet. You're kind of hard to miss, Fine-ly.

Ew, I thought. But then an unwilling part of my very human heart started beating a little faster. It had been a long time since a man told me I was attractive. Well, not if you counted strange men on the subway. But a man that I actually knew? It felt like forever. I was grossed out, but also flattered. But my heart slowed when I thought of how much better those words would have felt coming from someone else. Did Ben's sort-of asking me out and backtracking count as calling me pretty? Maybe that's what he'd meant, but I couldn't take that moment to the bank.

Thanks? I messaged.

Mitchell: Some people say the same about me.

Emma: I can't think of a pun for your name.

That was the best I could do. I couldn't say, *I know you're pretty, but I find you gross on a personality and moral level*, which is what I was thinking.

Mitchell: Hahahaha

It wasn't that funny.

Mitchell: We can try to think of one together.

Okay. Time to abort.

Emma: I gotta go. I'm meeting my mom. Bye!

I clicked out of the app. I went to preferences and requested it not send me any notifications.

"Did you let him down easy?" Mom asked.

"Yeah," I said, knowing that wasn't the truth. I could have handled it better. I could have said a firm no. He didn't have any power over me, not really. I should have said I was only on the app as a joke. I should have said a lot of different things. Any of the first responses I'd typed out would have been better than what happened. I wasn't stupid enough to think that this would just disappear. I'd have to say no eventually, unless he realized I wasn't worth the trouble. But I doubted I'd ever be that lucky.

"It's good that you're branching out, Emma. Even if Mitchell isn't the guy," she said as she dipped her last plantain into the garlic sauce.

I shrugged. I didn't know if I'd ever open the app again, but she was right. It was a start.

"Because, well, I've been wanting to talk to you about something. And now that you're a year sober, and you seem like you're a bit more open to things, maybe you'll be able to see the positives."

My stomach sank. I could tell by the tone of her voice that this was news. Like headline news. Her voice had become deeper, more solid. She was choosing every word carefully. I stared at her mouth, waiting for the bomb to drop.

"I'm seeing someone. A man."

"Oh! Mom, that's great. That's really nice." So she had a boyfriend. I really did think it was great. I wanted her to be happy.

"It's serious," she continued.

"Okay..." I guess I was going to have to meet him. Which would be totally fine. I'd never met one of Mom's boyfriends, but it was the kind of thing chill, grown-up women did all the time. I'd be able to handle it. I trusted myself.

"We're going to move in together." Her eyes were steady on me, like she worried if she were to look away for a moment, I'd pull the clip out of the grenade. But I didn't feel volatile. It was shocking, sure. It absolutely seemed quick. But I would adjust.

"He's going to move into Ninety-Sixth Street?" It would be weird having a strange middle-aged—well, I hoped he was middle-aged—man around the apartment I grew up in, but I could maybe get used to it.

"I'm going to move into his place. In Long Island City." Oh. This explained the tone.

"You're going to let go of Ninety-Sixth Street?" I tried to swallow my panic. "But it's such a good deal! You've always said it's such a good deal!"

She shrugged. "I'm going to be sixty soon. I won't be able to do the stairs forever. And he owns. So it'll be a better deal." She gave me a half smile, but I didn't reciprocate.

I was shocked. I couldn't imagine Mom's home being anywhere besides the apartment we'd lived in together for more than half my life. The place had held us through so much. I got my first period, lost my virginity, and discovered and deleted Tumblr. It had especially felt like an anchor over this past year when I had time to kill between work and Hudson Group meetings. But I couldn't imagine Mom was feeling any better about leaving. What about being a few blocks away from Gloria and Terri? And how would either of us live without Zabar's babka?

"When is all this happening? It's like a long-term plan, something that you're working toward in the next few years, right? I mean, you can't really move until you retire—you're so close to the school now. You don't want a long commute."

"Emma." She said my name like she had when I was a child and wanted to stay home from school even though I wasn't really sick. Like she knew something about me I didn't. "His name is David. He's an architect—or he used to be. He teaches at Pratt now."

"That's nice, that you're both teachers," I offered. I was supposed to ask about him, be more interested. But I couldn't think of any follow-up questions. I wanted to run back up to the apartment and throw myself onto the carpet where my bed used to be.

"Thank you for saying so. I'm going to move when the lease ends in February. It's September now, so we have about six months. It's not happening tomorrow." She was trying to reassure me. It wasn't working.

"September to February is five months. Isn't this all happening quickly? Do you think maybe you're rushing things? I mean, how well do you really know him?"

She took a deep breath. The waiter asked if he could take our plates, and I told him we were still working on it, even though I'd lost my appetite.

"We've been together for a little over a year."

"A little over a year!" I yelled it. Which I only realized when I saw people from the surrounding tables turn to us over their shoulders. "Sorry," I said in a whisper, overcorrecting. "I just don't understand why you haven't told me this."

"You've been so fragile. I didn't want to rock the boat. I wanted you to be well. But now, you had your big celebration, you're branching out— I thought you'd been doing better."

I wanted to tell her that I was never so fragile that she couldn't live her life. But it would have been a lie, and we both knew it.

"You're right," I said. "I'm better now." I took the last bite of my pork chop, looking forward to going home and licking my wounds in peace.

When I got back to my apartment, I called my sponsor, Lola. "Em-ma!" she said, pulling apart the two syllables of my name. "I was almost worried you'd miss your call today!"

I felt the same surge of annoyance that rose up when Mom rushed to tell the waiter we'd only be drinking water as soon as I sat down that afternoon. Did Lola really think that after a year of me calling her every day, I would suddenly forget? That my commitments were built on a fault line?

"I know it's a little late— I just got home."

"Did you go to Friday Night Drinks again?"

I'd caught her up about how it felt last week, and I'd sounded fairly optimistic on that call, so it stood to reason that she might think I'd go again. But every time I thought of it since, I remembered running into Ben as he leaned against the bar and the mirrored wall of liquor reflecting shards of our conversation back at me as we spoke. Nothing had happened since I mentioned lunch again at Friday Night Drinks. I assumed if Ben wanted to see me again, he would. But not going to drinks felt safer. "No. I had dinner plans with my mom." I didn't want to tell her about Mom having a boyfriend—a David—and how she was going to move in with him. I was hoping if I ignored it, it would stop being real.

"That's nice! It's always healing to nurture family bonds."

"Most of the time," I said, an edge of sarcasm creeping its way into my voice, unbarred due to the long day.

She caught it and tilted the conversation: "Has your dad finalized the plans for his trip yet?"

I took a deep breath and told her that he had. He'd be coming in two weeks and staying two nights at an Airbnb a few blocks away. When we first started emailing properties back and forth, I sent him things in the brownstone-lined streets of Brooklyn Heights that might've given him the closest thing to the quiet that he was used to upstate. He sent me something back, a place on Maple Street, just a short walk from where I lived. The question What do you think of this? was the only thing the email contained aside from the Airbnb link.

What did I think of it?

I thought it was a beautiful apartment. It was tastefully decorated. It was reasonably priced. And it was closer to me than anything else available for that weekend. I didn't understand what had caused his sudden interest in staying so near, but I'd seen him go through enough phases and radical changes in his life that I doubted I'd ever get the answers I wanted from him. My current theory was that he and Gaura were breaking up.

"Well, what's one thing you're looking forward to that's coming up?" Lola asked, wrapping up the call.

I paused. I wasn't looking forward to having to hear more about David and his apartment. And I certainly wasn't looking forward to my dad's impending visit. It felt like there were storms brewing on two horizons. Wasn't everything supposed to feel smoother now? Weren't the rocky bits supposed to be behind me? Why did it suddenly feel like all the parts were, instead of coming together, falling apart at the seams? I took a deep breath. "I'm going to a yoga class tomorrow," I said.

SEVEN

The fated calendar invite did indeed arrive. It was sent by Amy in HR, who was apparently the chair of the Fun Team. I'd spent an inordinate amount of time thinking about who else might be on the Fun Team, but I had not once asked Jermaine. I was proud of this. I might even have been pulling off pretending not to care. That's what normal people did, right? Lola wouldn't have balked at helping plan a large-scale event, and she was the most normal alcoholic I knew.

But this did cause one big problem. It was now Wednesday at 12:57 p.m., and I was walking into this meeting totally blind. In my continued desperate attempts at chillness, I hadn't even asked Vanessa what it was like last year. Did people get heated about venue choices? Was I supposed to do marketing work for the party? Or were the tasks a free-for-all? There were so many things I'd be bad at on a party-planning committee. I didn't even like parties when I drank, not really. I mean, obviously I couldn't get through them without getting drunk. Large groups of people had always made me nervous.

I walked through the door to the big conference room, caught in a terrible daydream about mandatory Fun Team wine tastings: I'd be standing with Amy from HR, refusing to take a sip, no excuses, other than the truth, left as the group assured me I could just spit it out. Although most of the conference rooms had been transformed into glass boxes, this was one of the only old-school ones we had left. It was surrounded by real Sheetrock and brick walls, making me feel like I was in an '80s movie about high-powered Wall Street dealings.

Richter & Thomas was the annoying kind of place where everyone was so streamlined that they knew exactly how many minutes it took to get from one place to another. It was now two minutes before 1:00 p.m., and it looked like I'd be the first person at the meeting. That is, until I turned left and saw a single other person sitting at the table: Ben.

He looked up at me and gave a tight smile, but he didn't look surprised. Did I look too surprised? Because I was. I was very surprised.

"Are you going to come in?" he asked.

I was frozen in the doorway. I hoped I wasn't also slack-jawed and wide-eyed. "Yeah. Of course," I said. But I was now posed with the difficult job of choosing a place to sit. The conference table was giant. It could seat fifteen people. Ben had placed himself in the corner seat farthest from the door. Should I choose the chair closest to me and therefore the farthest from him? That would be a statement. But I couldn't sit right next to him, either. That would be an entirely different kind of statement. Seconds were ticking by. I had to make a decision.

I sat down across from him. The table was long and narrow, so there were only about three feet between us. I had nowhere to look but right at him. He fixed this problem by looking at his phone. Genius move, but I didn't mirror him. Instead, while we waited the long two minutes in silence, I decided to look down at my outfit and judge myself.

I was wearing black jeans—fine. Leather boots with a slight heel—fine. A baby blue V-neck sweater that hadn't really fit me since college but was so soft I couldn't throw it away—not fine. It was currently showing about half an inch of midriff. But I knew if I pulled it down, the edge of my beat-up old bra would show. That would be worse. As it was, this was probably toeing the line of too much cleavage. I took another peek at Ben. His blue-checkered shirt was wrinkled in a way that made me think it had sat awhile in a laundry basket after getting washed. The top button of his shirt was undone, so I could see his Adam's apple bobbing. He'd slicked back his usually messy jet-black hair.

The conference door opened, and other people started to stream in. It must have been 1:00 p.m. on the dot. Amy from HR sat at the head of the table. She was followed by two other women, one from Reception and one from Finance. And then Mitchell Brady walked in. He pulled out a chair next to me. "Hey, Fine-ly," he said, an awkward reminder of our dating app conversation. I heard Ben choke back a guffaw across the table from us.

"Just call me Emma." For time immemorial, it has apparently been a cool, sought-after thing to be called by your last name. But I didn't like it. I had a complicated relationship with the man who gave me the name. And I liked to think of myself as just Emma. Like Cher or Adele but without the money, prestige, or talent. I also had no intention of being seen publicly flirting with Mitchell.

He started to say something else, but Amy from HR cut in. There were about ten of us now. "Okay, everyone!" Amy said. "Welcome to this year's Fun Team! Have any of you been on the Fun Team before?"

Three hands went up, including Ben's and Amy's. I knew this was Ben's first year as a department head, so he must have done it before his promotion as well.

"Yay! So many returnees!" Amy said. Three out of ten didn't strike me as great odds, but maybe that was a good Fun Team retention rate. "Ben, I was especially happy to see you nominate yourself on Monday!"

Ben blushed. He really, truly blushed, his cheekbones turning a furious red. I realized that the other times I thought he'd blushed, I'd been entirely mistaken. The light dusting of color when I flirted with him or when I apologized to him, they were nothing next to this. Did he have a thing for Amy in HR? She was probably midthirties, and overly cheerful, which didn't strike me as Ben's type, not that I should be assuming I knew anything about his type. Just because he asked me out for a drink did not mean that he only found awkward and overly serious twentysomethings attractive.

"I didn't want to—" Ben started, then stopped and said with a shrug, "I don't mind doing it."

"I want all the first-timers here to know the Fun Team is really about having fun. Yes, we do have a lot of work to do to get the party in tip-top shape, but I hope we'll also become friends," Amy said.

No one responded to her pep talk.

"With that in mind, let's play a little game to get started. One of my favorite things about chairing this meeting is that we have so many folks who don't work together regularly, and as such, we have so many opportunities to get to know each other better!"

I had not been warned about games. Had I been, I would have put up more of a fight when Jermaine told me I was nominated. My body heated, and I felt my palms begin to sweat. I remembered all the reasons I absolutely needed this job: the primary being my savings account was completely empty.

"Let's start with a classic— I assume everyone knows two truths and a lie?"

All the heads around me started to nod. I sat stock-still. I would not even condone this with a nod. A work get-to-know-you game was the worst kind of hell I could imagine. I thought that the marketing-and-communications office was hell that day Ben might have caught a peek at my speech, but if it was, Dante would have seen it very early on in his journey. This was a deeper kind of hell. This was like being forced to take acting for one semester in high school. I still woke up in cold sweats with the words *zip, zap, zop* on my tongue.

I racked my brain. As always, I could only think of horribly inappropriate things about myself, all of which were true: (1) I've sucked a guy's dick in the back of a bar, (2) I've sucked a guy's dick in the back of a movie theater, (3) I've sucked a guy's dick on the stern of a boat.

Oh god. People were starting to talk. Marjorie from Finance was saying she got engaged in Paris. I could imagine her on the top of the Eiffel Tower, surrounded by other Americans with flashy new diamond rings. Now people were starting to guess about her, but I hadn't listened well enough. I looked to Mitchell and nodded along with what his guess was. It worked. No one was looking at me. I guess Marjorie did get engaged in Paris, but she'd gotten married on Cape Cod, not in the Hamptons. A world away, as we all knew.

Now it was Mitchell's turn. So it would be mine next. Fuck.

"Okay." He laughed like he was enjoying this. "Um, I've been to Everest Base Camp, I was almost a pro-snowboarder, and I'm newly single."

I looked around. Somehow, no one was rolling their eyes.

Marjorie and Amy started laughing. "Well," Marjorie said, "I think you told me about that near miss in the Olympics qualifying round…"

"Oh yes! Isn't that where that photo of you and Shaun White in your office is from?" Amy continued. "Where you both have gold medals? Was that your medal or—"

"Okay, you got that one! It's true! Any other guesses? What do you think, Finley?" Mitchell gave me a flash of a wink; it was so fast I wasn't sure if I'd imagined it or not. "You might have a pretty good idea, actually."

Was he openly referencing that we'd matched? "Oh, well—I don't know. I mean..." I stuttered out the beginning of a sentence but didn't know how to finish it.

"You haven't been to Everest Base Camp," Ben said.

"Oh Ben! I think he's perfectly capable!" Amy chimed in, giggling.

Mitchell's face fell slightly. "No, he got me. That was the lie." Then he plastered his smile back on. "I haven't been yet, anyway."

"That's the attitude! Do you plan to climb Everest, Mitchell?" Amy asked.

"For sure. But I want to go farther than base camp."

"Doesn't it cost ten thousand dollars to get to Everest Base Camp?" Ben asked.

Mitchell laughed. "Yeah, I think around that. Luckily, I work here." He gave the table a smirk and got a few shallow smiles in return. Only the finance team got paid well enough to throw around cash on wild vacations. The rest of us sitting around the table—who were staff in Administration, Marketing, IT, or HR—got paid a living, but not an exorbitant, wage.

"How exciting," Amy cut in. "Don't we all feel like we know Mitchell better?"

I didn't feel I knew Mitchell any better. I'd known he was a dick, and he'd proved himself to be even more of a dick.

"So you're admitting it's more of a show of wealth nowadays than a physical feat?" Ben somehow pulled off asking this like it was a genuine question, not an opening shot.

Mitchell opened his mouth, but Amy cut in again. "Your turn, Emma!" she said.

My stomach revolted. A single drop of sweat dripped down my back. I had nothing. "Well, I don't know," I said. Suddenly, I remembered the dating profile Vanessa and her friends had written for me. "I've lived in every borough but Staten Island. I have four roommates. I don't know how to drive."

"Emma!" Mitchell immediately cut in before anyone else had the chance to respond. "You made it too easy. You know how to drive."

I shook my head. "That was true. I don't know how to drive. I might've missed sixteen, but I'll get there by thirty!" No one laughed. Whatever. I counted it as a win since I didn't mention sucking anyone's dick.

"You don't have four roommates," Ben said matter-of-factly.

"He's right," I jumped in so people would stop looking at me as though I'd revealed some pitiable fact.

"Ben! You keep getting the lie right away!" Marjorie said.

"Well, I knew Mitchell would have mentioned the Everest thing at some point if it were true," Ben said.

Mitchell furrowed his eyebrows like he was trying to determine if he was being insulted.

"And I know Emma lives alone," Ben finished.

"Yeah?" Mitchell said, suddenly looking aggressive. "How do you know that, Nowak?"

I should've found a way to de-escalate things. I opened my mouth to try, but only a weird guttural sound came out.

"She mentioned it once," Ben said. I'd forgotten how we talked about it the first day we met.

"I want to hear more about all the neighborhoods you've lived in, Emma!" Amy said, getting us all back on track.

"Yeah, anytime," I said. I could feel how red my face was. My skin was just reacting to being looked at—it had a hard time tolerating that. I wiped my palms against my jeans and kept my eyes down.

"Okay, Ben, why don't you go next?" Amy said.

Ben charged forward. "I own six pairs of boat shoes. My hometown once got thirty-five inches of snow. I've never been to Europe."

The lie was very clearly the boat shoes. I looked around. Everyone knew it. That's why we were all quiet. He was making fun of Mitchell. Hey, I got it. Mitchell was a total jerk. He probably did own lots of boat shoes. I just wouldn't have said it to his face.

Mitchell and Ben were staring at each other, and they both looked furious in that way straight men do when they're told that the film *300* is (a) bad, and (b) pretty homoerotic. I looked to Amy, but she blinked back at me, clearly at a loss for what to do. She was the chair of this meeting, and in HR, so handling it really seemed like her job. But what if Mitchell escalated things and brought me into it again? I couldn't let that happen.

"You're lying about the boat shoes," I said. "I've seen you wear at least eight different pairs."

Thankfully, they broke their eye contact. Ben looked at me and threw up his hands in mock defeat.

"Great!" Amy said, finally stepping back in. "Mark? Why don't you go?"

We didn't get anything else done at that first meeting. As soon as Amy dismissed us, we all scurried away like we were fleeing tenth-grade math class. When Jermaine asked me how it went, I told him it was fine, and I didn't mention anything about Ben or his bright red cheeks and angry looks. It's possible I was being vain, but it might have been Mitchell's wink at me that had set him off, which, if true, was silly—Ben had nothing to worry about, certainly not on that front.

EIGHT

When my dad knocked on my apartment door a few minutes after I buzzed him in, I didn't know what to expect, but I was still surprised. He looked different. It was the first time I'd noticed the gray streaking through his honey-blond, shoulder-length hair. We had the exact same shade, which a hairstylist had once called "taupe." A battered suede jacket hung off his frame, and the turquoise ring he always wore on his pinky finger had moved to his middle. Suddenly, it felt like two worlds: this small safe one I'd built for myself colliding with the unexpected one my dad always brought with him.

"It's so white in here," he said. His words were cramped in his throat, and his breath was shallow.

I wanted to laugh. That's how I felt every time I walked in, too—the white walls felt jarringly bright. I'd convinced myself that people didn't actually notice what you were afraid they would. Maybe that didn't work with family.

"It's a rental," I said.

He ran his hand over the old phone box now covered in globs of dried paint. His finger came away black with dust; I'd forgotten a spot. "But it's got good light," he said, walking toward the bay windows that I'd pushed my bed against so I could wake up with the sun.

I nodded and thought about how the last time I'd seen him, I'd been so early in my sobriety that I didn't say everything I'd meant to about it. I'd described the change to other people, how being in the program and my commitment to it shifted something elemental in me. I'd planned to show him my shiny new skin, but as soon as I crossed into the mountains and stepped into his house, the desire had faded. Trudging through his opinions about drinking was so nerve-racking that the only thing I could focus on was not drinking. I didn't have the bandwidth to also proselytize about how great not drinking could be.

This time, well, it felt like maybe anything could happen. The Big Book is clear on how you should talk about sobriety to people you hope will get sober: *Our public relations should be guided by the principle of attraction rather than promotion. There is never a need to praise ourselves. We feel it better to let our friends recommend us.* Would my mostly clean apartment (newly tidied for his visit), steady job, and general positive demeanor (after all, I had spent all of last night practicing casual smiles) show him that life could be better in sobriety? Probably not. Very, very likely not. But still, there was a chance, right?

We sat on the couch, which also served to separate my "bedroom" from my "living room and kitchen," with steaming mugs of chamomile in our hands. "Is there anything in particular that you wanted to do while you're here?" I asked, desperate to put words to the silence thrumming between us.

"Whatever you normally do, I'll tag along for," he said, and then added with a laugh, "As long as you don't mind being seen with your old man."

I imagined bringing him to the Saturday-night mediation meeting or to the "hangout" Mitchell kept asking me for. "But I'm here all the time. You must have something you'd like to do or see. Maybe there's a store or a class that you've been missing?"

"Anything you can buy here you can buy in Albany," he said. "I'm really just here to spend time with you."

"Don't you live over an hour from Albany?" When Ben and I first spoke, Albany and Phoenicia seemed like worlds away.

He shrugged.

What did people do with their parents when they visited? I remembered once seeing a list of restaurants "perfect for when your parents visit!" online. They were mainly white-tablecloth steakhouses and French restaurants that'd been New York staples for longer than I'd been alive. Those weren't the kind of places my dad would like. He'd be more interested in trying a new hole-in-the-wall raw-vegan place in Bushwick. Colin's parents had visited last month and he'd taken them to the Tenement Museum. They were apparently all enchanted by the history and how people could live in such small apartments. I was pretty sure my apartment was smaller, so I didn't know how interesting that would be.

But just as I was about to suggest it anyway, he spoke up again. "We could paint this place."

"My apartment?" My eyes bounced around the white walls, empty of paintings, framed posters, or family photos.

"It could use some color."

Somehow, I'd forgotten there was an era of my dad where he was an artist. It was that part of him that had brought him from South Jersey to New York in the '90s, that had put him in the downtown bars where he'd met Mom, and that enchanted my younger self with quick, effortless drawings of the trees, dolls, and faces that meant everything to my child-self. While most parents hung their kid's drawings on the fridge, I'd taped my dad's to my bedroom wall. All of those prior selves were still coexisting inside him, and they were all currently judging my bare apartment.

"I'd lose my security deposit." It hadn't exactly been an easy feat to gather enough funds for the first month's rent, the security deposit, and the movers while ensuring my credit didn't go to shit.

"Fuck the security deposit," he said with a shrug of his shoulders and a smile that looked like he was attempting a Harrison Ford impression.

There were a lot of reasons to say no, but the piece of me that missed the thrill of impulsivity ignored them all. "Yeah, alright. Fuck it."

The bus let us off right in front of the Bed-Stuy Home Depot. It was odd to see the suburban mainstay, which fit best in a strip mall, pushed between the tall towers of projects and protected by a chain-link fence. There were Hasidic Jews in traditional dress ambling by Central American guys looking for a day's work and a burly Black contractor speaking quickly in what I was pretty sure was Haitian Creole as he waited in line for a Depot dog. My dad seemed unfazed and uninterested. He was seamlessly settling back into Brooklyn life after over a decade away.

As we walked toward the interior paints section under the industrial lighting, I realized the thing that seemed different was that he looked really tired. His skin was so pale that the purple of his veins gave his entire body a supernatural glow. I thought of radioactive villains from old comic books who'd accidentally happened upon a nuclear testing site and transformed into something unrecognizable and then fixed themselves on revenge. Maybe I'd been right about Gaura breaking up with him. It would explain the weight loss and pallor. She'd driven him to the train, but maybe they were still friendly. Divorce took a long time, after all.

The paint chips were never-ending. Each color had multiplied itself and was hiding behind a thousand variations with differences I couldn't quite grasp.

"What were you thinking?" my dad asked.

I was surprised by the question. I hadn't been thinking of the color. I'd been thinking about him, about the twists of conversation that felt forced, and the few that felt as natural as new spring growth on a tree that had spent a long winter dormant. "Blue?" I said.

"Always a good choice." He gestured toward a section of whites that dove into blues and then deepened into greens.

On our way, a bright red peeked out at me, a baby bird's beak darting out of the nest. I picked it up, brushing my thumb against its smooth surface. It was called "100 mph."

"You won't be able to sleep with that color," my dad said.

"No?"

"I know it seems exciting. Like your apartment could be the inside of your body. But you can't paint your walls the color of blood. It's too stimulating. You'll have nightmares every night until you go back to white."

I had nightmares often enough as it was. Dreams so obvious I felt my subconscious could use a lesson in subtlety. At night I relapsed. Over and over again as I slept. When I woke up I could still hear myself, my own rambling voice explaining to dream people I had created why I deserved to drink again.

Just last night, me and my dream friends were in a bar celebrating something one of them did. A new job, a new boyfriend, a new haircut—even Dream Emma couldn't pretend to care. The room was dark, with dim yellow lights strung up against a mahogany wall. I could barely see my own hand reach for the beer. I could see the beer, though; it was the star of my subconscious. Lit up under a spotlight of my imagination. It was in a frosted pint glass, glistening gold like honey, bubbling like it was from a spring.

A friend, who was faceless, looked at me and asked, *I thought you didn't drink?*

And then it was clear: my hand—as true a depiction as my mind could ever conjure, ruddy and pink, nails chomped off and ragged—was grabbing the glass, was bringing it to my lips, was swallowing it whole.

Oh, I drink. I have for a while now.

And then, as quickly as dreams can move, I was at the bar. It was full of people like me, people who didn't need excuses, people who didn't ask questions. People who didn't answer calls for help, and who didn't cry for it, either.

When I reached the bar, I got a smile and a vodka from the bartender. The beer was foreplay; this was how I liked to drink. It looked like water, except it shimmered like old panes of glass, not quite even, not quite smooth. It hit my stomach like I remembered, ran through my veins like fire. My mind was quiet. I was home.

"I'll stick with blue, then," I told my dad, shaking off the memory of the dream. Sometimes it felt like my body hadn't caught up with my mind and my spirit. It craved something that the other two didn't anymore. When the dreams first started happening, they scared me. On days after, I wouldn't even let myself walk down the beer aisle in the grocery store, sure that I'd slip up and buy something. But I didn't feel that way anymore. They were no scarier than a graveyard; they, too, were just relics of the past. In any case, I didn't need to invite any more nightmares into my life. I didn't want to go a hundred miles per hour.

It was afternoon and my walls were still white. Everything had taken longer than we thought it would. The trip to Home Depot had lagged as we waited for someone to mix the paint. The bus took a detour. We'd forgotten to buy drop cloths and my dad had offered to run out to grab some. I couldn't think of an excuse not to let him, or to go in his stead. But it was small errands like this that would usually have him coming back tipsy. I thought of what Lola would say: that it wasn't in my power.

I couldn't control his actions; I could only control my own reactions.

All my furniture—which amounted to a bed, a couch, and a coffee table—was pushed into the center of the room in a tight clump. I sat on the coffee table and distracted myself with Instagram. I had a follow request from @urfavoritefinanceboi. I clicked on the profile, even though I had a very good feeling who it was. I was right: Mitchell Brady. I quickly scrolled through his photos. They were all of him on yachts. Sometimes he was alone, looking over the railing with his hairless chest in full view, and sometimes he was in groups of thirtysomething guys holding cocktails and wearing polos. It didn't surprise me that he was into yachts, but the sheer volume of photos of them was unfathomable. I mean, how often could he really be yachting? It wasn't like I'd ever seen this kind of boat docking on the Hudson River between the Intrepid and Chelsea Piers. I followed back, it was the only polite thing to do, and absent-mindedly scrolled through the people he followed. I was surprised to see a familiar name: Ben Nowak. I guess Mitchell handed out follow requests as easily as he did smiles. After I first met Ben I'd searched for him online, but I didn't find him in Vanessa's or Jermaine's followers, and typing his name into the search bar got me nowhere. I concluded that he must be unsearchable, like any real man of mystery.

I clicked Follow without thinking—his profile was private and I needed to see it. I hoped he'd follow me back. That he'd get the same flutter of curiosity from me as I got from him. What details would he reveal about himself online? Would there be pictures of him standing in front of a Christmas tree with his family, a picturesque snowy suburban landscape framed in the window behind them? Or would I see old girlfriends who looked nothing like me? Generic shots of music festivals?

I pocketed my phone as my dad walked back through the door exhaling staccato breaths.

I watched his every movement and analyzed them to puzzle together whether he was drunk or not. He was blinking slowly, almost as though it was taking effort for him to open his eyes again. That was a point toward drunk. But he'd come back in a reasonable amount of time with everything he said he was going to get. That was a point toward sober. I'd been playing this game my whole life—even before I could talk or walk, I was trying to figure out if he was drunk.

I'd only ever asked him once. I was twelve and he picked me up from a late bus, swerving his beat-up Subaru over the yellow line more times than I could count. I'd screamed when we got out of the car, my adrenaline forcing me to parrot words that my mother used to say. *Why do you have to get drunk to do this? Why do you have to be drunk to be around me?* He'd denied it, of course. In the morning, I wasn't mad anymore, I was just afraid that it was going to be like when Mom and he fought: days of aching silence. But thankfully, we both decided to pretend nothing had happened the night before. It was only this year, when I waded through agonizing hours in my own mind, that finally I understood it wasn't me he couldn't stand to be sober around—it was himself.

We worked in silence at first, only speaking about how to make sure the painter's tape was level or where I kept a screwdriver that he could use to open the paint. (I didn't have one, but he made do with a butter knife and a hammer.)

It wasn't until the first stripes of Sea Mist hit my wall that the conversation started to shift away from the immediate. "Do you like living alone?" he asked.

I didn't answer at first. I didn't want to talk about why I felt I had to live alone. That I couldn't take other people's drinking and drug use, and it didn't feel fair—or possible—to ask them to abstain in their own home. "I was really sick of living with a rotating door of roommates. And I haven't even ever had a real boyfriend, so that wasn't an option."

"What's a real boyfriend?" He let the word *real* hang out in his mouth, giving it quotation marks without using his hands to splatter paint everywhere.

"Someone I've lived with?" My mind drifted to Susannah and Brian, wherever they were now. I imagined them falling asleep with their arms around each other, his warm breath on the back of her neck so familiar it no longer gave her goosebumps. I wanted someone to reach out to in the night, to find someone warm and alive next to me instead of miles of cool cotton blend. "Or even just someone I've loved." My face blushed, but it calmed me to know that he couldn't see it. We were facing away from each other, painting back-to-back.

My dad gave a murmur of assent, and instead of dipping his brush back into the bucket, he set it down. "You know, after me and your mom split, I wasn't even with anyone until Gaura. I spent the next seven years in a period of self-isolation."

I was pretty sure he meant he hadn't slept with anyone between his two wives. I gave him a noncommittal grunt. I would be happier not diving too deeply into that subject.

"For some people, it's easier to be with someone, and for other people, maybe people like you and me, it feels easier—more in our comfort zone—to be alone."

I nodded. "Being alone is less complicated."

"But I'm really happy I'm not alone. There's a reason people write so many love songs, Em. Life is better with someone by your side."

"You say that like I can make the choice by myself. Like I can just walk out into the world and declare I'm ready for love." I imagined walking to my corner bodega and asking any of the guys in there if they wanted to settle into a long-term relationship with me, or if not, maybe they wouldn't mind putting the word out? I wondered how Mom had changed her mind about being with someone. How did David suddenly fall into her lap? I wouldn't bring it up in front of my dad. Even though they'd been apart for far longer than they were together, the lesson about not mentioning my parents' dating lives in front of each other had been etched into my psyche.

"No, but that's a bigger part of it than you might think."

"What do you mean?"

"Well, I mean that it's a requirement. You have to want something to get it. Life won't just hand it to you." He told me the story of how he met Gaura, which I'd never heard before, and I hadn't expected it to be online. I couldn't imagine the man I'd known when I was sixteen taking mirror selfies and nervously dressing for a first date.

"Please tell me you still have the pictures you used?" I could hear glee creeping into my voice.

"Oh god, no. They were destroyed long ago."

"Did you take the selfie in the upstairs or downstairs bathroom?" Until Gaura moved in, he'd kept the previous owners' hunter's theme of the master bath, complete with wallpaper depicting bounding hounds and fleeing ducks.

He turned to me. "Unfortunately, the upstairs," he said with a wink. We both started laughing.

The walls turned from white to power blue, and then a second coat transformed them into the deeper shade I imagined covered the sky on misty New England mornings. Along the way, my dad told me the story of why his parents got married: "They were both students at Rutgers. Grandpa and his roommate had a party, and my mom went." He never referred to his mother as "Grandma." She hadn't lived long enough to become one. "They didn't speak that night, they didn't even really know each other—she was a friend of his roommate's girlfriend. But she had a bit too much to drink and fell asleep on the couch. Nobody realized she was there until the next morning, and when they all did, when the morning light really blasted them in the face, they both knew what they had to do. They were going to have to get married."

"Even though they didn't know each other?" I was shocked. It was a funny story, but it couldn't have been true, right? Essentially, if my grandmother could've held her liquor better, I would never have existed.

"Didn't matter. If they didn't get married, she'd be disowned—her parents were very Catholic. Hell, they were all very Catholic."

"It sounds like the start to a romance novel, actually."

"Except for the part where they were miserable together for the next twenty years, I guess."

I laughed. "Yeah, we can forget that part and say they lived happily ever after." Then, after a pause, "How do you know if you'll be miserable or happy with someone?"

"Well, I think the first step is to not marry a stranger just because they fell asleep on your couch." He shot me another smirk. "And then, well, marry someone who brings out the best in you."

"That's what everyone says."

"Okay, think about it this way. When you're with someone, if you like yourself, then they're good for you. If you don't like yourself, then they're not. I think it's that simple."

I nodded, thinking about all of the different Emmas and whether or not I really liked any of them. I could at least say Drunk Emma was the worst of them. I dipped my brush back into the blue, letting a now-comfortable silence wash over us. This was the color that had greeted nineteenth-century whalers and now greeted lobster fishermen and Kennedy descendants alike. It suited my room on the top floor. It allowed me to imagine my bay windows were the bow of a ship. Me and my studio were going places.

"What is that?" I asked him. He was standing in my kitchen, tucked into a corner and tipping an orange pill bottle into his open hand. The sink was running water over the paintbrushes that he'd come into the kitchen to wash, but he was standing feet away.

He looked up at me, surprised. He swallowed. Was the pill already in his mouth? "New stuff the doctors have me on," he said.

"For what?" I asked. I didn't realize he took medicine that wasn't herbal.

"Blood pressure." He was lying. Or he wasn't. I couldn't control people's actions, only my reactions.

"Can I see?" I asked, barely above a whisper.

He didn't hand over the bottle. He pocketed it. But I caught the last three letters: *-ine.* The only things that I could think of that were spelled that way were opiates like codeine or morphine. My eyes darted to his pupils—they were pinpricks. How had I not noticed before? My heart beat faster. He was lying. But it was bright in here, under the harsh glow of the fluorescent light. Maybe I was being paranoid. What did I know about blood pressure medication?

He turned to the paintbrushes. "These are almost clean," he said. Sea Mist dripped from them into the stainless steel sink. Had he not heard me? Or was he just moving forward as if he hadn't? I looked at his back, my stomach in my throat. He was lying. Or I was insane. I knew I shouldn't think about either of those options—I should just be happy that he was here.

My windows were wide open, and my furniture was still pushed to the center of the room. It was early October, and the first hint of fall was flowing in with a cool evening breeze, but the smell of fresh paint was clinging to the room. My mind was racing. I couldn't stop thinking about the pills. It wasn't even the pills I was obsessing over, though—it was my accusation. How had those words slipped past my lips? Had I offended him? Where had I gotten off asking him to see the bottle? Did I seem insane? Like I didn't trust him? I'd just about convinced myself to call and apologize when I remembered his tiny pupils and the way his jacket had hung off his bony frame. I'd been looking for signs of drunkenness and not finding them because he'd been getting high.

A notification on my phone cast a blue glow over the darkness of my room. I reached for it, and out of the corner of my eye, I caught the Instagram logo. I thought of all the things Ben might say to me. There were a million different options. It could be anything from: *I'm recusing myself from the Fun Team, which previous to your joining, was the very light of my life.*

Or: *Amy from HR told me you're dating Mitchell Brady. Now that I know you have such bad taste, I will absolutely never be interested in you.*

But there was the slightest chance it was: *Hey, I can't stop thinking about you.*

I let my heart hope for the briefest of milliseconds that it was the last option, and then tapped my finger down.

The Instagram message wasn't from Ben. It wasn't from a random bot trying to convince me I'd won an iPhone. It was from fucking Mitchell. An option so bad, I hadn't even entertained it.

11:12 p.m.
Mitchell: hey, you around?

What the fuck did that mean? Around where? I knew I should ignore it. But it was, at the very least, diverting.

11:14 p.m.
Emma: I'm home.

Mitchell: You live in the city?

Okay. Great. Well, at least that offered some clarity. This was absolutely a "u up"–adjacent text, and while I was awake and losing myself to a fruitless thought spiral, I wasn't up for what he wanted. But I had very little experience saying no to men.

Honestly, I don't think I ever had before. If they were interested in fucking me, I was usually okay with that. When I was drinking, I felt so disconnected to my body that I didn't mind going along with anything. But now I was aware of every cell. When I sat too close to someone on the subway, or even felt a strong breeze push against my skin, the sensations resonated. I was awake to everything. I wasn't sure what my sex life would be in the future, but I knew I'd never be up for the kind of night Mitchell was suggesting again.

Emma: No

Mitchell: Where do you live then, cause I'm cool with coming to North Brooklyn to chill.

Was he sniffing out a lingering scent of my past as a good-time girl?

Emma: I don't want to chill, but thanks.

Mitchell: Not chill, huh? You wanna get crazy?

He probably wanted to take an Uber to my neighborhood and find a dive bar to snort coke in. After that, he might tell me that Brooklyn sucked, and we needed more coke, so we'd take a car to Tribeca or some other sleek Manhattan finance-bro enclave and he'd take me to his local "bar," which was probably a club with twenty-foot windows and taupe velvet curtains. There, he'd buy us twenty-nine-dollar signature cocktails named after '90s R & B classics that none of the patrons actually liked. Drunk Emma would have taken him up on the offer. But then she'd probably have gotten too drunk or tried to steal his coke from his pocket. When he caught her, she might offer to fuck him for it. If he said no, she'd get angry. It would be our one and only "date." But Drunk Emma wasn't in charge anymore. She got her keys taken away.

Or maybe I was underestimating him. Maybe that was basic finance-bro shit. Maybe he had ascended to the next level and actually did have a yacht docked somewhere off the island of Manhattan that he was willing to whisk me away on. Although that sounded like an interesting adventure, I wasn't interested in Mitchell.

Emma: No. I want to look up cats to adopt and then not adopt them or watch cult documentaries.

Mitchell: Is that how you decompress?

Emma: Generally, yeah.

Mitchell: Aren't you too young to want a cat?

Emma: People of all ages like cats?

Mitchell: Yeah but like you've heard of crazy cat ladies. You don't wanna start walking down that path too early.

I imagined a parallel-universe version of myself with doe eyes instead of my suspicious squinty ones, quickly writing "no cats!" on a flowery notepad with "How to Get a Man to Love Me" written on the top.

Emma: Actually, that sounds like exactly what I wanna do. I want to cover my path in fuzzy, untrained cats. Maybe I will apply to adopt one tonight!

Mitchell: Awww you're messing with me. But anyway, I get you that tonight's no good. We'll connect another time.

Emma: *thumbs up*

Mitchell: Did you type out thumbs up instead of doing the emoji?

Emma: yes that's how the kids do it.

Mitchell: Lol okay. *Thumbs up*

I hoped against all hopes that he would send that to someone else. That's what he got for trying to only date girls who were younger than him. Thumbs-fucking-up. But knowing that he was an option, an ugly temptation for me to refuse, kept me from obsessing about the pill bottle.

My dad and I had agreed to meet at nine the next morning, but it was now ten after nine and he was nowhere to be seen. The sky was bright and high, but the wind had a bite to it. I pulled my denim jacket closer to my body. Even though it was already October, it felt like the first real day of fall. If I'd known his bagel order, I could have saved time and started the long wait. The line was already extending outside the side entrance and was stuffed with tote bag–carrying hipsters and families wielding strollers erupting with baby supplies.

The bagel store my dad used to take me to on weekend mornings in Park Slope had long since closed, the storefront transforming into an organic pet-supply shop. But this newer place had Montreal-style bagels, which were, according to several food blogs, better than New York–style. I would have avoided it on account of my loyalty to New York–style everything, but I was even more loyal to convenience. And I honestly couldn't tell the difference between the bagels—they were both boiled, which was the only important thing.

I felt my phone vibrate against my stomach and pulled it out of my pocket. It was an Instagram notification. I slid my finger across the screen with a small amount of dread in my veins, expecting to see that Mitchell was still up on some sort of bender and had found himself in my neck of the woods. But that wasn't it. It wasn't a message at all. It was a follow request.

Ben had accepted my request and requested me in return. I accepted, and then rushed over to his profile, my father's lateness forgotten in my eagerness to see a new side of Ben. He didn't have many followers and wasn't following many people. There were only a few photos of him mixed in with pictures that he'd taken on the streets of New York: a box of VHS tapes next to a box of DVDs on top of a pile of garbage, a sign in the window of a random apartment that read Clean Bathroom $2.00, a half-eaten slice of pizza covered in snow. Scrolling further back in time, I found pictures of a trip out West documented by zoomed-in snaps, likely taken from a car. Red hills that I guessed were in Arizona or New Mexico. Even further back, almost a decade back, his page was dominated by a black cat sitting on the kind of big leather sectional that would be impossible to have in a small New York City apartment. None of those photos had captions, so I was left without the cat's name.

I maneuvered over to my own profile, wondering what Internet Emma looked like to his eyes. I'd deleted all the photos of myself out at a bar, holding a glass of wine, or with eyes set to half-mast and mouth curved into an easy smile. I couldn't bear to look at photographic evidence of me at my worst. But when I was done deleting, there hadn't been much left. I knew I didn't want to show the world Drunk Emma, but looking at my sparse Instagram, it didn't seem like I had anything else to show.

Now my most recent post was of a single tomato I'd been able to grow on my windowsill over the summer. Older ones were of my toes at the beach and a sunset through the windows of a subway car. Susannah had disappeared along with all my "going-out" photos. But I could still see the places where she'd been, between the beaches and the sunsets. Did I look boring? Did I look lonely? My stomach squirmed in fear. Maybe I shouldn't have followed him. I suddenly felt overwhelmed, knowing he was out there looking at me, or this online version of me, but without my real-life context.

I closed the app and tried to breathe. It was now 9:20 a.m. and I'd still had no word from my dad. I called him and he didn't answer. I walked away from the lamppost I'd been leaning against, my hands sweating with the swirl of sudden anxieties taking over. Was he too hungover to come get bagels? Would Ben lose whatever scrap of interest he had in me? Would the baby in the bagel line ever stop crying?

My feet led me toward my dad's Airbnb without much forethought. When I knocked on the door, there was no answer. Fears pulled at me from every direction: Had he checked out early and not told me because I'd insulted him last night? Were those pills indeed opiates and he'd overdosed? I'd never heard of people accidentally OD'ing on pills, but maybe it could happen. Or maybe that's why he'd actually come to Brooklyn, to get something he was having difficulty getting in the Catskills. I knocked again, this time louder, and felt the sting in my knuckles from the sharp raps against the solid wood.

Finally, the door opened. My dad looked haggard in a T-shirt and boxers, his hair standing in every direction. He'd overslept. Maybe if I stepped closer, I'd smell old liquor on his breath.

"It's nine thirty," I said, hoping that would explain my presence, my worry.

His eyes opened a bit wider, as though he was just starting to piece together the scene. He nodded. "I'll get dressed." The door started to close again, but I stopped it with my arm.

"I can pick up the bagels, just tell me what you want."

It was ten before I was back and carrying two everything bagels with cream cheese. When he opened the door for the second time that morning, he was showered, his hair was brushed, and the deep circles from under his eyes had faded slightly. Any sign of the side of himself he was hiding from me had been tucked away.

He led me to the backyard of the Airbnb, which had tall wooden fences covered in ivy and a small bistro table forced onto an odd angle by cracking concrete. I'd never had outside space in New York, but some of my earliest memories were of looking out at the gardens below my bedroom window. The woman who owned our Park Slope building had no patience for the mess plants brought, nor much patience for children. Her backyard was bricked over in a neat geometric pattern. She went out there every morning to hose it down and pull out any weeds that dared try and creep between the bricks. But other than that, it lay empty and tempting.

The reality of this garden felt different. Life was cracking into it and taking over. It was unkempt, and the human influence of the poured concrete was no match for the strong roots of the maple tree on the other side of the fence. The bistro table was dusted with pollen. I wiped it off with a swipe of my forearm.

"I think the travel yesterday took more out of me than I realized," he said. "I'm sorry."

That made sense. The train ride and all the prep work to paint, let alone actually painting, would tire anyone out. It made sense, but it didn't stop me from not believing him. All good lies are believable, after all. I knew that because I was a liar, too.

"Is your mother still living at Ninety-Sixth Street or did she move somewhere with a garden?"

He said it like it was an honest question. But I knew he was changing the subject out of desperation to avoid whatever it was I'd caught him sleeping off. I shrugged again.

"Having a garden makes a real difference in the city, I think," he said. "But I guess you don't really need a garden, being so close to the park. That's where you spend a lot of your time, right?"

"Yeah. I usually wake up early, 'cause I'm clearheaded in the mornings now, and take a walk." The more he acted like everything was fine and light, the more I wanted to scream. I'd put up with decades of silence. Pretending there was nothing wrong. Letting my paranoia eat away at me instead of pointing it back at him where it belonged.

He furrowed his brow, not sure what I was getting at. "Being close to nature is so important. It's how we remember we're human. That's been something I've been thinking about a lot lately, actually." He took a breath, like he was going to continue waxing poetically about trees, but I couldn't hear another second of it.

"I think the best way to remember I'm human is to not poison myself with drugs or alcohol," I snapped. To my dad, they were an opening shot, but I'd been fighting this battle since I saw him in my kitchen last night.

He put his bagel down. "What?"

"You know that I'm sober, right? That I'm a year sober?"

"That doesn't have anything to do with what I'm trying to say," he said, his voice rising to meet mine.

"Of course. Drinking or not drinking is never relevant to you. It's relevant to everyone around you, but never to you!"

"Because not everything is about drinking. Your mother was always like this—"

"Because she lived with you! A drunk!" There was very little doubt that anyone in a nearby garden wouldn't be able to hear us.

"I'm not drunk right now." He slammed his hand against the wobbly table. It shuddered in response.

"Only because you were sleeping something harder off, right?" I glared at him.

His breathing was labored, and he looked back at me with ferocity. "Never mind. We're not doing this, Emma. I refuse to do this. I have a train to catch."

"In hours!"

"Well, I don't want to spend them getting screamed at."

I almost said that he'd screamed, too. I thought it. But instead, I took a breath. This was going nowhere. I nodded. I couldn't will him to tell me the truth.

"Is there any way for us to have a nice morning?" he asked. He sounded genuine. Like that's actually what he wanted. I wanted him to tell me the truth for once, but it was clear I wasn't going to get it.

"The listing said this place has HBO?" I couldn't talk to him anymore. But I could sit next to him quietly in a dark room.

He nodded, and we went inside. We ate the rest of our bagels to the opening credits of *Game of Thrones*, which he'd never seen. The beats of the first episode were slower than I remembered, but there was something heartwarming about seeing all the Starks at home for the last time.

As the music of the last scene boomed and then faded, he turned to me and asked, "How was the light in your room this morning?"

It had been my first thought, actually. I'd wondered if the sky had bled onto my walls; the blues were such a perfect match. "Lovely," I said. "It's a great color. Thank you for suggesting it."

He nodded. "I don't think you lose your security deposit for making improvements."

I laughed. It was light, but it wasn't forced. "I guess not."

"I'm glad we did that. It feels nice to know I left you with something good."

"Do you still draw?" I asked.

He made a quizzical face at me and said nothing. I took this to mean that it wasn't something he could forget.

"Will you draw me a picture of my apartment, just as it is today?" I wanted to remember it, the good parts of yesterday.

Before I finished my request, he was up and looking for something to draw with. The best we could find in the Airbnb was a golf pencil and a calendar that was taped to the kitchen wall. He tore off January and started drawing on the back.

He angled it so that the bay window was front and center. I watched him cram the furniture into the center of the room, and then place me on top of the coffee table where I'd been when he walked in last night, looking out.

As I saw the lines forming, I knew they'd end up on my fridge, just as those long-ago pictures he'd made me had ended up on my wall.

In the afternoon, I watched him get into the Uber and wondered when I'd see him next. Would it be my turn to visit? Maybe we were slowly going to spiral back into each other's lives until our relationship mirrored something much closer to the fathers and daughters I saw on Cheerios commercials as a kid? Maybe whatever happened with the pills yesterday didn't have to matter.

My phone vibrated. It was an Instagram message from Ben: I'm so impressed that you got tomatoes to grow in a window box. All my attempts have failed. Three dots indicated he was still typing, and then a picture of a window box stuffed with herbs in varying states of decay filled my screen.

I smiled. If he wanted to talk about window box gardening, we could talk about window box gardening. I could put this whole weird weekend behind me and step forward into the future.

NINE

What I'd started with Mitchell wasn't evaporating as I'd hoped. He'd begun Slacking me at work. None of it was interesting or reject-able. It wasn't like I could say "Hey, I'm not into you romantically" in response to a message like this:

Mitchell B: Ugh I've been in this meeting for nine hours. No lie.

I never messaged him first and only ever gave him a word or two in response. But it was now Wednesday morning, the Fun Team meeting was in a few short hours, and my subtle hints that I wasn't into him were getting me nowhere.

Was he going to act like we were friends at the meeting? I really hoped he didn't make it seem as though we had some sort of flirtation going. It wasn't like I could say, in front of Amy from HR, "There's no way I would ever date you, and my days of meaninglessly fucking people are behind me." Who knew? Maybe that nine-hour meeting would keep him forever, and he wouldn't be able to come this week.

My dream was immediately dashed when I walked into the big conference room on twelve and saw Mitchell, Ben, and Mark from Reception already sitting there. None of them were speaking. They'd each claimed a separate corner of the table and had their phones out.

I wasn't sure where to place myself among them. I decided to not overthink everything—I'd just sit where I'd be most comfortable. So I walked over to the corner that was the farthest from Mitchell and pulled out the chair beside Ben. "Hi," I said in a low voice, sitting down.

"Hey," he said, giving me a nod.

Ben and I had been dancing around each other on Instagram for the past few days. We chatted a bit about window box gardening, and I told him about the groundbreaking innovations of not overcrowding your plants and watering them regularly. We reacted to each other's stories and commented on the rare post. He even sent me a post of a *New Yorker* cartoon depicting a subway car pulling up to the station, displaying a lowercase *a*, with the caption No, you want the A train. This is just a train. I responded with a video from SubwayCreatures of a man cutting his toenails on the A train and said, I think I'd prefer just a train. Things were light, friendly. Conversations were noncommittal. But every time I saw a notification light up my phone, I always hoped it was him.

I looked up to find Mitchell watching me, head slightly cocked as if the whole scene was curious to him, like the movie he was watching had just taken a surprising turn. "Hi, Emma," he said.

"Mitchell."

"There are plenty of seats over here," he continued.

My face flushed. All eyes, even Mark's, were on me now. "I'm fine here," I said. And then I pulled out my phone, hoping to end the conversation.

Amy from HR walked in with Marjorie, chatting excitedly about some new fashion company that was using ocean plastic as thread. I'd heard that recycling plastic bottles into thread and then making clothes from it was one of the major contributors to the microplastics problem, which was quickly poisoning all fresh water on earth, but I bit my tongue, reminding myself that no one liked it when you interrupted their joy with bad news, even if was true.

"Alright there, Emma?" Amy asked.

"Mmm-hmm," I said, refusing to look up.

"Oh, don't worry about her—Mitch was just teasing her," Mark said. I didn't know why Mark had read the situation that way. Mitchell had embarrassed me, yes, but I was equally, if not more, upset by the world's unsolvable plastic crisis.

I didn't respond. Not engaging felt like the best way to go here. I continued looking down at an email I'd already read, that Jermaine sent out a few hours ago about some copy text.

"Well, then," Amy said, her tone sounding almost gleeful, like she'd just popped a piece of candy into her mouth. More people piled into the room, but I kept my eyes firmly on Jermaine's words floating back and forth on my phone screen.

Mitchell turned to Amy and Marjorie, inserting his opinion on the climate crisis. He had recently invested in a luxury sneaker brand that used the very thread they were discussing.

I felt a soft brush against my foot. Another foot? I pulled my own back sharply, hitting my knee against the top of the table with a bang. I hissed in an effort not to curse.

"You okay there?" Mitchell asked, and anyone who hadn't noticed my slight accident now turned back to me.

"Yup!" I said, trying to sound cheerful as I rubbed my knee.

Mitchell nodded as if my response had satisfied him, then turned back to Amy and Marjorie.

Feeling his eyes still on me, I turned to Ben, who mouthed, "Sorry."

It had been his foot. Had it been a purposeful foot? "Don't worry," I mouthed back.

"You okay?" he asked, continuing to pantomime his words. I nodded quickly.

Amy checked her watch, gave up on the one straggler we were waiting for, and started the meeting. She stood, took out a dry-erase marker and wrote "$50,000" on the board behind her. "Okay, guys, this is what we'll be working with this year. I know it's not quite the cushion we had to work with last year, but I know we can do it."

I didn't understand. Every worry was erased from my mind, the 50K smoothing my anxieties like an enormous Zamboni. What would we be paying 50K for?

Amy turned back to the board and wrote a single word above the number: "BUDGET."

Fifty thousand dollars for one party? Would we be eating caviar off tiny gold-plated forks and drinking from champagne glasses made of Swarovski crystals? Or maybe we'd be hiring ten consultants to help us optimize growth while we danced awkwardly to Top 40 hits?

This was hilarious, because I was paid exactly $49,440 a year. This was after a 3 percent raise at my six-month review—hence that uncomfortable four hundred and forty dollars hanging out around the end. I mean, hey, I'd take it. Four hundred and forty dollars was about a third of my rent; it was nothing to sneeze at. But I'd just learned that a whole year of me—me coming in at nine and leaving at five Monday through Friday, me being squished into subway cars, me emailing my colleagues fanatically to get last-minute deadlines out, me getting dressed even though I wanted more than anything to stay in bed, me forty hours a week, fifty weeks a year, was worth five hundred and sixty dollars less than one night of an open bar. Good to know, I guess.

A little before five o'clock, Vanessa swiveled over to me.

"So..." she said.

"Yeah?" I asked. I looked up and noticed Jermaine and Colin were already gone.

"Do you have anything to tell me?" she asked, lips pursed expectantly.

"Did something happen with one of the Facebook ads? Was it not approved?" Our Facebook ads were terrible—filled with old white people drinking wine and looking at sunsets—but I thought they were too boring to really cause a stir. I always felt my gut sink when we targeted middle-aged, college-educated men, our bread and butter. We weren't here to explain financial investing to people, the content team always reminded us, we were here to make it easier for our existing customer base to use financial services.

"No, don't be silly. This isn't about work stuff."

"Then I really don't have anything to tell you," I said, trying to keep my tone light. We didn't really talk about anything besides work stuff. Except for that one time when Lola convinced me it was time to make friends, which led to the work night out where my phone was taken—putting me squarely in this mess with Mitchell. I tried not to think about it.

"I'm hearing things through the grapevine about you, Ems," she said. "And like, sure, you can have your secrets. But there's really no reason to not tell me if half the office already knows."

This moment felt like a crossroads. Like if I didn't tell her what was going on, we'd forever be stuck as work friends instead of real friends. And I'd recently realized that I did want to be real friends with Vanessa. She was funny, and kind, and made it feel natural to let my guard down. I wanted to tell her whatever she wanted to know—the only problem was, I truly didn't know what she was talking about. "Vanessa, I really don't know what you're talking about. I have no life updates."

"Amy from HR told Maria different," she said. I watched her thin, manicured hands press the off button on her computer. She was looking at it intently, as though it needed all of her focus. "I just wish you could trust me."

"What is this about? The fucking Fun Team? We haven't chosen a venue yet."

"The venue! Really, Emma! The venue!" She thumped the purse she had been packing onto her lap. A pack of mints fell out, bouncing against her knee and then dropping to the floor. I went to reach for them. "Just leave it. I'll get it," Vanessa said.

I pulled my hand back, but Vanessa made no move to bend down and pick up her mints. She just looked at me. After a beat of silence, she lifted her hand and made a come-on gesture, spinning it in a slow circle between us.

"The Fun Team is torture," I said. "Is that what Amy from HR told you? I hate every second of it." That wasn't completely true, but I wasn't going to tell her about Ben's foot touching my foot. Or that it might not have been accidental.

"She said that there was something going on between you and Mitchell Brady."

It hadn't occurred to me that this was what Amy from HR might have suggested. That Mitchell had pushed it into everyone's heads with his winks and his teasing.

"There's nothing going on between us. I haven't once seen him outside of work."

"Amy seemed pretty sure. I get why you wouldn't want people to know. He's a bit of a dick, but if you're enjoying yourself..." Vanessa said.

"I'm not fucking Mitchell Brady," I said. "He's like vaguely hitting on me, but it's really minor and borderline." Amy might have been this delusional, this gripped by Mitchell's smiles, but surely Vanessa could see things differently? I'd kept her at arm's length, but even from that distance, I thought the shape of me would be clear enough for her to understand that I wouldn't be interested in a guy like Mitchell. I had a sudden moment of panic. Would Ben think the same thing? What if he thought I was just trying to fuck any guy at R&T? That I saw him and Mitchell as interchangeable?

"Oh," Vanessa said.

"Sorry. I don't have any office gossip." I turned my computer off with a touch too much force and it slid a few inches across the desk. "Also, fuck Amy! She's in HR! What is she doing gossiping?" I slammed my desk drawer shut. The thin, spray-painted metal shuttered against my hand. The furniture wasn't built to be abused; it was weak and supple. I'd have thought a company like Richter & Thomas could have afforded sleek hardwood, but I had previously been delusional about many things, like the assumption that people in HR would remotely do their jobs.

"You're right," Vanessa said. "She shouldn't be talking about people like that. It's just life is so tedious here sometimes, isn't it?"

"Yeah, it is." I knew what she meant without her spelling it out. No one really wanted to be working at Richter & Thomas—well, except maybe Mitchell Brady or other people on the content and finance teams, people who wanted to go skiing in Aspen more than they wanted the oceans to be cleared of plastic. I imagined Mitchell lying in bed at night, staring at the ceiling, and just wanting. I could see him clutching his throat and barely being able to breathe because he wanted to say, so badly, that he'd been to Sundance, or on a yacht in the South of France. I knew what it felt like to want like that. Everybody in the rooms I went to after work did. It's what we all had in common.

"What did you want to be when you grew up?" I asked Vanessa.

She huffed, twisting in her chair. "You know this already—I wanted to be a pro figure skater. Hang eight gold medals off my neck."

"Okay, then, after that. When you had a better shape of the world—"

"You mean when I had a real understanding of what it felt like to wake up at three forty-five a.m. every day?"

"Yeah, sure, after that. In high school and college, what did you want to be?"

"Well, I didn't dream of *this*." She gestured around the windowless room. "But I wanted to move to New York, live a little bit like they did in *Friends*, as silly as that sounds. Never experience another Michigan winter. I didn't think about work as much as I thought about the rest of it." I nodded, and she kept going. "I don't really know how kids are supposed to make a choice like that and then go after it. I didn't know anything—even through college, I didn't really know what the options were."

"I don't think I know anything now, much less when I was a kid," I said.

"What did you want to be?" Vanessa slipped off her shoes and tucked her feet under her, settling in.

"I always hated the question. I would say something different every time someone asked me. I said I wanted to be a pop star one day and a lion tamer the next, but they were all made up." I couldn't mirror her and take my shoes off, too; I'd worn the same pair of socks two days in a row and I was worried my feet smelled foul.

"Okay, but what did you think and then not say? What was your secret internal answer?" She smiled at me, fully aware of the difficulty of her question.

"The only thing I really wanted when I grew up was stability, I guess. I liked to imagine having a family. Being part of a unit. A husband and kids." I felt my face blushing at the honesty of it. Was Work Emma honest? I wasn't sure. But it didn't feel like she was in the room with us. The only other person I'd said that to before was Susannah. When she was being kind and sympathetic, she'd hold me close and whisper that of course I'd have a family. When she was being impatient with Drunk Emma's soliloquies—which to her credit, were exhausting even to my own ears—she'd tell me that neither of us were meant for anything so pedestrian.

"Oh, Emma. That's so earnest," Vanessa said. "It's interesting, I kind of wanted the opposite. Life felt so steady growing up, I wanted adventures and independence."

"Maybe there are only two kinds of people," I said. I liked that Vanessa wanted different things than I did. Susannah always did. But with Suze, it felt like she was pulling me out my shell, waiting on the other side of the door, annoyed that I occasionally wanted to binge drink and rewatch *Jersey Shore* rather than binge drink at a new bar in Bushwick that was having a Y2K dance party.

Vanessa laughed. "And they find each other in marketing departments."

I picked up my purse and headed for the door. Before I lifted the handle, I turned back to Vanessa. "Good night. See you tomorrow," I said.

"Emma," she said, "do you want me to take your place on the Fun Team?"

"No. Thank you." It was kind of her to offer, but I couldn't accept. And a small part of my mind whispered that I'd lose any contact I had with Ben if I took her up on it.

"Okay. See you tomorrow, then," she said.

"Tomorrow," I repeated.

I called Lola on my way out of the building, and I could hear the quiet strumming of a guitar in the background. Probably her musician husband. I hoped he wouldn't be able to hear our conversation.

"I'm glad you called," she said.

Usually, I would have seen her yesterday, but she was visiting her husband in LA while he was working on an album this week.

"Well, how was today?" she asked.

"Not the best." I hadn't told Lola what was going on with Mitchell. In my voicemails to her since Friday I had just focused on my step work, what passages I was reading from the Big Book, and what prayers I was finding helpful. I'd only had quick stolen moments while my dad had been in town. The guitar was still strumming along; it sounded like an old song

Mom would play at full volume on our stereo system when I was growing up, but I couldn't quite place it.

I told Lola about re-downloading the dating app after deleting it at Friday Night Drinks. I told her about Mitchell messaging me, and how I didn't know how to reply. I told her there was now gossip going around the office about us, and I wanted it to stop, but I didn't know how to make that happen. I shouldn't care so much. People thinking I was fooling around with Mitchell didn't mean that I was. And it certainly didn't mean that Ben believed them. But still.

"Alright, Emma. I think it's important you don't focus on this too much," Lola said after my rant left me near breathless.

"I really don't see how that's possible."

"I think this is one of those situations where you believe you have more power than you do, right? We alcoholics are always getting ourselves into these situations. We think we have the willpower to stop drinking, and we don't. We think we have the power to force people to forgive us, but we don't. What can we actually do?"

"Give up our will. Release the false sense of control we have on the things around us."

"Exactly. People will talk about you, and they'll form opinions about you. We don't have control over what those opinions are," she said.

"I know that. But these are opinions based on a lie. It's not like when I was drinking and I didn't want people to see the gross sides of me, or when I lied about what I did. This is other people lying."

"So they're jumping to conclusions. What can you do about that?"

"I can make it clear that I'm not with Mitchell." I felt desperate. This wasn't the advice I'd expected.

"You can do that through your actions, right? You're not with this Mitchell. You haven't slept with him and you don't want to. So eventually, your actions will speak for you."

"People might think we're sneaking around. People *do* think we're sneaking around. Even Vanessa thinks that." Vanessa and Amy from HR, I could handle. The worst part was the thump of fear that Ben might be thinking the same thing.

"But you're not." The strumming was getting louder. It was "I Wanna Hold Your Hand." I wondered if Lola's husband was slowly seducing her while she talked to me. Was he walking closer? Making eye contact?

"We're not."

"So, when people ask, tell them the truth. If Mitchell asks you out, say no. But you can't reach into people's minds and stop them from making assumptions."

"Okay." The problem was that was exactly what I wanted to do. I wanted to reach into Ben's mind and understand what he was thinking about me. I wanted to erase all of the interactions we'd had thus far and start everything over.

"Listen, I think you should go to a meeting tonight. Are you still by work?"

"I'm feeling tired. I went to the big meeting yesterday."

"I think it'll help focus you if you go again tonight. I don't want you obsessing about this all night."

"It's just 'cause the thing with Vanessa happened like ten minutes ago, that's why I'm so upset about it." I felt like I would do anything to go home, take a bath, and watch the documentary I had in my queue about the Scandinavian journalist murdered on that submarine.

"Well, would it hurt for you to go to the Wednesday night meeting?"

"I mean, I'm just tired. I'll go tomorrow night."

"You're being a bit willful here."

I was supposed to be handing my will over. To whom we were supposed to hand our will could be a bit vague. Depending on the situation and the alcoholic's personal beliefs it could be God, a nondescript Higher Power, the Universe, or even your sponsor. I got the feeling that today Lola thought I should let her take the reins, as I was obviously too turned around to drive.

"It's only an hour, Emma. What could it hurt?" Her musician husband was now playing "When I'm Sixty-Four." I imagined her hand on his shoulder, rolling her eyes and mouthing that she'd be off soon.

"Okay," I said. I could always text her later and say I didn't make it. I could even lie. But I had to get off the phone. I couldn't stand to hear one more Beatles song.

"Great. Let me know what passages are discussed. I hate not being there!" She laughed.

Fuck. Other people she knew would be going. I wouldn't be able to lie. "Sure."

"Okay, good. I can't wait to hear about it. Fellowship always helps, Emma, remember that."

This fellowship call had certainly not felt helpful.

I looked around. The meeting was only about ten blocks from the street corner I was on. People streamed around me, a rat looked up from a garbage can, and gasoline wafted under my nose. I wanted to go home, but instead, I started walking south. Maybe Lola was right, this was no time to be willful.

The Wednesday night Hudson Group meeting was held in the gym of a private Catholic school on Twenty-Second Street. The ceilings were tall, I couldn't begin to guess how many feet high, and the paint was crumbling off in places that must have leaked when it rained. Banners from basketball championships from the early '90s dotted the walls.

There were circular tables set up every few feet, and people had already begun to crowd them with their Big Books clutched in their hands. I hadn't brought mine, since I hadn't planned on being here. I went to the table on the far right of the room, where they gave out loaners, and signed one out. The girl helping me was overly cheery and looked like she couldn't be older than twenty-one.

"Do you need help finding a table?" she asked, assuming I hadn't been there before. It must have been the waves of nervous energy pouring off my body.

"No. I'm good," I said. I heard Lola's voice in my head, saying my gut reaction shouldn't always be to refuse help. But I ignored it. I looked around the room and saw that the tables were filling up quickly. There were a few single seats scattered around, but I didn't immediately recognize anyone I knew. I sat at the closest to me, looked up, and gave everyone there a weak smile. I hadn't realized before I sat down, but they were all men. Gender segregation was common on Wednesday night, too, but since we weren't required to sit with our sponsor like we were on Tuesday nights, it wasn't as pervasive.

"Hi," I said.

Several of them said hello back, and a few introduced themselves. They were mostly middle-aged, wearing baseball caps and cargo shorts. I listened as a man with an unkempt graying beard told the group he was counting days, that he was working closely with his sponsor, but that he'd only been in the program for two months. My heart went out to him. I loved to see middle-aged men get sober. It was always nice to see proof that it was possible.

We went around the table and each read a sentence from the paragraph we were studying today. Big Book meetings in HG were similar to Bible studies. They were close reads of a now-sacred text. Sentence by sentence, we pulled together a paragraph from the chapter "The Family Afterward."

Family confidence in dad is rising high. The good old days will soon be back, they think. Sometimes they demand that dad bring them back instantly! God, they believe, almost owes this recom-

> *pense on a long overdue account. But the head of the house has spent years in pulling down the structures of business, romance, friendship, health—these things are now ruined or damaged. It will take time to clear away the wreck. Though old buildings will eventually be replaced by finer ones, the new structures will take years to complete.*

"I don't know if I relate to this passage," I said. "It's never sat right with me that the whole book is written like all alcoholics are men of a certain age." One of the men on the far side of the table released a soft chuckle. I continued, "And that men are always the heads of the household, or that every family is structured the same way. I don't know how I'm supposed to see myself here."

To my surprise, the man with two months sober responded, "You must have things you have to work on, though. I think that's how you relate. We all have wreckage to clear away."

"There's no cross talk allowed," I snapped, my face heating. AA meetings weren't like group therapy—you weren't supposed to respond to each other's shares.

"I apologize," he said, ducking his face from my glare.

"For me," the clean-cut man beside me started, "this passage is about patience. It's written for families, so not necessarily for us, the alcoholics, to read, but I think it can help us ask for what we need. I know my wife thought sobriety would be like a light switch. I was bad, now I can be good. But I still have bad days, even when I'm not drinking. And sometimes I need her to be patient with me. To believe me that I'm working on myself, even if it doesn't seem like it."

Eventually, the circle wove its way to the man who had interrupted me: "I destroyed my family with my drinking, I really did. I look at my kids, they're teenagers now, and they're not like they're supposed to be. They're guarded against the world like they expect nothing but suffering. I want them to forgive me, but I don't know how to ask for it, because I don't know how to earn it."

I swallowed, embarrassed that I'd snapped at him earlier when he was so clearly suffering. "Can I go again?" The meeting hadn't wrapped up and everyone had spoken once. It wasn't exactly protocol, but it wasn't against the rules, either. "I had a harsh first reaction to this passage. Maybe because I don't know which angle to read it from. I have an alcoholic father and I'm an alcoholic myself. So should I be granting him patience or working to rebuild my own life? Or both? He's not sober, so this passage doesn't really apply to my family in that way. Overall, it has me wondering if I can grant him patience—" I looked to the bearded man as I readied myself to go against the rule I'd chided him for breaking "—or forgiveness if he hasn't asked. Is that something I have to do for me?"

TEN

After a few weeks of debate, the entire Fun Team was going to check out the top three venues we'd chosen: Hillside BBQ, a restaurant with a large second floor available to rent out, but it was generally favored by people who'd just turned twenty-one, and therefore might not feel chic enough to any of the senior partners; Rue 30, a deluxe bistro that Mitchell and a few others thought would be a complete bore and might not have enough room for dancing; and the Flatiron Hotel, which would require outside catering—and therefore would be significantly more work for our team—but was otherwise the best contender.

At Hillside, Mitchell acted as though he was the one leading the tour rather than the manager, whose dark undereye circles suggested he may have been out all night. "Emma!" Mitchell called to me as soon as I managed to fall far enough behind the group to be in step with Ben. "Over here! You've got to see this."

What I had to see was a large plaster pig with dotted lines marking the different cuts of meat. It stood proudly in the center of the empty and spacious second floor. I ran my finger over the word *tenderloin* hand drawn in black paint down the pig's hind legs. "Cool," I said. I wasn't sure why Mitchell had thought I, in particular, would be interested in this.

"You know," he started, "I've hunted wild boar from a helicopter in West Texas."

"Intense," I said, taking my finger off the plaster pig and putting my hand back in my pocket.

"Absolutely. *Intense* is the right word. It was part of a young entrepreneurship and leadership program. One of the largest landowners in the country—he has eight hundred thousand acres, it's practically a county—brings out a group of young leaders and teaches them how to live off the land."

"Because if you ever had to 'live off the land' you'd have a helicopter?" As soon as the words left my mouth, I could tell they'd come out on the wrong side of sassy.

"Well, that was part of the weekend where we learned to view things from thirty thousand feet. See the whole picture, and all that. It helps when you plan to run a corporation one day."

"Do helicopters go up thirty thousand feet?"

Mitchell didn't pick up on my sarcasm. He raised his eyebrows and charged forward. "Of course not. I think you might need a physics lesson, Ems." From my periphery, I saw him reach out his hand as though he might lay it on my shoulder. There wasn't anything really wrong with a hand on the shoulder, but I reacted like a startled cat. I jumped out of the way, knocking into a passing waiter who was carrying a tray of perfectly poured beers. The waiter was agile, far more so than me, so only took a half step out of place. But it was enough for one glass to fall and tip out onto the pig. The yeasty scent wafted up as I watched the amber liquid drip over the pig's plaster hooves. I was horrified. The glass rolled away, unbroken.

"Oh! I'm so sorry!" I reached forward, wanting to help, but I had nothing to wipe it up with, and I didn't want to get the scent of it on my hands.

The tired manager, who I hadn't realized had only been a few feet away, shrugged and came over with a rag. "It happens," he said. He wiped down the pig, and the rag came away black. He was smearing the painted lettering.

"But your pig," I said. "She was so beautiful. And I ruined her."

"She's alright," the manager said at the same time Mitchell practically pulled me away from the scene of the crime with a hand on my elbow. Even with all the spilled beer, I hadn't gotten out of having his hand on me.

On our way out, I fell behind, pretending I needed to tie my shoe. Mitchell charged forward to direct the group to our next stop, but Ben waited and held the door open for me.

"Thanks," I said.

"So are you hanging out with Mitchell now?" Ben asked, his words coming out in a rush, almost like they hadn't waited for his approval before escaping his lips.

"No. Not at all," I said.

He made a noise of acknowledgment but didn't reply.

"Why do you ask?"

His face darted to mine, just for a second, then away. "Just wondered," he said.

"I only ask because I heard that from someone else as well, who's not on the Fun Team, and I worry it's become the new hot thing to discuss at the water cooler."

"No one's talked to me about it. We also don't have a water cooler. I just—at Hillside—"

"You thought that because of how we act, then? Because, really, it's not true," I said. We had slowed our pace, and the space between us and the group had stretched out. The string that held us all together was pulled tight. It would be so easy to snap it, to grab his arm and say we should go our own way.

"I'm sorry," he said. "I shouldn't have asked. I didn't realize it was a sore subject."

"Well, as sore as any falsehood—"

"Falsehood!" he said, interrupting me with a laugh.

"Well, that's what it is!" I stopped walking. The group crossed the street ahead of us. The string broke.

He looked toward them. Then, giving up, he stopped, too, and turned toward me, shrugging. "I believe you. I just like the word. It sounded old-fashioned."

"Oh, okay." I took a deep breath. Maybe I didn't feel ready to own being sober, but I could tell him the truth of this situation.

"I got that vibe. About Mitchell. Guess I was wrong," he said, turning back away from me.

"I don't like him—even as a person. He's gross and annoying. He wanted to tell me about shooting pigs from airplanes." I knew Mitchell would be horrified at my mischaracterization, that he would've stepped in to immediately tell me it was hogs and helicopters, but I used our distance from the rest of the group to let out my unfiltered thoughts. "And that beer spilling, it was really his fault. He put his hand on me and I didn't want him to—"

Ben's gaze snapped back to me. "You should have said—I mean, I should have said—I'm going to say something." His hands were flexing, his eyes locked on mine. "I'm not going to let him touch you—I mean, if you don't want him to, he shouldn't be touching you." His voice was growing louder. Would the rest of the group hear us across the street?

"Ben, no, Ben. It's not worth confronting him or getting into a thing over it, please." Ben flying off the handle about Mitchell touching me would only make him look insane. Or make me look insane for telling him about it.

"What are you talking about? You're worth confronting him over." He was angry. Even though he was looking at me and speaking to me, I could tell he wasn't mad at me. This was the first time that I'd felt someone's righteous anger on my behalf. It felt wholly unnecessary, but also undeniably sweet—like a dusting of powdered sugar.

"No, no. I'm not saying *I'm* not worth it. But what he did, I mean, he reached for my shoulder in a joking way. There's not really a reason to sound the alarms."

Ben took a long breath through his nose. "But you didn't want him to."

"I also didn't want to go on a tour of Hillside." An attempt at a joke, but it didn't calm him down. I reached for his sleeve. "Ben. Just please don't say anything."

He gave a stiff nod, and I knew him well enough to know that he wouldn't break his word.

"Thank you," I said, still holding on to his jacket.

He opened his mouth to speak, but Amy called to us from across the street. "Come on, dillydalliers!"

We stepped away from each other immediately and hurried across the street.

"We've been waiting!" Amy said when we reached them. The rest of the Fun Team was standing in a circle waiting for us outside Rue 30.

"Sorry," I said.

Ben nodded along, hands in his pants pockets.

"Let's head in," Amy said, as though she might actually be annoyed at us for delaying the rest of the group. "We only have an hour and we have a lot to do."

"Amy's right," Mitchell butted in. "I have a two o'clock. Some of us have more than just Fun Team meetings."

Rue 30 was busy, and several servers stopped by to tell us that they couldn't accommodate eight people for at least two hours. Amy asked to see the manager twice, but she came across as more of a Karen meme than a person who had an appointment with the manager. We ended up leaving before we met with them, as we were now running late for our next appointment.

I'd never been inside the Flatiron Hotel before. It was a hulking building of granite that sprawled half a block on Broadway. There was a red velvet staircase leading to the main entrance, and at least one uniformed doorman at every side and service entrance. It had a large and ornate brass awning that had to be original, but its name wasn't written anywhere—not on the awning, not etched on any of the windows. You were supposed to know what this place was; it wouldn't lower itself by telling you. It was old and prestigious, which meant it wasn't part of the New York I grew up in.

The front door was pulled wide for us, and I caught Amy's smile as we walked in. This was the level of glamour she wanted for our holiday party. We were greeted, then promptly whisked through an oak-lined hallway to an adjoining ballroom where a coordinator in a perfectly tailored pencil skirt was waiting to tell us about the possible rental options.

I excused myself, mouthing to Marjorie that I had to use the restroom. I didn't really, but ever since I was little, I'd loved to check out fancy bathrooms. If they were called something archaic, like "powder rooms," all the better. They were like windows into other worlds, the most personal of public spaces. The values of either a business or someone's home were impossible to hide when it came to bathrooms. Everything about a place was laid bare. Dive bars had to have a bit of grunge to the bathroom or people would know it was a poser of a bar. It should be unisex, with no way to dry your hands and a cheap mirror that was just warped enough that reality would start to blur around the edges. Downtown clubs that were built for the rich and the beautiful had small rooms for toilets instead of stalls and lighting so dim it was hard to see where the toilet paper was. I was expecting this bathroom to have some sort of old-fashioned flair. A large antechamber with a chaise longue you weren't really allowed to sit on or perhaps a tray of individually wrapped mints.

I got distracted on the way in a long hall filled with old photographs—black-and-white pictures of society groups sat on lush forest green wallpaper, with small museum lights above each one. I couldn't see a speck of dust on anything, and found myself thinking about the cleaning budget the Flatiron must have. I couldn't even manage to keep dust off the books on my one Ikea bookshelf, but the Flatiron had essentially eliminated it. Even the wooden frames shone. I peered close to get a better look at the faces in the photo closest to me. There were about twenty-five men in tuxedos. They all reminded me of young Mitchells: proud, broad smiles they might have taken with them to leadership retreats. They were the kind of men who owned the world, who climbed Everest for the hell of it, who created the intricate financial systems that I now sold to their grandsons with snappy hashtags.

Realizing I was lingering too long, I rushed down the hall to the bathroom. It wasn't quite as grand as I'd expected. There was an antechamber, but it lay empty and useless. It was a collection of off-white walls and a thin, green carpet that reminded me of what lined the halls of my middle school. I imagined that women lined up here during big events instead of in the hall, a queue of bodies in their best dresses curling alongside the corners. When I entered the actual bathroom, I saw I wasn't alone. There was an attendant leaning against the wall, looking at her phone. She quickly stored it in her vest pocket. I nodded at her, and she nodded back before I darted inside the stall.

On my way back, I didn't linger to look at photos or sneak down any other hallways. I didn't want to miss the tour of the big ballroom. The events coordinator would probably tell us juicy facts about Gilded Age New York, and I was always a sucker for celebrity gossip, even if it was over a century old.

Seconds before I opened the large wooden door to head back into the ballroom, I heard my name spoken in hushed tones. I pulled my hand back from the large brass door-pull as if I'd touched a hot stove. I couldn't think of anything more embarrassing than walking in on people talking about me. I'd feel bad for everyone: for myself, for the people who would surely be humiliated to be caught, for any passersby who might understand what had happened and feel their own face flame with the awkwardness of it all.

I hadn't been listening to the words that surrounded my name in the sentence, but I knew instantly they'd come from Mitchell's mouth. I could see just how he was holding his lips—slightly pursed. His voice came again: "So, not friends, then?"

"I guess sort of?" a second voice said, this one quieter, farther from the door. But I had a strong suspicion it was Ben's.

"But I mean like, *not* friends?" Mitchell stressed the word *not* in a way that felt immediately clear to me.

"I don't know what that means," Ben murmured. Apparently it hadn't been clear to him.

"Come on, man," Mitchell said. "Did you sleep with her?"

"What?" Ben asked, appalled by the question. Even listening in, I'd guessed this was where things were going. The only thing that surprised me was that Mitchell had used a phrase as refined as "sleep with."

"Hey, don't make that face," Mitchell said, and I would have died to see the face Ben was making. "I just want to know if I'm stepping on toes or anything."

"Nope," Ben said, and then there was nothing.

I thought I should count to ten, or maybe even twenty, before I opened the door. I hadn't gotten to four yet when I heard Ben speak again. "I don't think you guys have a lot in common, though."

"Oh, don't worry about that. I don't want to actually date her or anything. She's obviously too…not quite crazy, but not quite sane, if you know what I mean?" Mitchell said. "Like you can tell she's the right kind of crazy to fuck, but like way too crazy to date."

I didn't open the door. I didn't go back into the ballroom. Instead, like the grown woman I was, I fled.

I went back past the portraits of all the white men in tuxedos, and past the bathroom, and back out into the main entrance, stumbling down the red velvet stairs. "Thank you!" I called behind me to the doorman, who'd swiftly opened the door for me as I ran.

I got half a block away before I stopped walking. What was my plan here, exactly? To head back to the office and leave the rest of the Fun Team wondering where I'd gone? What would I say the next time I saw one of them in the office? I didn't think they'd believe that I, Marketing Assistant #2, had any sort of work emergency that would have called me back to the office. Could I go home? Call Jermaine and say I'd suddenly taken ill? Maybe I could say I had a bad breakfast burrito and had come down with intense diarrhea? But that wasn't the kind of thing you told people. That was the kind of thing you kept secret. I couldn't think of a non-humiliating excuse.

I took a couple deep breaths. I called Lola, but then hung up instead of leaving a message. I didn't want to say something weird and worry her again. But I knew she would tell me not to flee, either way. AA very much had a face-your-fears attitude. But AA was built for owning past mistakes, and this was an active one. The problem was I didn't know what I had done. So how could I own it? I clearly wasn't better. I'd thought that people thought I was normal, that I came across like everyone else did: well-adjusted and kind. But apparently, I had a visible stain that announced to all who looked that there was something off. Like perhaps all the alcohol I'd drunk was still slowly seeping out of my pores, or maybe my reactions to things told everyone that screaming fights had been my childhood lullabies. Maybe I just didn't smile enough, or in the right way. No matter how much I'd pretended, Mitchell could still tell. He still knew that I was crazy. I would forever be crazy.

I leaned against the corner of the building and felt the cool stone through my light fall jacket. Fleeing was crazy. I knew that. That was a solid fact I could grab on to. If I fled, Mitchell would only know he was right about me. Maybe he'd start to think I was even too crazy to fuck. And while being too crazy to date sucked, being too crazy to fuck would surely be worse.

I looked down at my phone. I'd been gone a weirdly long time already. I should go back in now. Once they started wondering what happened to me, my bravery would be for nothing.

I nodded at the doorman as he held the door open for me. "Thank you," I murmured. He gave me a light smile. I took it to mean that I was doing the right thing. As I walked past the concierge desk, the rest of the Fun Team came into the main lobby.

"Oh Emma!" Amy said. "We lost you!"

Ben and Mitchell were behind her, walking together. Mitchell was wearing an easy smile while chatting to Ben. I couldn't even look at them.

"Sorry!" I said. "I was taking a call outside."

"I sent Marjorie to the bathroom to make sure you were okay. We all thought maybe you got sick."

So they'd been discussing my body and its possible failings anyway. Great.

"I can go grab her?" I offered. "I should have told you all, I'm sorry." I chided myself for apologizing too much.

Amy shrugged. "No, I'm sure she'll figure it out in a second." She looped her arm through mine conspiratorially. I was suddenly aware we'd never touched before. "Em-ma! It's really too bad you got the call when you did, because we had the most amazing tour! Didn't we, boys?"

I cringed at Amy calling two grown men "boys," but neither of them had a physical reaction. They both nodded along but didn't speak.

Amy continued on: "I think my favorite part was learning about the ceiling. It's hand-painted! Can you even imagine?"

"Amazing," I said, feeling my arm begin to sweat where hers touched it. I didn't look at Ben or Mitchell. They were two dark-suited blobs ahead of me. But even being this close to them, I felt self-loathing roll over me.

Finally, after I'd heard all the details about how many men it took to paint a ceiling—quite a lot, it turned out—Marjorie joined us.

"Emma! We're so glad you're okay! I checked three bathrooms!" she said as we all walked out.

"Sorry," I murmured.

When we got to the street, Marjorie moved to the other side of me, and I felt I was being guarded by the two women. I was thankful—I couldn't imagine walking with Ben or Mitchell. I would have absolutely made a mess of it. Either I would have confronted them, or tried to catch them in some lie, thereby confirming Mitchell's analysis of me, or I'd be sappily sweet and lose my self-respect. Self-respect wasn't a thing that had come easily to me. I'd built it back up, brick by brick, from rubble over this past year. I wasn't going to let Mitchell, or myself, take a sledgehammer to it.

A realization occurred to me. Marjorie and Amy might have heard Ben and Mitchell, too. I'd assumed they were on the far side of the ballroom and Ben and Mitchell were hanging back. But maybe Mitchell had said all those things when they were mere feet away. I wanted my body to dissolve. Why else would Marjorie and Amy be treating me this way? Why else would they be flanking me like this?

It had been one thing for Mitchell to shit-talk me to Ben. He'd had a legitimate question. He wanted to know the personal details of my sex life that he thought maybe Ben could provide. But to ask that in public, in front of the entire Fun Team? That felt like an entirely different situation. That was cruel and callous in a way that I hadn't even thought was possible. Amy's hand squeezed my arm as we walked back into work, but I didn't feel self-loathing anymore. I didn't think something was wrong with me. I knew something was wrong with Mitchell.

Before the sobriety, and the AA, and the marketing job at a financial firm, I'd had a very different life. I worked in restaurants that operated like nightclubs. I snorted coke and did shots at work—and it was normal. I fucked colleagues in single-occupancy bathrooms, and that was normal, too. I took the train home with smudged eye makeup and cash tips in my wallet at 3:30 or 4:00 a.m. and I never felt weird about it. If someone had said something to me, anything close to what Mitchell had said, I would have opened that door and revealed myself. As soon as I heard my name, I would have swung that old oak door as hard as I could and told him I'd rather eat my own shit than fuck him. I wouldn't have run away, or quietly gone back to the office, or needed Amy to hold my hand.

But since then, my life had cleaved itself in two. That Emma was gone—or as Lola would say, she was a shield I didn't need anymore. Opening the door hadn't even occurred to me. But sitting at home that night, eating a pint of Mint Chocolate Cookie instead of dinner, I wished it had. I kept playing it over and over again in my mind. I knew, from Mitchell's self-satisfied smile, from our late-night Instagram interaction, and from how he spoke about me behind that door, that he'd sniffed out the girl I used to be. Somehow, despite my attempts at office attire and demure work-appropriate smiles, he could smell it on me.

I thought of Ben's face when he told me I was worth confronting Mitchell over. I'd spent the past year trying to take better care of myself, and there was no doubt I was succeeding. I was tending to myself, but I wasn't always good at being my own defender. I didn't champion myself. Seeing how Ben had wanted to defend me made me want to give that grace to myself.

I pulled up Slack—not Instagram or Hinge, Slack.

Wednesday 8:48 p.m.
Emma F: I just want to make it clear I'm not romantically interested in you and that I'd like our relationship to remain purely professional.

I wanted to tell him I hated him, and I hoped he had a horrible accident that decapitated his penis, but I left that part out.

ELEVEN

On my lunch break the next day, I called Lola. The air was misty in Madison Square Park, and I felt it collecting on my eyebrows. The granite of the surrounding towers blended into the gray sky. I walked the small paths in a long, winding circle.

"What's going on?" she asked, sensing from the tone of my hello that something was off.

I opened my mouth, but my throat closed. I wasn't going to cry about Mitchell being a dick. I refused. I opened my mouth again to rationally and calmly tell her why I was feeling weird, but I made a soft little gasp instead of words.

"Emma? Are you okay?"

I swallowed and worked to take a few deep breaths.

"You sound upset. Why don't you tell me about your day, from the beginning." I heard her closing a door wherever she was, steeling herself for a conversation that would be longer and more involved than she'd originally thought.

"Okay," I said. I could do this. I could talk about the Fun Team. I told her about what happened.

"Oh god. Emma."

"I didn't say anything or do anything. I didn't." My voice

cracked again. I looked around, wanting to make sure I wasn't eavesdropping-distance away from any other parkgoers.

"It's okay to have a reaction." It was something Lola had said to me before. But she meant it was okay to have a sad reaction. It was okay to weep. She didn't think it was okay to scream.

"So, that was yesterday. And when I got home, I messaged him on Slack. And I told him very politely that I wasn't interested."

"Good for you—that was very responsible."

"It was stupid. It came back to bite me in the ass today."

"Did he retaliate?"

"No. I don't know. He wants to grab a coffee to 'clear the air.'"

"Do you want to go?" she asked, like it was a simple question.

"I don't want to go. But I don't know how not to go."

"Remember what we say about people you reach out to make amends to, and they never respond, or they don't want to see you?"

I laughed. "Do I get to be the good person in this situation? Instead of the one making amends?"

"Emma. There is no such thing as good or bad people. Anyway, you don't owe him your time."

"I think it would make things too awkward if I didn't go. I already said yes."

"Okay. When is it?"

"In ten minutes."

"Okay. Say a couple prayers. You got this. You can leave at any time."

I pulled up the Slack conversation again.

Wednesday 8:48 p.m.

Emma F: I just want to make it clear I'm not romantically interested in you and that I'd like our relationship to remain purely professional.

Thursday 9:02 a.m.
Mitchell B: Goes without saying. Didn't mean to imply anything else.

Thursday 9:17 a.m.
Emma F: Great.

Mitchell B: There was a misunderstanding here, Emma. I'd really like to move past it.

Thursday 9:19 a.m.
Emma F: Of course! Let's never speak of it again 😄

Mitchell B: Maybe we should clear the air, actually? I'm a little confused as to where this came from.

Thursday 9:26 a.m.
Emma F: I don't know

Thursday 9:27 a.m.
Mitchell B: I don't want to accidentally have this happen again. For my sanity?

Thursday 9:43 a.m.
Emma F: ok

Mitchell B: Perf. Coffee today?

Thursday 9:50 a.m.
Emma F: ok

Thursday 9:51 a.m.
Mitchell B: Cool. Joe's at 1:30?

Thursday 10:04 a.m.
Emma F: ok

It was now 1:27 p.m. I'd said I'd go, so I had to go. Joe's was a block away. I walked south through the mist. The whole world was sheathed in gray, matching my trench coat.

Like the Catholic church, AA had a prayer for most situations that a recovering person might find themselves in. When we'd gotten off the phone, Lola had texted me the prayer for *When I am disturbed by the conduct of another.* This was a frequent occurrence for sober people, for the obvious reasons of being surrounded by drunk friends and family members. She'd sent it to me when we started working together as something I could say after I had a difficult conversation with my dad, but I'd never thought of it in another context.

As I crossed the street, I mumbled it out loud to myself: *"God, help me to show this person the same tolerance, pity, and patience that I would cheerfully grant a sick friend. This is a sick person, how can I be helpful to him? Save me from being angry."*

Sometimes when I said prayers, I edited out *God* and filled in the catchall terms like *Higher Power* or *Universe*, but it didn't really make a difference because I didn't believe in any of it. All the same, it felt good to say my intentions aloud. I didn't want to be angry. But I wasn't sure I wanted to be helpful, either.

I opened the door to Joe's and felt immediately stifled by the heat. It was late October, and it certainly wasn't a cold enough day for it to be on so high. The steam pouring from the latte machines wasn't helping. I looked around, but Mitchell wasn't here. I checked my phone. I wasn't even early. It was 1:31 p.m. He was the one who wanted to have coffee so badly. He should have been here at 1:20 p.m., scouting a table. I got in line, looking for one. But unsurprisingly, as it was lunchtime in Manhattan, there wasn't a single table left.

By the time I ordered, it was 1:35 p.m., and he was nowhere

to be seen. I would just wait for my tea and scone and then leave. I wasn't going to wait for him. Maybe he was late on purpose? So that I'd be more on edge than I already was? I still hadn't decided if I was going to tell him what I heard yesterday. It was an ace in the hole in one way, but it could also potentially escalate things. He might become defensive. He might go up to Ben and try to swear him to secrecy. He might flat-out lie and tell me I'd been aurally hallucinating. I might believe him.

At 1:38 p.m., they called my name and Mitchell walked in, smile as bright as ever. He walked right up to me as I reached for my drink.

"Ugh, the line looks long," he said, half to me and half to the barista. Just as she began to walk away, he turned his body fully toward her, his focus laser sharp, and said, "I hate to do this, but could I grab a cup of black coffee from you?" The smile got even bigger.

She started to speak. Or tried to, but all she managed was to open her mouth before he cut her off.

"Don't worry, I'm not a periodic line cutter, I was just already late to meet her," he said, gesturing his thumb at me and grimacing in a way that made me feel like he was doing a weird bit that cast me as a nagging girlfriend.

The barista raised her hand up to point to the back of the line, but he was quicker. He pulled out his wallet, then ever so delicately laid a twenty on the counter, pushing it toward her. "Keep the change," he said.

She dropped her hand and, without making eye contact, murmured her thanks. In the time it took him to turn to me and shrug, she'd swapped his twenty for a fresh cup of black coffee. The whole thing was so seamless, I didn't think anyone in line had noticed it. If I'd blinked, I would've missed it, too.

"Should we grab a table?" he asked.

"I don't think there is one," I said, but he was already walking ahead of me. Somehow, a table had appeared just in time for his arrival and he was now sliding onto the bench seat.

I took the seat across from him. My shoulders were a few inches from the man at the next table. Normally, I wouldn't have even noticed, but I expected that things were going to get awkward today, and the people around us would undoubtedly be able to hear. It was better than the office stairwell, but only just.

As I settled in, Mitchell adjusted his cuff, flashing his watch, and leaned his elbow on the table. "So, how's your day been?" he asked.

I wasn't sure how to respond. I'd been a nervous wreck all day because of him. What did he expect me to say?

"I have to get back to the office in twenty minutes," I said. I pulled my scone out of the small paper sleeve and broke off a corner piece.

"Do you like those things?" he asked, pointing to it as I put the piece in my mouth.

"I like them enough." Apparently, he wasn't going to say anything about why he'd asked me here. Well, I wasn't going to, either. I didn't want to talk about it, so if he would rather sit quietly across from me while I nibbled on my scone for fifteen minutes, that was fine.

"I think they're incredibly dry. Not to mention the empty calories."

I could tell he was trying to make me feel bad about myself. I knew why men would mention *food* or *fat* right before a difficult conversation. It wasn't going to work with me. He didn't know it, but he'd already hit the most sensitive nerve I had yesterday. I broke off a bigger piece of the scone and stuffed my cheeks with it, shrugging.

"I'm more of a clean-eating kind of guy," he said. "So, anyway, I was surprised to get your message this morning."

"Mmm." I was still making my way through the scone.

"I really didn't mean to give off that impression—that I was interested in seeing you…"

"Oh—" I shook my head "—don't worry. I know you're not interested in dating me. I never thought that."

"Then why did you send that weird Slack? Someone could have read that, Emma." His voice was vibrating at a different level, like it was about to blow out his vocal cords.

"I really didn't want to do this. I don't think it's going to be helpful." The same panic that had pumped through my veins yesterday when I ran out of the Flatiron Hotel was back. I had to get out of here.

He pushed his coffee to the side and put his other arm on the table. His body now took up most of the small, white, circular plastic surface. I moved my tea back.

"Okay. That's fine," he said. "Could you send an email and cc HR saying that you misunderstood and that we've since cleared it up."

I blinked. I imagined Amy opening that email. What would she think? I remembered how she squeezed my arm yesterday as we walked back to the office. How could I ever show up to a Fun Team meeting again? "You want me to cc Amy?" I asked.

"I mean, I guess Amy would do. The hr@richterthomas.com email would be better. You know, the general one."

"You want me to cc the entire HR department?" I could see them all opening the email in the bay they sat in together, looking around, making eye contact, wondering if it was okay to laugh.

"If you're gonna make a fuss, just cc Amy, I guess. She'll probably pass it on to the rest of the team, though."

"I'm not going to do that, actually. I'm not going to send any emails." I remembered Ben's rage yesterday, and I used it to fuel my own.

"Seriously?" His voice dropped another register. I wondered what he would have done if he had to wait in line today or stand around awkwardly looking for a table. Maybe something like this.

"Yeah, I'm really serious."

"Anyone could read that Slack, Emma. This isn't funny."

"I agree. That's why I put it on Slack. But you didn't say anything anyway—it doesn't look that bad."

"It looks like I hit on you somewhere else. Which I didn't."

"Is that true, though, Mitchell?"

"Is this because of fucking Hinge? You're throwing a fit because I hit you up on Hinge? You shouldn't have messaged me back, then. Or just said you weren't interested there."

"Okay. Whatever." He couldn't make me send an email. I wasn't going to do it.

"You're being so irrational. Like actually insane." There was nothing calm about his expression anymore. He couldn't make me send an email. But he liked to talk to people. And he would probably begin as soon as we got back from the office. I would be insane, delusional, maybe even obsessed with him. I knew I could take being a social outcast. But I shouldn't have to.

"Yeah, so I heard you talking to Ben yesterday." I wanted to look right at Mitchell, to show him that he wasn't intimidating me. But he was, in fact, an intimidating person. He had an unblinking gaze he'd probably mastered at one of his leadership retreats. I didn't want to meet it. I looked down and played with the crumbs of my scone.

"I talked to Ben a whole bunch," he said. But his voice had become quieter. I could hear the gears shifting, and him beginning to change tactics.

"Maybe. But once, when I was about to come back from the bathroom, you told him you would fuck me but not date me. 'Cause I'm so crazy. That's the time I'm talking about." I essentially mumbled the words. It was far from glorious. But it was the truth, and it was done.

"I don't recall that," he said, taking one of his arms off the table and leaning back, sitting deeper into the bench.

"Well, I do. And I would bet, if he was asked, Ben would as well." I didn't want to bring Ben into this. It wouldn't be fair to him. Sober Emma cleaned up her own messes, she didn't fling them onto the next available person like Drunk Emma did. Also, a small part of me couldn't help but think getting Ben involved in an awkward HR fight between me and a member of C-suite wouldn't really help us take things to the next level.

Mitchell was quiet for three whole seconds. It was unlike him. I looked up. He was sitting fully back now and moving his jaw around. Had I won whatever this weird moment was?

"I don't want to send any sort of email to HR. I would like to not talk about this again." I hoped that by asking for nothing I wasn't making an enemy of Mitchell. I didn't want him to feel like I'd pushed him into a corner. I just wanted to go back to not having him be a part of my life in any way.

"So, you are fucking Nowak, then? Can't say I really bought it, but I guess you never know."

I took a breath. I wished I could say I was. If I hadn't told Ben a weird lie about my friend's dead boyfriend, I would have jumped on this get-out-of-jail-free card Mitchell was handing me. Men respected other men's claims on a woman infinitely more than they respected a woman's decision not to sleep with them. I knew that if I said yes, I wouldn't have to say anything else. This whole situation would fade away. Mitchell would think we traded secrets and he would have been able to keep his pride intact. But I had to say no. I couldn't knock on Ben's door and tell him I'd gotten myself into yet another weird scenario.

"I'm not."

"Sure," Mitchell said, folding his lips into a tight square. He started trying to get up from the bench, but we were all closed in too tight. "Have fun with that story."

"Oh," I said, moving my tea, standing and scooting out from the table to make room.

He nodded but didn't say thanks as he put on his coat.

I was terrified he was going to make my life hell in some way. I wanted to fill the silence that had opened up between us. I thought of suddenly saying he was right, it was about Ben, otherwise I would have been happy to fuck him, just so he wouldn't walk away with everything still so unsettled. But instead, I picked up his coffee and the sleeve my scone came in, and I threw them away.

As he passed me on his way out, he leaned down and murmured, "You're crazy as fuck." With that, he marched out the door.

Maybe he was right and a humiliating email to HR would have been less difficult than whatever was about to happen.

I got back to my desk and saw I had a Slack message from Ben. Who I had tried desperately not to think of since yesterday. I'd replayed the memory of hearing him and Mitchell on the other side of the door so many times that I could visualize the whole thing. I imagined Ben silently laughing, giving Mitchell his tacit approval with a wink. Ben didn't really seem the type to wink, but somehow I was sure it had happened. That right then and there, he'd decided to start winking because me being a crazy slut was something that was simply too wink-able to resist.

I took a breath. Ben probably didn't care. He might have already even put the incident from his mind. He didn't have to have a weird coffee meeting with Mitchell about it. He was able to scoff or wink or whatever and then move along.

I didn't open the message. I was still shaken from my conversation with Mitchell. I didn't have the emotional bandwidth to deal with anything Ben might want from me. Our work didn't overlap in any way, shape, or form, so it couldn't be a professional request. It had to be something personal. I was really done with personal at work.

Instead, I went about the quiet tasks I had to do. We had a lot of GIFs to make for our Instagram stories. GIFs were wonderful because InDesign was slow if I had too many tabs open, so I would close out of my browser and maximize the GIFs I was working on. I put my headphones on, listening to a murder podcast that was horrifying enough to distract me from my own problems, and edited stock photos of white men laughing at restaurants to have moving text about financial services overlaid. It was work. It was fine.

At a certain point, I checked my phone and saw that I had a bunch of emails. I responded to one from Amy—she'd included a poll, so it was easy—and then saw that Ben had emailed me. The subject line was weird.

Thursday, 11/02/21, 1:26 p.m.
Subject: Phone Number
From: Ben Nowak bnowak@richterthomas.com
To: Emma Finley efinley@richterthomas.com

Hi Emma,
I reached out over slack, but perhaps you haven't been checking it. When you have a moment, could you respond with your phone number.
Thanks,
Ben

Why did Ben want my phone number? I opened Slack and saw that he'd messaged me four times.

1:03 p.m.
Ben N: Hey sorry this is weird. Can I have your cellphone number?

1:14 p.m.
Ben N: Not to be weird, but it's a little bit pressing?

1:24 p.m.
Ben N: ?

2:56 p.m.
Ben N: I think if we could still talk that would be great.

The Slack messages were even more confusing. Getting my phone number was pressing? It was now 4:15 p.m. He must have thought I'd been ignoring him. To be fair, I had been ignoring him, but I'd also been ignoring everyone else.

I turned to Vanessa, who also had her headphones in. But after I looked at her intensely for three seconds, she took them out. "What?" she asked.

I pulled up the email from Ben on my phone and handed it to her. I was tired of trying to figure everything out on my own. I wished I had let her talk me through the Mitchell messages on Hinge. None of this would have happened if I'd been writing by committee. I was abandoning the facade of Work Emma. I needed real advice from a real friend for Real Emma.

She hunched over my phone, her eyes moving quickly over the screen. She turned back to me but didn't hand the phone back. "I think Ben is asking for your number. And being really weird and formal about it," she said.

"For, like, a personal thing, you think?" I asked.

"Yeah, Emma, for a personal reason. I mean, he's clearly into you. It's very obvious to anyone with eyes. So it's probably about that."

"What are you talking about? It's not obvious at all!"

"I saw you guys at Friday Night Drinks. There was weird energy. A vibe."

"Vanessa, there really was not."

"Well, you don't have to give him your number! Say no and cc HR on your response!" Vanessa had broken away from our whispers and finally caught the attention of Jermaine.

"You guys talking about HR?" he asked. "Is everything okay?" He slowly rolled his chair across to us.

"Everything's fine!" I said.

Vanessa made pointed eye contact at me that was so obvious Jermaine couldn't ignore it.

"Emma, do you want to speak with me about an issue?" He changed his voice into something calm and professional.

"I don't, but thank you for offering." I matched his tone.

He nodded, looked from me to Vanessa again, and then knowing he couldn't push the issue, wheeled back to his side of the room. But he didn't put his headphones back in.

I opened Slack.

4:32 p.m.
Emma F: It's fine.

Vanessa Z: Do you want to give him your number?

Emma F: I was just confused. I didn't know if it was personal or professional.

Vanessa Z: It was a deeply weird and formal email.

Emma F: Yes, hence the confusion.

Vanessa Z: Are you going to reply?

Emma F: Yes I will reply.

Vanessa Z: With your phone number?!

Emma F: I guess so. It's been a long weird day and now that I know this isn't for work I don't feel like I have to deal with it this second.

Vanessa Z: Romantic.

Emma F: Well, it wasn't a very romantic email.

Vanessa Z: No, but I think that was the subtext.

Emma F: Really? Do you?

Vanessa Z: Aren't phone numbers always romantic?

Emma F: No. Sometimes they aren't. I would guess he sent such a formal email so I didn't get the wrong idea.

Vanessa Z: What? You think he'd be so concerned with you getting the wrong idea?

Emma F: He might.

Vanessa Z: Nah, I think he's into you. He might have a weird excuse for the lame email but I believe the TRUE subtext is still romantic.

The door to our office opened after a single knock, and Ben popped his head in. Vanessa's fingers started typing furiously. I dropped mine from the keyboard.

"Hey," Ben said, looking at me. His hair was slightly messy, like he'd been running his fingers through it all day.

"Hey, buddy," Jermaine answered, spinning his chair to talk to Ben. "How can we help you?"

"Oh, I wanted to talk to Emma, actually," he said.

"Is this about work?" Jermaine asked, dropping out of his usual friendly tone and back into the professional one he'd used earlier. He'd really missed his calling as a voice actor; it was amazing the range he could convey with his delivery.

Ben looked panicked. He started to speak but then stopped, opening and closing his mouth several times. This would probably be the only time in my life I felt like a girl in a country song with an overprotective dad. Jermaine's expression would be fitting if he was standing on a porch with shotgun in hand.

"It's fine, Jermaine," I said, standing. "Me and Ben are friends." I'm sure everyone in the office knew that was a stretch, but it was the only reasonable thing to say.

Ben's shoulders sagged in relief. Jermaine's expression didn't change—now he just included me in his suspicious gaze. Vanessa's fingers continued to type. Her all-caps light went on.

"I'll just be a minute," I said to Jermaine. Then I nodded to Ben to leave the doorway and followed him to the staircase.

The door closed lightly but pulled all the air out with it. Ben looked bigger than I remembered as he stood on the landing, like this wasn't a natural space for him. He seemed to innately realize that as well, and hunched his body. He didn't look at me. Instead, he started biting his cuticle.

"Ben? Is everything okay?" I asked.

He dropped his hand to his side. No words came out of his mouth.

"I'm sorry I didn't respond to your messages. It's just been a long day. I didn't mean to ignore you." We were standing about two feet apart, which is farther apart than I'd stood with Jermaine in this very hallway, or than I would have with Vanessa, but I didn't think I could step closer to Ben. He was like a nervous cat; I didn't want to spook him.

He sighed. "That's okay. It doesn't matter."

"Is this about my phone number? I'll give it to you—I just

didn't realize it was urgent, I guess." I hoped he planned to explain why it was so urgent.

"No. I wanted your phone number to talk with you about something not work related. But now that we're talking, I don't need it." He started biting his nail again.

"Okay?"

There were several beats of silence, then he looked at me, full on. "I fucked up," he said.

"I'm sure it's okay, Ben."

"I don't know."

"Well, you can tell me. It can't be worse than the time I lied to you about my friend dying."

"Your friend's boyfriend," he corrected, lifting an eyebrow.

I laughed. "Yes, exactly. So it can't be worse than that."

"It might be."

"It doesn't matter. Really." I waited until he made eye contact with me again before I continued. "You can tell me. After all, I just declared that we were friends to my entire team."

He looked down at me, his brown eyes large and nervous. "Okay. So yesterday. At the Flatiron Hotel," Ben said, every few words accompanied by a dramatic pause.

But I didn't need any more words from him. As soon as "Flatiron Hotel" came out of his mouth, I knew what he was trying to gallantly tell me.

"Ben. If this is about what Mitchell said… You don't have to tell me."

His eyes opened wider. "Did he tell you? At coffee?"

"How did you know we went to coffee?" I asked, then changed my mind. I didn't want to know. "Never mind. But no, I overheard you two. When I was coming back from the bathroom."

"Oh. And you're not mad at me?"

Even as my mouth moved, I knew I should just say no, and leave it there. I knew I shouldn't pull at threads that might be potentially hurtful. But I couldn't help myself. "Well. I didn't really hear what you said. But I heard Mitchell say what he said about me being crazy or whatever."

"Oh," Ben said, his relief washing away. So that wasn't what he was nervous about. He was nervous about whatever he'd said in response. He'd probably tossed and turned about getting this off his conscience.

"Ben. Whatever you said, I don't think I need to know."

He nodded slowly. "Yeah, I think you do. It wasn't my smartest moment—"

"If you agreed with him, or piled on, really, let's just let it be water under the bridge." I thought I might spontaneously combust from embarrassment if I had to listen to Ben—who, let's admit it, I had a huge crush on—tell me I was a crazy slut to my face.

"No! I didn't. At all." He sounded surprised, maybe even desperate. "Look at me," he said.

I hadn't realized I wasn't looking at him, I was so lost back in that stupid awkward moment where I'd spent so much of the last twenty-four hours. But as I came to, I was staring at my shoes. When I finally made myself look at him, he stepped closer. Where there was once two feet of space, there was now one.

"I got angry, actually, when he said that."

I nodded, totally captivated by his eyes. I didn't think we'd ever been this close.

"At first, I told him to shut up, but he just laughed it off, and kept going on about this stupid theory about women that was truly vile. I wanted to shut him up. 'Cause he's such a dick."

I nodded again. We were in agreement there.

"So I told him you were my girlfriend."

I stopped nodding. I hadn't seen this coming. "What?"

Ben backed up, and suddenly, we were back to two feet, or maybe even a full yard of space between us. "I know! I know!" he said as though that was some sort of answer.

"I don't get it," I said.

"Because he was saying you weren't...girlfriend material, or whatever. And so I said you were. By saying you were my girlfriend." He started to subtly pace, not full laps around me, but just a step back and forth.

"Well. That explains his reaction at coffee."

"Yes!" he said, as though another part of this debacle had just occurred to him. "Coffee! I heard you were going with him today, and so I wanted to tell you beforehand—"

"Wait. Ben, were you not going to tell me I was in a fake relationship with you until you found out I was getting coffee with Mitchell?"

"Well, it's not really a whole fake relationship. It's not like we have to take Christmas photos in July to get you a green card or something."

"Oh my god, this is such a mess." I ran my fingers through my hair.

"I guess he asked you if we were dating and you said no?"

"Well, I didn't want to create a weird giant lie! So yeah, I told him the truth, which is that we're not dating." I took a breath. I was talking too fast. I was arguing with him like I was mad. But was I mad? I closed my eyes against the scene; I let it all fade away. So what if Mitchell thought we were dating? So what if I lied to him? Mitchell didn't matter. What mattered was this weird beat my heart had added to its melody. Ben had called me his girlfriend. That was worth noting. I opened my eyes and changed course. "I'm sorry, I'm overreacting. I'm not mad."

"You're not?" Ben didn't seem like he was quite sure I was telling the truth.

"No."

"Even though I lied?"

"It was a very nice lie."

Ben made a noise like he'd caught a laugh in his throat. Like he was somewhere between feelings and wasn't sure which to choose. "Okay, then."

"Okay." The disaster had dissolved; there was only smoke and no fire. "So, do you still want my number? You never know when you might need to tip me off to a fake-dating situation."

Ben's laugh released. "You should have mine, too. I'm not the only one known to create an outlandish story."

"No, certainly not."

We pulled out our phones. His face had a goofy smile on it, big enough to show the small imperfection of his twisted incisor. I could feel cool air against my gums—my smile was as big and wide as his.

Ben's number had given more weight to my phone. I was aware of it in a way I hadn't been before. It rubbed against my leg in the pocket of my jeans for the rest of the day while I worked. On my way home, I clutched it in my coat pocket. I was terrified of the possibility that I might accidentally text or call him, although I'd never made that mistake before. I had pretended that I'd butt-dialed people when they asked me why I called four times at 2:30 a.m., but to my knowledge, I'd never *actually* made that mistake.

I just couldn't believe that I held a small string connected to him. I felt like a cat; I wanted to reach out, grab the string, and run away with it. I wouldn't let myself, though. The crush on Ben, while it felt like progress that I was now able to admit it to myself, was maybe not a good idea. Everything that happened with Mitchell proved just how bad an idea it was. Anything that happened with me and Ben would be blown up, each morsel of information spreading like a dandelion on the wind. Our relationship would never be our relationship alone. And if things went bad, work would become tense and awkward. The Fun Team would be a no-man's-land, filled with land mines of sexual tension and sudden bombs of hurt feelings dropped from above.

But there was another side to me, the side that I imagined as a devil on my shoulder, that thought I could deal with anything, no matter how messy. That thought if everyone already assumed I was fucking Ben, then I should just go ahead and do it. If I was being punished for something, I might as well have the fun of committing the crime.

That part of me had been cooing ever since our hallway conversation. It jumped to conclusions, believing that Ben's choice to stand up for me with Mitchell—in that particular way, with that particular lie—meant he'd be very willing to fuck me, and perhaps even willing to date me. Yes, things had become muddled and confusing between us. And yes, he'd walked away from me at Friday Night Drinks and never mentioned the lunch I said I'd like to get. And yes, for a while there, it looked like I'd messed everything up. But the confident, dangerous part of myself rejected that idea. It only remembered the way Ben's eyes roamed over my face in the stairwell. The way he clenched and unclenched his hand when he was listening to me. The desperation that poured off him when he was trying to explain himself. How he didn't want me to be mad at him. That was his worst-case scenario—not that he was made a fool of, but me being angry or upset. Ben told Mitchell we were dating because the thought of dating me had occurred to him—to him I was something I'd never been to anyone before: *girlfriend material.*

Maybe I could text him and he wouldn't find it clingy and desperate. He might still be nervous that I was mad at him. Maybe he'd be happy to hear from me.

The loudspeaker came on in the subway car, announcing my stop. I hadn't noticed how long I'd been on the train. I hadn't even seen the people entering and exiting around me. I pulled myself out of my daydreams and opened my eyes.

The string to Ben was still there, in my hand. And I was going to tug on it.

I got home, and the small objects that filled my everyday life had been transformed in my absence. My Ikea couch with the cheap throw I got as a party favor at a wedding were cozy and welcoming. I opened my freezer and happily realized I was out of single-serving salmon filets. I could order in. Make a whole nice night of it.

Since I'd told her I would, I called Lola before I did anything else. I kept it brief. Didn't go into too much detail, but she could hear my smile, and she asked about it. And despite how humiliating it was, and how much my skin crawled at the thought of sharing myself in this way, I told her. I told her I planned to text Ben, that I thought he liked me.

She told me to center myself, to meditate, but that she was happy for me. Her voice sounded more surprised than happy, but I didn't care. I looked out at the quiet brownstones as we talked and imagined how lovely they'd be when winter came. I wondered if Ben would walk through the snowy streets with me. Maybe I'd be able to look at him under the streetlights, snow falling on his dark hair.

A few minutes after I ended the call with Lola, my phone rang again. I was expecting the pad thai I'd ordered online, so I picked up.

"Hi, is this Emma?" It was a woman's voice, her vowels stretched, her tone serene. She wasn't from New York. She certainly wasn't the delivery guy.

"Yes?"

"Hi, it's Gaura."

"Gaura?" I asked. I'd heard her. I knew who she was, of course. I just didn't understand why she'd be calling me.

"Yeah, Gaura. Your father's partner."

"I know, I'm just— I didn't expect you to be calling." We'd never spoken alone. I didn't even have her number.

She let out a wheeze of a laugh. "I know, I wasn't sure you'd even pick up. Have you spoken to your father since his trip down to Brooklyn?" That wasn't Gaura's business. She'd never involved herself in our relationship before. What horrible things had my father told her about the visit that she felt compelled to step in now?

"No, we haven't spoken." I looked over to my fridge, to the drawing of my apartment stuck to it. Sure, we'd fought over the visit, but there had been good moments, too.

"Oh. He said he called you." She sounded disappointed. "But I wasn't sure…"

"I mean, we just saw each other a few weeks ago." It was more like a month, but that wasn't unusual for us—it was closer to a good stretch than to a bad one. Another call started coming through, from a number with a New York area code. It had to be the delivery guy. I declined it.

"It might be nice if you gave him a call."

"Excuse me?" How fucking dare she.

"Not to pressure you, or say you have to!" I'd made her nervous.

"I'm sure I'll speak to him again, Gaura." Another call from the delivery guy. "I have to go."

I quietly retrieved my food from downstairs. Went back up, ate it with the same few thoughts spiraling through my mind: How dare she? Something is wrong. She's wrong. I'm a bad daughter. He's a bad father. We're bad at being a family. How dare she?

Emma: Hey

I texted Ben. I couldn't help it.

I tried to forget all of the possibilities behind Gaura's call by staring at the white screen of my phone. I wanted to focus on this nervousness. It was more fun.

Ben: Hi

Three dots appeared.

Then disappeared.

Then nothing.

Emma: How are you holding up?

Ben: I'm totally fine. I feel like I should be asking you how you are instead of you asking me.

Emma: You can ask me too.

Ben: How are you?

There was no part of me that was even tempted to tell the truth: that I was nervous about a strange call I'd received from my stepmother, out of the blue. I knew there were some people out there who'd unravel their feelings and secrets to someone as kind and honest as Ben. But I'd never really done that with anyone besides Lola, and she felt more like a priest or a therapist than a friend. I'd certainly never talked about feelings with a man I was interested in.

Emma: I'm okay. Actually, I'm feeling fairly nonplussed about the whole thing.

That was true. The phone call from Gaura had put Mitchell out of my mind. And maybe Ben would be able to do that for the phone call. It would be like the layers of paint in the kitchen at Ninety-Sixth Street. The walls were a pale gray now, but if you moved the fridge out to clean behind it, bands of color appeared, telling the story of the paint fads of the Upper West Side. Seventies avocado had been replaced by a nineties Tuscan orange, which had been replaced by the omnipresent millennial gray. I needed an emotional millennial gray—something that could be slapped up over my subconscious and mask everything else.

Ben: Really? I'm still playing everything over and over in my head. Like the whole day is a horror movie stuck on repeat.

Emma: Maybe you should try meditating.

Ben: Does that really work? I feel like without distractions I would only obsess more.

Emma: Any of those distractions working out for you?

Ben: Uh, no not really.

I could turn this toward something sexual. I could hint at it. Right here, this was my moment. Say something like *Maybe I can think of a better distraction.* Did that sound like something a real human woman would say, or was that more Sharon Stone in *Basic Instinct*? Was it silly and cloying and cliché? Also, what if he wasn't into me? Or what if he was into me but not into flirtatious texting? Knowing Ben, I could imagine that being a very real possibility.

Emma: But I thought that's what your large collection of coffee table books about New England architecture was for.

Better to keep things aboveboard. The last thing I could take tonight was a rejection. Friendly banter wouldn't be shot down.

Ben: Hahahaha you know I don't believe New England has a distinct architectural style. But I think I need something stronger.

It was so many *ha*'s. He must really think I'm funny. Or he was nervous.

Emma: Lemme guess, a Ken Burns documentary? What's your favorite one?

Ben: You're exactly right about me. Ken Burns is who I always turn to in a crisis. Hard to pick a favorite, but I'm an all-American boy, so I'd probably say Baseball.

Emma: Baseball! Haven't seen it! And here I had you pegged for a National Parks kind of guy.

Ben: Ken Burns's Baseball is the perfect movie to watch if you have like, I don't know, maybe 32 whole hours of your life to spare and you've always wanted to know a great deal about the lives of early-20th century Americans.

Emma: I don't think I even know any of the rules of Baseball (the game). Could I still enjoy?

Ben: (Can anyone enjoy?) But yes, the development of the rules is covered in great detail.

Emma: (Ha!) I could use some slow zooms onto historical photos tonight. Is this on streaming?

Ben: Yeah, amazon I think. You're really going to watch?

Emma: Why not? I have nothing better to do.

Ben: Yeah fuck it. Maybe I'll start it over too.

Emma: Should we time it and press play at the same moment?

Ben: Sure!

That was the first exclamation point I'd ever seen Ben use, and it seemed he was using it earnestly.

Emma: Gimme a minute to pull it up.

It was kind of lame, what we were doing. It wasn't what I'd imagined when I clicked his contact in my phone tonight. But it was more comforting than sexting. Possibly.

Emma: Okay, I've cued up episode one. You ready?

Ben: One, Two, Three…

Emma: Play!

Ben: 🎉

After a brief message from PBS's funders, the screen opened on a black-and-white photo of a jumbled city street. Brick buildings jutting out this way and that, it looked like the city had grown naturally, as a tree would, with branches sprouting up and growing knotted for no reason a human eye could discern.

Then white text filled the bottom of the screen. It read BROOKLYN.

And just like that, as if it was the easiest thing in the world, as if I did it every day, I started to cry. I didn't sob, or heave, or make any noise. Tears simply started to fall from my eyes, like the drip of the tap.

Tinny church bells were the only sound coming from my laptop as the screen started to zoom over the landscape. Although it was my home, I didn't recognize a single building. There were churches that could've been in any neighborhood, and buildings with sloped roofs that would have been out of place anywhere in the borough in this century.

A Walt Whitman quote washed over me, and then a crackling film jostled us over the Brooklyn Bridge in a train car.

Emma: Subways on the Brooklyn Bridge?!

Ben: What? Do they not go over the bridge anymore?

Emma: You're joking.

Ben: I'm joking. But, honestly, when I first moved here I thought they would still be there. You have no idea how disappointed I was that it's just a mob of tourists and none of them wear old-timey clothes.

Emma: I think I have no idea how many times you've seen this movie.

Ben: Oh, god. I'll never tell.

Emma: Haha it's okay, I like it so far.

Ben: We're only two minutes in. There are approximately 1,440 minutes left.

The next two minutes covered the building of Ebbets Field in Flatbush, Brooklyn, then we quickly saw Jackie Robinson take the field as the first Black player half a decade or so later. And then Ebbets Field was being torn down. The first few minutes were just broad strokes. But I couldn't help myself, a girl who'd never been to a baseball game, from crying a little bit harder when the voice-over started talking about Brooklyn's broken heart when their team moved three thousand miles away to California, as the camera panned over a half-destroyed ballpark covered in 1950s ads.

I'd spent too many years debating whether or not I was better off that my dad had moved away after the divorce. But in this moment, I felt much worse off. I felt like the fans who were shown as no more than blurry black-and-white dots watching the Dodgers leave. Maybe my dad would have taken me to a baseball game. As it stood, I didn't even know if I was supposed to like the Mets or the Yankees.

All those people in the images playing on my screen were long gone. I found the idea incredibly relaxing. All these issues and anxiety whirling in my mind would eventually quiet. I, too, would be as insignificant as the blurred faces in historical photos. My feelings about Mitchell, and our conversation today, and what he said and thought about me, would all disappear with time.

Emma: Are you crying about the Dodgers? Cause I'm crying about the Dodgers.

TWELVE

On Friday, I sat at my desk, trying to think about how best to design a LinkedIn campaign aimed at people in entry-level jobs, getting them to think about the future. It should have been easy to design with this market in mind. I was currently in an entry-level job. But I could barely comprehend the next few weeks. It seemed impossible that I would eventually be sixty-five and wishing I'd started saving for my retirement earlier. If I couldn't even convince myself, how could I convince others? Jermaine thought GIFs were the answer.

I was still distracted by the night before. My flirtation with Ben was blooming. Maybe we could now be classified as "talking," or we had at least talked once. And that was exciting and also terrifying. But Gaura's unexpected call had tipped my nerves into a category I would call frayed. Why was she suddenly concerned with my relationship with my dad?

I spent most of the morning and afternoon designing one GIF that transformed a young man into an old one—it had a little sliding door, and suddenly the photo of the young man, head thrown back in laughter, transformed into a gray and wrinkled man, lips in a tight frown. The bold black text appeared last:

Tomorrow is coming sooner than you think. It's time to make a plan.

"Hey, wanna come look at this?" I called back to Jermaine, who was the first of many approvals that our designs went through.

He rolled his chair over. "Sweet, I didn't think you'd have a draft this soon," he said. He cocked his head as I played it for him. "One more time?"

I played it for him again, the screen holding the last image of the older man, and the text I'd placed around him.

"Hmm," Jermaine said.

It was at that point I realized he hated it. In my six months or so at Richter & Thomas, I hadn't yet made anything he hated. I always had to do additional drafts, but there was usually at least an element or two he liked.

"I mean, I can start over..." I said, answering his silence.

"Oh, well, yeah. Maybe that's best," he said. He bit his lip, clearly looking for the right thing to say. Jermaine was only in his early thirties—I don't think he'd been a boss for longer than a couple years—and he wasn't well practiced in giving critique yet. "It's just, well. I think it'll make everyone who sees it depressed. It's forcing people to think about their own mortality." He paused, turned to me for the first time, and added, "No offense."

I shrugged. "Don't worry about it."

"The text should also be less ominous, maybe something along the lines of 'Have Your Own Back.' And I think we can skip the age-progression thing entirely."

"Okay, cool. I see what you're talking about."

"Great," he said, and then just as he started to scoot his chair away from my desk, a Slack notification popped up on my desktop. It was from Ben. Jermaine's eyes flicked up to it—it would've been impossible for him to not read the flashing white box on the top of the screen.

12:22 p.m.

Ben N: Hey. Did you already have lunch?

I minimized it as quickly as I could. But my awkward rush only brought more attention.

"You know," Jermaine said, leaning back in his chair and crossing his legs in a figure-four shape, clearly no longer planning to scoot his way to the other side of the office, "I've never really been able to get to know Ben. And we've worked together for years now." That's the kind of thing that would've bothered Jermaine. He wanted to be everyone's friend, and he generally succeeded. "But I guess it tracks, you two hanging out. You're both a little quiet, not into the whole Friday Night Drinks scene."

How insane that I was now being billed as quiet and not into the party scene. Drunk Emma and Work Emma were polar opposites. "I mean, I don't know if I'd describe myself that way. But Ben's nice. I think he's a little shy."

"So, you gonna go to lunch?" he asked.

"With Ben?"

He laughed. "Yeah, with Ben. Will you go?"

I hadn't really thought about it. I'd only thought about not having Jermaine see that Ben was messaging me and then having Jermaine stop talking about Ben. I hadn't thought about the actual content of the message.

"I don't know," I said.

"Might be nice, though, right?" Jermaine said.

I felt like he was a kind-hearted uncle pushing me to make friends. And fuck it, he was right. I did need friends.

"Yeah, I think I'll go," I said. And then, finally, I got the conversation-ending pat on the shoulder, and he scooted away.

Emma F: No, have you?

I thought of my rice and beans in the communal fridge. I could eat it tomorrow.

Ben N: No.

Was he going to make me ask him? He was typing, so maybe he'd hit Send too soon.

Ben N: I didn't bring my lunch either. Do you have a usual spot? Meet by the elevators in ten?

Emma F: Sounds good!

It wasn't a date or a not-date. I didn't have the capacity to untangle those knots today.

Eleven minutes later I walked up to the elevator bay. Ben was already there, long hair hiding his eyes as he looked down at his phone. Maria and Izzy were there, too. They were speaking quickly to each other, slightly behind Ben in line for the elevators, which meant that for me to go say hi to Ben, I'd have to walk around them.

I really didn't want to deal with their awkward glances, much less their opinions, so I hung back, staring holes in the side of Ben's head. I was sure it was Maria, who'd heard it from Amy, who told Vanessa I was flirting with Mitchell. I hoped Ben would just turn to me, I'd wave, and he'd walk this way. We could stand toward the back of the growing mass of people, and maybe even get into a different elevator than Maria and Izzy. If he'd just look at me, the whole problem could be avoided. But he wouldn't look at me.

"Ben," I said, but it came out as a soft whisper, not loud enough to get his attention. A man I didn't recognize from Content looked over at me suspiciously. If Ben didn't acknowledge me soon, this man was going to think I was a real creeper.

Izzy and Maria still hadn't noticed me, so I tried to slide around them, up to Ben. There was nothing else to be done. The crowd had gotten thicker, and still no elevators had come.

"Excuse me, hi, sorry," I said to Izzy as I walked around her.

She moved in toward Maria without comment, and for a brief instant, I thought I was in the clear. Ben looked over at my slight ruckus. He smiled and I smiled back.

"Emma!" Maria said as I snuck toward Ben. "Are you heading out?"

Izzy made a little about-face, making room for me in their circle. I didn't step closer to them or to Ben; I stood suspended in the middle.

"Yeah, going to lunch," I said.

"Do you wanna come with us? It's half-price tacos at La Cantina," Izzy said. Maria's friendly smile had spread to Izzy's face. They were wearing the same J.Crew-striped cardigan. Izzy's was maroon and Maria's was navy. I really needed to add more cardigans into my work wardrobe.

"Oh, I have plans, but thanks anyway," I said, gesturing behind me with a thumb toward Ben.

Izzy cocked her head. Maria furrowed her brow. "With Ben?" Maria finally asked.

I turned. Ben gave us all a stilted wave and a tight smile.

"Yeah, with Ben," I said.

"Oh," Izzy said. "Okay."

"Um, well, have a good time?" Maria said.

"Thanks." I nodded and walked the three steps to Ben's side. I could feel Maria's and Izzy's eyes on me.

"Hey," he said.

"Hi."

He twirled his phone in his hand. I was desperate to reach for mine.

I could feel Izzy and Maria staring at us as we stood awkwardly together, unable to make conversation. We were finally saved by the *ding* of the elevator's arrival.

The elevator ride was quiet and painstakingly slow. The car was already half-full with people from other floors, but me, Ben, Izzy, and Maria managed to squeeze on. It was always like this during the lunch rush. People piled in and poured out. Older executives were headed to dark steakhouses with private oak-paneled rooms, younger executives went to new shining Michelin-starred fusion restaurants, and people like me sought out lunch specials and cheap take-out salads wherever we could find them. Ben was still playing with his phone. I stared silently ahead, trying to ignore the feelings Izzy and Maria had brought up.

Whatever. The worst that could happen was they'd tell people that Ben and I got lunch, but since Mitchell was already probably telling people that we were dating, it would only work to confirm the rumors. Which Ben seemed to want to confirm? So he didn't look like a liar, I supposed. And confirming them wouldn't be so bad for me, either—Mitchell wouldn't talk to me anymore, and he wouldn't be able to call me an "undatable crazy slut," because everyone would think someone was dating me.

We stopped at a few more floors on our way down. By the fourth, the small space had become a sardine can. Everyone murmured and shuffled and tried to make themselves as small as possible. I had to step into Ben's space. I looked up at him and mouthed, "Sorry."

He nodded, put his phone in his pocket, and pressed his large frame as tightly as he could into the corner to make more room. Without thinking of any possible consequences, I molded my body—as stiffly as I could—onto his. They were just the ghosts of touches, nothing meaningful, the passing brushes of a stranger on a train. My pulse clearly didn't understand it shouldn't have been racing the way it was.

Stepping out into the lobby was a shock of personal space.

My mind couldn't catch up with my body, and before I realized I'd taken a step, we were hitting the curb and Izzy was calling back to us with a wave—somehow she and Maria were already crossing the street—"Have fun, you two!"

"Oh yeah, thanks!" I called back. My face was beet red, I could feel it. But the small, normal interaction with Izzy had brought me back to the present.

"So, where are we going?" Ben asked.

On the rare times I did take myself out to lunch on Fridays, I went for half-priced tacos, but since that's where Izzy and Maria, and probably two-thirds of the office, were headed, I settled for plan B. "I thought we could just go to the sandwich stand in the park. Maybe eat on a bench?"

"You won't be cold?" he asked, following my lead toward the park.

"No." I hunched my shoulders up in my black jean jacket. It was a windy October day. "My coat is warm enough. But will you be—"

"No," he said, cutting me off, and even though he wasn't smiling, I could hear the edge of laughter in his tone. "I think I grew up too far north. I've lost the ability to get cold. Especially when it's sixty degrees."

"So I have to admit I fell asleep to *Baseball* last night. I woke up on my couch this morning," I said.

His eyes darted to me and he smiled. "I figured, after you stopped responding."

"Did you stay up and watch the whole thing?" Ken Burns had felt like a bedtime story to me, not something that would keep me awake.

"Episode one." He shrugged.

We got our sandwiches and found a bench with room enough for the both of us to squeeze onto, which was truly blind luck at lunchtime in Bryant Park. People packed onto these benches like they were on the subway—no care for personal space while on their hour-long lunch break. We had to sit so close that I became very aware of Ben's thigh against my own. The length of it shocked me. His knee extended at least half a foot beyond mine. I didn't realize until he spoke that I'd been staring at the place where our legs touched. It was hard to look away.

"So..." was all he managed. Was the difference in our thigh sizes also too much for him?

"How long have you lived in New York?" I asked.

"I came here for college. NYU." He paused and smiled. "What's with the face?"

"Am I making a face?" I'd tried to school my expression to something neutral.

He laughed. "It's okay. If you're thinking what I'm thinking, then I feel the same way. NYU is buying up all the real estate, increasing gentrification—"

"Exactly! They own more city land than the Catholic church. They're insanely overpriced and bring in these rich kids who see the city as some kind of playground for their youth and not as a real place where families and regular people live." I took a breath. "Not to say you're an evil rich kid."

He gave me an indulgent smile as though I wasn't insulting his alma mater. "I'm really not. I went there after the army. The GI bill paid."

"If I'm being honest, I don't think I've ever met a soldier before. Or, like, someone who served who's young and not someone's grandfather."

"City kids are so weird." He shook his head. "You know the army is a thing that a lot of people in this country do, right?"

"Maybe it's that I just can't imagine you in a uniform. I want to see some proof." The truth was that, of course, I could imagine him in a uniform. But because I knew absolutely nothing about the army, I imagined him in a 1940s uniform similar to what Edward Burns wore in *Saving Private Ryan*, complete with the BROOKLYN, NY, USA on the back of the jacket.

He raised his eyebrows at me and pulled his phone out of his pocket. "I've got pictures on here somewhere." It took him a minute of scrolling through years of photos. While his eyes moved over his own memories, I watched the bones of his face. It was almost embarrassing how beautiful I found him.

"Here," he finally said and handed me the phone. The picture wasn't what I was expecting. I had imagined he'd show me a portrait of him sitting in full regalia with flags behind him—something staged, like you'd see on the news. But this wasn't like that at all. It was an awkward selfie with him and a few other guys. They were all in beige camo and were looking at the camera unsmiling. They were trying to pose like they were in a music video. One of them was throwing up a weird hand gesture that looked like he was trying to do a *W* for *Westside*, but it looked more like the *Star Trek* greeting. Ben had a lit cigarette in his mouth. All of them had close-cropped hair.

"Huh" was all I could manage.

"Yeah," he said, taking the phone back. "The army sucked. But I made some friends."

"It wasn't what you were expecting?"

"Of course not. I was a good Catholic boy who earnestly thought I was doing God's work by spreading freedom. And then I went to Afghanistan and sat behind a computer to shoot rockets. I hated it."

"And then you went to NYU to find yourself?"

"Well, I got it in my head that because I didn't like the army and because it was so clear we weren't helping anyone or anything by being over there, I should move to New York and be an anticolonialist intellectual."

"What? It was easier to picture you in the army!"

He shook his head and laughed. "I wrote this essay for NYU about how the army had made me a Marxist, and they ate it up. I was a philosophy major for one year, until I realized that rant-ing in classrooms about socialism and how we need an intersectional revolution also felt totally meaningless to me."

"So what does have meaning?"

"That's a hard question. The only answer I have is cliché."

"That's okay."

"Family. That's the only thing that's been a constant for me, at least. What about you?"

"What has meaning for me?"

"Or you could tell me your whole life story. I'd also accept that as an answer." He smiled, his eyes alight with interest. Would they dim if I told him I'd been a party girl who thought of nothing but how best to get drunk until a year ago? He'd had all these quests to find himself and took his life and his role in the world seriously, whereas I'd spent those years trying to find the best price for good cocaine in the five boroughs, avoiding looking too closely at myself or the world around me.

"I think you're right. When I think about history, even just of this little patch of land—" I gestured around the crowded park "—and all of the people who've walked through it, going back millennia, they've believed countless different things: in different gods and different systems of government. But family, love, caring for each other—they all believed in that. So what could have more meaning? It might be a cliché, but it's also true."

Then he blinked hard, squeezing his eyes together tight. Had I sounded incredibly dumb? Was he annoyed that I'd skirted around my own life story? But then I saw a suspicious-looking white drop beginning to drip down his forehead. Looking up, I saw we were sitting under a branch full of cooing pigeons, which would explain why the spot was empty.

"Oh!" I said.

"Is it bad?" he asked, eyes still closed.

"Um..." I wasn't sure whether to lie or not. Surely he must have felt it? "There's a napkin in the sandwich bag. Hold on."

Ben's cheeks were bright red. I sympathized with how reactive his skin was; it afforded him no emotional privacy. There was no way he could pretend he wasn't embarrassed. Whatever he'd intended to happen during this lunch, getting shit on by a pigeon clearly wasn't on that list.

Napkin in hand, I leaned forward and wiped the drop off his forehead.

"Oh," he said, blinking his eyes suddenly open. I looked at him, then looked down to see his open hand. He'd wanted the napkin. He hadn't expected my hands on him.

"Sorry," I whispered, "it'll just be a second." I moved on to the second napkin and wiped at his raven hair. He angled his head down at the slight suggestion from my hands.

I was now just inches away from cradling him against my chest. I could feel his breath hot on my neck. He didn't say anything, but the flush on his cheeks rose higher. His eyes followed me. I was cleaning bird shit out of his hair, but he looked at me like I could say anything and he'd believe me. Like he'd pick up a sword and run into danger if I asked him to. It was a heady power, one that excited and terrified me in equal measure.

"All done," I said, keeping my voice low but breaking eye contact and sitting back down.

Only someone as sexually deprived as me would feel their heart start fluttering in this situation. But whatever. I knew I may as well accept it: I was swooning for Ben Nowak.

"Thank you," he said, his voice low and hoarse.

"Sure thing," I said.

We looked at each other, and I felt heat rise in my chest. I thought I might be sweating under my jean jacket. Was he thinking about kissing me on this bench while I held bird poop–filled napkins in my hand?

"Our sandwiches are going to get all soggy and gross," I said. "We should eat them." I didn't think I was ready to start making out with my coworker on our lunch break. If that even was what he was thinking? Never in my whole life had I had a boyfriend. I'd never let a man close enough to be nice to me. Even though I'd thought about Ben constantly, I was suddenly terrified of the reality of him. His thigh against mine, his breath on my neck, his eyes on my face. Suddenly, it all felt real. Like this was already maybe happening, like something had already been put in motion.

He raised his eyebrows and blinked, shaking himself out of a trance. "Yeah, of course. Let me take those," he said, reaching for the napkins. I gave them to him, our fingers brushing, and the swooning started again.

Back at the office, I needed to distract myself from remembering how warm Ben's breath felt against my chest, which was becoming problematic to think about at work, so I pulled out my phone and looked at Instagram. I scrolled until I saw Susannah's face. Since I'd spent the past year avoiding her account, it rarely popped up on my feed. The algorithm had caught on to the distance between us. But I immediately knew why this specific post had beat the odds. It was Susannah standing with Brian, the guy I'd used as a tool to destroy our friendship, in front of city hall. She was wearing a white tea-length ballerina dress. He was in a three-piece suit. They were both looking at the camera dead-on. Susannah's eyes were watering, but if you were anyone else, you might not have been able to tell. It was just that I'd seen her cry so many times. I'd wiped the mascara from under her face after she'd vomited. I'd held her the night her mom died when we were fifteen. Maybe someone else would have stopped looking once they saw her megawatt smile. But I didn't. I stared at her glassy eyes and hoped they were happy tears. And wondered how she could do something like get married without me.

Comments were streaming in, but the thought of being just another person in her comments made my throat feel tight. Me, the girl she lived with for seven years, becoming nothing more than a generic social media comment to her? I couldn't deal with this as Instagram Emma. That felt somehow worse than nothing. I couldn't do nothing, though. She'd loved Brian enough to move out of our apartment to be with him. In a way, it was good that she also loved him enough to marry him. The boy who had changed both our lives so fundamentally should be worthy of marriage.

I pulled up her contact. I hoped she hadn't changed her number.

Emma: I saw the picture on Instagram. You both look great. Congratulations! ♥

It was generic, yes. But it was less generic than saying that in the comment section. I couldn't say all the other things that were pounding against my skull: *Have you been planning this a long time, or was it spontaneous? Was your dad there? Did he ask about me? How many dresses did you try on? Did you go to the vintage shop in Bushwick you always said you would?*

She responded within moments.

Susannah: Thank you ♥

Would that be it? A congratulations and an acknowledgment of the congratulations? Was there nothing else for us to say to each other? I scrolled up to see our last texts. It had been when we were arranging meeting up for me to make amends.

Susannah's name was first on my list when it was time to do my ninth step. Hurting her was a big part of the reason I got sober, and apologizing to her was something I'd been both looking forward to and dreading for the first few months of my sobriety. She didn't even know I was sober, it wasn't the kind of thing I posted about publicly, and we hadn't spoken since our big fight. I'd drunk-dialed her, leaving long winding messages about our sisterhood, but she hadn't called me back.

When it was time to make amends, I'd texted her a message that I'd spent hours drafting with Lola.

Emma: Hi Suze, I really hope you're doing well. I know you want your space and I completely respect that. I'm not expecting anything from you, not even a reply. I'm reaching out because I know I hurt you and I'm deeply sorry. I'm currently in a program that's helping me take responsibility for my actions, and if you're open to meeting, I'd like to apologize to you in person.

She asked me to pick a place, and I chose a quiet coffee shop in the West Village. Between the two of us, it would be hard to find a block in downtown Manhattan that didn't have at least one ghost lingering in a doorway. She'd lived in almost as many apartments as I had. As far as I was aware, I still had her beat at my eleven to her eight. But I didn't think Charles Street had ever meant anything to either of us.

I had been so nervous to apologize, I'd rehearsed my little speech in the bathroom mirror at least a hundred times. I arrived early, stationed myself at a table with a view of the door, and schooled my face into a serene expression.

Then she walked in and gave me a hug immediately. It was something our bodies had done again and again. But this time, I was trembling in her arms, my nerves forcing a physical manifestation. I still wonder if she could tell. We sat, and my apology went as I scripted it. She forgave me with ease and grace. But after that, things felt so specifically weird in a way that I hadn't anticipated. We didn't know each other anymore, and worse, it felt like we might not even like each other.

"So you're sober? Like on a yoga kick or something?" she asked.

"No, like, I'm going to AA. I haven't had a drink or a drug

in two hundred and five days." It hadn't really occurred to me that she wouldn't have picked up on what "the program" I kept vaguely referring to was.

"AA?" Her voice rose. A little frown appeared between her eyebrows. The same one I'd seen in math class and when a man wasn't interested in her. She was puzzling it out.

"Yeah. Alcoholics Anonymous."

"Yeah, I fucking know what AA means. I just can't believe you're going." As soon as those words were out of her mouth, I was relieved I'd waited until my ninth step to reach out to her. If I'd been earlier on in my sobriety, I might've heard those words and thought: *She knows me best, if she says I can drink, then I can totally drink.* But I had amassed just enough clarity in the past two hundred and change days to remind myself that I knew me best, and drinking had never led me down a good path.

"Really? I mean, I haven't had control over my drinking in, well, ever," I said.

"Who has control over their drinking?" she asked.

I laughed, thinking she was joking like all the new people I met in AA would have. She didn't laugh with me. "Most people, it turns out."

"Oh fuck that," she said like I'd told her I'd seen Bigfoot. "But this is just something you're doing to get control or whatever, and then you'll go back to normal?"

"No. I want—I hope that this can be my new normal. No more drinking."

"Ever?" I wondered if she was thinking about how Sober Emma might fit into her life and finding no space for her. Sober Emma liked long walks in the early morning when the city was just opening its eyes. Susannah liked late-night parties that the Safdie brothers might or might not attend.

"If I'm lucky."

"Well, shit. Isn't that harsh? Like, were you so bad you have to punish yourself for the rest of your life?"

"It's not a punishment."

We weaved the conversation away from my sobriety, and on to what was going on in her life: a dispute with the guy her and Brian were subletting from over an irreversibly stained couch; her boss had switched to a cheaper exterminator at the restaurant and they now had rat droppings, and there was really no reason he should have threatened to fire her just because she mentioned it in front of a customer; she'd gained fifteen pounds since moving in with Brian and wasn't sure why—her usual tricks to drop weight weren't working.

Did Sober Emma have a place in her life for this Susannah? Just hearing about her day-to-day felt like it had introduced an element of chaos that I wasn't sure I could take on. The truth was, we'd already moved on from each other, and there wouldn't be any going back.

The rest of the workday passed in a blur. I only made the mistake of pulling up Susannah's Instagram post twelve times. It felt like a victory. On the way home, Ben's words played on repeat in my mind. Family was the most important thing to him. It was to me, too. Both blood and chosen family. I'd tried my best to do right by Susannah. Whatever happened between us in the future, and no matter how painful it'd been to feel the distance between us, I was so glad she'd been willing to meet me so I could make amends. If the guilt of what had happened between us was still rolling around in my stomach, I don't think I'd be able to walk anywhere; its weight would have pinned me down.

This all suddenly made me remember Gaura's call. I didn't know what was going on with Gaura or my dad. But I didn't want to be the kind of family member that closed doors. Gaura wouldn't have called me without a reason, and it was my responsibility to at least call her back. As I walked toward the subway from the office, I dialed her number. It rang. And then, every cell of my body stiff with apprehension, her voice came on, directing me to leave a message.

By the time I'd hung up—no message left, I'm not a monster—there was a text waiting for me.

Gaura: Hey sorry for calling you yesterday. It wasn't my place. Sending you peace.

What do you know? Sometimes things just work out.

THIRTEEN

On Monday, the email at the very top of my inbox was from Amy.

Subject: Relationship Disclosure Form

Dear Ben and Emma,
I've attached the employee relationship disclosure form for you both to review. Now, although you are in different departments and have little interaction, this form is required for anyone at the Director level and above, which Ben is. I ask you to read the form over and return it to me signed if you decide it applies to your relationship.
As the form dictates, our sexual harassment policy is also attached.
All best,
Amy

I opened the first attachment.

Benjamin Nowak, employed by Richter & Thomas Financial Consulting as Director of IT, and Emma Finley, employed by Richter & Thomas Financial Consulting as a Marketing Assistant, hereby notify Richter & Thomas Financial Consulting that we have entered into a voluntary and mutually consensual social relationship.

In entering into this relationship, we both understand and agree to the following:

- Our personal relationship is voluntary and consensual.
- We are both free to end the relationship at any time.
- If the social relationship should end, we both agree that we shall not allow the end of this relationship to negatively impact our job performance.
- We will act professionally in the workplace without public display of affection.
- We have received and reviewed Richter & Thomas Financial Consulting's sexual-harassment policy, a copy of which is attached.
- We acknowledge that the social relationship between us does not violate Richter & Thomas Financial Consulting's policies and that entering into the social relationship has not been made a condition or term of employment.

Employee A (print name):

____

Employee A (signature):

____

Date: ____________________

Employee B (print name):

____

Employee B (signature):

____

Date: _________________

I'd been prepared to be aghast, to flush at words like *sexual* and *romantic* that I was sure the form would be covered in. But they weren't there. And I supposed we were in a "voluntary and mutually consensual social relationship." That could describe anything. It could describe me and Vanessa.

I texted Ben.

Emma: Did you see Amy's email? Thoughts?

Ben: I don't think we have to sign. Just because there are rumors doesn't mean HR should get involved.

Emma: Our HR dept seems to run on gossip.

I wanted to mention that he had created and confirmed the rumors, but he clearly didn't think that made them any more serious.

Ben: It's incredibly inappropriate.

Emma: So are we going to…refuse?

Ben: Well, she left us an out. "If you decide this applies to you."

Emma: True. Do you have time to respond?

Ben: Yeah. Of course.

I wasn't disappointed. After all, why would we sign something that signified we were together when we'd only been on a single friendly lunch date? That would be a crazy thing to do. But, well, it was something I, for no reason at all, wanted to do. It's not that I'd wanted him to sign it and then swing by M&C and drop it on my desk. That would freak me out. It would be beyond jumping the gun. I didn't want to sign this stupid form in this context. But if I was honest with myself, I did want a reason to sign it. To be in a relationship so steady and significant that it was worth putting pen to paper over. I'd never had someone call themselves my boyfriend or even admit to seeing me regularly. I certainly didn't have someone who'd let their bosses and HR know that they were in a "consensual social relationship" with me.

Subject: Re: Relationship Disclosure Form

Hi Amy,
Thanks for sending this along. But I don't think Emma and I have the kind of relationship that would require us to sign a disclosure form.
Thanks anyway,
Ben

That was fast. I should move on to making GIFs. I was still having issues with our new Facebook push—even though Jermaine had quite literally drawn out two people sitting and looking at a sunset with glasses of wine in their hands, somehow, when I made exactly what I thought he was asking for, it came out too cheesy or melodramatic. What could I do? The idea was bad. But I had a new idea. We didn't want to show retirement as everyone thought of it: gray hair, Florida porch. So what about a sunset on a mountaintop? Just as I was starting to pull copyright-free images, I got a new email notification.

Subject: Re: Re: Relationship Disclosure Form

Hi Ben,
Thanks for your quick response. I know the form is vague, but just so we're all on the same page, this is required for two employees engaging in a romantic or sexual relationship. I know there are many ways people define relationships these days, but this form isn't only for people who are in an "official" or "serious" relationship.
All best,
Amy

What the fuck did Amy think was happening between me and Ben? Had she been talking to Mitchell?

Ben: She's insane.

Emma: What does she think she knows? Is this from Maria seeing us go out to lunch?

Subject: Re: Re: Re: Relationship Disclosure Form

Hi Amy,
As I said, this form does not apply to Emma's and my current relationship. Furthermore, I wonder why you believe it does? Neither Emma nor I came and reported a relationship. In all my years at this company, I've never heard of HR picking up on office gossip and insisting that it had any basis in fact.
-Ben

I could imagine Ben sitting in his office, fingers clacking against his keyboard as he wrote back to Amy. His righteous anger pulling his spine straight. It made me feel relaxed, like he had things in hand.

Hi Ben,
Full disclosure, we received a written notice from a member of C-Suite about this relationship. Now, if this employee was incorrect or misinformed, I apologize. Emma, would you also confirm that this is the case?
Best,
Amy

Ben: I'm going to fucking kill Mitchell.

Outside-of-Work Ben had the mouth of a sailor.

Emma: I don't think that would help us get out of this.

I paused. Considered. Decided for once to try to be somewhat brave.

Emma: It might be simplest to sign the form.

Three dots appeared. Then disappeared.

Ben: Yeah, maybe that would be easier.

Did it sound like I was telling him we should date? Did he not want to date? I didn't want to talk him into dating me, obviously, but I also didn't want him to think that the form was a big deal to me.

Emma: Do you think she'll tell Mitchell if we refuse? Since he's C-suite and reported us?

Ben: I wonder what he fucking said.

I had never heard Ben utter a single curse. I'd never seen him type one out, either. But now he couldn't stay away from the f-bomb. It brought a smile to my lips.

Ben: But, yeah, I mean the form doesn't stipulate what kind of relationship, anyway. We went to lunch voluntarily and consensually.

Emma: Oh, thank god. I was worried I had coerced you onto that horrible bird poop bench.

Ben: Onto the bench, maybe. Out to lunch, not at all.

Emma: So, are we signing this thing?

Ben: Yeah, I guess so.

Emma: Now, the only question is...how can I print it out without alerting my entire team?

Ben: You would e-sign it like any self-respecting twentysomething, Emma. Don't you do graphics? Aren't you well-versed in the adobe suite?

Emma: Sometimes people don't accept electronic signatures!

Ben: I promise Amy will. Okay, sending mine.

Emma: Me too.

Ben: Should we celebrate over coffee later?

This trip to Joe's would not be as terrible as the one last week. First, and most importantly, Mitchell was nowhere in sight. Second, there were plenty of tables. Coffee shops were not generally as crowded after 5:00 p.m. as they were during lunch rushes. And, well, it was a date. Wasn't it? We'd signed a form.

I sat down at a small table in the back with a chamomile tea and a cranberry scone. It wasn't dinner, but I hoped it'd be enough to stop the weird tremors in my hands. On the way here, Ben and I had chatted about work. Ben talked about the upcoming new systems update and how people were oddly nervous about it. He said he'd been getting emails all day from coworkers convinced their files would get lost. We'd laughed about how silly people could be. But now, as he was about to sit down across from me, I felt like those ridiculous people worrying over nothing. How long could a person be nervous in the presence of another person? Surely his charm would have to wear off eventually.

Ben sat down after me, carrying a black coffee. He brushed his hair back from his face. The charm had not worn off yet.

I picked up my tea to take a sip and burned my tongue. I clenched my fist, trying not to react. But then I accidentally knocked my fist into the bottom of the table, and the rickety thing tilted, spilling both our drinks before I could right it. My pale golden tea clashed with his black coffee and then began to drip a drought-plagued September dirt color onto the floor.

"Shit. Shit. Sorry." I grabbed the single napkin I'd gotten with my scone and started to mop up what I could.

"Really, it's fine." Ben's hands joined mine, adding napkins, wiping away the mess.

"No, no, it's not fine." I stood. "We need more napkins." The three we'd had between us were sopping wet, and we'd yet to even tackle the floor. "And I'll get you a new coffee, and maybe a cake pop, because you've been so nice about this—"

"Emma. Sit." Ben stood, briefly towering over me. "I'll get the napkins."

I did as he told me, listening to the slow drip of liquid onto the floor.

Then things got worse.

"Emma?" a voice asked.

I looked up.

A man who was not Ben had walked up to my table. He looked like a finance bro who'd discovered himself in Costa Rica and now made TikToks about NFTs. He wore slim-fitting flannel and had a leather bracelet wrapped around his wrist.

"Yes?" I asked. Ben was coming up behind him, a cloudlike pile of napkins in his hands.

"It's Luke," the man said, pointing at himself. I noticed that his beard was impeccably manicured.

"I'm sorry?" I said. Luke, or whatever, was talking to me like he knew me. I was sure I'd never seen this man before in my life.

"Luke Torrance," he said, and gestured to himself more energetically.

I shook my head. My cheeks bloomed.

"We know each other."

"I really don't think so." A sense of dread was growing in my stomach. I gestured behind him to Ben.

"Oh, sorry, bro," Luke said, stepping closer to me to let Ben take his seat. He plopped the napkins on the table, and we both started cleaning up.

"Yeah, we do know each other." Luke sounded like he thought I might be joking…or lying. "We met a couple years back at Gov Ball? We watched Ed Sheeran perform together?"

I was now humiliated on several levels. The first and most important was that Luke was outing me as someone who partied and didn't remember people I met. The second, and honestly almost as important, was that he was falsely painting me as someone who'd be into seeing Ed Sheeran live.

"I'm sorry. I don't remember," I said.

"Oh, for real?" Luke said. "Your friend Susannah was there, and my buddy Jacob. We all hung out like all day." There was a certain tone to Luke's "hung out" that I didn't appreciate. I was sure Ben heard it, too.

I was becoming increasingly worried that I had fucked this man either in a porta potty or in some shrubbery. I knew I'd gone to Gov Ball with Susannah two summers ago. Or at least, I knew I'd bought the tickets, got dressed, poured a pint of vodka into a Poland Spring bottle, ate some acid, and then somehow turned up at home the next day. I didn't remember Luke, Jacob, or Ed Sheeran.

"Sorry," I said.

Luke, however, was not deterred. "I've thought about you a lot since. It's been one of those big regrets hanging over me, not getting your number." He chuckled to himself, almost shyly. But there was nothing shy about Luke Torrance. He was here hunting me as if I were his white whale, chasing me into places he had no business being in. But I, like Moby Dick before me, was ready to drown him.

"Well, honestly, I've tried not to think about that time in my life."

He laughed as though I was inviting him in on a joke and said, "I'll have to try harder to make an impression next time, then, huh?"

"I don't think so," I said.

"Well—" Luke began.

"She's seeing someone," Ben said, cutting into the conversation for the first time.

"Oh, I get it," Luke said, looking at Ben as if seeing him for the first time. "Sorry, man."

"Bye, then," I said.

Luke gave Ben a pat on the shoulder as he walked away to the other side of the coffee shop.

"I'm so sorry," I said to Ben.

"Not your fault. At all. I'm sorry—I shouldn't have said anything. But I thought you wanted an out?"

He wasn't wrong. But also, I was the one who'd decided to fuck a stranger (allegedly, I reminded myself) at a music festival two years ago. Of course this would happen to me. There were probably men lying in wait all across New York City, ready to jump out and surprise me with the worst side of myself whenever I tried to move past it. I imagined men hiding in bistros, bookstores, and subway platforms ready and eager to remind me of long-forgotten nights. The scenarios could even be worse than this one—I could walk my kid to school one day and some guy like Luke might be their teacher. Or what if I was about to get an emergency surgery, and the doctor walked in, winked, and before putting me under, asked if I remembered dancing with him at House of Yes? Eventually, if I was sober long enough, the memory of Drunk Emma would have to fade from the city, right?

This date was becoming a disaster. We were sitting with a pile of trash between us, and all around us lay my other, more metaphysical trash. My present anxiety and the terrible way I'd dealt with it in the past were both visible, and I couldn't think of a good story to explain it all away.

Except for the truth. Surely it would be easier than enduring this piercing silence. Ben wasn't even looking at me; he was looking somewhere past me, at a spot on the wall to the left of my face.

"I'm nervous." That was a good start. His eyes darted to mine. "It's because I'm sober," I blurted out.

He raised his eyebrows, as though that statement had only added confusion rather than clearing anything up.

"I told you already that I don't drink. Do you remember? At Friday Night Drinks?"

He nodded.

"And that's because I'm in recovery. As in AA."

AA was the magic word. Ben raised his eyebrows again, but this time in understanding. "Okay," he said.

"I don't know if you know this, but in AA, we're not supposed to date for the first year of sobriety. And I'm just past that mark, so I haven't been dating. And before I was sober, well, it was different then, but dating wasn't something that I had room for in my life. Or that my life was stable enough for, I guess." I took a breath, hoping it would fill me with continued courage. "I don't remember that guy, but it's entirely possible I watched Ed Sheeran with him, although, now sober and sitting here with you, I feel like I hate both him and Ed Sheeran."

"I also hate that guy and Ed Sheeran," Ben said. His face twisted into a wry smile.

I laughed hard and loud, throwing my head back. I hadn't expected him to say that. My head swirled. The truth wouldn't stop coming out of me now that the dam had burst: "That morning, when we first talked and you were setting up my computer, that Word document that came up, I was writing a speech for my one-year sober celebration. So when it came up in front of you, I panicked."

"Oh," he said, and surprisingly, he blushed. "That makes much more sense than what I thought."

"What'd you think I was writing?"

"Well, you said it was creative writing, but then you were super cagey about it. So I thought it was maybe fan fiction and you were embarrassed."

"Fan fiction?"

"Yeah, like when people write about Draco and Hermione falling in love…or whatever." He glanced away, and I could tell that the "or whatever" was something he didn't want to be talking about publicly in a coffee shop. That it was a loaded, sexy "or whatever."

An awkward giggle escaped. "Do you write fan fiction? Is it like, porn?"

"No, no. I don't. Not at all. I don't read it, either." He was flustered. "I had an ex who was into it, is all. But yeah, it can be kind of porn-y. From what I gathered."

"Oh," I said. And now, next to the pile of napkins and the mess of my past was a sexy, porn-writing ex-girlfriend.

"I've heard that before, about the first year of sobriety," he said, and I was grateful for the change in subject.

I wanted to ask him how he knew that, where he'd heard it from. I wanted to ask him every thought he'd ever had about addiction and sobriety. Did he believe it was a disease? Or did he think it was a moral weakness? "I just don't know what I'm doing," I said.

"You're doing fine." His voice was calm and sure. He rested his open palm on the dry side of the table, and I placed my hand in his. It was sturdy, with callouses I couldn't see. "I haven't dated in a while, either."

I nodded, at a loss for words. I wanted to know everything about every woman who'd ever touched him before me. But I wouldn't ask. I'd undoubtedly shown enough of my less-desirable sides that I didn't need to add irrational jealousy to the mix.

"Did the form freak you out? 'Cause it doesn't have to mean anything. We can take things however slow we want. This is still just coffee."

In truth, taking things slow was the opposite of what I wanted. I wanted to run to the bathroom and have him bend me over the sink. But that wouldn't have been good for me or him, so I nodded and said, "Slow sounds good."

By the time we left, the air was starting to get that night-time chill. The wind had picked up, pouring leaves onto the pavement. I pulled my coat tighter around my shoulders. The neighborhood's buzz had quieted. Flatiron wasn't a residential neighborhood, and it wasn't full of bars and restaurants. People usually came here to work and then disappeared into the farther reaches of the city by the time the streetlights clicked on.

"What train are you taking?" Ben asked as he slipped his

hands into his pockets. I regretted removing my hand from his at Joe's. I wished I could dip it into his pocket now. But I wasn't sure how he'd react. Or, well, I was pretty sure he'd be fine with it, but I didn't have the courage.

"The 4. I'll walk down to Union Square."

"I'll walk you," he said.

"What are you taking?"

"I live in Gowanus, so the F."

The F was much closer. It was only a block away. I wanted to tell him not to bother, but instead, I heard myself agreeing.

"If you could live in any New York neighborhood, which would you choose?" I asked as we started toward my train.

"Money's no object?"

"Of course not. The game is moot otherwise."

"I guess Greenwich Village. But I don't know if that's 'cause I actually want to live there or because it's the New York I imagined before I moved here."

"Big *Friends* fan?" I asked.

"I was more of a pretentious Bob Dylan fan, but sure, *Friends* was set there, too."

"Ah, this must have been the philosophy-bro era?"

"Of course. What self-respecting Kantian Marxist doesn't love Bob Dylan? What about you?"

"I'm more of a Hannah Arendt girl myself, if we're choosing philosophers."

"We were choosing neighborhoods, but I'll make sure to read *The Banality of Evil* sometime soon so I can impress you."

"Park Slope."

"I get it. What's more romantic than a brownstone?"

"Few things. But I also love Ditmas Park, the big old Victorian houses, with their backyards and garages. But I'd probably need a car." I remembered when I first saw Ditmas Park as a kid, I couldn't believe we'd taken the subway to get there. The houses looked like monuments to another time with their wide porches and bulbous wooden frames.

"You can learn to drive," he said like he had the utmost confidence in me.

"Well, someday." We'd arrived at the north end of Union Square and, with it, a slight surge in crowds. Union Square was never empty. I stopped and looked up at Ben. Tiny drops of mist were sticking to his hair, making it look jet-black against the navy blue sky. "This is me," I said, pointing toward the nearest subway entrance.

He nodded, and for a moment, we stood staring at each other.

He leaned in. His head ducked down and his hand spanned my lower back as he pulled me closer to him. I gripped his shoulder, and even through the damp wool of his coat, I could feel the muscles that surged there. He pulled me up farther onto my tiptoes, and I felt entirely enveloped by him, as though he could wrap his body around mine and I would feel none of the wind or rain that filled the air around us.

But then, when I was sure his lips were about to meet mine, he paused. His eyes darted over my face. He tucked his bottom lip into his mouth, biting it. Was he stopping himself? Was he trying to be gentlemanly? Was this what he meant by going slow? I might be sober and fully aware that it would be better for us to wait to have sex, but I could kiss. Certainly I was allowed that much.

Before I overthought it, I closed the rest of the distance between us. I might have surprised him, but he certainly didn't react like I had. He met my kiss with an urgency I hadn't expected. I felt like Baby in *Dirty Dancing*, and he was Patrick Swayze, solid and waiting to catch me when I jumped. There was no toppling this man. As soon as my mind started catching up to the fact that I was actually kissing Ben and not just dreaming about kissing Ben, my feet were planted back on solid ground and he was tucking his hands back in his pockets. I wished they were still on my waist.

"Oh," I said.

"I guess this is good-night," he said.

I really wanted him to come over. I wanted to slide my hands under his coat and touch the heat of his skin. I wanted to pull him back toward me and whisper indecent things in his ear. But I was very grateful that my sink was full of dishes and I had a pile of dirty clothes on the bathroom floor. Because taking things slow was a better idea. A great idea, even.

FOURTEEN

Taking things slow was killing me. It'd been over a month since we'd signed the form and we'd first kissed. We went out to lunch. We went out to dinner. We went to museums (okay, we went to one museum). We held hands. I got to know the small rough patches of skin at the base of his fingers. He told me about how his parents were high school sweethearts, and by the time his memory kicked in, they'd grown so far apart and liked each other so little it made him wary of committing to someone when he was too young. I told him about my parents' divorce—about my dad moving away and changing his name, and Mom closing herself off from anything serious until recently. That my childhood had made me confused about love and relationships, and scared of all the ways they could go wrong.

We made out under scaffolding, on street corners, and at the end of subway platforms where only the rats dared dance. He didn't invite me over, and I didn't invite him over, either. I wondered if he had some set date of when we'd be able to venture up staircases and past first base, but I didn't want to ask.

What I did want, something I was spending an embarrassing amount of time thinking about, was to see him naked. I'd wrapped my arms around his waist and run my fingers through his hair and even trailed my hand up his stomach under his shirt. His skin felt hotter than I remembered anyone's feeling before. And lying in bed by myself, I could remember where the trail of hair met his skin and how the clash of textures felt under my fingertips. It made me painfully aware of how unaware I'd been in all of my previous encounters.

I'd never had sex sober. Sure, there were some morning afters where my head was still spinning, and I was still coming down, where I'd been with people. But that wasn't sober sex. Everything was still clouded by a veil of drugs, maybe not actively making me high but slowly seeping through my pores, exhausting my system. Even kissing Ben felt like electricity I'd never known was possible. It was as though I'd gone from watching lightning strike on a faraway mountain to having it hit my skin, sizzling and shocking its way through my body.

What would it feel like when we had sex? I couldn't wait to find out. I was terrified to find out.

We'd finished watching *Baseball* in our separate apartments and were now working our way through *The National Parks: America's Best Idea.* It didn't have the narrative pull or New York exceptionalism that *Baseball* did, which in some ways was best. There were no Dodgers to cry over, so I could stare at the words Ben wrote me as often as I stared at the beautiful wide shots of Yosemite Park.

As I sat in my apartment now, a picture came through of the dinner he was eating: a sizzling pork chop next to sautéed carrots.

Emma: Did you make that?

Ben: Of course.

I sent back a picture of my own dinner, which consisted of a frozen burrito I had microwaved and a heap of undressed lettuce.

Emma: Yours looks better.

Ben: I can't even be nice about that, it looks...not particularly appetizing.

Emma: I didn't know you were out there *cooking*

Ben: I mean, I've lived alone a long time. Takeout gets sad.

Emma: Did you grow up with a home cooked meal every night? Because I've never thought of takeout as sad. Takeout is life!

Ben: Yeah, I can't lie, dinner was a whole thing when I was growing up.

Emma: Maybe you'll have to show me how to make dinner a thing. I should be graduating from sad frozen single servings.

Ben: I can cook for you.

Emma: At your place?

Ben: Of course at my place. This weekend?

Emma: Will you put out candlesticks and everything?

Ben: If you want candlesticks, I'll get you candlesticks.

Emma: I haven't been to your house before.

Ben: Yeah, I'm aware of that...

The phone felt hot in my hand. I couldn't wait to see what he'd say next. I wasn't sure what we were talking about. Was this dinner, or was this dinner and me spending the night? I couldn't imagine getting to his house, eating dinner, and then just leaving. The siren call of the bedroom would surely be too strong to resist.

Ben: Doesn't have to be this weekend.

He was giving me space again. Seeing if I still wanted to take it slow.

Ben: My kitchen isn't going anywhere.

Emma: This weekend sounds great—let's do it this weekend.

Why the fuck did I say "Let's do it"?

Emma: The dinner. That's what we'll be doing. 😊

Ben: Haha, yeah. Of course.

We would be having dinner, with subtext. But subtext didn't have to mean anything, right?

My search history was full of questions that the internet couldn't come to a consensus on, including brilliant queries such as: *What do you wear to go over to a guy's house for the first time? Do grown men expect you to shave?*

And, of course: *How to have sober sex*

There were answers out there. Pages written in *Cosmo* about how best to please a man, and long Quora threads with men telling strangers on the internet why they prefer women bare. None of it was helpful. It wasn't context-specific enough. I thought of making a Reddit post about my exact situation, but the idea of random people judging me was far too terrifying.

I only had two options:

1. Go with my gut. Do what felt natural to me. The problem was that what felt natural to me was not to do this sober. That was how I'd gotten to twenty-six with the nerves of a virgin but the body count of, well…someone on the other end of that ancient spectrum. So that was out.

2. Ask someone in real life who knew the situation. That would be embarrassing and awkward, but would it be as embarrassing as grossing Ben out by wearing the wrong kind of underwear? No, it would not.

I texted the only person who fit the bill. After all, she knew me. She knew Ben. She was a hot, young, single woman living in New York City. I pulled up Vanessa's contact.

Emma: Hi, I have a very weird and embarrassing favor to ask you.

Vanessa: I can't wait to hear it! What an intriguing text!

Emma: Can I call?

The phone rang a moment later.

"Hello?" I answered.

"I'm so ready. What an honor to be the recipient of an embarrassing-favor request!" Vanessa sounded giddy.

"Okay, you can't tell anyone—"

"It'll go from your lips to my ears and then to God's ears. No stops in between." Her voice reminded me of being fourteen, curled on the floor of Susannah's room and vibrating with that special high only secrets could provide.

"Okay, so I'm going over to Ben's house this weekend." A slow pause grew between us, filling the space with Vanessa's obvious confusion. "For the first time…"

"Oh, does he have, like, roommates or something?"

"We've been taking it slow. So neither of us have been to each other's places yet."

"Wait, are you telling me you guys haven't slept together yet?"

"Yeah." I exhaled a large breath, hoping that the most awkward part of this conversation was now over.

"So you're telling me he just looks at you like that without having ever seen you naked?"

"I don't know what you're talking about, but yes, we haven't seen each other naked yet."

"Emma. Come on. He looks at you like you're the only girl he's *ever* seen naked! His eyes, like, glow at you. It's honestly kind of disgusting."

"How would you even know how he looks at me?"

"Well, you know I'm there, next to you, also leaving the office when you meet him by the elevator every day for lunch and every evening when you guys walk out together. He's always there first, waiting for you. It's almost like he doesn't go to his office anymore. He just waits by the elevator all day, hoping you'll appear."

"Vanessa—" I didn't know what to say. Had I noticed that he never made me wait? Yes. But Vanessa must not have noticed my face any of those times, because I was sure I looked like a puppy hoping to catch sight of its favorite person.

"It all means you have nothing to be nervous about if that's why you're calling."

"I haven't done this before, with this much buildup. It's killing me."

"Okay, there's something called the bullet, and it'll help out with that. Especially if properly combined with season one of *Outlander*."

"No, not that kind of killing me. I haven't been with a guy fully sober before, and I'm suddenly so aware of all the choices I have to make. What underwear do I wear? Should I bring an overnight bag? Or am I supposed to leave afterward? Do I have to wax my whole body?" I hadn't needed this much guidance in tenth grade when I *actually* lost my virginity. That time, I'd gotten carried away with a senior I was hooking up with one Friday night when his parents were upstate, and he'd invited a bunch of people to hang out. He'd lived in a tiny tenement apartment, and since his bed was a twin, we'd gone to his parents'. Their room was really a glorified closet stuffed with a queen-size bed. There wasn't enough room for a door with hinges, so they'd used a frosted sliding glass one instead. Everyone else at the apartment that night could hear us, could see the outlines of our bodies, but Drunk Emma didn't care. The whole thing was exciting and hilarious. I couldn't imagine doing that now. My stomach coiled at the thought.

"Okay, hold up. Are you going over with the spoken intention that you're going to sleep with him?"

"No, he invited me over to cook me dinner."

"Okay, you can't see it, but I'm rolling my eyes at how gone he is for you. But more importantly, you don't have to sleep with him if you're not ready. I'm sure he's hoping you will, but I'm also sure he won't stop talking to you if you aren't." Vanessa's advice was kind, delicate. I couldn't keep myself from comparing it to what Susannah might have said. We never talked about not being ready for things or going slow. By the time I lost my virginity that Friday night, she'd already had three boyfriends and had told me she was starting to worry that I might be sexually stunted. We were always like two freight trains, plowing through walls to keep pace with one another. I caught up quickly.

"Vanessa, I am so ready. Like, beyond ready. I'm just also nervous and need guidance."

"What underwear would you have worn last year? Would you have gotten a wax then?"

"No, I never knew if I was going to fuck someone. And I pretty much only slept with strangers I met that day and then never saw again. So I'd wear tattered period underwear I bought at CVS a decade ago."

"Wow. Were guys into that?" She sounded genuinely surprised that I could've pulled that off.

"Well, it never stopped any of them." I thought of Luke Torrance. I doubted he'd been treated to anything as dignified as CVS underwear. It was very unlikely underwear had made it to Gov Ball that year at all.

"See, you've revealed an important aspect of the male psyche. If they're attracted to you enough to get to the point where they're taking your underwear off, they don't really care what the underwear looks like."

"But I don't want him to just not care. I want him to care in a positive way. But I also don't want to look like I'm trying too hard or like I'm not myself."

"Okay, now I'm rolling my eyes at how gone you are for him. But I'd also say you should scratch the Brazilian wax, then. That doesn't seem like you."

"It's not."

"Then wear a black bra and black underwear without any holes. Extra points if it's black with a bit of lace."

I rustled through the top drawer in my dresser, but nothing fit the bill.

"I've gotta go, Ems. Take some deep breaths. I really don't think there's a way this can go wrong."

I could think of a million-and-a-half ways, but I hoped she was right.

Ben had a department heads' meeting at one o'clock on Tuesdays, so I was on my own for lunch. As soon as Jermaine left the office, Vanessa leaned over to me and whispered, "Should we go shopping?"

"During lunch?"

She shrugged, but her lips lifted in a smile. "Why not? I'm

pretty sure R&T owes you for all those sad lunches you ate at your desk."

I rolled my eyes. "Fine. Where?"

"There's a Victoria's Secret at Herald's Square," she suggested.

"Aren't we supposed to hate them for giving us all eating disorders in the mid-aughts and being owned by, like, a creepy old man who gave half his money to Jeffrey Epstein?"

"Yes, of course we hate them. But there aren't any cute independent boutiques in Midtown that are budget friendly. So it's either that or Macy's."

"Macy's it is, I guess," I said.

"Look at you, being so moral at choosing a different giant corporation, Emma."

"What can I say? I'm perfect."

It was a quick walk up to Macy's on Broadway, but as soon as we walked in, we were accosted by samples and offers of spritzes of perfume. The scents all clashed together to make something monstrous, with a heady sweetness that could only be achieved through chemical alchemy. Christmas music pounded out of speakers discreetly hidden in every nook and crevice. It wasn't classics. Bing Crosby's ghost had long since been laid to rest by the Macy's marketing team. Now it was all Mariah Carey and Kelly Clarkson and ballads sung at impossible octaves about gifts given and received. This was my least favorite version of Christmastime. It was the kind that demanded Instagram pictures around Christmas trees covered in color-coordinated baubles with families and their new poodle mixes, wearing matching Christmas-themed pajamas. It was the kind of Christmas that made me sneer down at people who'd grown up in the suburbs with bay windows that seemed to have been built for showing off their perfectly decorated trees to their neighbors. A single thought stopped my snarky spiral: Did Ben grow up with a window like that?

I kept that question with me as Vanessa and I made our way

to the intimates section. Did Ben's family go to church and then pile around a tree for an annual family photo? Did they smile and laugh and then fight just a little bit? Was there a version of my life—a version I might even be heading toward—where I'd find out for myself? Not this year, of course not this year, but maybe at some point in the future?

My phone rang as Vanessa held up a bra with an uncountable number of straps. It would make me look more like a fish caught in a net than a sexy, confident woman. I shook my head at her as I pulled my phone out of my pocket. My jaw clicked open in surprise. Gaura's name was flashing across the screen.

"Who is that?" Vanessa asked, reading the surprise on my face.

"My stepmother."

"Are you guys close?" She tried to hang the contraption back on the rack, but it kept tangling itself with other bras, the straps reaching out like tentacles.

"No, we're really not. I don't know why she's calling." My stomach dropped. That other call from her all those weeks ago pushed itself to the front of my mind. Had she changed her mind about minding her business?

"Do you think it's an emergency?"

"I don't know," I said, the last word of my sentence catching at something in my throat and only making it out as a whisper.

"You should pick up." Vanessa's voice pulled my eyes to hers. She looked so certain that that was what I should do. It was like my plan to not answer and never think about it again wasn't even something that could occur to her. The phone kept ringing between us. I was frozen. "Pick up!" Her voice flipped into a higher register, as if the mystery of Gaura's call was affecting her as much as it was affecting me.

"Hello?" I answered, hoping my voice sounded normal and keeping my eyes on Vanessa's.

"Emma? It's Gaura." Her voice was quiet.

"Is everything okay?" There was no reason to pretend this was a normal situation or a normal call.

"It's your dad. I thought he would tell you. He meant to tell you when he visited, but… I don't know what happened." This was it, actual bad news. Were they getting divorced? By the sound of her voice, it didn't seem like it. I knew what divorce sounded like. It had undeniable accents of bitterness and rage. Gaura didn't sound angry—she sounded helpless.

"Is he okay?"

"I don't know quite how to say this. I've been meditating on it, but the words aren't coming naturally to me. It's as though they don't want to be said."

"Say it. Whatever it is. Rip the Band-Aid off." Whatever it was, it couldn't be worse than the suspense of this moment.

"Where are you?" she asked instead of putting me out of my misery.

"Macy's. Is it loud?"

"I think I can hear Mariah Carey?"

I'd stopped paying attention to the constant stream of Christmas music pumping out of every nook and cranny of the store. It was doing its work on my subconscious.

"Well, it's December at Macy's. I think Mariah Carey is just part of the deal."

"Right. I haven't been at a store like that in so long." I looked at the stiff lace and spandex all around us. It was leagues away from Gaura's preferred natural fibers.

She took a breath in. A deep one. I could almost hear the one-two-three-in, one-two-three-out count. "Your father's sick. Over the summer—"

"The summer?" I cut in. The leaves had long since fallen to the sidewalks and been turned to dust by the parade of never-ending fashion-forward leather boots.

She ignored me, pressing forward. "Over the summer, he started feeling sick. There was something wrong. Nothing was helping. His skin yellowed. We finally decided to go to a Western doctor, and they did a biopsy of his liver. It was malignant."

I paused, trying to remember the definitions of her words. *Malignant.* As opposed to *benign.* The root words were clear enough. Benign was good. *Bene, Bonne, Benefit, Benevolent.* And malignant was bad. *Mal, Malfunction, Malpractice, Maleficent.* But I couldn't help myself: "So that's bad news?"

"Yes." Her slow yoga voice had returned. She was gaining back her control.

"Cancer?" I said, stuttering through the second syllable.

"Yes."

"Fuck. Does he know you're talking to me?"

"I've been hoping he'd tell you. He said he would tell you in New York, and then he said he would call. He can't bring himself to do it."

He said he'd tell you in New York. He said he'd tell you in New York. He said he'd tell you in New York. The sentence echoed through my mind, bouncing off the memory of our last breakfast in the rented garden apartment. It was me this time. My fault. I didn't let him tell me.

"So, should I call him?"

"That would be best. I know it's a shock, but the sooner, the better. The timelines they've given us haven't been encouraging."

Timelines. I had enough knowledge of my dad to know his timeline wasn't good. He must have been in a terrible way to go to a real doctor. For Gaura to drive him there. I wondered which of the two of them broke first. Who had decided to travel in, wait in hospital lobbies filled with people they didn't trust, and have my dad's blood drawn? He must have been so scared to agree to turn toward the exact thing he'd railed against for so long.

Suddenly, there were thick chunks of the bagel I'd had for breakfast in my throat. In my mouth. And then I was rushing toward the closest cashier, pushing myself behind the register, and grabbing the small receipt-filled trash can. I heard voices. The cashier was squealing in shock. *Oh my god*s ping-ponged around the lingerie section, from customer to customer. The smell of my vomit was mixing with the thick clouds of perfume.

Vanessa was behind me, touching my back lightly, making excuses and apologies. I heard her mention something about pregnancy and morning sickness hitting worst in the afternoon, and the other voices quieted just in time to listen to me vomit again.

I had lived in New York for too long. A whole life was too long. I couldn't walk through any neighborhood without seeing ghosts or having to hide from old memories. I wanted to find somewhere quiet—somewhere quiet that wasn't my apartment—to call my dad. If I went in there and heard the news I knew he was going to tell me, it could infect the place. I might never be able to get the stain of the memory out of my walls. It would drip down and seep between the floorboards. The scent of it would be there no matter how many times I mopped or scrubbed. I'd heard enough bad news in my life to know this was true. The place the news is heard is changed forever. It's why Mom moved us out of that Park Slope apartment after my dad moved upstate—the fights they'd had kept floating back at us or rearing their heads when we watched *Dawson's Creek*. It's why I moved out of the apartment I shared with Susannah, too. The memories, the good and the bad, were plastered all over the walls. They'd been thrown up there in thick globs. The entire place felt like a palette painting, the memories lying there heavy and unblended. I couldn't take it anymore. I couldn't handle trying to make a cup of tea and suddenly remembering that she'd chipped the mug in my hand while imitating Dumbledore running to ask Harry if he'd put his name in the Goblet of Fire. And I really, really wanted to stop stepping into the shower and remembering the time I'd taken a bath after a long night, passed out, and woke up only when my head slipped under the cold water.

So for this phone call, I needed to find a place I wouldn't mind destroying. That I could avoid until I died or moved. It couldn't be somewhere I walked every day, like Madison Square Park, or I'd start avoiding whatever bench I'd foolishly chosen. My lunch walks would lose part of their path. I didn't want to choose a place that was already special, infused with good feelings, like Prospect Park. That had to stay pure.

It was Tuesday, so if I was being a good girl, I'd meet with Lola and then go to the Tuesday meeting. But I wasn't going to do that. I wanted to lick whatever wounds I was about to earn, hide under a bed like a cat, and not let anyone touch me.

Emma: Hey so sorry, I don't feel well. I can't make it today. I'll call tomorrow. Everything is okay.

I had never done that before. This would be the first time since meeting Lola that I missed Tuesday night. I had gone to that Starbucks on the corner of Sixty-Ninth Street with migraines, an ear infection, and blinking away tears more times than I could count.

Lola: You'll be in my prayers ♥

I didn't respond. I'd talk to her tomorrow. I'd tell her everything. I'd be a good girl. Just not today.

My feet turned toward my usual subway, not having any other ideas. The perfect place was eluding me.

Once I was on the train, it started to press in on me. The subway car was crowded. I was standing between two construction workers having a rapid discussion in Spanish and a girl who looked like she'd stepped out of the pages of *Vogue*. She was taller than everyone else, and I couldn't understand whether the buckles on her jacket had any use.

The conductor announced the next stop was Brooklyn Bridge–

City Hall, and before I knew it, I was on the platform and heading up the stairs. I hadn't walked across the bridge in at least ten years. Susannah and I used to do it after long nights out in high school, when we couldn't get enough of New York at night, when crossing the river on a lit-up landmark made us feel like we were on top of the world, when coke pumped through our teenage bloodstreams and we couldn't imagine sitting still or going to sleep, when it was just the two of us.

I remembered how empty it was. One January night, with winter air blowing through our coats and lights of skyscrapers blinking on the dark river, we climbed up on the ancient steel beams. We looked down on the cars—certain death was only twenty feet away. A tumble or two, and my body would have spun into the dark depths below. But those twenty feet felt like infinity. How could we fall? The capillaries in my cheeks had been bursting like cellular fireworks trying to keep me warm. My boots were steady on the rusted steel. Death was twenty feet and an entire lifetime away. There was no way it could touch us.

Those boots and that coat and that girl who had climbed were gone, but the bridge was still there. And I needed the memory it carried. I wanted to feel impervious again.

I realized my mistake as soon as I started up the ramp. People were streaming off and on in numbers that reminded me of the crowds that poured in and out of Times Square at rush hour. This was no small creek bubbling by; it was the smooth and steady force of the Hudson. The Brooklyn Bridge was very different on a warm-for-December evening at sunset than it had been on that icy January morning. Still, I walked on.

The ramp was steep. I didn't remember that, either. I was out of breath when the concrete gave way to wooden planks that blinked black as cars passed quickly underway. I was grateful for the constant delay of families taking group photos. I started to sweat under my wool coat. To my right, New York Harbor opened out into the ocean. The East and Hudson Rivers wedded and poured into the orange horizon where they'd eventually meet the sun as it set over Staten Island. To my left, there was the clog of bridges piled on bridges, the suspension wires of the Manhattan, Williamsburg, and Fifty-Ninth Street Bridges all crossing over each other in my view. Nothing was still. People, water, and cars were churning around me. There was no way I could climb up on the railings of this version of the Brooklyn Bridge.

I found a scrap of space on a bench under the first tower beside a couple with their legs intertwined. I put on my headphones. I pressed the call button. I listened to three rings.

"Hello?" There was a slight buzz to my dad's voice. It wasn't too thick, though.

"Hi," I said.

"Gaura said she called you." I could never guess what he expected from me.

"I'm sorry—I didn't know if you had wanted to talk to me yourself or not, but—" A young woman was setting up a ring light and tripod a few feet away from me. I watched as she did a TikTok dance as people moved around her. Such a big smile.

"Well, I don't know what she told you. But it's cancer."

"She said. In your liver?"

"Yeah." His voice had changed, gone softer. A lump rose in my throat. I wiped my palms on my jeans. I wanted to know how bad it was, what stage it was, and how much time was left. But I didn't know how to ask.

"I'm really sorry, Dad." My voice was softer now, too. I was speaking around the tears that were stuck in my throat.

"No man can live forever, but it's like that's news to my consciousness. I keep having nightmares, and they're so on the nose, Em, you'd laugh."

"Yeah?"

"I'm in a hallway filled with clocks, and they're exploding one by one as I pass. And I'm running and tripping over myself like a fool, trying to get out, but I guess I keep running out of time."

"Are you scared?"

"In the dream? Or right now?"

"Both." The tears in my throat had somehow found a way to silently stream out of my eyes. I mopped them up with the sleeve of my sweater.

"I'm terrified." I'd never heard him say he was scared before. We'd only really spoken of death once. I was sixteen and trying to date a guy who was trying to be a graffiti artist, so I'd brought thick-tipped markers upstate with me on the bus, and I'd stashed my tag everywhere: the Port Authority bathroom, the grimy Trailways bus windows, and even on the tile of the kitchen backsplash in my father's house.

He'd laughed when he saw it the following day. I didn't expect him to reprimand me—he never did. I thought he might critique my style (I never could match his natural talent with a pen), but he hadn't done that, either. Instead, he'd grabbed the graffiti pen and put the last stanza of a poem next to my crudely written name.

Do not go gentle into that good night.

Rage, rage against the dying of the light.

"It's Dylan Thomas. Did they teach you that in school?"

I shook my head and rolled my eyes, annoyed that another attempt at teenage rebellion had been ignored. Murmuring to himself about the state of public education, he went to his bookshelf and shoved a book of poetry into my hand.

"Read it," he demanded.

My eyes had skimmed over the stark black text on the yellowed page.

"Do you get what it's about? There are two ways a man can face death, with gentleness or rage, and eventually, we all have to choose."

"I can come up there," I said, my breath bringing me back to the bridge, but my head was still full of Thomas's poem. In it, he begged his father to rage against the dying of the light, but I wished gentleness for mine.

"Good. Gaura's planning a celebration of life for the twelfth. Twelve/twelve and all that."

"I'll be there." I wanted to ask what a celebration of life was, if it was something they'd invented or something they'd seen on their travels. The Christmas party was on the ninth, so I'd take the bus up right after. It was ridiculous planning anything around the Richter & Thomas holiday party, but after all these months working on it, a part of me wanted to see all our work come to life.

In the moment of silence between us, I heard the breathing exercise he was doing. A hard inhale for one-two-three and then a soft exhale for one-two-three-four. I wouldn't have been able to manage it.

"Are you going to get treatment?" I couldn't help but ask.

"Not anymore. It wouldn't buy me much time." He swallowed hard. "It's not a comfortable thing, cancer."

I wanted to say I wished he'd told me earlier, that I wished I could have been there to hold his hand during chemo. That I would have been a good daughter, if for this moment only. But those words didn't come to the tip of my tongue. Instead, my body remembered the breathing exercise he was doing, the memory of learning it in that class in Chelsea floating around me like smoke. I was able to count our breaths; even over all the noise of the city, they shared a beat.

FIFTEEN

I cried getting off the bench. I cried walking down the ramp. And I cried the whole walk from the foot of the bridge to my apartment in Crown Heights. A few people's glances lingered on me, but most people let me walk by without comment. I wasn't sobbing—there was no sound coming from my throat. I felt like I was in the hallway from my dad's dream, running with him as clocks exploded all around us, the shattered glass and machine mechanisms piercing themselves into my feet. There wasn't enough time for our relationship to change. This was it. It was going to have these miles, these resentments, these failures. This was us.

I'd thought in big moments like this my mind would flash to drinking, that I'd remember the best way to escape painful thoughts was to not have them at all. In AA qualification after AA qualification, I'd heard about bad news interrupting a sober life and forcing it backward. But that wasn't what came to my mind. Instead, I thought of my first full day sober.

I'd woken up with vomit all over my shirt. It was crusted onto my chin. It had pooled in the hollow of my throat. A half-digested two-inch piece of pizza crust was on the pillow next to me. I didn't jump out of bed and start cleaning myself up. That wouldn't really have been possible, as you know if you've ever thrown up all over yourself in your sleep. No, I just stared at my popcorn ceiling and felt my skin grow tighter under the weight of my vomit. My body didn't feel like it could move. But my mouth was so dry; my lips were cracked with thirst. I didn't get up. I could only move my eyes from one brown water stain on the ceiling to the next.

This wasn't the first time I'd woken up in a pool of vomit. But it was the first time Susannah wasn't in the room across the hall, the first time she wouldn't be there to help me change my sheets and make light of it. My new roommate, Sydney, who worked at a financial firm, wouldn't think it was very funny. She might even be repulsed—or worse, worried.

As the sun rose higher in the sky, my room filled with unfiltered light. I had venetian blinds stuck at such severe slants they looked like cartoon ski slopes. Most days, I could sleep through the sunrise, but on that morning, I watched the tiny slivers grow brighter and brighter from my bed.

People were waking up and going about their lives. And I wasn't. If I didn't show up to work, people would assume I was sleeping off a bender. It'd happened enough times before. If I didn't show up for a few days, they might think I'd run off somewhere. Eventually, they might realize I was dead. They'd be disturbed in the moment, but I'd soon fade from their memory. Honestly, I bet it would only take a few weeks.

If I never got up again, it would be the hardest on Sydney. She'd be the one who would smell the weird scent pouring from beneath my door. Who wouldn't see me for days and then eventually realize a mouse hadn't died behind the stove. She'd be the one who would have to gather her bravery to open my bedroom door—I glanced over; it was unlocked, so she wouldn't have to break it down—and see my rotting corpse. She might scream. But then she'd call 9-1-1, or was a drunk's dead body not an emergency? She might get transferred to 3-1-1, I suppose. But the city would eventually come. For the rest of her life, she'd remember me as the dead body she found—the horror of it—but she wouldn't feel my loss.

Mom would feel like a failure in some way, I'm sure. But her frustrations with me would be over, and she'd soon be free to gallivant around Europe as a retired and unencumbered woman in her sixties should. She'd be fine. She would find some peace.

Same with Susannah. By the time she found out, it might be weeks later. She wouldn't have to deal with the immediacy or the shock.

I lay there, watching the sunrise, and knew it could go on rising without me.

Did I want to keep doing this? There was no one and nothing I was living for. It felt like it would be so easy to die. The more I thought about it, lying there until the shadows started growing long in my room, the more it felt like the best option.

Then I realized I had to shit. Like, badly enough that I was going to shit the bed if I didn't get up. And for a second, I thought, okay, well, that's part of death. People shit themselves. When Sydney found my body, I would be covered in both vomit and excrement.

But I just couldn't tolerate that. There was still some part of me that longed for dignity, a part that raged against death instead of accepting it. So I got up and went to the bathroom.

Then I started going through the motions of life. I took a shower. I threw my clothes away and took out the garbage so Sydney wouldn't smell vomit in our kitchen. I drank a glass of water.

Those simple things took hours.

But finally, I'd sat back down in my bedroom, looked in the mirror, and decided that if I didn't want to die, I would have to live very differently.

In the past year and change I'd done that. I became a person I could have barely imagined as I stared up at that ceiling.

I turned my key in my apartment door and opened it to the new, different life I'd built for myself. Here was my hard-won little room on the top floor. I was proud of it, but it wouldn't be enough to comfort me tonight.

Mom picked up on the first ring. "Emma? You okay?" She always answered the phone like that. As if she was constantly expecting me not to be okay, which, if I was very honest with myself, were usually the times when I called her.

"Where are you?" I asked, kicking off my shoes and sitting down on my couch.

"Home. What's going on?" Her voice sped up; I could hear her anxiety, always at a constant buzz when I was around, kick up a few notches.

"I got some bad news from my dad." I placed my hand under my sweater. I could feel my body under my fingertips. There were organs there, breath moving in and out of my lungs causing my whole body to pulse. I was alive. The skin cells of my hand and my stomach recognized each other, warmed each other.

"What does he want? Whatever it is, don't go up there again. You don't owe him anything—and the last time was such a disaster." I'd called Mom from the bus station on my way home from the Saturn's Return party.

"He doesn't want me—" I stopped. I was about to say he didn't want me to come upstate, but that wasn't exactly true. "He's sick."

"So? What the fuck is his wife calling herself again? Gupta? Tell her to take care of him." I could feel Mom's anxiety turning to rage. It was unlikely she'd have a change of heart when she heard the whole story. Her sympathies—long hidden these last twenty years—wouldn't suddenly burst from under floorboards and out of forgotten flowerpots. They were gone forever. Nowhere to be found. The flowerpots had cracked. The floorboards had no secret compartments. What you saw was what you got. What she said about my dad, she meant.

"He's like really sick."

"What does 'really sick' mean?"

"Cancer."

"What kind?"

"A bad kind."

"He's dying?" she asked. Her voice hadn't lost its edge.

"Yes." I went back to trying to feel my breath through my fingertips. That thing that had lodged itself in my throat on the bridge was trying to claw its way through my esophagus again. I was going to cry. There wasn't any stopping it. I tried to take a gulp of breath instead.

I could hear Mom's breath on the other end of the line. Her fiddling—whatever it had been—had quieted. For a moment, we were both still together. "Oh, Robert," she murmured. It was good to hear him called by his old name. Sometimes I played a sentence in my head when I was around him and he introduced himself as Kirtan. He had made me memorize it before my first field trip in kindergarten. *My name is Emma Finley. My dad's name is Robert Finley. We live at 311 Fourth Street in Brooklyn.* I could still see the way he nodded seriously when I got it right. And then Mom said, "Can I come over?"

"Please."

I thought that when she sailed into the room, she somehow also would have stopped the earth from spinning. That all this pain floating around me would be erased when she laid her palm on my forehead. It wasn't. She came to me, rushing to the couch to give me a hug. But the sun kept setting, and the dried salt on my cheeks from my earlier sobbing didn't evaporate.

"I brought Zabar's," she said. And that, at least, was something. She pulled out everything bagels, lox, cream cheese, and babka, setting them in a line along my coffee table. They looked like little toy soldiers. In Mom's house, comfort food was always the first line of defense against any overwhelming feelings.

"So," I said, watching her cut into a bagel. "I'm going to go up there."

"Emma," she said, "you still don't have to. It will be horrible. It won't be safe. You have to put your sobriety first. I don't think you should go."

"Mom. I have to."

"You don't have to. You don't. It will be terrible."

"It already is terrible."

"He was always so healthy," she said. "Healthy as a horse. Never got a cold. Never even a headache. He could always keep going."

"You haven't seen him in a long time," I said. I remembered how tired he looked walking through my apartment door. How had I not known?

"That's true." She had a bagel in her hand, schmeared and lox-ed, but unbitten. "When you go up there, will you call me every day?"

A ghost of a laugh slipped out of my mouth. "I'll try." I had no idea what it would be like when I got up there. His body would have deteriorated more. He'd be sicker, frailer. The only other person I'd seen with cancer was Susannah's mom. But I didn't know her when she was well. By the time I met Suze, her mom was walking with a cane and wearing brightly colored silk scarves around her scalp. When she passed, I helped Susannah put together the slideshow for the memorial. It was only then that I saw what her mom looked like before, what she really looked like. She'd been so full of life. The difference between the woman in the photos and the woman I'd known was stark. We pulled particularly sweet or funny pictures of her mom out of albums and took them to school to scan them. Where were all the old photos of my dad? I could feel the lump in my throat begin to rise when I realized I didn't have a single picture of him.

"Will you distract me?" I asked Mom.

"Of course," she said. But no distractions followed. I knew her mind well enough to see it spinning, trying, and failing to think of anything but my dad. It broke my heart a little bit that this situation was beyond even my always-capable mother.

"With something nice," I continued. "How's David?" We'd met for lunch a few weeks back; this was the first time I was seeing her since then. Time, and the pleasant diversion of starting things with Ben, had eroded the panic I'd initially felt at learning about David, and his and Mom's plans to move in together, miles from Ninety-Sixth Street.

"Are you thinking of David as something nice?"

"Well, he's nice to you, isn't he?"

She nodded in response, her mouth full. He was nice to her; I could see it. There were little moments where love burst between them: when they laughed about a terrible theater production, when he spilled a drop of coffee on his crisp white button-down and she wordlessly dipped her napkin into her water glass and began to dab at it, and when he eagerly showed me he followed Richter & Thomas on Instagram and made sure to like every post (something I most certainly did not do). I felt a little uncomfortable that closeness between them could bloom like this without me knowing anything about it, but I couldn't be mad. Not when she seemed so happy.

"Since when are the walls blue in here?" Mom asked.

"It's Sea Mist."

"Okay, when did the walls get Sea Mist–ed in here?"

"Dad and I did it together. When he was in town that first weekend in October."

"Oh, well, it looks nice. He's always had a good eye."

I nodded, and shoved babka into my mouth, hoping it would dull the ache in my throat.

★ ★ ★

I emailed Amy and Jermaine in the morning, telling them that whatever had sent me home yesterday had only gotten worse. It was the first time I'd called out since getting my job. I just didn't want to leave the apartment, and I really didn't want to smile tightly and nod as I passed people in the hall. I didn't want Jermaine to tell me to take one more stab at a new header image on an email. I didn't want Vanessa to look at me wide-eyed, wondering why I hadn't requested leave or told the rest of the office about my dad. I wouldn't be able to do any of it. I'd fuck up somehow. Crack. Lines of tears would drill themselves into whatever makeup I caked on to cover up my pallor. I would say something weird. I'd run out.

Lola had texted me after the meeting last night and wanted me to call to check in today. She asked me to let her know a time I'd be free. She had caught on to me calling her when she was hosting meditation classes. She knew something was up.

Instead of calling her, I weighed the pros and cons of taking up smoking again.

Pros:

- It would feel great.
- It's not considered a drug in AA, so it'd be like getting a freebie.

Cons:

- It took weeks of giving myself hiccups from aggressively chewing Nicorette to quit last time.
- Cancer apparently did run in my family.

After a few hours of pacing around and listening to Taylor Swift while I cried, Ben texted me.

Ben: Hey, I heard you're sick today. Hope you feel better soon!

I thought about how it would feel to put my head on his chest as I tried and failed to fall asleep, or how his warm hands would feel against my back as he pulled me toward him. I hadn't thought about the reality of looking him in the eye and telling him what was going on with me. That I knew he'd been waiting for me to be a normal adult woman for over a month, and that we finally had this romantic evening planned, but there was something else wrong with me now. What would I even say? *Hey, Ben, I'm actually not sick, I just needed a day off because… Well, do you remember me telling you about my somewhat tense relationship with my father? Turns out he's dying. Bummer, right? So rain check on the sex!*

He was Ben, so he'd be kind and understanding. It wasn't that I was afraid of his reaction. How could I be after the steady way he held my hand when I struggled to find the words to tell him about being sober? But I wanted to stand strong next to him, not collapse and be carried by him.

I'd told Vanessa what Gaura had told me as we made our way out of the brightly lit labyrinth that was Macy's during the holiday season. The vomiting was so weird, and she'd covered for me. I remember how she'd tried to politely swallow her questions but a few snuck out. *It's late stage but they're just telling you now? Did you talk to him or only to her?* I told her I'd tell Jermaine another time but couldn't handle speaking to anyone else about it until I spoke to my dad. But even now that the conversation was over and my bus ticket was bought—I was going up there a week from now with no return ticket—I still hadn't found the words to tell Jermaine. And I suddenly realized that I couldn't tell Jermaine if I hadn't told Ben. It'd be terrible if Ben heard it from someone else. God knows Amy was never going to keep her mouth shut.

So, it was settled. I couldn't tell the people at work until I told

Ben. And I couldn't tell Ben until after our date, or it would be ruined. So this news would have to sit inside me until the weekend was over. No big deal. I'd always been good at withholding information and keeping secrets close to my chest.

It would only be a few days.

Emma: Just a bad headache. I couldn't take the thought of looking at screens all day. I'll be back tomorrow!

In my kitchen, I checked my phone with my hair dripping a trail of water behind me. I had notifications. They weren't from Ben. They were from Lola. She wanted me to call her. She'd texted, and she'd left a voice message. The repeated efforts didn't make me feel cared for. I felt like I was in trouble, like a small child who'd caused too much mischief in class. Clicking on Lola's name to call her felt like a similar act of courage to opening the door to the principal's office, knowing that I'd have to report my own crimes.

"Emma?" she answered immediately.

"Hi."

"I'm so glad you called. I've been worried about you. It's not like you to miss a Tuesday meeting." I didn't know if I'd imagined it, or if there was judgment in her tone. Was she worried? Or was one of her sponsees not showing up just a bad look for her? In HG, sponsorship groups sat together. Lola's own sponsor and her sponsees sat ahead of us. Just like Lola checked in on me, there was someone else to check in on her. If the women she was responsible for didn't show up or didn't seem to be on a good path, it might reflect badly on her. Or maybe she was genuinely concerned, but I didn't have it in me to face that.

"I didn't feel up to it, like I said."

"Emma, Tuesday meetings are important. It's the one day a week our whole community comes together. I know you know this."

I didn't want to talk to her about my dad. I never did. Ever since I did my fourth and fifth steps, where I wrote down all my resentments that I'd ever felt and then confessed them to Lola, I'd hated to talk about him with her. We'd sat together in a diner, neither ordering more than coffee, the waiter hovering close by and continually offering slices of pie. My list was long, and "resentments" were loosely defined. This list was how HG decided to conduct the fourth step: *Made a searching and fearless moral inventory of ourselves.* It was essentially a confession. What had I done wrong? What was I still upset about? What thoughts were poisoning my soul? I was supposed to write them all down and tell Lola. She was supposed to tell me that I wasn't alone, but also point out what character defects had led me astray. The idea was that I could move on after I'd confessed. My misdeeds and my misthoughts wouldn't weigh me down anymore. They wouldn't drive me to drink.

I had a long list about my dad. Most were childhood memories. Moments when I wanted a dad like I saw in the movies, or like my friends had, and the difference between him and the ideal felt like an unbearable bitter taste in my mouth. Eventually, I grew used to it. But even thinking back to being eleven and standing on a chair to reach the kitchen phone only to hear his slowly spoken excuses about why he wouldn't be able to make my middle-school ballet recital was unbearable.

When I told Lola this memory, when I said it still made me want to throw a fist into the cold laminate table below us, she told me that I had "unrealistic expectations." That my father had showed himself to me and that I should only expect what he was capable of. That he was sick with his own alcoholism, that he should be pitied, not punished. I nodded. I crossed the memory off my list, as I was supposed to after voicing it aloud, but I didn't snip the strings that tied it to my mind. She was wrong. Lola was wrong. She had a dad who made her paint the porch when she stayed out too late. A dad who taught her to fucking drive. All I'd ever expected was what she had. How was that unrealistic? Lola didn't understand that. She didn't understand what felt so true to me—I had been wronged. And yes, I had also grown up to wrong others. But both things could be true. Some things weren't the fault of my disease. They were the fault of someone else.

I felt fiercely protective of the girl whose feet dug into the smooth wood of the kitchen chair and listened to a grown man's excuses, hoping they were true. Grown-Up Emma, who got so drunk from the liquor I stole from the bar I worked at that I threw up during my shift, deserved to be examined, but Kid Emma, who wanted a father who showed up, was righteous. So I didn't want to talk to Lola about my dad. But his news was the reason I'd missed the Tuesday meeting. It was the truth, and it was a good reason. It was a solid excuse. It would make me righteous.

"I had a very difficult call with my father right before," I said, taking a deep breath before I continued. "He has cancer. Late stage."

"Oh, Emma. I'm so sorry."

"Yeah," I said.

"I'm sure that was a terrifying call."

"It was." I didn't want to dig further into it. Exploding clocks crashed into my mind.

"I completely understand that you didn't feel like you could come to the meeting, but, Emma, now is the time to lean on your community."

I closed my eyes against her words.

"I don't want you to isolate—if you hide your pain away, it will feed your disease. When we're struggling is when we need the program."

"I just need a few days, Lola."

"Emma, I'm going to make a recommendation. You don't have to take it, of course, but I think it would be for the best. I think you should still try to go to three meetings this week. If you can, I think you should make up Tuesday's meeting. Push yourself to be in community. It will be healing." She said all the words quickly, as though they'd been pressing up against the dam of her teeth and then, with a breath, were finally released.

"Okay," I said, hating the sound of the word and hating Lola.

SIXTEEN

Because of the vomiting-in-Macy's incident, I had no cute underwear to wear for my date with Ben. I hunted for acceptable underwear in my dresser but only found collapsed elastic and jokey thongs covered in sayings like *Yes, Daddy.* The closest thing to respectable I found was pair of high-waisted shapewear that I longed to put under whatever it was I decided on wearing. But even if they would make me feel more confident during dinner, the inevitable moment when Ben ran his hands toward my stomach and was greeted not with soft skin but with tightly woven nylon would be awkward enough that it would ruin whatever moment we were creating.

Not that we hadn't had enough awkward moments already. They seemed to be constant in the lead-up to this dinner, crashing against our shoreline with the steady beat of waves rather than the surprising interruptions of wayward ships. Just today, he'd surprised me by swinging by M&C at 4:57 p.m., easily chatting with Jermaine for a few minutes, and then with a light smile and a hint of color in his cheeks, asking me if I was ready to go. I couldn't do anything but agree, not in front of everyone. So it wasn't until the office door latched shut that I looked up at him and said, "I thought I'd go home and change first."

"You don't have to." He shrugged and pulled my hand into his own.

"Oh, but I haven't shaved my legs," I said. This was, surprisingly, not a lie. I had planned on shaving them tonight after work because the longer I waited, the smoother my skin would be. But more importantly, and not mentioned, was that I hadn't showered in three days. The time kept slipping past me when I was at home. Hours spent googling what late-stage liver cancer felt like (spoiler alert: really bad) became late nights watching videos about people getting stuck in caves and dying: trapped, panicked, fingers raw from desperately trying to claw their way out.

I'd seen one with a dignified British man giving a tour of the Yorkshire Mossdale Caverns, where six men died in 1967 when the caves suddenly flooded after a storm. He pointed to a little crevice in the ceiling of a tunnel, no larger than a New York sewer pipe, and said that two of the bodies were found there. It was interesting, he claimed, that the two men had chosen that spot, squeezing themselves together. As they were experienced cavers and knew Mossdale well, they knew it wasn't a passage out of the cave. Had they been trying to escape the floodwater? he wondered, or were they acting as dying animals do and simply moving forward and upward? Even though the crevice held no hope for them, they couldn't help but search for a way out.

The story calmed me because that was certainly a worse death than the one my dad was facing. I didn't want to search for any hopeful stories with miracle turnarounds. I wanted to be sure that people had faced worse than what he was about to. That they'd been in more pain, that their fear had settled more deeply into their bones. But all of these rabbit holes took time, and I couldn't bring them into the shower with me; the water would have drowned out the sound of my laptop even if I left it playing on the toilet seat. It wasn't normally a huge deal if I didn't shower every day—I just had to put more perfume on before going to work. That wouldn't cut it tonight.

"I don't care if you don't shave your legs." Ben laughed and gave me a lasting smile. I wanted to join him in it, to drink his expression down like ice-cold vodka and dull my pulsing thoughts. But I had to clean myself first and put on my best pair of CVS underwear.

"But I do," I said, trying to make my smile flirtatious and knowing. It worked because his cheeks turned a deeper pink. Poor Ben with his transparent moods. If my skin were that reactive, he would've been able to tell what I was feeling wasn't exactly flirtatious.

The extra time might not have been worth it, though, because it left me here, with my hair only puffier from having been blow-dried, standing naked in front of a closet that held nothing that would make me feel sexy and beautiful, and a never-ending number of useless scraps of cotton. I wanted to burn them all.

I sat down on my bed and closed my eyes, trying to take in all the advice and say all the prayers I'd learned this past year at once. Fragments of the Serenity Prayer—*accept what I cannot change*—and Third Step Prayer—*relieve me of the bondage of self*—danced across my consciousness, but Vanessa's voice lingered the longest: *You can always just wear black.*

Ben lived on the third floor of a small brick building in Gowanus. All around, there were new blocky buildings, each a copy of the next except for one mutation. When he gave me his address, that's what I expected to walk up to, something with wide glass doors and a doorman in a jean jacket rather than a double-breasted gold-buttoned coat. And although those buildings surrounded his block, there wasn't a single one on it. Carroll Street between Third and Nevins was still full of bricks that had been placed there in the building boom of a century and a half ago, when industry and the men who made its wheels spin filled Gowanus. Now it was full of Whole Foods and tech workers in three-hundred-dollar sweatshirts. There was a coffee shop on the ground floor, and I couldn't help but wonder if Ben was a regular. If the baristas knew his name, his order, and the way his top left canine folded over the tooth next to it, only visible when he smiled wide.

It couldn't have been more than thirty seconds from when I texted Ben to let him know I was downstairs to when he flung the door open—the wide smile I'd just been thinking of on his face.

"Hi," he said, almost breathless from running down the stairs. He was in a black T-shirt and black jeans. Had Vanessa given him advice, too? He wasn't wearing a belt. His jeans were hanging on his hips, revealing just the edge of his boxers. The way he was holding the door open gave me a view of the tendons in his bicep. I'd seen him in a T-shirt before. Surely I had.

"Hi," I breathed back. The way his smile got wider when I spoke pushed everything else out of my mind. There was no bad news to tell him. There was no world outside of this block and this apartment. Here, everything would be still except for the energy pulsing between us.

"Is this a two-bedroom?" I asked as soon as he opened the door to his apartment at the top of the stairs. I couldn't help myself. I should have said something about the elegant way the table was set—with unlit candles standing tall in brass candlesticks—or the delicious smell of caramelizing onions that hung in the air. Instead, I wondered immediately about the square footage and what price he was getting; I was a New Yorker after all, and it's not a sport that unites us here, it's the love of the hunt for a great apartment at a good deal.

"I got super lucky. I took the second bedroom from a guy I met on Craigslist when I first graduated, and then he happened to be moving out to live with his girlfriend right when I got a promotion, so I didn't need another roommate."

"It's huge." I was standing in the center of the living room, still wearing the black peacoat I wore every day.

"It's eight hundred square feet on a good day," Ben said, stepping closer to me.

"And on a bad day?" He was close enough that I could feel the warmth of him, but not close enough to touch.

"Seven hundred and fifty," he whispered into my ear as he reached for the top button of my coat. I turned to him, unthinking, and then our lips connected and his hands were slipping my jacket off, dropping it to the floor. I was on tiptoe, surging up toward him, my body begging for the kiss not to end before my mind was even aware it was happening.

"I came for your coat," he laughed, leaning his forehead against mine.

I looked at it, a pile of black wool stark against the shining walnut floor. He must have mopped for me. "You got it."

"There's dinner." His voice was low and quiet, darting toward hoarse.

"Is there really? It wasn't just a ruse?" I asked.

He stepped away from me, picking up my coat from where it had fallen. On his way to the neat hooks by the door, he looked me over. Our outfits matched almost exactly: black jeans, black shirt. Only mine wasn't a well-lived-in black tee, but an ancient American Apparel long-sleeve scoop-neck shirt I'd probably stolen in high school. It had rarely been worn because when I was drinking, I thought it wasn't sexy enough, and now that I was sober, everything about it felt too tight. "You look good," Ben said. They were simple words, but it seemed like he was restraining himself, like he wanted to say more or touch me more. That's what I wanted, too.

"Thank you. You do, too." I took a step closer.

He turned away with a slight cough. "I just have to finish one thing, and then we can eat." I wondered if I was making him nervous. It was clear from the table settings and the mopped floor that he had a careful plan for this evening, a well-thought-out order of events. I didn't want to disturb them, so long as they turned off the racing part of my mind, the part still stuck back in my apartment, thinking about caverns and cancer.

"What's for dinner?" I asked, following him into the kitchen.

"Roast chicken—do you know Thomas Keller's salt-and-pepper recipe?" he said, bending over to open the oven door. I could see the heat rush out as he closed his eyes against it.

"Not at all." I thought of Mom's failed chicken. I could tell based on the scent that this would be something else entirely. My mouth watered. "I almost expected dinner to be burnt, the way it is in all the movies."

"What movies?" he said, taking the chicken out. The skin had bubbled and broken.

"You know, the movies that star, like, Meg Ryan and Katherine Heigl, or whoever's the Meg Ryan or Katherine Heigl of Gen Z."

"So, romantic comedies?" His voice was teasing.

"The girl invites the guy over for dinner and fucks it up somehow because she's so nervous or like a working woman who doesn't cook, but then it's okay because he likes her anyway, even though they can barely see each other through the smoke. That's how it goes."

"So there's not one where the guy invites the girl over and he doesn't fuck it up?"

"Must have gotten stalled in production."

He shrugged. "Real life is too boring."

As we sat down to eat, my gaze snagged on a small Charlie Brown–style Christmas tree sitting in a too-big stand in front of his living room window. He'd put it on an out-of-place-looking end table, the kind of thing that belonged next to a bed, not in front of a window. "You have a Christmas tree?" I asked, as though I thought my eyes might be deceiving me.

"Old habits die hard. Breast or thigh?" Steam poured out of the chicken as he cut into it.

"I haven't had one in years. Where'd you get the ornaments?"

"I stole my favorites from my mom's house." When my eyes met his, he turned a pointed gaze to the chicken.

"Oh, breast. Thanks. Is your mom a big Christmas person? Are you going up there for the holidays?"

"Yeah, Christmas is her primary hobby. She puts a Christmas tree in every single room of the house." He took a bite of his drumstick, but quickly swallowed it down at my shocked expression. "Half of them are fake. It's not like she drags real-live, six-foot trees into the bathroom."

"But there is one in the bathroom?" I asked between bites of broccoli.

He nodded. "It's tiny. And plastic. It goes next to the toothbrush stand."

"I'm honestly kind of jealous. We only had a tree when I was, like, a kid-kid. These days my mom and I just trade presents over the coffee table."

"Are you gonna be at your mom's place for Christmas?"

"Oh no. She's going to be celebrating with her partner, David. They're going away just the two of them." She'd offered to cancel their Vermont Airbnb when she'd come over earlier in the week, but there wasn't a need since I'd be away, also.

"Oh, do you—"

I saw it on his face. He was so kind, he couldn't bear to think of me alone at Christmas. "I'll be up at my dad's."

Tension eased from between his brows. "Sweet. In Phoenicia, right?"

"Yeah." Now was the moment. Hand-delivered to me by the Universe. I could tell him why I was going there for Christmas, about what would greet me in Phoenicia. It wasn't as if I could disappear from the office after the holiday party. He'd wonder why I was gone. I had to tell him. Now. My hands were sweaty against my silver-plated fork. It would just be words. They would come out of my mouth, and he would react to them. He would be kind. But then what? All the mopping and the cooking and the putting of candles in candlesticks that he'd done would be ruined. No, it could wait. What was one more day? "I can't believe the holiday party is finally next week. What will Amy do with her time now that it's over?"

He laughed. "Did you hate the Fun Team?"

I thought for a moment. "I guess it wasn't all bad." I almost said more, but I stopped myself before telling him I was grateful for the opportunity to have planned the world's most mediocre office holiday party, since it meant I got to sit next to him once a week. "Did you hate— Oh wait, you nominated yourself, so you must like party planning at least a little bit."

He paused his fork on the way to his mouth and raised his eyebrows.

"What?"

"You must have figured out why I'm on the Fun Team."

My heart started to beat faster, but I still said, "I haven't, honestly."

"Emma." He paused as if giving me one last chance to say it myself. I wouldn't. I couldn't tolerate being wrong. "I nominated myself after Jermaine nominated you."

My heart exploded, but I tried not to show it on my face.

"Is that too weird?" he asked. "Should I have kept it to myself? I thought it was obvious. It wasn't like I thought about it beforehand—I heard your name and then my own popped out. I couldn't stop thinking about you. You were so funny, and cute, and beautiful." He was rambling.

I put my hand on his. "It's so nice. It's what I was hoping you would say, but I didn't want to assume." I gripped his hand tighter, trying to make sure he knew how I felt: "I loved being on the Fun Team with you, Ben. It was my favorite part of every Wednesday, and Wednesday became my favorite day of the week."

I couldn't quite express the depths of my feelings, but it must have been close enough because he stood up and asked, "Are you done with dinner?"

I looked at my plate. I'd barely started, taken two bites at most, but I stood with him and said, "God, yes."

And then, we were on the bed.

All I could feel was the weight of him on top of me and the heat of his hands against the soft skin of my stomach. Want pooled between my legs—something deep and dark I wasn't sure I'd ever felt before. He left wet kisses up and down my neck, the sound of them mixed with his strained breathing eclipsing anything else I could hear. Gone were the usual wail of sirens and hum of chatter that covered New York in a constant blanket of sound. It was just him and me. I could taste him on my tongue, smell the musk of his deodorant, and below that, just faintly, his own masculine scent. It felt ancient, primordial; how badly I wanted that entire scent, the smell of a man, of *this* man, to cover me completely. And how I could feel him. His lips against mine and then moving across my neck, my collarbone, just below my ear and back to my lips again. His hands moving across my body, leaving everything he touched aflame: my waist, my denim-clad thighs, my hips. And his skin below my hands: the muscles of his biceps rippling beneath my fingers, the smooth expanse of his back, the damp silk of his hair. The strain of him pushing against his jeans, and pushing the seam of my own pants into me, a tiny hint of what it would feel like when we took off our clothes. Because we were still wearing all our clothes. I was completely out of my mind from *kissing.*

I opened my eyes to see him looking down at me, his lips a deep shade of maple-leaf red. He reached for the button of my jeans, asking, "Is this okay?"

I nodded and reached for his in return. We separated briefly, him rolling over to hurry off his pants as I peeled mine down my legs. He ripped his shirt off while he was at it, pulling it over his head from the back of his neck in the way only men do. I reached for the edge of my own, wanting to mirror his every movement.

And then suddenly, he was back on top of me, the heat of his skin searing my own. His lips felt wetter against my neck, his body slotted between my legs, and what I'd felt earlier when we had two pairs of jeans between us was now solid and real and hot. Cotton on cotton was an entirely different feeling than denim on denim.

"You're so beautiful," he said. His eyes were closed, but his hands were everywhere, running up my legs and down my arms, resting and squeezing at my waist and breasts. He was seeing me with his hands instead of his eyes. "So soft."

I believed him. I must have felt soft because everything about him felt the opposite. His chest, his stomach, his thighs were all firm and unyielding. We were so close to very much not taking it slow anymore.

My CVS underwear was going from damp to soaking where our bodies met. I'd never felt any touch as electric as his. It was all-encompassing, but I wasn't sure if it was because I'd never had anyone touch me when I was in full capacity of my senses before or because I'd never wanted anyone to touch me as badly as I wanted Ben to.

But as his hand dipped below the loose elastic of my underwear, a wave of thoughts crashed in my mind, breaking through the haze of lust. *What if I'm bad at this sober? What if I get too clingy and intense? What if my vagina is deformed in some way and I've just never noticed before?* I took a shuddering breath, and he misunderstood it, pulling me tighter against him. The breath didn't come back into my lungs. The sudden fear I couldn't name had frozen my body. My heart was thumping to the beat of *what-if,* and I couldn't take all the possibilities coming to mind. Especially the ones answering the questions: *What if he doesn't like me as much as I like him? What if we break up in two weeks? What if this all means so much more to me than it does to him?* The worst part of my mind whispered back: *You'd be broken all over again.* I felt like those men stuck for eternity in Mossdale Caverns. I needed to claw my way out of this.

"Ben," I said, but it was too quiet. It was almost a whisper.

He whispered my name back to me, rough as sandpaper in my ear.

"Ben. Ben." I pushed up at his chest.

His lips left my body. His hands left my body. His weight left my body. "Sorry. Too fast?" he asked, rolling over to lie next to me. I looked over and saw his chest blotched with pink and rushing to the speed of his heartbeat. It was just like his cheeks when he was embarrassed or flirty. Clouds of rose-colored skin bloomed where he'd been pressed against me. He was fully here, in this bed with me.

I turned from him and looked to the ceiling. There weren't any water stains or spots where mold was creeping through. It was smooth. I'd never seen a ceiling so perfect.

"Emma?" Ben ran a finger down my arm from my shoulder to my elbow, leaving goose bumps in his wake. "You okay?"

"I… I just…" No more words came out. I couldn't look at him. I was suddenly sure that he was going to change his mind about me. He'd see the fear in my face and realize this was too complicated for him. He of the silk hair and toned abs and perfect ceiling didn't need this much drama to sleep with a girl.

"We don't have to do this tonight. Let's go finish dinner, huh?" He sat up and reached to put his shirt back on.

I wasn't even looking at him, but he knew anyway. I was lying on his bed in my bra and underwear, inches away from a panic attack. The rest of dinner would be a nightmare if I stayed. He wasn't kicking me out because he didn't want to be rude. If I looked at him, I'd see pity in his eyes.

"I should go," I said.

"What?" His voice flipped into another register as he stood. I heard the swish of his fly as he zipped himself back into his jeans.

He was dressed. I should be dressed. I reached frantically for my shirt and my jeans. Tugging them on too quickly, misaligning seams as they slid their way onto my body.

"Emma, please don't go. Let's finish dinner, or we can get out of here and get some ice cream or something. The original Ample Hills is like two blocks away."

"No. I should go home." I couldn't find my socks.

"Emma." He reached for my shoulders, forcing me to look at him. And I could tell he was being earnest. He didn't want me to leave. But he didn't know. If he kept waiting for me, he'd be waiting forever. I was never going to be normal.

"It's okay. Whatever you're feeling, it's okay," he said.

"I'm feeling like it's just too much, with you being a director and me being an assistant." I looked him dead in the eyes and swallowed back everything that wasn't serving me getting out of here as soon as possible.

He dropped his hands from my shoulders. "Are you being serious?"

"Yeah, I'm being totally serious, Ben. It's just inappropriate." I moved to sidestep him.

"I don't believe you. You're lying. That's not what's happening in your head right now." He moved to block me, putting his stupidly giant body between me and the door.

"You have no fucking idea what's in my head!" We were fighting. This was a fight. And if I had been training for anything my whole life, it was winning a fight like this.

"Just tell me what it really is! Did I do something you didn't like? Was I moving too fast?" His words were coming out quickly now. I'd never seen him desperate like this.

"I told you. I don't want to do this." I searched my mind for any excuse. "We're just too far apart in the org chart." I moved to pass him.

He put his hand on my wrist as I walked away. "Emma," he said. A plea.

"Don't touch me." I ripped my wrist away.

"Okay," he whispered. "Don't make this about something dumb. Tell me what happened."

I shook my head. Horrible things to say rushed to the tip of my tongue. Lies I would tell to devastate him. I could cut deeper. If I wanted to, I could. I'd say I'd just realized I found him unbearably unattractive, that as soon as he touched me, breathed into my ear, any arousal shriveled away. "Let me go," I said.

He nodded, all fight having fled from his body.

After I gathered my stuff, the silence aching through the apartment, I looked back at him before I walked out his apartment door, my leather boots chafing against my sockless feet. He was sitting at the perfectly set dinner table, elbows on his knees and face in his hands. His hair was sticking up in every direction. He looked like he'd been hit by a tornado. That's what I was to him, a tornado of complete insanity.

I closed the door without saying goodbye. Running down the stairs, my breath came quickly, in fits and starts between laughter and tears. It was tragic because I'd ruined everything, like I always do. But it was hilarious, too, because Mitchell had been completely wrong about me. I wasn't too crazy to date; I'd been good at going on dates with Ben. It turned out I was too crazy to fuck.

SEVENTEEN

Days passed. Ben didn't call me and I didn't call him. Most moments, it felt easier having erased the complication from my life. Things with my dad were complicated enough; I didn't need to invite potential heartbreak into it. It was for the best. I repeated that to myself like a mantra until something would crack my mental armor. On Sunday, I walked past the Ebbets Field Apartments, midcentury housing projects built where the Dodgers used to play. I reached for my phone but stopped the motion before I took a picture. It was for the best.

I'd emailed Jermaine and Amy on Saturday morning, finding no reason to delay since I'd fucked everything up so intensely with Ben.

Hello,
I'm writing with a bit of unfortunate news. I recently found out that my father has been diagnosed with liver cancer, and the prognosis is quite poor. I am planning on traveling to be with him on Wednesday morning and staying there through the Christmas and New Year's holiday. I will keep you both abreast of my plans, but I know you will both be understanding about me taking this

extra time off right before the holidays. Please let me know if you have questions, concerns about my workload, or anything else.
Best,
Emma

I was glad of corporate norms and coldness when I got their responses. They were sorry, approved the time off, and asked no questions. Jermaine mentioned during our weekly team meeting Monday morning that I'd be taking some time off but said nothing more about it. Colin looked confused. Vanessa looked relieved.

She pulled me aside when I went to microwave my leftovers for lunch to check in with how I was doing, and how the night with Ben had gone. I told her I canceled it with everything going on with my dad—I just wasn't up to a romantic evening, I said. She thought that made a lot of sense. I gave her a tight smile. I wished I could run home early, but since it was the day before the holiday party, the Fun Team was having an all-hands-on-deck meeting after work to make a few final decorations. I would be stuck at work awhile longer. My new mantra would be harder to repeat if Ben was standing next to me.

I got to the conference room before he did. When I arrived at five o'clock, Amy was the only one there, organizing large stacks of colorful construction paper and laying out scissors and thick heavy-duty Sharpies. I smiled at her, and she smiled back. I felt a little shy after the weird exchange of emails about my dating life and then about my dad's cancer, but thankfully, she was able to fill the silence, a real talent of hers, and get me to start tracing the stencils she'd printed out.

Every time the door opened, I looked for Ben. I felt silly sitting and playing with crafts, hoping for someone to open the door, and then praying for it not to be him walking through it. It felt like being back in school, with terror sitting deep in my stomach and thick construction paper flopping against my palm.

The room eventually filled. People chatted about holiday plans and traditions, gossiped about who had gotten too drunk, who was surprisingly fun or unsurprisingly messy at holiday parties past. I was quiet, a bag placed strategically on the seat next to me, waiting for Ben. I didn't mind the conversation around me. Jermaine was right; although I'd hated the idea of joining the Fun Team, it was okay. Mitchell was annoying, but he hadn't shown up tonight, and the rest of the people had their own complex lives and problems but were by and large kind. I could take deep breaths in this room. And they felt like victory.

Fifteen minutes after the time when Amy had asked everyone to meet, Ben walked in. His eyes didn't immediately meet mine, even though my gaze followed him closely as he went to take a seat on the other side of the room. And then, as I continued to look, he struck up a very un-Ben-like conversation with Amy. He questioned her intensely about the stencils, which markers to use, what he had missed. He was avoiding me.

I fastened my eyes on the table. I wouldn't look at him again. Three seconds passed. I looked at him. He still didn't meet my eye. I wasn't finding breathing as easy as I used to.

When we were done making giant fake Instagram squares for people to take pictures in with #happyholidaysfromR&T written in Sharpie on the bottom, Ben fled the room. He was the first one to leave. I couldn't help myself—I never could, not with anything—and I grabbed my bag and ran after him.

"Ben!" I called.

People gave me questioning looks, but I kept going. Ben didn't stop or turn around. "Ben!" I ran to catch up to him, and he was far too polite to run away from me down the office hallway. I reached out and touched the arm of his well-tailored suit jacket.

He turned to look at me, and I saw something close to fear in his eyes.

"Please, can I talk to you?" I hadn't released my grip on him, afraid if I did, he'd dematerialize.

He paused, as if trying to think of a way out, and then gave me a stiff nod.

Without speaking, we opened the door to the same staircase we'd been in a month and a half ago when he confessed to telling Mitchell I was his girlfriend. When the door latched closed, I knew I had to start talking, start apologizing. Over the weekend, I'd wanted to tell him how sorry I was, but I was sure he would never forgive me and never want to hear from me again. That was what I deserved. I wasn't fit for romantic relationships. But watching him from a distance in that conference room was torture. I couldn't put him out of my mind, not when he was just out of reach.

"Ben, I'm so sorry." My voice was quiet, near breaking. "I freaked out. I just panicked. I haven't been with someone sober, you know that, and I got scared, and I handled everything so badly. You didn't deserve any of that. It wasn't true what I said when I was leaving..." I knew there should be more to my apology. There was more I wanted to say. I wanted to tell him he was kind and understanding. That he hadn't done anything wrong. But no more words found their way out of my lips.

"Here's the thing—I obviously really like you." He ran a hand through his hair, adding static to the strands. They didn't fall back into place, instead remaining upright.

I nodded, feeling my eyes widen, desperate for any and all of the words he might say. My mind was at war with itself. *He really likes me!* one half of it screamed. This man, the one I obsessively think about, whose hands I imagine running down my body, under whose warmth I pretend to huddle, really likes me. The other half, the one that could still process complex thought, picked apart the words *here's the thing. Here's the thing* was not the kind of phrase one starts an outpouring of love and affection with. It's the predecessor to a *but*. It's the beginning of a contradictory phrase. Him really liking me? It wasn't simple. Not anymore. Not after Friday.

"And because I liked you and I thought we had a good time together, I thought whatever else—" he motioned to the air around us "—would be fine. But when I first asked you out, you panicked and lied. Then I decided to try to get close to you anyway—"

"I'm so glad you did! Ben, please, I'm so happy we got to know each other," I interrupted, and my voice was so desperate it made me sick.

"What I was trying to say was I think I kind of ignored you when you said you didn't want this. I tried to spend more time with you anyway, and I thought I understood, and that taking it slow was working. But I don't think I did understand what you were going through, not really. I ignored it as a minor obstacle we could overcome. But I'm not ignoring it anymore. I'm going to listen to you."

"What?" I was so confused. He wasn't listening to me. "I want this. I'm so sorry I freaked out," I said slowly. "I really like you." Softly.

Something had changed. I could feel it in the air around us. There was no way I could reach my arms around him anymore. The space that had once been filled with something akin to warm water—a barrier, to be sure, but something that I could easily push my hands through, that would feel smooth, soft, and welcoming against my skin—had turned to ice.

"Emma. It's just… Maybe you need more time, and I'm so sorry if I pressured you in any way. But instead of being honest with me, you lied. You were like a cornered cat, and I couldn't reach you. We couldn't talk about it."

If I talked, I would cry, so I stayed quiet. But I knew he was right; I hadn't handled anything like a remotely normal or responsible adult. I could have talked to him. I could have told him what was happening with my dad, and how unsteady it was making me feel. We could have just had dinner.

"Please," I said.

After a long pause, he said, "I don't know, Emma."

"Okay," I said.

"Let's take some time. Cool off, be friends?"

"Some time," I repeated. I knew *some time* meant forever. That, at least, I knew. I looked over to the wall. I didn't want my gaze to touch him. "Cool."

"I think you're on the right track, Emma." And then, from the corner of my eye that was trying to avoid his body, I saw movement. He was going to walk away. That might be the last sentence of our relationship. The next time we spoke we'd be cordial coworkers. I couldn't let him have the last word, especially when it was such a patronizing turn of phrase. What did he know about my life? What was the right track? And why the fuck did he keep saying my name like he was my fifth grade teacher?

"I don't know what that means," I snapped.

The black of his coat moved further into my line of sight. "You're trying to improve yourself. I get it. I've been there. It's a good thing to do. A worthy goal."

I hadn't been happy with myself when I left Ben's on Friday night—far from it. But I had felt like I'd spared him the worst vitriol I could spit out. Obviously, that didn't matter. I'd still hurt him, even though I wasn't at my worst, even though I could have done more damage—all that mattered was that I'd done enough. It was almost funny. I thought I knew everything bad there was to know about myself, that this whole year I'd been cleaning house. Getting on my hands and knees and scrubbing my psyche until even the grout gleamed. But all this time I hadn't realized I'd somehow missed an entire room.

"I'm sorry," I said. I didn't know what else to say.

The door opened and then closed again, and I was alone. I hugged myself. I tried to breathe in for four seconds and then out for four seconds. It seemed to take an uncountable number of tries to get it. But finally, I could breathe, and I could think. And one thing became perfectly clear to me: even a year sober, I was the fucking asshole.

Lola hadn't told me I had to go to the meeting tonight, not directly, anyway, but she did say she thought it would be good for me. And that she really hoped I would. That kind of indirect pressure worked. I didn't want to disappoint her. I wanted to be a good sponsee. I wanted to be good at being sober. And good sober people did what their sponsors recommended. They didn't dread going to meetings with their entire body. It didn't feel like the worst possible fate to them. Apparently, or so I've been told, it felt healing. If it were any other day of the week, I wouldn't have minded quite as much. But it was the Monday meeting. Held in the School of the Future, where each speaker would point to the next at random. The worst of the week. The one I'd been able to avoid for months.

But I got dressed. All black, of course. I might be trying not to be the asshole, but that didn't mean I wanted to get picked at random and forced to get onstage and spout words of wisdom about my sobriety. I had no words of wisdom, no stories with silver linings. I was going to listen, not talk.

I walked up the narrow school staircase. The halls were filled with students' work. Posters written in Magic Marker about the power of recycling, photo boards with smiling teenage faces promoting the chess club. I wonder if the kids who put these together had any idea that hordes of grown-up alcoholics poured into their school in the evenings and read about the work they were doing in Earth Studies.

I was late enough that the seats in the auditorium around Lola and her sponsorship family were full. I gave them a smile and took an empty seat in the middle of the back row. I felt safe. No way would I get picked back here. Lola's seats were closer to the front; they had a much higher chance of the person onstage noticing them. But all the way back here, in my oversize black sweatshirt? The speaker would have to have really great eyesight—full-on higher than 20/20 LASIK shit—to notice me.

We breezed through the reading of the opening preamble and the steps. Almost everyone raised their hands to offer to be sponsors. The speaker, in a red satin dress and black blazer, started talking about the seventh step: *Humbly ask Him to remove our shortcomings.* In that step, as interpreted by HG, God removed all of our flaws. All we had to do was be willing to have them removed, to give the power up to him rather than hoard it for ourselves.

Each step had an accompanying prayer, and the seventh one went like this:

> *My Creator, I am now willing that You should have all of me, good and bad. I pray that You now remove from me every single defect of character which stands in the way of my usefulness to You and my fellows. Grant me strength, as I go out from here, to do Your bidding. Amen.*

The woman in the satin dress was talking about how she was no longer envious, vain, or obsessed with status. Like a good member of HG, she didn't want to focus too much on what life was like before she got sober. She focused on the solution. How now that she knew she had value to her fellow recovering alcoholics, she didn't need to go out, get drunk, and put other people down. She trusted her sponsor. She trusted God. She was different now. "It's simple," she said. "I gave my will over, and I was rewarded with miracles beyond my imagination." As she finished, she extended her arm and pointed her finger sharply forward. She reminded me of Winona Ryder in *The Crucible* as she pointed to someone in the first row with a raise of her eyebrows. "Come on up!" she called.

My stomach tensed and then eased again. My strategy was

working, I told myself. Look at that first-row chump. He was a tall man in yellow basketball shorts and a black T-shirt. When he got to the mic, he wiped his palms against his thighs. They must've been sweaty. "Well," he said, looking straight at the woman in the satin dress, "you really know how to pick 'em. This is my first-ever meeting." I let out a breath. His first-ever meeting! I couldn't imagine the horror. He hadn't known what was going to happen to him. He hadn't known about the accusatory fingers that would come pointing around the room. "So I haven't done the seventh step..." He laughed, and the room laughed along with him. His palms came off his thighs. "But I want your life," he said, gesturing to the woman. "I don't want to be a dick anymore. I don't want to be a drunk anymore. I want to be free of all this shit that bounces around in my head. I guess to get there I have to start somewhere. So I might as well start with step one. Which I think is to admit I'm powerless over alcohol?" The room murmured its agreement; I could feel everyone holding their breath. This was theater, and all eyes were focused on him. He was a natural. "So here goes. You guys, I am so fucking powerless over alcohol."

Everyone cheered. Their clapping rumbled the ground beneath me. I wiped my hands against my jeans.

He pointed to someone in an aisle seat. They talked about how without the seventh step, they would never have had the courage to apologize to their kids in the ninth step. How they needed to be a different person before they could apologize for who they used to be. A few more people had similar messages about the power of the seventh step. About the power of God. I discreetly checked my phone. Only twelve minutes left. I was going to get out of here unscathed.

"Hmm, I always like to choose whoever looks like they want to get up here least," said the newest speaker, a middle-aged woman who looked like her day job might be on Wall Street. "We gotta pull people out of their comfort zones, right?" My eyes met hers. Shit. She smiled. She reached out her arm. She pointed right at me. "You! All the way in the back, get on up here!"

My heart jumped. I pointed at myself, just to be sure. I was praying that there was someone a few rows ahead that she meant instead.

"Yes! You!" she said, nodding and pointing at me again. People were turning around. I was going to have to stand up. The people in my row started adjusting their knees, curling up on themselves to make way for me. Somehow, I found my feet. Somehow, I crawled out of my row. I walked to the stage. I didn't fall.

My face was bright red. I could taste vomit in my throat. Everything I had ever thought was correct: this was hell. Of course. Of course today would be the day. This would be the meeting.

The mic loomed before me, a heavy black planet shadowing the entire sky.

I didn't have anything to say. I didn't care about the seventh step.

"Um," I started.

The auditorium looked back out at me. Wide expectant eyes. Patient smiles. Far-off gazes.

"I don't really know what to say."

I looked like an idiot. A fish moving its mouth pathetically in the bottom of a boat about to have its throat slit, desperate for relief that would never come. They weren't going to let me off this stage without their pound of flesh. I had to say something. I had to say something about sobriety.

"I'm still an asshole," I said.

The room laughed, the sound bouncing from mouth to mouth, across aisles, and through wooden chairs. Everyone wanted to hear my jokes. I wanted to tell them one; I just didn't have anything funny to say.

"I thought maybe I wouldn't be, after I gave my will over. After I wrote down every single bad thought I ever had and told someone else about them. But here's the thing—I kept having bad thoughts. And I keep having to write them down. And that's okay—I mean, like, whatever." I could feel my heart hammering in my chest, beating wildly against my rib cage. I stopped my palms before they made for my thighs again; I forced them to grip the mic stand. "But what really sucks is that sometimes I'd rather be the asshole than show the world anything else, anything soft. I slash through people's feelings, and I do it with my eyes wide open." It was torture to stand there—to talk with distant expressions as the only feedback. Did they hate me? Did they not give a fuck? Did it not matter? "I was promised all these things when I got sober. For fuck's sake, we read a list of promises before every meeting. I paid attention. I wasn't supposed to still be an asshole. That was a defect of character I wanted removed.

"And you might be thinking, well you must not have done the other steps right if the seventh isn't working. But I promise I tried my hardest. I scratched them all into my brain's gray matter: *One, we admitted we were powerless over alcohol—that our lives had become unmanageable.* Of course, of course, of course I am. I couldn't live the way I was living. The choice was death or sobriety. I had no allusions of moderation. So, check number one off.

"Two, came to believe that a Power greater than ourselves could restore us to sanity." I gasped a breath. "This was a bit harder because I wasn't raised with religion. But I believed in AA. I believed that you all were telling the truth. I did what my sponsor told me.

"*Three, made a decision to turn our will and our lives over to the care of God as we understood Him.* Okay, I always forget that this is a different one than number two, but I feel like I covered it. I did everything my sponsor said. I went to every Watch, every meeting. Even when she didn't understand that prayer wasn't always helpful to me or that sometimes I needed to lick my wounds alone, I listened to her more than I listened to myself. It's why I'm here right now, at this meeting that I hate more than anything, talking to all of you.

"*Four, made a searching and fearless moral inventory of ourselves.* I filled a whole fucking composition notebook, you guys. I thought about every single bad thing I'd ever done. I wrote them down. I claimed responsibility for my side of the street during every fight or fallout, even the ones with my parents, even the ones from when I was a child.

"*Five, admitted to God, to ourselves, and to another human being the exact nature of our wrongs.* I sat down, I did the fucking thing. I told my sponsor. It was humiliating, and we didn't even order pie.

"*Six, were entirely ready to have God remove all these defects of character.* This is honestly why I came to AA—I wanted to stop drinking, God, did I want to stop drinking. But I also wanted to be a shiny new person. I had no attachments to my defects, I didn't want to feel jealous, or lonely, or afraid. I wanted to feel whole, perfect. I wanted to be like the girls I watched fall in love and get married and have babies and live a normal fearless life. I didn't want to be famous or rich or important, I just wanted to be able to feel my skin against my body and not want to tear it off.

"*Seven, humbly asked Him to remove our shortcomings.* But here we go—"

The spiritual timekeeper motioned at me; I was over my five minutes. Their phone was chiming. They wanted me to get down, to pick someone new.

"Give me a second, I'm almost there." I couldn't believe I was arguing for more time. "Step seven. Trust me, I asked. Trust me, I wanted this shit gone. But here I am, still desperate to rip my skin off. Terrified of love, like, and anything in between. I don't know if I've ever felt lonelier in my whole life. And worst of all, I don't want to take any blame for it. I want to lash out at the world. I'm still absolutely, unequivocally, an asshole. And I don't think this place—" I gestured around the room "—is going to help me." My throat dried up. I thought I had more to say, but maybe I was just done.

I started to walk off the stage. Someone called to me, "Hey!" and for a second, I thought they were going to tell me, one drunk to another, that they'd felt the same way but got better. That they found a way out with some sentence buried in a paragraph of the Big Book that I hadn't read. I looked up. "You have to pick someone!" they finished.

I didn't walk back to the mic. I pointed at the guy calling out to me. If he wanted to talk so bad, he could have at it.

I walked down the aisle back toward my row. The guy started talking, but I didn't hear what he said. Eyes turned toward him and away from me. I kept walking, then pushed open the door. I felt some gazes snap to the back of my head, but I walked on. I had to get out. I couldn't spend another second in that auditorium.

Back home, I threw clothes in my bag and ignored Lola's fourth call. Would I need a black dress at the celebration-of-life party? I threw something red and floral in there, too, just in case black was forbidden by Gaura.

This was a terrible idea. I should pick up the phone, and I should apologize. I should say I was just blowing off steam. I should deal with the world around me, the world I created. Anyone and everyone would tell me this was self-sabotaging. Who the hell did I think I was, going to my father's deathbed without the support of a sponsor? This sounded like what people talked about when they warned against relapses in their qualifications or in whispers about friends they'd lost along the way.

I sat down. I took a deep breath.

Last time I'd worn the red floral dress was for my Watch ceremony, and it still had the coffee stain on the right hem. That was just this September. Only a few months had passed. It was supposed to be the start of the rest of my life. I was going to open myself back up to the world. To set out, free, whole, and perfect. But it didn't work out that way. Instead, I was bringing a dirty dress to my father's deathbed, and instead of being honest with the man I was falling in love with, I'd pushed him away and jumped overboard.

My phone started ringing again. It was Lola calling for a fifth time.

The red floral dress slipped onto the floor. I slipped into my bed.

Back to basics. It was time to *keep it simple, stupid.*

I wouldn't drink tonight. Just for today, just for tonight, I wouldn't drink. Worse would be not going to see my dad, worse would be losing my job, worse would be what happened a year and a half ago.

I just had to take it one day at a time. That sounded doable until I remembered the next day was the holiday party.

EIGHTEEN

"You should go dance!" Amy said, her cheeks flushed from using up her two drink tickets. She eased herself into the seat beside me and leaned into the coats hanging behind us. We'd pushed a table in front of several wheeled clothes racks the hotel had provided to create a makeshift coat check.

"Oh no. It's okay," I said. The last thing I wanted to do was dance. I'd only ever danced in the most drunken moments of my previous life, and even then, I didn't enjoy it. I never felt swept away by the music. And today, with my bus trip tomorrow morning looming and everything between me and Ben in tatters, the idea was entirely laughable.

"Emma! You've been checking people's coats all night! Have a little fun!" Amy refused to be dissuaded. She moved her glass of white wine with floating ice cubes to her throat, cooling herself.

I wasn't sure how I was going to get out of this. I felt safe behind the coat check table. The different perfumes mixing at my back, the soft brush of the occasional cashmere against my wrist, the folding chair that I would have bet came off the exact same assembly line that the ones at my Saturday night meeting did—it all soothed me. And that's what I needed to get through this party. I didn't need to wonder where Ben was or stand awkwardly while Vanessa's long hair trailed behind her spinning body on the dance floor.

I shook my head. "I'm happy here."

Amy put down her wineglass and looked at me. "Really?" she asked.

I nodded and then started organizing the tickets by number again. Just to give my hands something to do.

"Are you nervous?" Amy asked with an expression that reminded me of my high school guidance counselor. Amy, who'd never acted much like an HR professional, had suddenly turned on her you-can-trust-me face—apparently all it took was a couple glasses of white wine.

I shrugged, doing the only thing I knew how to do in response to that precise tone of voice: I transformed into a surly teen. I fixed my gaze on the front doors. I couldn't trust Amy. Anything she knew was immediately common knowledge among half the office.

Amy leaned in. "Lots of people get nervous at parties," she whispered. "I bet half the people in there are a little bit nervous."

"Not like me," I said.

She smiled softly. "Sure, like you. You didn't invent feeling awkward in groups, hon."

I gave her an attempt at a laugh, but it came out as more of a wheeze.

"How about this? Go in there, do a loop of the room—after all, you should see your decorations in action—and grab us two glasses of water. I need to cool down from all my dancing." The ice cubes had melted in her wineglass and her cheeks were still blooming.

I couldn't find a reason to refuse her, not without getting into my entire backstory. I weighed the two options in my mind. Grabbing two waters seemed like the lighter one compared to confessing my alcoholism. The silence lapped at me, pushing until I finally broke and said, "Sure thing. I'll be back in two minutes."

I opened the very same heavy door I'd heard Ben and Mitchell whispering behind all those weeks ago. It was carrying even more weight today. I walked one step forward and let the door close behind me.

The ballroom was dim. The warm lights turned to an intimate level that wouldn't be out of place at a side-street French bistro. All I could make out were bodies. For a second, everyone's faces blurred together. People were more anonymous than they ever had been. They were suits and cocktail dresses. Stiletto heels and wing tip oxfords. I couldn't walk past the doorway. I couldn't enter the fray. Everything was dark and flushed with motion. It would be like walking into a choppy sea without knowing how to swim. I would drown.

Cold air enveloped me from behind. The door had opened again. Fuck it. I couldn't get the bottles of water. I'd turn back around and tell Amy there was too long of a line at the bar.

"Earth to Emma," a voice from behind me said. Mitchell Brady. My least favorite person at Richter & Thomas was standing inches away.

"Oh, sorry." I moved forward into the ballroom.

"Looks pretty good, doesn't it?" Mitchell said, scanning his eyes across the room. "We did a good job." Did Mitchell think we could now be friends? Have pleasant chats? Pretend nothing had happened? "You got anything going on for Christmas?" It seemed that was exactly what he thought.

"Uh, no," I said. I decided to play along. "You?"

"Yeah, I'm headed up to Pound Ridge to see the fam, and then off to Pohnpei to get my surf on."

"Pompeii? The Italian city destroyed by a volcano thousands of years ago?"

"Ha! Good one, Em," he said, slapping my back, and then without explaining further, he swam through the crowd with practiced ease; the groups of dancing people moved aside like the Red Sea parting for Moses. He was heading for the bar, and as curious as I was about what he'd just said, I'd rather take a moment for myself than wait with him while he got drinks.

I slunk to the far corner, the perfect place to watch the world move around me. It was a shadowy enough spot that it would hide the tension tattooing itself between my eyebrows. Even far from the crowds, I could feel body heat bouncing off the walls and creating a thin layer of sweat between my skin and the green silk fabric of my dress.

It was a stupid dress to wear. Sober Emma had never worn it. I tugged the neckline up in an effort to cover my cleavage. It was too revealing. Too fluttery. I had tried too hard. But I wanted some piece of the confidence I used to have when I walked into these rooms—dimly lit rooms containing bars and dancing and people twisting about with drunken half-baked thoughts. I might feel out of practice with socializing, but I'd figured I could at least be wearing a pretty dress the next time I stood near Ben.

I saw Jermaine out of the corner of my eye. He was heading my way. I worked to twist my mouth into a smile.

"Emma!" he called, his ever-broad grin even larger than usual. I could now see his first and second molars.

I stepped away from the wall to meet him. "Hi," I said.

"The place looks great," he said, gesturing to the decorations that we'd made on Monday. Paper flowers fluttered around the bar, the photo booth had a line of people waiting to use our silly dreidel and Christmas-tree props, and a cut-out mistletoe wreath had been tied to the center chandelier. I doubted we were allowed to do that.

"You guys must have done a lot of work," Jermaine said.

"Yeah," I said. "It wasn't too bad, though." I was at a loss for what else to say to him. It was far too late to suddenly start asking him about his personal life, right? Or was the holiday party the place to get deep with your boss? These were all uncharted waters for me.

"I'm glad," he said with genuine warmth. "I know the Fun Team can be a taxing assignment and that you weren't looking forward to it. But it all worked out!" He put a damp hand on my shoulder. He was far sweatier than I was.

"Yeah!" I tried to mirror his warmth, but I wasn't sure I pulled it off. "I think the bar has cleared up, and I came in here to bring Amy something, so have to run. Can't leave my post for too long!" I started to walk toward the other side of the room before I finished my sentence, leaving a still-smiling Jermaine in my wake.

The bar hadn't actually cleared up. Mitchell was leaning over it, and the blushing bartender was ignoring anyone else in her periphery. I'd have to wait a little longer.

I saw Vanessa taking a break from the dance floor, where she'd left Izzy and Maria—both decked out with candy cane earrings—and quickly changed direction to make my way to her. I glued myself to her side before noticing that she was standing with Darren, Ben's IT friend. And oh god, oh no, Ben was on his way over to this circle. He was too close to back out of his decision. He couldn't change course now without being blatantly rude. And he definitely wasn't blatantly rude.

"Emma!" Vanessa said, throwing her arm around my waist. "Don't you look gorgeous!"

I blushed. Thank god Ben was just reaching us now. Darren was half-stepping to allow him to join us. "Thank you," I murmured.

Silence spilled between the four of us. Vanessa cleaned it up. "So, have you all been dancing?"

"I'm not much of a dancer," I said. I wanted to get there first, to have her understand that not dancing was a choice I made independent of what Ben and Darren would say. She had a glimmer of mischief in her eye that worried me. I could imagine her pushing us all out onto the dance floor, willingly or not. She didn't know how things had ended between Ben and me. She probably thought if she gave us some alone time, it would be the cute, friendly thing to do.

"Me, either," Ben said, and I let myself look at him for the first time since he'd walked up. And, of course, my body, being entirely unaware of how he'd clearly said he wanted to cool things down, reacted. My breath shallowed, my cheeks heated. He was just as handsome as ever in a well-tailored three-piece suit.

"Two left feet over here," Darren joked.

"Oh come on!" Vanessa said. "No one out there is a pro. It's just nice to move around to some music." There were no murmurs of agreement. Had Vanessa and Darren been having an easy time of it before Ben and I walked over carrying armfuls of tension?

"Is everyone so excited for Christmas?" Vanessa asked, trying a different tactic.

"I'm Jewish," Darren said.

She got no other responses.

"Anyone going away?" she tried.

I didn't know what to say. I was going away the next day. Two weeks before the office closed for Christmas. But Vanessa knew that. "No?" Vanessa said. "Me, either."

"I'll be going home," Ben said. "To Albany."

"The capital!" Vanessa said, clearly glad to have a topic to glom on to.

"Yep." Ben nodded.

Vanessa ran out of follow-ups. She looked to me and bulged her eyes, silently asking me to insert something into this dying conversation. But I couldn't help. I wondered if Ben's mom would make a big Christmas dinner after they all came home from the local church, where everyone knew everyone else's name. Did each Christmas tree have presents underneath it?

Maybe she wrapped bath bombs and put them under the tiny plastic tree that lived on the bathroom counter.

"Well, I'm going back out to the dance floor. Anyone wanna join me?" Vanessa was greeted with shakes of heads. "Okay, well, I'll catch you later, right, Em?"

"Yeah, for sure." She'd have to come get her coat back when the night finally ended, after all.

Darren suddenly piped in. "I'm gonna run and grab a drink! See you guys later!" His feet darted away from us before either Ben or I could respond.

Well. I wasn't about to join Darren and Mitchell at the bar. That would have been too much to handle. A rocky coast of jagged boulders waiting for me to crash into them. But standing here with Ben just might have been a whirlpool. There was no safety at sea.

We hadn't spoken since yesterday, since he left me alone in the staircase. In the interim, I had humiliated myself in front of all of HG, ignored all communication from my sponsor, and used the office copier to print a one-way Trailways bus ticket to my father's deathbed.

"Hi," I said, reveling in having the chance to tilt my neck toward him. But I wasn't greeted by the smile I'd grown used to. I looked to the floor.

"Hi," he said.

"I've been thinking about you," I said. It was true. But I hadn't meant to say it. "I know I said I was sorry, but I didn't say it in the right way."

"Oh," he said.

"I'm sorry, Ben." I reached out, placed my fingers on his forearm, and quickly removed them. I shouldn't have touched him. I forced myself to tilt my face back up toward his. To deal with whatever expression I found there. "You were probably so confused that night."

"Yeah..." He sounded suspicious.

"So I feel like in the spirit of our possible friendship, and not being an asshole, I'd like to explain myself. Could I?" This was giving Ben what he was due.

He nodded, and it was as if his head pulled his body closer to mine. Changing the distance between us from spacious to friendly.

"You know I'm sober, and you know this is my first relationship in sobriety and that I haven't been with anyone as my full self before."

"Yeah, Emma, of course, I get it."

"Just wait, please." He didn't want the backstory. He needed to know what had changed. "On Tuesday, I found out my dad has cancer. And…" I thought of all the possible metaphors and clichés that could make this lighter, like *the battle can't be won* or *his journey is coming to an end.* But Ben didn't need those. I thought of the Post-it notes I'd found the first day I'd met him. He wasn't a platitudes guy. "He's going to die. Soon. I think he tried to tell me when he visited in October, but we fought like we always do, and I guess he couldn't bring himself to tell me what was happening. So his wife called on Tuesday and told me I should come say my goodbyes. I'm taking the bus up there tomorrow." It wasn't lost on me that my father had made the situation worse by not telling me something and that I went and did the same exact thing. Like father, like daughter, through and through.

"Emma—"

"You're probably thinking that I should have told you. That we could have just gone to the Ample Hills two blocks away and nothing needed to happen on Friday night."

He opened his mouth to speak again, but I held up my hand to stop him.

"And I thought of that, but I didn't do it. I didn't do it because I was excited, and I wanted everything to keep being normal, and also because I didn't want to show you any more of my damage. I wanted to be as normal, as perfect, as I could be. But instead, I bottled things up, panicked, and then exploded, hurting you in the process." I took a deep breath. "I'm sorry."

"I'm really sorry about your dad, Emma." There was even less distance between us now. Had it disappeared while I was talking? "Death—or sickness—can make us act in ways we don't want to, I get it." Was that forgiveness? Did that mean we could go back to where we were before? To taking it slow? I tried to quiet my anxiety and nodded.

The music changed. They weren't playing songs people could jump around to anymore. It was something slower.

"Do you wanna dance?" he asked as Judy Garland's voice cascaded from speakers all around us.

"What does the dance mean?" I whispered. I hadn't immediately realized, but the song was "Have Yourself a Merry Little Christmas."

"I don't know," he said.

I took his hand. We didn't make our way to the center of the dance floor, where Vanessa, Izzy, and Maria were swaying as they sang along. We just stayed where we were at the edge of the room. It was just a dance, I told my galloping heart. But my heart didn't listen.

Ben's hands were on my waist, and my hands were on his shoulders. Even with my heels on, I had to stretch my toes up an extra inch. He leaned down toward my face, and just as I thought he might kiss me, he brought his lips to my ear and whispered, "We can decide together what it means."

I gripped his shoulders tighter, pulling him closer to me.

Breath echoed between us. I heard Judy's voice sing about golden days.

"I want it to mean something," I whispered back.

The song ended, and we stepped away from each other. "I Saw Mommy Kissing Santa Claus" had come on.

"Emma—" Ben started, not letting go of me. I fell farther

into him, burying my face in his chest, the sound of his heartbeat loud in my ears. I let out a breath. It felt so good to be held. "I do, too," he said.

The sound of Amy's voice booming through the PA system shocked us into separation. "Everyone!" she called. I looked around and found her standing on a chair, mic in hand. "What a great night we've had— I know, it's not over yet, but before we serve dessert and everyone starts to head home, a few people wanted to say a few things, myself included. So I'll hand the mic over to Mr. Richter in a bit, and he'll tell you what a fantastic year we've all had, and what a special team we are."

I looked around the room, still feeling the warmth pouring off Ben's body as he stood a few inches behind me. People were smiling, looking at Amy, chatting among themselves, and sipping drinks. I hadn't seen the whole office together like this before. Everyone in one room, with nothing to do but enjoy themselves. I didn't think of this job as my identity—far from it. But these were the people I spent my days with, and being in this room with them, it did feel a bit like home.

"But I want to take a moment to thank my team, the Fun Team! Where are you guys?" Amy squinted around the room and waved us forward. "Fun Team members, get up here!"

Ben put his hand on my back and pushed me lightly forward. "Come on," he whispered in my ear, his breath warm and intimate.

"This year's Fun Team has been truly spectacular, as I think you can all see—" she gestured around the room as the rest of the Fun Team gathered "—so I want you all to give them a big round of applause!"

The room erupted. People were just tipsy enough that they'd abandoned polite claps for hoots of appreciation. My face heated with so much attention on me, but I also couldn't stop myself from letting out a laugh. The Fun Team had been ridiculous. This party with its open bar and hotel chandeliers was also ridiculous. I felt Ben reach for my hand. I intertwined my fingers with his and looked up to find a smile on his face. It might be ridiculous, but it also warmed my grinch of a heart that we were all together, celebrating the end of a long year.

NINETEEN

Some people wished for travel to take seconds. They wanted to be able to fly across the world in hyperspeed jets, to blink and magically transport their body across continents. I wished for the opposite. The bus ride was hours long, but I could have sat in my window seat for days and still clung to it when the bus pulled up in the small mountain town of Phoenicia.

I hadn't taken a vacation day the entire time I'd been working, so I had a "full bank" and could take as much time as needed. I didn't know how much time I needed because death had no schedule. It was impossible to place on a corporate calendar. Society did its best to organize it anyway with a mixture of boxes checked—"floating holiday" and "vacation." I saved the "bereavement" box until I'd really need it.

The last time I'd been up here was early spring when the mountains were a rich, full green. They'd teemed with breath; every inch of the wild was alive. With trees, with moss, with hikers, and bears and deer. With tens of thousands of species of insects. All moving, crawling, building, and breaking. I'd hoped for a rebirth between my dad and me as he celebrated his second Saturn's return, but our planets hadn't aligned. Upstate had seen flowers bloom and die again since I'd last been here. I wondered, not for the first time, if the cells in my father's liver had been mutating even then. If while we talked, leaning against his kitchen counter, their DNA was twisting upon itself, ripping things to shreds, devouring everything they could find. They must have been, for him to be so sick five months later in October when he came to visit me.

Now, from my tinted bus window, everything looked different. It was past the season where there were leaves on the trees, but I knew the ground would still be littered with them. A blanket of orange and red slowly fading to brown on the forest floor.

The first summer my dad moved up here, I was nine years old, and I came with him. That was the plan at first: I'd spend summers away from the steaming concrete of New York, in the lush stone hills with my father. But I didn't do well that summer. Everything scared me. The spindly limbs of daddy longlegs outside my window wouldn't let me sleep. The scream of cicadas wouldn't give me a moment to think. My dad would take me on long walks up the mountain at the back of his property. He'd stretch out his arms, throw his head back, and breathe deeply, telling me to do the same. To feel the mountain mist on my skin, to smell the fresh air. But the air didn't smell fresh to me. It smelled wrong. Fresh meant young, alive, ripe. Those were the things that described New York. The smell of gasoline pushing against sweat cooked in spices from every corner of the earth, all of it underpinned by the brine of the Hudson, which moved with such power it could never freeze—that was what fresh smelled like to me. These ancient, crumbling mountains were miles off.

I lasted two weeks before I called Mom and begged her to bring me home. I was lonely and scared. She waited one more week and then took the bus up, and we both left my dad and upstate behind. After that, I'd only ever visited for a week or two at a time.

The local taxi I'd hired at the bus station pulled over at the bottom of the long ice-covered driveway. No one had been doing the shoveling or salting.

"This alright?" the driver asked. He'd done his best to chat with me when I first got in the car, but he eventually took the hint from my one-word responses.

"Yeah. Fine." I got out and immediately stepped into a puddle, cold water smudging into my suede boot.

The driver took my suitcase out of the trunk and placed it on a dry patch of ice for me.

"Thank you," I whispered, unable to make eye contact. My stomach was in my throat. My muscles were trembling. I wanted to get back in the cab. I wanted him to drive me all the way home to my little studio oasis, all decked out in Sea Mist. I couldn't look at him because I was afraid if I did, I'd get on my knees and beg him to take me back. Excuses even popped into my mind: *I could say I forgot my phone on the bus, I could pretend that I got confused between Phoenicia and Palenville and I shouldn't even be here, that I was just now remembering I'd left my stove on all the way back in Brooklyn.*

The driver gave me a nod, and before I knew it, my only chance at escape was rolling away. I stared until he turned the corner, looking for his next fare.

I walked up to the house. When my dad first moved in it was a bright royal purple, but the years had turned it a pale lavender. The steps were so weatherworn they showed no color. All that was left of them was water-clogged wood. I felt a hint of give under my feet.

Gaura stepped outside before I reached the top step. She didn't match her surroundings. She looked dried out. Her skin was wrinkled in places I hadn't remembered. It wasn't only her charming smile lines and constant crow's feet dotting her face anymore; a deep chasm between her brows now joined them.

"Hi," she said, so quiet it was almost a whisper. She pulled a hand-knit shawl tightly around her shoulders and exhaled deeply as she looked at me.

"Hi," I said. Gaura and I had never had an individual relationship. She'd always been the woman by his side, not someone I knew as her own person.

"I wanted to say something before you saw him," she said. "I don't want you to be shocked."

I expected Gaura to say more, to tell me how he looked, to prepare me. But she just closed her eyes and tilted her face toward the sun. The empty beats of conversation let in the sounds of the neighborhood. Someone was taking out the trash. Someone else was working on their car. Someone jogged by, their feet echoing on the asphalt—so many people living other lives and not noticing the sorrowful reunion taking place on their neighbor's porch.

Finally, she opened her eyes, and her arms with them. "Emma," she said. I went to her. The wool of her shawl scratched against my cheek. She smelled of yoga mats, like she'd rubbed an essential oil—sandalwood maybe—over her sweat-soaked skin. I wondered when she'd showered last.

I followed her in. She led me to the guest room so I could drop my stuff. She didn't offer to let me settle in for a few minutes, and I didn't ask to. I wanted to go straight to my dad.

She'd been right to warn me. As soon as my eyes landed on his body, I steeled my expression so none of my shock would show on my face. He was lying on the couch, a patchwork of pillows and throw blankets propping up his body.

"Is he asleep?" I whispered to Gaura.

She nodded beside me.

"He's yellow," I said, my voice dropping from a whisper to a hush. Only his face was visible beneath all of the blankets, and I was immediately glad I couldn't see more of him; his face was more than enough. His saffron skin was plastered to the bones of his skull, and any flesh that had acted as a border between the two had disappeared.

She nodded again. "Has been for a few days now." A pit opened at the bottom of my stomach. Was I too late? He was still alive, yes. But I'd been hoping we'd have time to talk, to rush as much healing as we could into whatever time we had left. My mind recalibrated. I'd have to take what I could get but accept that it might not be much.

I gripped a steaming mug of tea as guests began to pour into the house for the celebration of life.

"One last sunrise," Gaura had called it. It wasn't as if my dad was going to die the next day. It wouldn't exactly be the last sunrise that he ever shared with the world—the last time his consciousness understood that a day had ended and a new one had begun. But it would be the last time his community gathered around him.

I heard someone speak at a meeting once who said they finally felt really sober when they realized they wouldn't drink if they were dying. That if a meteor was heading toward the earth and death was certain, they wouldn't drink—even if they were alone, even if there was no one to catch them, even if there could never be a consequence. It could be them, the bottle, and the end, and it still wouldn't matter. They didn't want to anymore. That, they said, was true sobriety. No more counting days, no more counting years. No more anxiety when they walked past a liquor store.

I remember thinking to myself, sweating through a too-tight sweater in a damp church basement, what a fucking joke. What a blissful joke.

But there was something about their face. I don't remember their name or what else they said. Not even their gender. I only remember the expression: a soft smile. There was nothing tight or forced about the muscles in their face. There was no performance. They were just out there. Existing. The weight they'd been tugging around behind them had disappeared—now they got to walk like everyone else. I didn't understand how they were doing it, but I believed them. Back then, I knew myself well enough to know that I wouldn't last next to a bottle of wine watching the last hour of twenty-four-hour news as we all awaited the second big bang, but I wished more than anything that I could look out at the big burning sky with clear eyes and hold my own.

Today, I'd bet on me rather than the bottle. After all, this wasn't the end of the world, but it was an ending. The sun's golden rays were peeking through the clouds, and I was looking at them. People churned around me, exhaling plumes of smoke, sipping glasses of red wine, dancing slowly to the falling notes of discordant jazz.

I hadn't spoken to Lola since the meeting on Monday. It'd been four days—the longest we'd ever gone without speaking since she became my sponsor. I would call her. I would. As soon as I knew what to say. She was so helpful to me when I didn't know what else to do but think about drinking and sit where she told me to in unfamiliar church pews. But I wasn't sure she'd be able to help me through this next part.

My tea had gone cold. I put the handmade ceramic on the floor next to me. Gaura made her own mugs. She etched stars and moons into every one. They were each unique, thrown and baked on-site. They had never traveled far. Kind of like me. I wasn't a traveler. I lived where I was born. My bones were made for long walks on concrete sidewalks and my lungs had grown accustomed to breathing in fumes and pollution. What did I know of mountains and crisp air?

Without the tea, I didn't have something to occupy my hands. Or, more importantly, to occupy my gaze. It locked on to my dad like it'd been pulled by a magnet. Like it needed to see him.

He was in a leather chair, far away from the center of the action. His face looked a shade beyond pale, as if it was already purpling. It was almost as if some of his skin cells had started dying, shutting down and drifting off his body. I knew that wasn't how death worked. I knew that his heart would stop, and that would stop everything else. But it looked, from where I was sitting across the room, as if it was happening in reverse. Like he was dying from the outside in, like something strange and black would spread from his skin through his muscles and finally reach his heart.

People were milling about. Wine in their hands, teeth and lips purple from it. There was quiet music playing—some playlist Gaura had made of all my dad's favorite songs. She'd asked me if I wanted to add any, but none had crossed my mind. Although my dad was sitting alone, there was a constant stream of people kneeling next to him. They whispered words I couldn't help begging my ears to make out, and where they failed, pleading with my eyes to make sense of the motions of their lips.

I looked at him, and the people who cared for him, and I felt a constant ache in my throat threaten to open up in a sob. When there was a pause in the stream of people, and he was alone for a moment, he brought his gaze to mine. Four blue eyes bleeding together. He lifted his hand slowly—was it a wave, or was I being beckoned? I hadn't talked to him yet, not alone. Gaura was always there, twisting her busy hands into knots and boiling a never-ending amount of water for a never-ending amount of tea.

The hand beckoned me. I stood and walked my socked feet across Persian rugs overlapping across the wide-planked wooden floor. I kneeled to him, just as the others had done.

"Help me up," he said. He placed his hands on the armrests and tried to push himself forward but could barely raise his body an inch.

Without thinking, I reached my arms around him and lifted. "Where are we going?"

"Grab my cane. And the blanket."

I reached across the chair and handed the cane to him, then threw the blanket that had been covering him over my forearm. Was he hoping that I was going to take him to the bathroom? I looked around for Gaura, who was, for once, not hovering close by.

"We're going to the deck," he said. "I want a moment with you."

My heart shuddered. Was this the scene in the movie where he'd hand me family heirlooms? Or dark secrets he couldn't take to his grave. People turned toward us when we started to walk across the living room. No one said anything; the quiet mumbling we'd been surrounded by vanished. I saw from the corner of my eye that Gaura made to stand, but her friend—Mary Beth, I think?—pulled her back down to the couch by her hand.

Someone opened the sliding glass door just as we reached it. I would usually have said thank you, but the words died on my tongue. Houdini, their cat, tried to follow us, but he was scooped up and returned to the house.

I wished for shoes as soon as my socks met the cold, damp wood of the deck. It was a cool evening, bordering on bitter. I pulled the blanket my dad wore tighter around his shoulders. He looked at me. "You cold?" he asked.

"I'm okay," I said, even as the wind raised goose bumps on my arms. I didn't want to go back in, to face the stares without him. I didn't know where we would go now that we were outside. Surely my dad couldn't stand for very long. As soon as the thought crossed my mind, the deck light clicked on. Someone from inside the house must've still been watching us.

We reached two Adirondack chairs that had begun to grow a thin layer of moss. I helped him into one and then gingerly placed myself in the other.

"Thanks," he said.

I brushed it off with a twist of my wrist. "Of course."

"Thanks for coming, I mean," he said. He wasn't looking

at me. He was trying to pull the blanket where it had gotten stuck under him.

I didn't know what to say, so I used my previous answer: "Of course."

"Can't be easy." The blanket was unstuck. He was smoothing it against his legs.

"Harder for you." I looked at his skin again. It was paper thin.

"I don't know about that. As soon as I knew this was the end, I wanted to see you," he said, his eyes intently focused on the tree line. "I needed to know a piece of me would still be out there. I needed to be sure of it."

I looked over at him. At his nose that bumped in the same place mine did, at his wide forehead and broad shoulders. "I'm undeniably yours," I said.

He turned toward me, his eyes grazing over my face, possibly marking the same things I had a moment ago. "It's true," he said with the shadow of a smile. "You're mine. But it's not just the looks. You were always more mine—or more like me." He turned back out to the darkness between the trees. "The way you'd pop up in the morning, how you'd sink your teeth into a meal, or obsess about one thing like it was your whole life. That was all me. Even when I moved up here, you kept acting more and more like me, less like your mother. It was like the distance didn't matter at all. You were growing into your old man."

I wanted to laugh. How could two people experience the same event and come out believing entirely different things? The distance was my defining feature. It mattered more than my blue eyes or broad shoulders. It mattered more than my last name or home address. I was Emma, the girl whose dad moved away. Of course I kept acting more like him. What he believed was genes, I believed was a pathetic attempt to get him to come back to me. We'd never really know which was true.

"The distance mattered. So much. It mattered." Bitterness

rose in my throat. Not quite anger, it was a feeling forbidden to me: a deep despair.

He turned to me. "Okay." He took his hand out of his blanket and put it on my knee. It was warmer than I expected it to be. Warmer than my skin. Blood was still pumping through his veins. "But there were good times, too, right?"

This I couldn't deny. I nodded at him. "There were."

He lifted his hand to my cheek and wiped away a tear I hadn't realized had fallen. His hands were still rough and callused. I tried to remember the stories behind all his scars, the ones he used to tell me when I was little. I think one of them involved chopping wood, but I couldn't be sure.

"All those Sunday mornings in the park," I said.

"Or the first summer I moved up here," he continued, "when the septic needed to be replaced, but you were too scared to use the old outhouse—"

"That was terrible!" I interrupted, laughter replacing my melancholy. "I didn't poop for like a week."

"Oh please. It was three days at most." He threw his head back with a loud laugh. "I showed you all the constellations that summer, too. Do you remember? You'd never seen stars until then, not really. Not like we have up here."

I tipped my head back. He was right. The sky was cluttered with stars. Some dim and distant, and others sharp and bright. "Yeah," I said, even though I couldn't remember the stars from that summer, there were enough here now that I could paint a memory back into my consciousness.

"Can you see any now?" he asked.

"Orion." I pointed. His shoulders stretched across the sky. His body was so broad I could almost tell that the earth was round as I traced the curve of him.

"That's the easiest one. Go again."

"Orion's belt." I moved my finger a centimeter.

He laughed with me, but it was softer than before. "Do you see the bright red star above Orion?"

"No." It was hard for me to make anything out of the clutter.

"Follow his bow. Right above the stars that make up his bow." He leaned closer to me and lowered my extended arm. "Just look with your eyes. You don't need your hands to see."

The red star blinked at me, calling my attention. "I see it."

"That's the bull's red eye. One of the two eyes that make up Taurus."

"Oh." Taurus was my sun sign.

He smiled. "Yeah. That's your constellation. And that star, the big red one, is how you can find it. I've always thought of it as your star. My baby girl's star."

Silence rose between us. But the wind and rustles from the forest kept any awkwardness at bay. The world was alive all around us.

I don't know how long we sat before the sliding glass door opened again.

"Aren't you cold, Emma?"

I didn't turn around. There were tears in my eyes that weren't meant for Gaura to see.

"She's alright," my dad responded for me.

"Can I help you in, Kirtan?"

Some communication passed between them voicelessly, and my dad was taken back into the warmth.

I kept looking up at the stars even without my dad to guide me. But the night didn't feel the same without someone by my side. I'd spent hours walking through New York alone, my footsteps only accompanied by the millions of others going their own way. But there was something about the crowded starry night sky and the clouds of my breath fading into the darkness that made me hug myself and wish I had someone else's arms around my own.

I called Ben.

"You okay?" he asked. His voice was deep and sleep-filled. I realized we'd never spoken on the phone before. Guys' voices always sounded deeper over the phone. I wondered if the reverse was true for me. Did my pitch hike up to something girlish and frivolous? Or maybe my voice sounded sultry, soft, and smooth.

"What's your star sign?" I asked. My voice came out rushed.

"What?"

"Your horoscope?"

"Oh, uh..." I could hear him fighting back a yawn. "Capricorn. Is that good?"

"Wait. Doesn't that mean you just had your birthday? December, right?"

"No. January eighteenth. It's in a couple of weeks. Why?"

"I'm looking at the stars. They have real stars upstate. Did you know that?"

He laughed. "Yeah, of course I knew that. You see anything interesting?"

"Well, if I knew what the Capricorn constellation was, I might look for it."

"I can't help you there. I'm not sure I even know what Capricorn's animal is." He took a breath. "How's your dad?"

"Bad." My voice hitched. I didn't want to tell him about the details. About arriving here and feeling further from my father than I ever had, but also seeing him with crystal clarity that I'd somehow lacked my whole life.

"Do you want to tell me about it?" Ben's voice wasn't tired anymore. He was listening.

"The whites of his eyes—they're yellow," I whispered. I wasn't afraid that anyone could hear me from inside the house. I just didn't want the words to be true. Maybe if I spoke quietly enough, the truth of them might also disappear with the vapor of my breath. Loud words were leaden with a somberness you couldn't take back. I needed to be able to take mine back.

"Oh wow," he said.

But it was as if that little detail was all I needed to start talking. Ben hadn't hung up. I hadn't spontaneously combusted. Maybe we could go further.

"You know how people say they knew they were grown up when they realized their parents were people, not just parents? That quote is in tons of movies, and people talk about it all the time. You know it, right?"

"Yeah, I know it."

"Well, I feel like I always knew that. My parents were so obviously people to me. I mean, they weren't that great of parents, so it wasn't hard to imagine them as something else. I wasn't really their first priority. And with my dad, it was like he was barely a parent at all. At a certain age, I stopped idolizing them. I saw them as people." I took a breath.

"Yeah?" he whispered, a nudge for me to continue.

"But over the years, my dad became something else—a villain. He was this giant shadow over me, and after I gave up doing everything I could to get his attention when he first moved away, I built my whole life around his absence." I didn't know how to explain it to Ben. I didn't know how to tell him that it'd been a key part of my identity, having a dad who'd moved away, and who used alcohol to be absent even when he was in the room. I used it to excuse all sorts of my own bad behavior. I'd wake up with a crippling hangover that had me glued to the toilet for most of the day and think to myself that I'd never had much of a chance to be any other way.

"I used to believe my parents had set me up for only one kind of life, that my drinking had been fate," I continued. "But that gave them, especially my dad, far too much power. When I got up here, I came looking for this giant evil villain, this towering darkness, but all I got was a frail, sick man. And it just occurred to me—he's human. He's dying, and he's human."

"Is it worse that way?"

"I don't know. If he's just some guy trying his best, and I've been treating him like he's something terrible and evil all these years, what does that make me? A fool? Or worse?"

"Emma, you're not a fool. And you're not a villain, either."

I thought of how desperately I'd tried not to be an asshole to Ben, how all my feelings got confused until the only thing I could breathe out was venom. I didn't know how to love. I didn't even know how to fucking like.

"You're a person. He's a person," Ben said. "There's nothing as simple as villains. Or as fools."

I didn't want to exhale. I didn't want to inhale. Any change in breath would tip Ben off that I was crying.

"Emma?"

"Are your parents heroes?" I asked. I wanted to be whisked away into another family's dynamics and dysfunctions. I needed a break from my own.

"They're just people. Like anyone else."

"How old were you when they split up?"

"They got divorced as soon as my youngest brother left for college. They were waiting for us to grow up, I think. My dad moved down the road, though. And my mom has the house we grew up in."

"That sounds nice."

"Well, my dad moved in with his high school sweetheart, which is weird. I guess he'd been carrying a torch for her all those years."

"When did he meet your mom?"

"Also in high school. I think he felt like he couldn't marry the woman he's with now because she wasn't Catholic. So he just waited a whole lifetime for his parents to die and then did it anyway."

"Maybe not that nice?" I asked. I imagined the gossip that the small suburb of Albany must have enjoyed when Ben's dad left one high school sweetheart for another.

"It's okay. He's just a person, right?"

"And your mom?"

"Maybe a little more heroic. But what can I say? I'm kind of a mama's boy. I mean, I'm packing for Christmas and I'm bringing a whole load of dirty laundry with me."

"Are you going to make your mom wash your dirty laundry on Christmas?"

"Well, I'll tell her not to…but she'll probably do it anyway."

"Maybe you're the villain."

"Do you think so?"

"Not a bit."

When I went back in, my fingertips had lost feeling, and I caught the purpling of my lips in the reflection of the glass door. Somehow, though, I didn't feel all that cold.

TWENTY

"I can't take another commercial," Gaura said, as the second commercial break and the tenth slick car zooming through mountain passes filled the screen. She looked at me. "I'm going to rest. Is that okay?"

A few days ago, when conversation had slowed and my dad spent more time asleep than awake, Gaura had uncovered a TV from a hidden area behind a collection of bright silk fabrics. She said she didn't like it out because she hated how so many Americans used their TV as the centerpiece of their room like it was an altar to corporations they prayed to in the evenings. I wondered if she didn't like it out because she didn't want people to know that she, like the rest of us, used the modern opiate of escapism to get through the days. But as my dad got sicker, it was the only opiate available to the two of us. We lived and breathed only because the TV provided something for us all to look at. My dad, of course, had actual opiates to dull his pain.

They were far enough behind the times that they had no streaming services, only basic cable and a DVD player. Unfortunately, the DVD player was not accompanied by any DVDs, so we were stuck with whatever content the gods of cable could provide. This evening, TBS had decided to gift us with *Field of Dreams*.

Gaura was in an odd state of pregrief that had hollowed out her cheeks and left her eyes constantly bloodshot. The night before, as my dad slept between us on the couch, a deep opiate-induced sleep that we knew mere words wouldn't wake him from, she stared at him but spoke to me. "When I look at him like this," she said, "I can't believe it's him. I keep seeing my father as he died, and in the back of my mind, that's who I'm next to, not my beautiful, strong husband who never even got a cold."

Tonight, though, he was awake, and he responded even though Gaura's question was meant for me. "Go rest. We'll be here after." She still looked to me for an okay, and I gave her a nod.

There was an awkwardness that I wanted to fill after she left the room, so when TBS announced we'd only have to listen to two more commercials before the movie came back, I said, "I've never seen this movie before."

My dad looked at me. "Really? It's a classic. It was huge when you were a kid."

I pulled out my phone, quickly looking it up. "It came out in 1989. I wasn't even born."

He made a noncommittal grunt.

"I didn't know you liked baseball movies," I tried again.

He shrugged. "There's something nostalgic about it. The cornfields, the farmhouse."

"You grew up in suburban New Jersey."

He smiled and wheezed out something that might have turned into a laugh if he wasn't so weak. "You can be nostalgic for things you haven't lived through. As long as it speaks to an essential part of you."

I thought of watching Ken Burns's *Baseball* with Ben and crying as they knocked down Ebbets Field and moved the Dodgers to LA. All of that happened before even my father was born, and I had no connection to the Dodgers except that they were from Brooklyn and I was from Brooklyn, but because of that, it felt like a piece of them belonged to me.

During the commercials, my dad had to explain the White Sox scandal to me so I could understand who was emerging from the cornfields to play ball. They were baseball players banned from ever playing in the Majors again after throwing the World Series for a bet. "Baseball players didn't make the kind of money back then that they do today. These weren't rich men. They were just a bunch of guys who saw an opportunity they had a hard time refusing. I think they were paid double their annual salary for throwing the game."

"But this main guy," I said, pointing to Ray Liotta as Shoeless Joe Jackson, "he wasn't in on it, right?"

"It's hard to know. Maybe, maybe not. Does it matter to the movie?"

"Well, if he was innocent, it makes sense that it was such a tragedy that he never played again, to the point where this guy would build a whole field for him in the afterlife or whatever, but if he was guilty... I don't know, he broke the rules and got fired. Why are we still talking about it one hundred years later?"

"Redemption stories are more interesting if the guy fucked up. If the guy was innocent and wrongly accused, what's the risk in giving him a second chance?"

"And if he was guilty?"

"Well, it takes a whole different kind of faith to believe he won't fuck up again."

"Like the kind of faith it takes to build a baseball field in the middle of nowhere and expect ghosts to come play?" I wasn't watching the screen, even though Kevin Costner was on it, making an impassioned speech to his frazzled wife. I was looking at my dad, whose breath seemed shallower than it was yesterday.

He gasped a laugh. "Exactly. It's a hell of a lot of faith."

"Did you play baseball as a kid?"

"Of course. I was a boy in, as you reminded me, suburban New Jersey in the '70s. Of course I played baseball."

My dad came from a messy, big, Irish Catholic family that sputtered out kids all over the contiguous United States. I didn't know much about them, except that his mother died when he was in high school and his father was an asshole. The picture I'd created for myself with those facts had been one-note: dark and dreary. Little League was hard to fit into that image.

"Who'd you root for?"

He smiled at me, but his lips looked frail. They couldn't fully push up his cheeks. "Guess."

"You love an underdog and the road less traveled, so I'd have to go with the ever-losing Mets." I kept my voice light, trying not to show the fear I felt as I looked at him. If he was this weak now, what would the next few days bring? A hospice nurse was supposed to be coming tomorrow morning to set up a hospital bed in the center of the room. It would be a new kind of altar. I hoped we could keep the TV.

"True. But I inherited my team from my father, and he loved a winner. We were a Yankees family." I could see, through his jaundiced skin, that he was happy to have surprised me.

"By those rules, does that make me a Yankees fan, too?"

He nodded. "You can't choose your family, and you can't choose your baseball team. Not really."

I was sitting next to Dad as he slept when my phone buzzed. The only people I was regularly hearing from a week and change into my trip upstate were Mom and Ben. I was surprised to see Vanessa's name on my screen.

Vanessa: Hey, I've been thinking of you ♥ But also, I had to tell you… Colin accidentally unplugged his headphones without pausing his music and he was listening to DJ Khaled???

I hadn't given much thought to the day-to-day of the office since I'd been gone. I'd disabled Outlook notifications on the bus ride, not wanting to feel the pang of anxiety when I saw all the work I was missing. But it was nice to be reminded that this world, the one surrounded by bitter rocky hills and a house sagging under the weight of sorrow, wasn't the only one I existed in. There was a little office in Manhattan, doing work that wasn't particularly important or groundbreaking but could occasionally be fun, waiting for me to come home to it.

Emma: No way. I've always assumed it was some super cool indie band I've never heard of!

Vanessa: He's had us all fooled! How are things up there?

This wasn't a conversation Work Emma would've been comfortable having. But Work Emma had disappeared around Vanessa. Probably around the time I asked her for advice on my sex life, but certainly by the time I'd thrown up in Macy's.

Emma: It's hard up here.

Just because I wanted to open up to Vanessa didn't mean I knew how to open up to Vanessa.

Vanessa: Do you wanna tell me in what ways it's been hard? You don't have to! But if you want to, you can.

Emma: I do. I'm just not sure where to begin.

Vanessa: Why don't you tell me about your dad. What was he like before he got sick?

A few months ago, this would have felt like such a complicated question. But here, surrounded by his things, with him resting beside me, it didn't feel as knotty as it once had. He was Dad, and that was complicated. But it was nice for once to just focus on him as a man. How would I describe him if I wasn't describing his relationship to me?

Emma: He's a painter.

I wasn't sure if he had painted recently, but even if he hadn't, he'd never stop being a painter to me.

Emma: He paints the details of things. Extreme closeups. The kind of painting where you can't quite tell what it is you're looking at, and then suddenly it comes together that it's a tiny piece of a curtain covering up a blue sky. Or the veins of a fallen leaf. Or a half-bitten cherry.

His paintings were all over the house. There were canvases in stacks leaning against the walls in closets and framed pieces hanging over the fireplace. I loved them all.

"Your father changed his mind last night," Gaura said as she stepped out of their bedroom, closing the door lightly behind her. She had a multicolored duster sweater wrapped around her shoulders and as she came toward me, I understood how the garment had gotten its name: small dust balls were riding her coattails.

"About what?" I picked up a sticky wineglass I'd just noticed, which must have fallen underneath the couch during the celebration of life. It had been lying on its side, the dregs of wine turned to syrup, for a week now.

"We'll be going down to Kingston today," Gaura said. She followed me but kept her arms tucked around herself. I didn't blame her. She was so tired she'd become almost otherworldly.

Like a specter floating above the mortal realm, or a ghost manifesting herself just for a moment.

"What's in Kingston?" I turned the water on to wash the dishes, but it was so cold it was close to ice. I snatched my hand back, red and splotched.

"Hospice. It's its own building, near the hospital." She seemed like she might have been trying to make eye contact with me, but the best she could manage was my right cheekbone.

"Oh, I thought the nurse would come here?"

"We're not going to do that anymore." Her eyes drifted farther down, to my collarbone.

"I thought he wanted to be at home?" Dad had made it clear these past few days that he didn't want to die in a sterile environment. He wanted to be home, where he was safe and loved.

"It's too hard, Emma."

I nodded. The house was a wreck. Gaura was a wreck. She couldn't watch him die in their home. I understood that. I thought of my now–pale blue walls. How would they feel to me if Dad died looking at them? Home was a precious place, and every memory colored it.

I opened my arms to Gaura, and she fell into them. She didn't unfold her arms, she just let me hold her body as it closed in on itself.

Then she stood tall again, her eyes not showing any sign of having cried, and said, "The ambulance will be here around noon to take us. Can you follow in my car?"

"Oh, I can't drive." I forgot that Gaura didn't know that about me. Shame flushed my cheeks. I wasn't a very good support system. I added it to my to-do list.

She shook her head slightly as if to clear it. "Well, I suppose you'll ride in the ambulance, then. And I'll follow behind."

"I'm sorry."

She waved me off. "I'm going to take a shower," she said.

★★★

I opened the front door to two young men on the stoop. One was tall and hunched; I could see the curve of his scoliosis through his uniform. The other was middling height with a plastered-on smile. They both had brown hair and pale sun-starved skin.

"Hello," I said, stepping through the screen door.

"Hi, ma'am," the shorter one said. "We're here to pick up a Mr. Curtain Finley and take him to Kingston Hospice?"

"It's Kir-tan," I said. But I wasn't sure why I bothered; these men didn't need to know the correct pronunciation of his name. "We need a few minutes. He's getting dressed."

"Alrighty, then. Do you want us to come in with a gurney?"

I swallowed. I thought gurneys were only for dead bodies. "He'll walk out," I said.

Walking wasn't easy for him. But I thought he'd want to walk out of his house for the last time. I knew that mattered. He hadn't said, but I knew because I wouldn't be able to bear it if I didn't cross my own threshold for the last time standing on my own two feet. Maybe that was genetic. Or maybe that was some Finley pride he'd instilled in me without my realizing.

"Does he need assistance coming out?" It was the short one again. I wished he'd stop smiling. Who smiles while they come to pick up the dying?

"He'll walk out," I repeated, my hand sweating around the handle of the tote bag filled with a few days' clothes Gaura had packed for Dad.

The medic asked me a few questions. I didn't answer him. His words were hard to understand. They were in the wrong tone. He was speaking in a frequency that my ears couldn't determine. All I could hear was a hiss of positivity. My mind was moving at a slower pace, my neurons were stiff. I stared at the door, desperate not to miss a moment of looking at my father.

Houdini stared at me from the kitchen window, his eyes reflecting off the snow. Then, just before I heard the jangle of Gaura's keys, he jumped off the counter and went to say his final goodbye to Dad.

The three of them—Dad, Gaura, and Houdini—appeared in the doorway. Gaura propped open the door and took the walker from Dad. She quickly carried it down the three steps, left it on the snowy lawn, and then ran back up to help him. Houdini was weaving between his legs and meowing. "You're alright, kitty," my dad said. "You're alright." Houdini seemed to disagree; his circles through my father's legs became tighter, as if he couldn't let his body lose contact with his human's.

"Houdini!" Gaura called, and she started to push him away. "You'll trip him!"

Dad was leaning against the doorframe, his body weak and his eyes glazed. "Hold him up to me for a sec," he said.

"You can't hold him—he'll wiggle and you might fall." Gaura was still trying to push Houdini away, but Houdini was escaping her.

"Just hold him up to me, I said." His hands were plastered onto the doorframe. He wouldn't be able to let go, to hold his cat. "Let me look into his eyes."

Gaura took a breath. "Fine," she said. She stopped her frantic shooing of the cat and picked him up. The medics and I watched as Houdini bumped his forehead into Dad's. "Wish I could take you with me, pumpkin," he murmured.

"He's purring," Gaura said.

Dad nodded.

"It's sweet," the smiling medic said a touch too loudly, cleaving the magic moment open and reminding us all of his presence.

Gaura wordlessly put Houdini down, and he trudged into the house. "Okay, then," she said. Dad began his descent down the stairs and into the ambulance.

I'd never been inside an ambulance before. The only time I'd had to call for one was when Kenny D'Amato fell down a flight of stairs after doing E and broke his head open in senior year of high school. There was blood everywhere, and while my friends and I were fuckups and burnouts, we did manage to call 9-1-1, pick him up, and cross our fingers that he wouldn't die.

This was an entirely different experience. There was no adrenaline pumping through my body, no smell of sweat, no fear of getting in trouble. There was exhaustion, misery, and a drum of panic to let me know that every minute that passed was going to be tattooed onto my soul. That they were all important by virtue of being close to the last.

I was thankful that the tall medic strapped my father in and pulled down a seat for me without a single comment. The talkative one had jumped into the driver's seat.

As we started to pull out, I reached for Dad's hand. They'd draped a thin white hospital blanket over his clothes, and under it his body suddenly looked like it was carved in relief. He was so thin, so fragile. "Are you comfortable?" I asked.

"No," he said. His eyes were closed.

Maybe that was a stupid question. Like asking someone "How are you?" at a funeral.

"Is there anything I can do?" I asked, holding tighter to his hand.

He didn't respond.

How did things change so much so quickly? Every minute of every hour of every day he was closer to death. As Gaura said, he was spending less and less time on this plane of consciousness. The walk down the stairs had probably exhausted him. Maybe that smiling asshole was right and he should have been carried out. Maybe that would have given me another moment to talk to him. I looked at where our hands were clasped. He'd curved his fingers back around my own—it wasn't fully a hold, but it was the gesture of one.

I knew dying of cancer was painful. Why else would they always be creating new powerful painkillers for this exact scenario?

I remembered hearing someone qualify in a meeting about their father dying of cancer and how they pocketed one of the vials of morphine as they said goodbye. I didn't quite judge him for it, but I didn't forget it, either. But being here, in this cornucopia of painkillers, with the presence of death a suffocating veil over every thought, it didn't just seem like an easy thing to do; it seemed almost sensible. I counted to five to clear the thought.

The ambulance bounced onto the highway and jerked us into a higher speed. And then, suddenly, I had no room inside my mind for thoughts. The only thing I could hear were sirens. They filled the room, bouncing and echoing off the small chamber in the back. Dad's eyes opened a few moments after my own widened in shock.

His breathing skipped a beat.

What did that motherfucker think he was doing up there?

"Slow down," I said, glued to how every sudden movement tensed Dad's body.

No one responded. I could hear them chatting together, voice-like murmurs carrying through the metal and plastic divider. What were they talking about? I knew that people could get used to anything, that this was their job, not their personal tragedy, but they should be a little more aware that it was ours. We switched lanes with a forceful jerk.

"Slow down." I banged my hand against the wall to grab their attention. The tall one looked back at me and furrowed his brow like he didn't understand what I was saying. The sirens wore on. "Slow." I hit my hand hard against the plastic near his face. "The Fuck." I slammed it again. "Down." My palm was tingling.

"Whoa," the talkative one said.

"You're hurting him." I looked down at Dad's jaw clenched in pain. "And we don't need the sirens. It doesn't matter how quickly we fucking get there. Okay?"

"Okay, okay. Jeez." The sirens quieted. "I'll just use them when I need to pass someone, okay? No reason to sit in traffic."

I looked back down, and Dad's jaw wasn't so tight anymore. He murmured something that I couldn't make out. I bent my head to him. "There's my Brooklyn girl," he whispered.

TWENTY-ONE

Gaura, Dad, and I lived in the Kingston Hospice Center for five days.

Two of us walked out.

TWENTY-TWO

Nothing was holding Gaura and me together. Or maybe it was that after five days in the hospice, we both needed time apart to process and grieve. Silence filled the car as she drove back to the house—her house.

We had the funeral to plan, stuff to clean out, and calls to make. But all that wouldn't take longer than a week—at least, not my part of it. After that, I'd probably take a bus back home to New York City, go back to work when I ran out of bereavement time, and restart my life. Dad's world upstate hadn't been a major part of my life, and so the absence of it shouldn't be, either. Still, it felt like nothing would ever be the same again.

"Do you wanna turn on the radio?" Gaura asked, shaking me out of my stray thoughts.

"Sure," I said. It was only 9:00 a.m., so I was slightly afraid there'd only be loud, boisterous talk radio made by vulgar men with ridiculous nicknames like DJ Morning Wood and Daddy Hot Takes. But when I turned it on, the first station was playing "Silent Night," the second was playing "I Saw Mommy Kissing Santa Claus," and by the time we heard "Little Drummer Boy," I turned to Gaura with a realization. "Is it Christmas Day?"

"Oh," she said. "Yeah, I guess so."

I switched the radio back to "Silent Night."

Hymns and church music kept us company as we wove back into the round snowy hills. Houdini chirped at us when we walked in. Gaura went to him, picked him up, and dipped her head into his fur. Wordlessly, she carried him upstairs and shut the door to her bedroom. We hadn't discussed what we'd do for the rest of the day, but we didn't need to. We were going to sleep.

But as I lay on my futon, with the morning sunlight reflecting off the snow and into my eyes, I found myself completely awake.

I reached for my phone, and even though I doubted she'd be awake this early, I called Mom.

"Hello?" Her voice was breathless, as if she'd run to her phone. "Emma? Is that you?"

"I'm surprised you picked up so quickly." A migraine was starting to bloom behind my eyelids. I wished the curtains could block out the winter sun.

"Are you kidding? Emma, all I've been doing these past few days is waiting for your call. Where are you?"

"We're back at the house. Gaura and me. Dad died early this morning." It was the first time I'd said the words out loud. My voice sounded shallow and numb.

"Fuck," she whispered.

I didn't say anything else. I sobbed, and she listened. I heaved out tears, dumping them down my face by the bucketful.

"Emma," she murmured.

I couldn't speak. My throat was only capable of making one noise. I held the phone tightly to my cheek, even as my tears coated it.

I don't know how long we stayed like that, Mom murmuring my name as she listened to me cry, both of us clutching our phones as our only lifeline.

When I quieted, she asked me what I would do that day.

"Nothing. I'm going to try to go to sleep, I guess."

"Emma, I hate to ask, but—" she paused "—is there alcohol in the house? Do you think you should maybe get a hotel room?"

I took a breath. She was worried about me. She loved me. It wasn't that she didn't trust me, not exactly. "I'm not going to drink."

"I'm sure Gaurel would understand—"

"You know her name's Gaura," I snapped.

"Of course. Isn't that what I said? I didn't mean to offend you, my love. I just—these are the situations you hear about, when things become too much."

She meant that this was when people relapsed. But it wasn't when I would. I still felt like I was looking up at a meteorite crashing into earth, and the only thing I had to hold close was my choice to be sober. "Mom, I think I need to go to sleep. The funeral's going to be Sunday, the twenty-eighth."

"I'll be there," she said quietly.

"Are you going to bring David?" I hoped David would come. If she had his shoulder to lean on, then I could use hers.

"I think so. Would that be okay?"

"Of course. I want you to have someone to support you. How's packing up the apartment going?"

"We still have a month, so I haven't started. Are you going to bring your new guy?" I didn't know if Ben qualified as my new guy. Or my anything. We'd gone from taking it slow to taking a pause. We'd made up at the Christmas party, but I wasn't sure if we'd pressed Play.

"This isn't the kind of thing you ask a guy you've been kind of dating to."

"There aren't any rules about what you can ask people to do. And I thought you said he was upstate anyway?"

"Hours away." I wanted to tell her that she didn't know anything about modern dating, and that things were more complicated now. But I guessed that wasn't really true—she was also a woman dating in the modern world.

"You could ask him. You don't have to be beholden to how you think people act when they date. You can ask for what you want, and he'll do what he wants. It's really that simple."

"What would I say? If I wanted to?"

She took a breath before starting. "You'd just say 'It would mean so much if you could make it.' It's scary, I know. Of course it's scary. But it gets easier every time you invite someone in."

"It's easier for you now? With David?" I paused, but before I let her answer, I started again. "Why did it take you so long?"

"I had an idea of myself, I think. As a mom, a teacher, someone who'd seen enough about marriage to never want to be involved in it again. I think I was ready to be with someone long before I was ready to let go of that image of myself." She sighed. "But it didn't have anything to do with you."

In a way, I knew what she meant. Sometimes it can feel like disloyalty, letting go of past versions of yourself. Even though I'd changed so much about myself, even though I'd worked so hard for it, I still wasn't sure who I was going to be or what exactly I was working toward.

"I have to go to sleep. Really." I didn't usually bring people closer, or ask them to come further into the mess of my life. But I was so tired of trying to hold everything together by myself.

"Okay. I love you, Emma."

"I love you, too."

When I woke up, the sun had quieted and Houdini was purring on my chest.

I texted Ben without thinking.

Emma: Hi. Merry Christmas.

Ben: Merry Christmas

His text was accompanied by a photo of a Christmas tree weighed down by tinsel and glass ornaments.

Emma: Which one is this?

Ben: What if I told you this one was in my childhood bedroom?

Emma: I honestly wouldn't know how to handle it. It's huge!

Ben: No, joking. This one belongs to the living room—it's my mom's masterpiece.

Emma: The one in your bedroom has all the ornaments you made as a kid, right?

Ben: Ha, if only. My mom doesn't want anything that sentimental when she could have shiny plastic made thousands of miles away.

Emma: It's good to know no one's perfect. I was starting to get worried for a minute.

Ben: How are you?

I wasn't quite sure how to respond. I was terrible. I couldn't imagine being worse.

~~He died this morning~~

~~My Dad's dead and its Christmas which I already hated but now I hate more~~

I was apparently taking too long to respond because I got a double text.

Ben: Are you still in hospice?

I'd told Ben before we went in a few days ago and had asked him to periodically send me random funny memes. He'd complied, and even made me smile once, which was quite a feat inside the Kingston Hospice Center.

Emma: No, my stepmom and I are back at the house

Ben: I'm so sorry

He understood enough for me not to have to write it out.

Emma: Thank you

Ben: Please let me know if there's anything I can do to help.

I thought back to my conversation with Mom. Ben was offering to help. I could ask him to come to the funeral. Because the truth was, I wanted him there. I wanted someone to stand next to me who was only sad because I was sad, not because they'd lost something themselves. Someone whose only reason for coming was because I needed them to.

And if it was too much, he was allowed to say no.

Emma: I understand if you can't, and please don't feel like you have to, but the funeral will be on Sunday, and it would be nice to have you there.

His name flashed across my phone. Was he calling to let me down easy? Tell me I was pushing things too fast and too soon?

"Hello?" My voice was still croaky from sleep.

"I'll be there," he said.

"Don't feel obligated—"

"I don't. You're only about an hour south, but that doesn't matter. I'd drive all day."

Something weird happened to my heart when he said that.

It was as if it took its first beat in days. “That’s really nice of you, Ben.”

“Of course.”

“Well, I guess I’ll text you the details—”

“Wait, text them to me later. Stay on the phone for a minute. It’s good to hear your voice… I was worried.”

“I’ll stay,” I said.

“There are boxes in the basement of all his old stuff,” Gaura said. “If you want to go through it and take a few things, you’re welcome to.”

I’d never been to the basement of this house before. I remembered when Dad first bought it, he tried to show me during the big tour, but as soon as he opened the door, the damp smell of mildew wafted out and the stairs creaked as he trampled down them, and I simply refused to follow. I was a city kid, and the only thing I knew about basements were that mice (or worse, rats) and serial killers (or worse, serial-killing ghosts) favored them, and I was not going to risk my life entering one.

I’d grown up since then (mostly), and now the only thing I had to fear were objects that triggered painful memories. I thought maybe I’d prefer the rats. It was a toss-up.

“There’s no light on the stairs,” Gaura continued as I opened the door, and the same smell of mildew that I remembered greeted me once again. “When you get down there, there’s not a switch—it’s just a string coming from the light bulb.” I felt like I’d made the right call at age nine. This basement sounded terrifying.

I started down. The wood was soggy and weak—ready to dissolve at any moment. The last thing I needed was to fall through the basement stairs, to be trapped here in this decaying house in Phoenicia. After the car ride, I’d felt time ticking by. I wanted to go home. I was ready to sleep in my bed, surrounded by my things. Sit on my mattress and feel like I was on the stern of a boat, propped up by Sea Mist.

"I'm going to close the door behind you, okay? I don't want Houdini following you. He might find a mouse."

"Okay." But I wished for Houdini's company and his protection from the now-confirmed rodent population.

She shut the door, and everything fell into darkness. I blinked my eyes, but it didn't help. The dark was a vacuum. I tiptoed the rest of the way, taking deep breaths.

The floor surprised me when I found it; I'd been ready for another step. I held my hands out in front of me, searching blindly for the string that would be my salvation. When I found it, the light revealed a room covered in '70s wood paneling, thick forest green carpeting, and one wall of floor-to-ceiling boxes in different stages of decay.

Were these the things I was supposed to look through? Long-forgotten things that had lost any meaning. How could I ever get through them all? I didn't know where or how to begin.

I took a picture and texted it to Ben.

Emma: I truly know how to celebrate boxing day.

Ben: Holy shit. And here I am only packing up the argyle sweaters my mom bought me to return to Kohls. Do you have to go through all of that stuff?

Emma: It's not mandatory, but I'm going to try to. What will you exchange your assuredly very flattering sweaters for? Can anything truly desirable be bought at Kohls?

Ben: Socks? Underwear? Onesies for my niece that talk about how she's a "daddy's girl"?

Emma: Please, no.

Ben: I would never. Where are you going to begin with the boxes?

Emma: I'm at a loss. Choose for me?

Ben: I'd probably go top left.

I took a deep breath and walked over to the tower of boxes. They were unlabeled, but their differing states of disintegration gave me some sort of clue as to the time period of Dad's life they were from. The boxes on the bottom had burst under their burden. The cardboard bore signs of water damage and simply couldn't support the weight of the tumbling tower above it. The ones at the top were crisp and unbothered, as if they'd only just been placed there and had all the confidence that they would be picked up soon. They were certainly newer and so probably had little to do with the part of Dad's life that meaningfully intersected with mine. It would help to ease myself in and work backward in time.

I pulled the one on the top left down. Or, more accurately, it fell on me as soon as I jostled it, as it was far heavier than I'd anticipated. I cut the packing tape from the box, lifted its lid, and revealed a collection of books on Zen meditation. I shuffled through them and found them overwhelmingly uniform. *Peace Is Every Step*, *Beyond Thinking*, and Richard Gere's *Pilgrim*. My father was the kind of man who picked up and put down passions that he wore as identities every few years. I had a vague memory of Zen meditation leading to yoga, which led to Gaura, but I couldn't be sure.

The next box was lighter. I opened it and, at first, had no idea what I was seeing. It seemed like a mass of small plastic ziplock bags filled with dirt. Had he been soil testing? I picked one up to look closer. It was just brown dust. I was tempted to open and smell it, but I thought I should probably proceed with caution. I put it down and reached for another. This one had more of a shape. It was a dried mushroom. Although my mind briefly short-circuited, I realized that this was not, in fact, a cardboard box full of magic mushrooms; it was simply a box full of different kinds of wild, dehydrated mushrooms. I mean, some of them might have been hallucinogenic, but a few looked like the hens of the woods I remembered seeing here when I visited in the fall.

The third box was full of office supplies, random receipts, and leaky pens that had long since dried. It looked like he'd poured the contents of a kitchen messy drawer or an old work desk into a box and then forgot about it. I picked up a bag of rubber bands and found them crisp with age.

So far, there was nothing I felt I had to keep as a memory of him. Books on meditation that he'd certainly disavowed? Mushrooms so old they'd turned to dust? Post-its? I'd been worried about wanting too much from Gaura, but now it seemed more likely that I'd come away with nothing.

Ben: How's it going?

Emma: More banal than I thought. It turns out going through ancient office supplies is boring even if those office supplies once belonged to your recently deceased father.

Ben: Is there no situation in which staples are worth crying about?

Emma: Well, I couldn't say no situation, but so far not this one.

I sent him a picture of one of the mushrooms to see if he could guess what it was. He failed miserably.

The next few boxes were cut from the same cloth. They didn't contain anything that struck me as *him*. Maybe I'd have to keep Richard Gere's meditation book after all. If the basement had a window, I knew I'd be able to see the sky start to pinken and dusk appear over the snowy mountaintops. But I was only half-way through, and I was stuck with nothing to look at except cinder block and mold.

I heaved the next box off the stack, and I could tell it was books again. The first few were Civil War histories. Then books about the ecological history of the Catskills, probably from when he first moved up here. There was one of those photo books of Old Phoenicia complete with images of stern-looking nineteenth-century homesteaders and survey maps of roads that were now paved and lined with highway markers.

Just as I put the photo book back, ready to tape the box up and add it to the pile of forgotten things, I noticed something that was incredibly familiar to me but had no place here among my father's things: the Big Book. I had the same edition in my bag upstairs. The one that I carried with me to countless meetings, the one I read from at night, that I'd highlighted and annotated and prayed to for salvation. Why did he have one?

I snatched it up and flung it open. There was a list of names on the first page.

Jim P. 7/09/01
Marc B. 12/29/02
Jackson R. 11/30/04
Robert F. 5/11/06

I brushed my finger against my father's old name. There he was in writing, my very own Robert Finley.

It was tradition in AA for sponsors to pass their books on to their sponsees, so the sponsees could see what passages mattered most to the sponsor. The names in the front acted like the names in a family Bible. They told the story of a sponsorship family and how a book was passed down from one man to the next. HG didn't do that tradition—Hudson Group members were asked to sponsor so many people that it wouldn't have been possible—

so my book had always just been my own. But I'd seen books like this one before.

He'd been where I'd been. Not to the exact same rooms, but that didn't matter. He'd been there.

These boxes in front of me told a story of an unsatisfied man, one searching for something he couldn't name. He didn't find it in AA, or in mushrooms, or even in meditation. But he'd tried. How had I not seen it before?

I had no idea he'd ever quit drinking, even for a month, even for an hour. I had no idea that he'd ever admitted he had an issue with it. But suddenly, memories of that summer I'd spent up here when I was nine came flooding back. The summer of 2006. The long walks in the woods, the hours spent on gin rummy by the fire, the complete absence of a raised voice. He was sober. How had I not realized he was sober?

Suddenly, I wanted the mushrooms, and the rubber bands, and the books about the Catskills. I could push aside last summer when he told me I should've just stuck to beer and wine, because I knew some part of him knew that was bullshit. He'd done that, over and over again, and it hadn't worked. The fact that AA hadn't worked for him didn't matter, either. It worked for a few months, and those few months gave us our best memories. I wished I hadn't gone home early. I wanted to go back in time and shake myself into loving how the cold air hit my lungs. AA worked enough. Even though it stopped working, or he stopped working, he tried.

I flipped through the book, and a small piece of paper fell out.

I read the top: "Pine Hill Community Center Group Meeting Schedule."

Every day of the week had a 7:00 a.m. and a 6:00 p.m. meeting. I checked my phone. It was 5:10 p.m. on Friday, December 26.

I left the rest of the boxes unopened and flew up the stairs.

★ ★ ★

"Thank you again for driving me," I said as Gaura's GPS warned that we'd arrive at our location in five hundred feet.

She turned on her signal and began to pull over. "You can stop thanking me. You don't need to."

I hadn't let the book out of my hands, but I hadn't told Gaura where I'd gotten it. I wondered if she knew, but I couldn't bear to talk about it with her. What if she repeated all the things Dad had hated about AA? What if she said it was just a gift and he'd never been to a meeting? Her hands were full of needles that might burst my bubble, and for the moment, I needed it to breathe.

"But I'm really thankful," I said, unbuckling my seat belt.

She reached over and placed her hand on top of mine. "Emma, I get the need for a spiritual practice."

I nodded, looking into her eyes. Maybe I was wrong on our last drive, maybe we weren't going to be strangers.

"So, I'll pop into the yarn store over in Margaretville and be back in an hour?"

"Perfect. I'll see you then."

I glanced around as my feet hit the crisp snow that lined the shoulder of the road. It was dark. Phoenicia's lack of streetlights had followed us to the next town west. I could make out the burning red cherries of cigarettes about fifty yards away. I couldn't see the people smoking them yet, but I knew I was in the right place.

As I walked inside, I looked around the room. It was a far cry from the palatial churches where HG had their meetings. There were no old oak pews, stone arches, or hanging tapestries. There were chairs and people. Someone was setting up an easel to display a yellowed poster of the twelve steps. The rusted folding chairs were arranged auditorium style, which was a small mercy. I didn't know if I could cope with sitting in a circle and being forced to look everyone in the eye. I knew I was being regarded as new here. I could feel everyone's eyes continually drifting toward me, a curiosity. New people in AA were sacred, something to be huddled around and protected. A few people gave me tight smiles. I nodded politely back at them.

It was as if a statistician had taken a random slice of the local population and plopped them down into this room. There were women with close-to-translucent skin, long unwashed hair, and an unknowable number of layers of knit fabrics. One was even wearing an ankh necklace. Next to her was a man with unintentional stubble, hands so deeply callused I could see their coarseness from my seat across the room, and a hoodie that was in no way warm enough for the bitter wind outside. I took a few deep breaths. There was a woman whose body spilled over one seat and onto the edges of two others, and she was holding the hand of a smaller woman and leaning her head against the wall behind her. Her breaths were short and heavy, and I wondered if she was okay, if she was ill in a way other than the one that had brought her inside this room. There were all of these faces who wouldn't otherwise be together, and I was here. I was with them.

These were my people, and they, however briefly, had been my father's people. I grazed my eyes over the white paint chipping off the cinder block walls and timeworn flyers advertising local events that had long since passed. Had they been here when Dad came to this very room?

Time passed, and I kept losing track of it. I couldn't remember what someone said five seconds after it floated out of their mouth. Until finally, the woman who'd been so clearly struggling moved her head. She raised it with her hand in one fluid movement. The qualifier gestured to her, and she began.

"I've been clean eight years. It's a long time, but it's also not enough time. I lost my son a week ago. He was twenty. He knew me sober, but before that, he knew me using. I couldn't take that back. That had already happened. I tried to be a good mother, but I couldn't change what happened. He'd already been born into that life." She paused heavily. When she began speaking again, her voice had a new strength. Her sorrow had an added bite. "Now, I don't wanna talk about how he died. It wasn't doing anything good, that I'll say. But he wasn't doing anything that was foreign to him, either. He wasn't doing anything he didn't grow up around." She paused for a second time, taking a heaving breath before continuing. "Now I gotta live with this. And I'm not gonna use. But this is what I want to say about it all. If this isn't an excuse, then none of you got an excuse." It was an accusation, but not an unfair one. If this woman could come to a meeting instead of getting high, if she could bury her son sober, then I felt sure I could make it through whatever I had to make it through. That we all could, every single one of us in this room.

These weren't the shares I was used to hearing in HG. She didn't mention a spiritual solution or any solution besides not using. She'd gotten too high, fucked up her life, and faced real consequences. Consequences that brought bitter grief. Now she was trying not to fuck up and use. That's all it was. And in trying to do that, she brought her pain to the room so we could help her hold it. I couldn't imagine the rooms of Hudson Group trying to hold that kind of anguish; I was sure it would slip through everyone's fingertips as they tried to find the right passages in the text to explain it away.

I raised my hand, and the speaker nodded to me.

"Hi. I'm Emma, I'm an alcoholic, and I'm grieving, too," I said. "My father died yesterday."

There were a few murmurs of sympathy around the room, and one woman turned to face me, her eyebrows furrowed in sympathy.

"I spent my life either trying to be exactly like him or nothing like him. We didn't have the easiest relationship. He moved up here when I was a kid, and I didn't see him much. And when

I did, he was either on some new fad that was going to change his entire life, or he was drunk. But mostly, it seemed like he was drunk.

"And then I grew up, and I still didn't really see him, but then somehow, I was drunk half the time, too. And life was racing past me. People were moving on, getting married, contributing to society, and all I could do was work at bars, black out, and throw up my dinner. I found my way to these rooms spurned on by how much I didn't want to be Dad. I didn't know what I wanted, but I knew I didn't want to be him. So because he was drunk, I had to be sober.

"I've heard that miracles happen when you get sober, and I haven't found that to be true. All of my hopes and dreams haven't fallen out of the sky—I've had to work for them, to try to be a better person every single day. But the closest thing I've had to a miracle happened to me today. I was going through Dad's stuff, and I found this book." I held it up, the sweat on my palms almost causing me to drop it. "And it has his name in it, and it had your meeting schedule from 2006. I've spent the past year and change feeling like I got sober because I wanted a better life than he had. But at some point, not forever, but at some point, he was sober, too. And it didn't heal him, not perfectly or completely.

"Now I feel like I can't be sober just because he was drunk. I have to be sober because I want to be sober. Because my life is better when I don't drink. Maybe it's that simple—or at least just for today, it feels that simple."

There weren't many places to walk, but I bundled myself up anyway and set out. I wanted to be walking when I made this phone call. As soon as I stepped outside, I could feel the cold air bursting the capillaries in my cheeks. The snow crunched under my winter boots. I didn't want to make this call. I wanted to simply never speak to Lola again. Ghosting felt more natural to me. It was so much easier to ignore a problem than deal with it.

But I knew I should call her. Not because that's what a sober person did, or because I had to stay spiritually fit, or even because that's what someone told me to do. No, I knew I should call her because I didn't want to be a coward. I wanted to be the kind of person who owned up to their mistakes. It would be easier to walk down the streets of New York if I wasn't worried about running into anyone. If I didn't have to hide from the things that made me ashamed.

When I got to the end of the driveway, I hit Call.

The phone rang a couple of times, and I blissfully thought that I might be able to leave a voicemail and end it at that. I started crafting a monologue—

"Hello?" Her voice was crisp, almost staccato. She usually spoke languidly, as if each word deserved its own breath—but not now.

"Hi, Lola."

"I'm glad you called, Emma." She didn't sound glad, not exactly.

"I wanted to apologize."

"You've been gone from meetings for quite a while. I honestly didn't know if you'd be back."

"Well, I've been upstate. My father passed."

"Oh, Emma. I'm so sorry. I wish I had known. Prayer and community are what you need now more than ever." Her vowels were stretching. I realized this was probably a way to get back into her good graces, but I didn't feel like I needed Lola's absolution anymore.

"I haven't been praying much lately."

"I've heard that many people who go through loss in fellowship lean on the third step prayer—"

"I don't think prayer is what I need. But I really didn't call to talk about that. I know I made a scene at the last meeting I went to. And I'm sorry, that wasn't the proper way for me to talk about what I was feeling." I started walking up the road toward the mountain, my calves burning at the incline.

"You were under a lot of stress with your father's illness. We all say things we don't mean sometimes."

"I did mean it."

"Oh."

"Lola, you've helped me a lot, and I'm grateful. I don't know what this past year would have been like without you. But I don't think HG is where I want to be. So I don't think we should work together anymore."

"This is a very dangerous time for you, Emma, and the words you're saying are very dangerous. I want to help you—"

"And you have! But I don't think you can help me anymore. I want to be sober. I want to go to AA. I just want to do it a little differently."

"HG is solution-based, Emma. In those other meetings, people just complain, they don't try to change." I felt the way her voice cooled off again, changing with her perception of me.

"I don't feel that way."

We weren't getting anywhere. But maybe there was nowhere to get. I didn't want to call Lola and tell her my resentments every day. I wanted to let them go.

TWENTY-THREE

The funeral was at a Buddhist temple at the end of a winding mountain road. I felt like a child as I sat in the back seat of David's rental car with him and Mom up front, but I didn't mind the heated leather as it warmed my thighs. They'd picked me up from Gaura's early in the day so we could get breakfast in town before the ceremony.

David was wearing a pressed suit, and Mom was wearing gray slacks and an oversize sweater. I slipped on my red floral dress—the same I'd worn two weeks ago when Dad showed me the red bull's-eye in the sky.

"Well, I'm glad I have four-wheel drive," David said as we drove over a patch of road covered in ice. We were in the mountains in late December—they would have been impassable without it. "I don't think I've ever been to a Buddhist temple before, so this will be a new experience for me."

I raised my eyebrows at him in the rearview mirror but bit back a snappy retort about how we were all having new experiences today. He was nervous. This was weird for him. "Are your parents alive, David?"

"Oh, um. Yes, they are. Thankfully. They live together in a retirement community." David was over sixty.

"That must be nice for them to be together." The usual pang of jealousy that gripped me when I wished for another family didn't come and didn't infect my voice. I'd meant what I said. Holding one person close for all those years? It might not have happened in my family, but the fact that it happened anywhere made me feel a little more hopeful.

Mom reached her hand back and squeezed my knee.

"Have you heard from Ben?" she asked. She had an amazing ability to know what I was thinking before I did. It was as if she could see the thoughts forming like clouds in my eyes, and by the time they rained down on me, she'd already walked ahead of me into the storm.

"Yeah, he's there. He got there early." According to David's GPS, we were only five minutes away, and Ben had texted me eight minutes ago that he'd arrived. I'd looked at the message every ten seconds since it came in, and I hadn't been able to decide how I felt about him being there. The fact that he'd driven down was possibly the nicest thing someone had ever done for me. I felt like a cat who'd found a patch of sunlight, and I wanted to roll and revel in it. But at the same time, I'd never been so naked with anyone. I thought of the night at Ben's apartment and how everything felt like it was moving a mile a minute—that didn't hold a candle to this. I might not have slept with him yet, but this would be the most intimate I'd ever been with a man.

The GPS started to sing out. Mom kept her hand on my knee. Whatever happened next, I would get through it. The woman from the Pine Hill Community Center meeting flooded my mind. She'd run out of everything but persistence. I borrowed an ounce of bravery from my memory of her.

As soon as we pulled up, I saw Ben pacing in the parking lot next to an enormous black pickup truck.

"Is that him? The tall one with the truck?" Mom asked.

I saw his eyes catch on to our car, search it for me, and then lock on to mine in the back seat. He stopped pacing.

"Yeah. That's him."

After I introduced everyone, the four of us stood in the parking lot.

"Thank you again for coming," I said to Ben. He was wearing a suit, because of course he was, but his hair was curling around his ears in a way I hadn't seen before. He looked ruffled.

"Of course." He nodded. His eyes hadn't left mine.

"That's quite a truck you have!" Mom said. She sounded cheerful, and I knew from her tone of voice that she was trying to get him to like her. I was touched.

"Oh," he said, turning from me for the first time, "it's my dad's. I just thought it'd be easier with the mountains."

While he was looking at the truck, Mom turned to me and mouthed, "He's cute!"

I blushed just in time for him to look back at me. Confusion passed over his face.

"We'll head in, get seats," Mom said.

When I heard the door open, I hugged Ben around his waist, burying my face in his down coat. He held me tightly.

"Are there a lot more people coming?" he asked. He sounded nervous.

"I don't know." His coat smelled like crisp air and coming snow.

"Should we go in? I don't want your mom to think—"

"In a minute. I just need a minute." Even though I was terrified before I saw him, I felt my heartbeat slowing now. I looked up at him. "My mom likes you. She's not going to think anything but that."

His lips turned up in a half smile. "How could she like me already?"

"It would be very easy. You're completely likable."

Another car's wheels moved over the gravel parking lot. I let go of Ben, and he tucked my hand into his before we walked up the temple stairs.

Once the service was over, I stepped outside immediately. It had been fine, but it didn't mean as much to me as finding the Big Book, or looking at the stars, or watching *Field of Dreams.* It didn't feel like my final goodbye to Dad. I'd be saying goodbye and hello to him all my life.

I hadn't asked Ben to stay beyond the service, so as we found ourselves wordlessly walking to his truck, I knew it was time for me to give up my hold on his hand and start saying my goodbyes.

"So, should I follow your parents' car down to the house, or do you want to ride with me?" Ben asked.

By *parents* he must have meant David and Mom. "Down to the house?"

"To Gaura's house? She said everyone was welcome to come over?" He took his time pronouncing Gaura's name but didn't mess it up. I knew that Gaura was having a potluck of sorts at her house, but I'd hoped to briefly make an appearance and then run away with Mom. I'd told Gaura I'd go back to the city after the funeral, and I meant it.

"Oh!"

"I don't have to come, of course. If you want time with your family, I completely understand—" Ben was beginning to ramble.

"No! I don't want time with them! I'll ride with you." I couldn't believe I was inviting Ben further into the weirdness of my father's past life, but the last thing I wanted was to see him drive away.

He nodded and unlocked his car. I texted Mom that I'd see her at the house and climbed into Ben's dad's Ford.

"You'll take this road until you hit the highway again," I said, strapping myself into his car. "Everyone's probably going to the same place, anyway."

We talked about the service, the history of the temple, and Dad's many attempts to find the meaning of life as we drove up and down the snow-grayed mountains. Ben was unfazed by the winding roads, cementing himself as an upstate boy in my mind.

We had to park on the lawn next to a sea of '90s Subarus. We stood out. "Before we head in there," I started, "I hadn't planned to stay very long. I think Gaura and I are both ready for some time apart."

I looked out my window to see a blonde woman with dreadlocks and wine-stained teeth, who I remembered making a speech about my father's spirit of integrity at the celebration of life. I couldn't bring myself to unbuckle my seat belt. Before Ben had a chance to respond, I started speaking again. "Actually, I don't think I want to go in there at all."

I expected him to talk me into it. But he just said, "Okay," and switched the truck into Reverse.

"Wait!" I put my hand over his. "I need my stuff. I don't want to come back."

"I can grab it," he said, putting the car back into Park.

"But you don't know where my room is, and I haven't packed, and I should tell Gaura I'm leaving." I would run in, say I couldn't stay, grab my stuff, and leave.

"We'll run in like it's a heist," he said. "In and out."

I hadn't even told Ben why I didn't want to go in. Or why I needed a break from Gaura and her friends. Thankfully, he wasn't asking me to explain, because I don't think I'd have been able to—I was moving with my feelings instead of my thoughts.

The house was filling up as we stepped inside, and Ben's hand glued itself to the small of my back. The temple had felt sparsely populated with everyone spread out on individual meditation pillows, but now that people had poured into the living room of Dad and Gaura's small home, it felt like a rush hour 1 train. We swerved our way through people I didn't recognize—everyone held small, compostable plastic cups of red wine and gluten-free seed crackers crumbling onto napkins.

I led Ben to the bedroom I'd spent the last few weeks in. The door was ajar, and heavy winter coats had been piled on the bed. I hadn't remembered making my bed before I left for the funeral. Someone must have pulled the comforter up for me before they threw the first coat down. It had stopped being my room and returned to its true nature as a guest room, a transient space belonging to no one, least of all me. It took me less than a minute to shove my crumpled clothes into my suitcase and zip it up. Ben wordlessly took it from me as we started to push our way out of the house. I looked around for Gaura and Mom, wanting to tell each of them that I was leaving. Where I found them surprised me.

They were tucked against the same corner of the counter that Dad and I leaned on only six months ago, where a march of ants died under my thumb. Mom had her hand on Gaura's forearm, and Gaura's mouth was moving as steadily as a mountain stream. I'd never seen her talk that much. Almost as shocking was Mom's stoic silence, the steady beat of her nodding head. I could have gone up to both of them at once, said my goodbyes, traded hugs and sorrow. But something about the little bubble they'd created for themselves made me want to leave it intact rather than disturbed. So instead, I walked out without any notice. One last Irish goodbye to honor my father.

Snow started to fall just as we hit the main road. Big fat flurries landed on Ben's windshield and began to dust the asphalt.

"Do you have a place where you want to go?" Ben asked.

I hadn't thought that far. I'd only managed a quick text to Mom that I didn't think I'd make the potluck after all. She hadn't responded yet, but I knew service was spotty here for her. She hadn't considered rural reliability when choosing a phone plan—nor had I, for that matter.

"Maybe we could just grab a bite?" I suggested.

"Sure. There's a diner in town that's pretty famous, right?" He was talking about the Phoenicia Diner, where I'd been countless times with Dad, and just this morning with Mom and David. I couldn't take yet another meal there.

"Would you mind if we went one town over? I'm feeling ready to be done with Phoenicia."

"Sure, I bet they have a diner in Margaretville." He turned the car around, and we headed deeper into the Catskill Mountains as the sun dipped below the horizon. Now that night was falling, the snow was the only source of light. Tumbling flakes flashed white against the sky, cleaning the landscape around us. What had been gray and rocky mountains were becoming fluffy and bright. The night felt cartoonishly beautiful.

"I'd only been to one funeral before today," I said. I looked at my phone, but Mom still hadn't responded. I hoped she'd gotten my message.

"Whose was it?" Ben kept his eyes on the road.

"My friend's mom when we were in high school." I saw Susannah in her too-big black dress as I blinked. There was a long time in our lives when we did all the big moments together, but this year had seen us both go through monumental things without each other. This felt more like the end of our friendship than when she actually moved out. Before, it always seemed like there might be a way back. Now, with a wedding and funeral between us and the past, I wasn't so sure. "Have you been to a lot?"

"A few."

"I bet all the girls ask you to be their date to family funerals, right?"

He laughed. "No. They don't." Then he paused. "Last year, right around this time, I went to the funeral of my army buddy. Came from a big military family. It was intense."

I imagined horns played by men in uniform and flags laid over a grave in Arlington. "Did he die overseas?"

"No. He died of an overdose a few years after we came home."

I thought of all the times Ben fixed me with kind eyes when I talked about sobriety. I was surprised he hadn't told me this yet. "Were you close?"

"Yeah." His fingers twitched against the steering wheel. "He might've been my best friend."

"I'm sorry." I didn't know Ben was grieving when I first started at Richer & Thomas. Was that why people thought he was shy? Why he didn't feel up to making new friends and going to get drinks every Friday night? I thought about him alone in his apartment, watching the world go by with the constant company of a lead weight in his chest.

He dropped one of his hands off the wheel and onto my knee. "Me, too."

"What was his name?"

He didn't move his hand off my knee, but he didn't look at me, either. "Jason."

"Do you want to tell me about him?" My voice was quiet in the darkness of the car, lingering just above a whisper. I thought of how I'd been relieved when Vanessa asked me about Dad, not just his sickness or my grief, but when I got to talk about who he actually was.

He raised his eyebrows. "Oh. I mean, I don't know. What would I say?"

"You can say the good parts. What were your favorite things about him?" I put my hand over his. There were so many ghosts with us in the car already, it seemed only fitting to invite one more in.

"He was good. Like a genuinely good person." He glanced at me finally. "God, that's a stupid thing to say."

"It's not. How was he good?"

"You have to understand, it's rare for a guy in the army to

be that kind. We'd walk down the street, and he'd give every single homeless person a dollar. He'd go to the bank and make sure he had singles, just for that purpose. I mean, I don't know anyone else like that. Sometimes I honestly found it annoying."

"Did you feel like you had to start doing it, too?"

He laughed. "Not at all. Not until he died. That first week, after I heard, I gave anyone who asked for money twenty bucks."

"Twenty! Were you trying to one-up him?" I laughed with him.

"No, no. I knew I couldn't keep it up, so I wanted to give enough while I could. While it still felt like he was with me."

I nodded. "What else was good about him?"

"He made the best fried shrimp. He used seltzer in the batter. I've tried to do it, but I can never get it right."

"I can't help you there. I've never once fried shrimp."

Ben put both his hands back on the steering wheel as he made his way around a tight curve, shrugging. "It'd be impossible to replicate anyway."

Margaretville was a narrow valley town carved out of the rock of Big Indian Wilderness. Houses were built on slopes and a different hill jutted out above each storefront. I hadn't realized how much it'd snowed until I saw the dunes piled on sidewalks. It was only supposed to take twenty minutes to drive there, according to the GPS, but with the unplowed snow, it'd taken us at least double that.

As Ben pulled into a restaurant parking lot, my phone started ringing. I answered to Mom's frantic voice on the other line: "I've been trying to reach you!"

I stayed in the car while I talked to her, and Ben got out and gave me some space. The phone call only took a few minutes, but by the time I was done, snow had coated Ben's dark coat and hair. Even his eyelashes were painted white. Somehow, it was only six o'clock. The quiet of the country night was coaxing me into believing the sun had set eons ago.

"My mom and David are heading back to the city. They're worried about the snow." There was a pit in my stomach. I had accidentally forced myself upon Ben. "I'm sorry—I didn't realize how late it was getting. Do you have to get back to Albany?"

"No." He shook his head as if the one word was enough to stifle all my worries. "Let's get inside." He nodded to the restaurant.

I followed him, still at a bit of a loss. Ben could drop me back at Gaura's on his way home. I hadn't wanted to go back, but it wasn't that big of a deal. She would drive me to the bus station in the morning. I could give Houdini one last kiss.

The diner was almost empty, and the waitress, who was on the upper end of middle-aged, looked at us like we were the very thing stopping her from closing early and going home.

"We'll be quick," Ben said. "Do you want a coffee?" he said, turning to me.

I nodded, and he held up two fingers to the waitress. She raised her eyebrows in wordless understanding and headed for an industrial-sized coffee maker. But coffee turned into fries, which turned into pie and conversation.

Slipping my fork into whipped-cream-covered pumpkin pie, I asked the question that had been nagging at me since our drive. "Why didn't you tell me?"

He kept chewing, having put a too-big bite in his mouth a moment earlier, but furrowed his brows.

"About Jason," I continued.

"It's not an easy thing to talk about."

"I get that."

"I bet you do," he said, a smirk twisting his lips upward.

"Are you insinuating that I keep things close to my chest?"

"Maybe."

I threw a fry at him, laughing. He caught it and popped it into his mouth.

"It's natural, you know, to want to put your best foot forward.

And I guess I was keeping things close to my chest, too. But I feel like I've been better about that since he died."

"How so?" I asked.

"I was just kind of floating, you know? Not making any big decisions. But then everything seemed more serious when I realized how fragile it all was. That anyone could be gone at any moment. It suddenly felt like I was wasting my time going out, playing video games, or doing anything that wasn't meaningful. If I only have so many breaths, I want to take each one with intention."

"What are you serious about?"

He gave me a smile. He knew what I was up to, what I was fishing for. But then his eyes lost their laughter, and he said, "I'm serious about you, Emma."

I'd felt safe with him before. But those words made me sure in a way I didn't think I'd ever felt before. I got up and slid in next to him, on his side of the booth. He welcomed me, curving an arm around my shoulders and tucking me into his suit jacket.

"I'm serious about you, too," I said.

While we were in our own little bubble, talk drifting from death to childhood snow-day traditions and back again, the world kept changing outside.

"This is crazy, right? This is unsafe?" I was gripping the dashboard, trying to keep the panic out of my voice. What had once looked beautiful and magical now felt slippery and dangerous. Didn't people die in these situations? Was getting plowed over a thing? I felt like I remembered a story about people dying because of snowplows. Or maybe they slid out and crashed? Or maybe it was after they crashed that they were plowed over? I tried to remember everything I'd heard as a child watching network news and hoping the New York City public school system would close for a snow day. They always gave tips about how to stay safe while driving through the snow. How could I have known that was actually important information?

"We're fine, Emma. The truck can handle this kind of snow." Ben was focused now in a way he hadn't been when we were driving over. His hands were at ten and two.

"But the woman at the restaurant told us specifically to 'stay safe out there' and 'be careful.'"

"She was just being polite. That's what people say on snowy nights." He sounded confident. Calm, collected. Maybe I was being ridiculous. Maybe this was something he did all the time.

We were only two minutes out of Margaretville, heading back toward Phoenicia. I'd told Ben he could drop me back there before he went home. He'd asked me a few times if I was sure I wanted to go back to Gaura's, but as he didn't offer another solution besides—I nervously assumed—going to his mother's house, I told him Gaura's was fine.

I wondered if this was what people called "a whiteout." The black of the asphalt was buried. Snakes of snow were whipped together by the wind and slithered on top of what was already packed down. There were no other cars on the road.

"How far is Albany from Phoenicia?"

Ben gave me a quick glance. "A little over an hour."

I remembered him telling me it was an hour and a half the other day, so he was underestimating now. "Longer in this weather?"

"Yeah, longer. But when I get to 87, it'll be totally clear. This is the toughest driving now, over these mountains."

Toughest driving. I was vacillating between thinking we were insane for doing this and thinking that only I was insane for not knowing anything about cars or snow and especially cars in the snow, but those words opened my eyes even wider, if that was possible. There was nothing I could do, absolutely nothing. Ben was a grown-up. He had a big truck. All the same, I started mouthing the serenity prayer to myself. *God, grant me the seren-*

ity. The words helped me take my first deep breath in minutes. *Accept the things I cannot change.* I could not change the weather. I could not change the situation. *Power to change the things I can.* What could I change? Would it be my moral obligation to make Ben stay at Gaura's with me? But, oh god, the house would be full, wouldn't it? The woman with wine-stained teeth might already have claimed my bed, her husband with the salt-and-pepper hair spooning her tightly, their skin on the sheets my skin had been on. *The wisdom to know the difference.*

A vacancy light flashed in front of us. "A motel!" I cried. "Ben! There's a motel!"

He slowed. "Do you want to stay there?"

"Yes! Let's stay there." Maybe this was my second AA miracle of the week. After finding Dad's Big Book, I thought I'd gotten all I needed, but now another sign was appearing before me. I wouldn't have to sleep at Gaura's, and Ben wouldn't get plowed over on the interstate. A win-win if I ever saw one.

He pulled into the parking lot. It was a single-story motel with room doors that led right outside—the kind of motel from countless horror movies, the kind of motel that Janet Leigh shouldn't have stopped at. There was a man bundled up to the point of looking like a black Gore-Tex Pillsbury Doughboy shoveling the path to the office.

"Does this place look okay?" I asked. Ben hadn't sounded as relieved as I had. Maybe he thought motels were creepy. I'd certainly understand. "Would you rather sleep in the car?"

"Sleep in the car? Emma, I can drive us back. I can drive you all the way to the city if you want. It's seven o'clock. We're in an F-150."

I didn't know what to say. I just looked at him. Drive back to the city? He was insane. His eyes roved over my face.

"But if you want to get off the road, I'm happy to stay here. I don't have anything I have to get back to. We can spend the night here." His voice took on a softer tone, as if he were calling to a kitten stuck in a tree.

"I want to get off the road," I said. Maybe he could drive me all the way to my Brooklyn apartment. Maybe he could even parallel park this massive truck on Flatbush Avenue. But I didn't want him to. There were warm rooms and springy mattresses right here, and even though Ben and the clock said it was only seven, my body knew it had to be hours later.

"Then let's check in."

I nodded.

Neither of us moved to open our doors. Ben's hand found its way to the back of my neck, and he pulled me forward. His lips felt so warm against mine. I could tell he'd meant for it to be quick, a fraction of a kiss, a statement rather than a moment, but I leaned farther into him. I felt his breath escape from his lips and dust across my own. His bottom lip felt full and tender, and I danced my tongue across it. We hadn't kissed in weeks. We'd fought and made up, but there hadn't been any of this. My breath caught. How had there not been any of this? I should have kissed him the moment I saw him in the parking lot this afternoon. I should have kissed him at the holiday party. I should have kissed him in every Fun Team meeting and—

Ben broke us apart and leaned his forehead against mine. "Let's check in," he said again.

The two queen beds took up the entire small room. They stared out at us like the giant bulbous eyes of a toad. The ancient green comforters looked like blinking eyelids, and the lumps of pillows a brow bone.

"I don't think I've ever stayed in a roadside motel before," I said.

Ben closed the door and then stepped around me and farther into the room. "I didn't think you had, either." I could hear the smile in his voice even though his back was to me.

"Are you teasing me, Ben?"

"I might be, city girl." He turned around to face me and then shook his head ever so slightly, as if clearing it. "I'm going to throw some water on my face." He pointed toward the bathroom.

I wanted to say something dumb like "I'll miss you." Thankfully, I still knew it was ridiculous to miss a man while he washed his face. So I didn't say it. I just thought it, and meant it.

I sat on the bed closest to the bathroom and farthest from the rather flimsy door that stood between us and the outside world. I kicked off my shoes, peeled off my tights, and slipped my bra out from under my dress. I didn't want to go back outside, even for my forgotten pajamas. My dress was made of soft cotton. It didn't have any buttons that would push into my flesh.

Ben walked out of the bathroom and draped his suit jacket on the room's solitary chair.

"I'm just going to sleep in my dress," I volunteered. "You're wearing fancier clothes. You should probably sleep in your underwear." We didn't need to be talking about what to wear to bed. As exhausted as I was, I still knew we wouldn't sleep for a few more hours. But I couldn't leave the matter open.

He nodded, but I saw his eyes flick to my chest, taking in that I was no longer wearing a bra. The room was cool. "I have an undershirt," he said. I remembered the heat of his skin underneath my fingertips and wished he'd forgo the undershirt.

I patted the bed next to me. He looked from my hand to my face and unbuckled his belt. It swooshed from his belt loops, and heat ran to my face. Had he interpreted the pat as a sexual gesture? I hadn't meant it as one. But I longed for the feeling of his body next to mine, the feeling I'd gotten when we were wrapped around each other back at the diner. Now that we were here, in a room with beds, a strange shyness had overtaken us both. Last time we'd been in a room alone with a bed, I'd freaked out. I didn't know if I was very different now than

I was then. I'd still never had sex while sober. I felt more nervous about being here with him than I had when I lost my virginity over a decade ago.

"I'm not expecting anything, Emma. I didn't think anything like this would happen today." He looked like he needed me to understand. His brown eyes were warmer, yet more insistent, than I'd ever seen them.

"I'm not expecting anything, either." I wasn't. I just wanted to feel close. To have him hold me. I didn't think I'd suddenly be overwhelmed and lustful. The day had been too long already.

"We have two beds," he said.

"Let's just use one."

He nodded and unbuttoned his pants.

Maybe I'd had too much bravado, been too sure that sleep was what my body needed most. "There's a TV," I said.

"Do you want to watch it?"

I nodded, and he kept taking off his pants. He must have caught something in my expression because he said, "I don't want to lie down in my suit pants." He kept his boxer briefs on.

"Of course," I said, standing up to look for the remote.

There was nothing on basic cable. After surfing the twenty channels ten times, we settled on watching the last act of *Dances with Wolves*, filled with ample commercial breaks that cut the tension.

My eyes started drifting closed as Kevin Costner got interrogated. I liked it better when he played with the magic baseball team.

"Should we get under the covers?" Ben's voice was soft and close. I'd drifted to sleep on his chest. The TV was off. The movie must have ended. Ben stood like a grown-up and pulled down his side of the bed, but I just wiggled my body under the stiff blanket and pilled sheet. Dreams started to play behind my eyes but stopped when I felt Ben's leg brush my own.

"Will you hold me?" I asked.

I could feel him nod as he wrapped his arm around my waist, his thumb landing on my rib cage. "I'll hold you."

"All night?" I whispered.

Always. He didn't say it out loud. He mouthed it into the back of my neck. I wasn't sure if I could hear him or just tell what the word was from how his breath felt against my skin.

I arched back against him, and I felt his body respond to mine. My dress was bunched up and I could feel the heat of him. There was hardly anything between us. I pressed back once more without thinking. He held me tighter to him. The pace of his pulse doubled.

"I'm going to fall asleep." My voice was hoarse, but I meant my words.

He placed the ghost of a kiss on my neck. "I know." He didn't let me go, and my dreams started where they left off.

Sunlight beat against my eyelids. The starch of my dress had left imprints on my skin. There was snow piled high against our window, and the storm had blown graceful curves into it. I tiptoed to the bathroom, but once I got there, I realized I had nothing to change into. Ben hadn't brought a suitcase since he didn't think he'd be sleeping anywhere overnight, and so when we parked, I hadn't thought to take mine out of his trunk. I looked at myself in the mirror. My hair had tied itself in one massive knot. I needed a shower. I slipped my dress off. I'd have to change back into it to grab the suitcase, but I couldn't bear to leave this room again as I was. I needed to be clean of yesterday and of the last few weeks. As long as I was in the limbo of the Margaretville Motel, I could let it all go. I could drop the weight of grief for just a moment.

I didn't know how long I let the hot water pour over my back with my eyes closed and my temple resting against the recently bleached tile. My mind drifted back to last night and falling asleep in Ben's arms. My pulse raced just from the thought of it. Things felt so different between us now. I couldn't imagine the lengths I went to hide what I thought were the worst parts of myself from him. Could I have had this all along? His rough palm on my waist, his lips on my neck, his soft gaze as I spoke—were they all just waiting for me to fall into them?

There was a knock on the door accompanied by "Good morning." I shut the water off. I didn't want to hog the bathroom.

"One minute!" I called, wrapping myself in a blush-pink towel I hoped hadn't started out as white. When I opened the door, Ben looked at the towel. He didn't even try to glance up to my face. He just moved his gaze over my water-warmed legs to my bare shoulders and back down again. And while he was looking at me, I looked at him. The bright morning sun uncovered the amber strands hidden within his dark hair. And although his posture was relaxed, I could see tension finding its way to his shoulders, accenting the muscles it met there.

"Good morning," I said.

"Hi," he replied, his eyes resting where the towel settled on my upper thigh.

"Hi." I released a shaky exhale.

He blinked. "I didn't mean to rush you," he said.

"You didn't. You look very pretty this morning, Ben." I'd meant to tease him, to sound light and flirty, but when I heard the words come out of my mouth, they didn't sound lighthearted. There was a heaviness to them; they fell to the floor between us.

"Pretty?" He was looking at my collarbone, at the water pooled in its hollow. His voice was brambled, trancelike, as though he was caught between waking and sleeping.

I nodded.

"You're prettier." Finally, his eyes met mine. And I could have sworn that there had been space where my words had fallen—feet of space even. But it was gone. Now there was nothing between us but a few breaths, an ancient terrycloth towel, and an unappreciated undershirt.

"Emma?" Ben's coarse palm was running from my shoulder to my elbow, and my skin erupted in goose bumps. He was touching so little of me, but I could feel him with every part of my body. I closed my eyes.

"Please," I whispered. My breath heated the centimeters between our lips, and he erased them.

He palmed my hip, pulling me close to him. He brushed his tongue against my lips, then my tongue. I was on my tiptoes, but they were unnecessary. Ben was holding me so tightly he was almost lifting me off the ground. His hands kept roving, and my towel didn't stand a chance. It dropped without argument. I stood bare, pushed against him. I could feel how much he wanted me. Probably almost as much as I wanted him. "You're so soft," he whispered into my throat, dropping kisses between his words. My mind was blank; it could only trace the path of heat he was making with his hands.

"Take your shirt off. Take these off." I thumbed his boxers. I felt like I was begging. He stepped away, and the second he came back, I could feel the heat of him. I ran my hands through his hair and kissed every mole that dotted his cheeks, mapping his constellations with my lips. He pushed me back until my knees hit the edge of the bed. The wrinkled sheets felt rough compared to the fever of his skin.

He was holding himself above me, putting more distance than there had been since I'd opened the bathroom door. I tried to pull him back. I wanted to feel the weight of him against me. I watched his muscles tense as I ran my hand across his chest and down.

"Do you have—" I started. That wasn't a question I usually asked the men I hooked up with, but I thought if I was going to do this sober and responsible sex thing, I might as well try to really do it.

Ben shook his head. "I didn't think to bring a condom to your father's funeral." There was a hint of laughter in his voice.

"I would call that being severely underprepared." It was okay. We could still touch each other. We could still be intimate.

"Evidently." He eased some of his weight off me, releasing a sigh. And it suddenly didn't feel okay at all. I wasn't the kind of girl who could be satisfied with a slice of cake. I wanted to eat the whole damn thing.

"It's okay," I said. "I'm on birth control. And my last STI panel was clear—you're the first person since then. So long as it's the same for you..."

"It is. But are you—" He was going to ask me if I was sure. He loved to ask me that, to check in. To make sure each step we took was one I wanted. And this time, I was very, very sure.

"Please."

He nodded, a single jut of his chin, and then went back to kissing my throat, and then caught my nipple between his lips, and then moved lower and pressed his lips against me.

I'd imagined sober sex to be solemn. I'd thought of wincing women in period pieces lying back and thinking of England. I thought I'd be more inhibited, that everything would feel cramped and awkward. Even though everything else I'd experienced sober had been more, I somehow still believed that this would be less. But of course, of course, of course, the opposite was true. Every part of my life had gotten better and richer when I stopped drinking, but this, this alone was a reason to never drink.

I was feeling things I'd never felt before. Parts of my body were responding that I hadn't even known had nerves. I kept thinking I'd been completely burned alive, then finding there were new places that had spent a life untouched and were suddenly ablaze.

Please, please, please. I didn't know if I was speaking out loud or not, but Ben understood, and his mouth was back on mine.

I arched toward him, and he finally pressed into me. I gasped and closed my eyes, tangling my hands through his hair, brushing my nails against his scalp. A shiver raced through me as he brushed his lips behind my ear.

Our eyes met, and I felt like I did when I wrapped my arms around him in the temple parking lot: so glad he was here, that he was with me, and that it was him holding my heart.

EPILOGUE

Can taking your boyfriend to an AA meeting count as a date? Maybe since we got coffee on the way here from the office? But after the meeting, we were heading to Mom and David's place for dinner. I wasn't sure if I could count that—a mother's presence generally negates date vibes. Still, it would be nice. I had a sneaking suspicion that Mom had bought a cake. Ben had asked me earlier in the week if Magnolia's banana cake was still my favorite. Since I'd never told him it was, I knew he must be in secret communication with Mom over my cake preference. The very idea of them planning a celebration for me—one that was my speed, in that it had no crowds and lots of cake—felt fantastical.

I was a half step ahead of him as we walked through the church doors. I looked back, and he gave me a reassuring smile. It would be fine. This was an open meeting. He was welcome here. I'd told him exactly what would happen from start to finish. There wouldn't be any surprises. He knew about the steps and the preamble and that he didn't have to say or do anything. He knew about me. He knew where we were.

We found seats, and suddenly, I was talking again. "At the end, we're going to get up and hold hands."

"I know," Ben whispered back.

"And we make a circle—" I continued.

"I know," he said again, giving my knee a squeeze.

"Oh, and they'll pass a collection basket. They're not making money—don't worry—but they have to pay rent on this space." While I was talking, I reached for my wallet. "I don't know if you have a single—"

"I do. Put your wallet away!" Ben looked like he was on the verge of laughing at me.

I thumbed to where I kept my cash, grazing my finger over the drawing Dad made of my apartment the last time he'd visited Brooklyn. After the funeral, I'd taken it off my fridge, folded it, and put it in my wallet so I could carry something he made with me. I didn't need it in my kitchen, now that I had a few of his paintings to hang. Gaura told me I could take any of them that spoke to me, and I ended up with a collection that was food themed: the half-bitten cherry, an onion skin, and the wrapper of a fun-sized Milky Way I was pretty sure had been stolen from my Halloween candy—he'd painted it when we lived in Park Slope. I pulled out a dollar bill and shoved it into Ben's hand. "Just in case you don't have one!"

That was enough. I didn't need to say anything more. Except I hadn't warned him about how bad the coffee always was, and it seemed like he was eyeing the snack table. I leaned over to whisper to him, but a cough from the front of the room interrupted me. Tim was a middle-aged guy wearing two layers of flannel and an expression that screamed that he'd lived in the East Village since 1985 and had devoted much of the past twenty years to complaining about how the musical *Rent* had brought tourists to his block. He led the meeting. I'd found this one in January after coming back to the city and hadn't missed a week since.

"Good evening, everyone," he started. "And welcome to the

Saturday evening meditation meeting." He asked if anyone was counting days or needed a sponsor. And then, finally, he asked: "Is anyone celebrating an anniversary of a year or more in the month of September?"

My hand went up.

Tim nodded at me.

"Hi, my name is Emma, I'm an alcoholic and I have two years today."

There was pleasant applause. Jenn, my new sponsor, was sitting a row ahead of us. She turned around and mouthed, "Congratulations!" Then someone named Mike was celebrating ten years, and the room's gaze moved to him.

And that was it. Tim hit the gong he stowed in his backpack every week, and it was time to meditate. I didn't think I'd be very successful tonight. It was going to be hard to get my mind to focus on anything outside of this moment. Ben was familiar. We were familiar to each other. This room and this group of people were also familiar. I loved them both: Ben and the room. It would be fine. It was actually, in fact, already fine. Ben's thigh was leaning against my own, and his hand hadn't left my knee. The whole thing was starting to feel unbearably nice. My mind drifted in and out of happy endings for us. I imagined us living out our lives in a Park Slope brownstone, or a remote cabin in the woods, or even a South Florida retirement community, and they all felt strange. But wonderful and absolutely possible.

★★★★★

ACKNOWLEDGMENTS

So many hardworking and creative people helped make this book a reality. A huge and heartfelt thank-you to:

My agent, Jamie Carr, whose kindness, vision, and surefootedness always made me feel safe in the journey towards publication. And to Elisabeth Weed, who stepped in at the final stages with grace and support.

My editor, Leah Mol, who understood the book and Emma with such empathy and whose sharp eye strengthened the book and my confidence in it.

The entire team at MIRA Books, particularly my publicist Sophie James, Puja Lad and the marketing team, Tara Scarcello for her pitch-perfect cover design, and Jerri Gallagher for her all-star copyediting.

Serkan Gorkemli, Kathleen Fletcher, Kirk German, and Lila Flavin, members of the writing group that formed in a Gotham Writing class in 2016 and helped me feel like a real writer for the first time in my life.

Jochebed Smith, Jillian Eugenios, Kyle Rea, and Anna Munro read early versions of this book when it was still a thesis project and helped me see its shape. Extra kudos to Jo, who read it again a year later and left me an audio message that made me feel like this story might actually be something.

The brilliant professors I had at The New School, whose support inside and outside the classroom has been life-changing. Including Helen Schulman and John Reed, but especially Luis Jaramillo, who worked on *DBN* for a year with me, pushed me when I needed it, and gave me the confidence to believe it really could be published.

All the wonderful people I worked with, both at the Healthy Materials Lab and at Sarah Lawrence College, who allowed me to be both a writer and coworker and always encouraged my creative side.

The early readers who posted reviews on NetGalley and Goodreads and wrote about how this book made them laugh and cry; it is such an honor to have made you feel something.

My family, who are all artists, creatives, and storytellers themselves. Especially my mom, dad, and aunt, who told me I was a writer long before I thought of myself as one, and my sister, Anna, who was my final reader before I sent *DBN* to agents and gave me the courage to do so.

Caroline Shifke, my dearest friend, for giving me the prompt that inspired me to start writing this book, caring about how many words I wrote every day, letting me stare at you on FaceTime instead of the blank pages, and always making me feel like everything I wanted in my life, and for the book, was possible. I could not have asked for a better writing partner.

Geoff, who shows me how transformational love is every day.